"THERE HAVE BEEN ALMOST THREE HUNDRED ARRESTS SO FAR," SAYS SHADRACH.

"Ninety-seven sent to the organ farms. And still the arrests continue."

"Avogadro's men bring them in d___
night," Katya L_____
the Khan be sa___

"When he dec___
tors have been c___

"Conspirators!___ ___ingly.
"What conspirators? The whole thing is insane. Mangu killed himself."

"You talk as if you were there when he jumped."

She is silent a minute. She studies him. "Walk with me across the plaza. Keep your back to the tower."

"There are cameras everywhere. It doesn't matter which way we face."

They start across the plaza. Lindman raises her arm, holding it across her face as though to scratch her nose with the back of her wrist, and says, mouth covered, "I saw Mangu the night before he jumped. We talked about Project Avatar. I told him he was going to be the donor."

ROBERT SILVERBERG

SHADRACH IN THE FURNACE

BERK science fiction BOOKS

SHADRACH IN THE FURNACE

This is a work of fiction. All the characters and events portrayed in this book are fictional, and any resemblance to real people or incidents is purely coincidental.

A Baen Book

Baen Enterprises
8-10 W. 36th Street
New York, N.Y. 10018

First Baen printing, June 1985

ISBN: 0-671-55956-7

Cover art by Jael

Printed in the United States of America

Distributed by
SIMON & SCHUSTER
MASS MERCHANDISE SALES COMPANY
1230 Avenue of the Americas
New York, N.Y. 10020

For Norbert Slepyan

1

It is nine minutes before sunrise in the great city of Ulan Bator, capital of the reconstituted world. For some time now Dr. Shadrach Mordecai has lain awake, restless and tense in his hammock, staring somberly at a glowing green circlet in the wall that is the shining face of his data screen. Red letters on the screen announce the new day:

MONDAY
14 May
2012

As usual, Dr. Mordecai has been unable to get more than a few hours of sleep. Insomnia has plagued him all year; his wakefulness must be some kind of message from his cerebral cortex, but so far he has been unable to decipher it. Today, at least, he has some excuse for awakening early, because great challenges and tensions lie ahead. Dr. Mordecai is personal physician to Genghis II Mao IV Khan, Prince of Princes and Chairman of Chairmen—which is to say, ruler of the earth—and on this day the aged Genghis Mao is due to undergo a liver transplant, his third in seven years.

The world leader sleeps less than twenty meters away, in a suite adjoining Mordecai's. Dictator and doctor occupy residential chambers on the seventy-fifth floor of the Grand Tower of the Khan, a superb onyx-walled needle of a building that rises breathtakingly from the dusty brown Mongolian tableland. Just now Genghis Mao sleeps soundly, eyes unmoving beneath the thick lids, spine enviably relaxed, respiration slow and even, pulse steady, hormone levels rising normally. Mordecai knows all this because he carries, surgically inlaid in the flesh of his arms, thighs, and buttocks, several dozen minute perceptor nodes that constantly provide him with telemetered information on the state of Genghis Mao's vital signs. It took Mordecai a year of full-time training to learn to read the input, the tiny twitches and tremors and flickers and itches that are the analogue-coded equivalents of the Chairman's major bodily processes, but by this time it is second nature for him to perceive and comprehend the data. A tickle here means digestive distress, a throb there means urinary sluggishness, a pricking elsewhere tells of saline imbalance. For Shadrach Mordecai it is something like living in two bodies at once, but he has grown accustomed to it. And so the Chairman's precious life is safeguarded by his vigilant physician. Genghis Mao is officially said to be eighty-seven years old and may be even older, though his body, a patchwork of artificial and transplanted organs, is as strong and responsive as that of a man of fifty. It is the Chairman's wish to postpone death until his work on earth is complete—which is to say, never to die.

How sweetly he rests now! Mordecai runs automatically through the readings again and again: respiratory, digestive, endocrine, circulatory, all the autonomic systems going beautifully. The Chairman, dreamless (the motionless eyes), lying as customary on his left side (faint aortal pressure), emitting gentle hhnnorrking snores (reverberations in the rib cage), obviously feels no apprehension about the coming surgery. Mordecai envies him his calmness. Of course, organ transplants are an old story to Genghis Mao.

At the precise moment of dawn the doctor leaves his hammock, stretches, walks naked across his bedchamber's cool stone floor to the balcony, and steps outside. The air, suffused now with early blue to the east, is clear, crisp, cold, with a sharp wind blowing across the plains, a strong southerly breeze racing through Mongolia from the Great Wall toward Lake Baikal. It ruffles the black flags of Genghis Mao in Sukhe Bator Square, the capital's grand plaza, and stirs the boughs of the pink-blossomed tamarisks. Shadrach Mordecai inhales deeply and studies the remote horizon, as if looking for meaningful smoke signals out of China. No signals come; only the little throbs and tingles of the implant disks, caroling the song of Genghis Mao's irrepressible good health.

All is quiet below. The whole city sleeps, save for those who must be awake to work; Mongols are not given to insomnia. Mordecai is; but then, Mordecai isn't a Mongol. He is a black man, dark with an African darkness, though he is no African either; slender, longlimbed, tall—some hundred centimeters in height—with dense woolly hair, large wide-set eyes, full lips, a broad though highbridged nose. In this land of sturdy golden-skinned folk with sharp noses and glossy straight hair, Dr. Mordecai is a conspicuous figure, more conspicuous, perhaps, then he would like to be.

He squats, straightens, squats, straightens, jack-knifing his arms out and in, out and in. He starts every morning with a calisthenic routine on the balcony, naked in the chilly air: he is thirty-six years old, and even though his post in the government gives him guaranteed access to the Roncevic Antidote, even though he is thus spared the fear of organ-rot that obsesses most of the world's two billion inhabitants, thirty-six is nevertheless an age when one must begin conscientiously to take measures to protect the body against the normal unravelings time brings. *Mens sana in corpore sano;* yes, keep on bending and twisting, Shadrach; make the juices flow; let the old yin balance the yang. He is in perfect health, and his bodily organs are the ones that were in him when he popped from the womb one frosty day in 1976. Up, down, up, down, unsparing of self. Sometimes it seems odd to him that his vigorous, violent morning exercises never awaken Genghis Mao, but of course the flow of telemetered data runs only in one direction, and as

Mordecai puts himself through his fierce balcony workout, the Chairman snores placidly on, unaware.

Eventually, panting, perspiring, shivering lightly, feeling alive and open and receptive, hardly worrying at all about the coming surgical ordeal, Mordecai decides he has had enough of a workout. He washes, dresses, punches for his customary light breakfast, and sets about his morning routine of duties.

So, then, the doctor confronts Interface Three, through which he daily enters the residential suite of his master the Khan. It is a ponderous diamond-shaped doorway, two and a half meters high. From its silken-smooth bronze surface jut a dozen and a half warty cylindrical snouts, three to nine centimeters high. Some of them are scanners and sensors, some are audio conduits, some are weapons of ineluctable lethality; and Shadrach Mordecai has no idea which is which. Most likely, what serves as a scanner today may well be a laser cannon tomorrow; with such random shifts of function does Genghis Mao contrive to confuse the faceless assassins he so vividly dreads.

"Shadrach Mordecai to serve the Khan," Mordecai says in a clear firm voice into what he hopes is today's audio pickup.

Interface Three, now emitting a gentle hum, subjects Mordecai's announcement to voiceprint analysis. At the same time, Mordecai's body is being checked for thermal output, mass, postural stress, olfactory texture, and much more. If any datum should fall beyond the established Mordecai-norm, he could find himself immobilized by loops of suddenly spurting webfoam while the guards are summoned to investigate; resistance at that point might lead to his immediate destruction. Five of these interfaces protect the five entrances to Chairman Genghis Mao's chambers, and they are the wiliest doors ever devised. Daedalus himself could not have forged more clever barriers to guard King Minos.

In a microsecond Mordecai is recognized to be himself, rather than some cunning lifelike simulacrum on a king-slaying errand. With a smooth hiss of perfectly machined joints and a gentle rumble of flawless bearings the interface's outer slab glides open. This admits the doctor to a stone-walled inner holding chamber hardly larger than himself. No welcome vestibule for claustrophobes, this. Here he must halt another microsecond while the entire surveillance is repeated, and only after he passes this second muster is he allowed to enter the imperial residence proper. "Redundancy," Chairman Genghis Mao has declared, "is our main avenue of survival." Mordecai agrees. The intricate business of crossing these interfaces is a trifle to him, part of the normal order of the universe, no more bothersome than the need to turn a key in a lock.

The room just on the far side of Interface Three is a cavernous sphere known as Surveillance Vector One. It is, in a literal sense, Genghis Mao's window on the world. Here a dazzling array of screens, each five square meters in area, rises in overwhelming tiers from floor to ceiling, offering a constantly shifting panorama of televised images relayed from thousands of spy-eyes everywhere on the planet. No great public building is without its secret eyes; scanners look down on all major streets; a corps of government engineers is constantly employed in shifting the cameras from place to place and in installing new ones in previously unspied-upon places. Nor are all the eyes in fixed positions. So many spy-satellites streak through the nearer reaches of space that if their orbits were turned to silk they would swathe the earth in a dense cocoon. At the center of Surveillance Vector One is a grand control panel by means of which the Khan, sitting for hours at a time in an elegant thronelike seat, is able to control the flow of data from all these eyes, calling in signals with quick flutters of his fingertips so that he may look at will into the doings of Tokyo and Bangkok, New York and Moscow, Buenos Aires and Cairo. So sharp is the resolution of the Khan's myriad lenses that they can show Genghis Mao the color of a man's eyes at a distance of five kilometers.

When the Chairman is not making use of Surveillance Vector One, the hundreds of screens continue to function without interruption as the master mechanism sucks in data randomly from the innumerable pickup points. Images come and go, sometimes flitting across a screen in a second or two, sometimes lingering to provide consecutive sequences many minutes in length. Shadrach Mordecai, since he must pass through this room every morning on his way to his master, has formed the habit of pausing for a few minutes to watch the gaudy, dizzying stream of pictures. Privately he refers to this daily interlude as "Checking the Trauma Ward," the Trauma Ward being Mordecai's secret name for the world in general, that great vale of sorrow and bodily corruption.

He stands in mid-room now, observing the world's griefs.

The flow is jerkier than usual today; whatever giant computer operates this system is in a twitchy mood, it seems, its commands moving restlessly from eye to eye, and pictures wink on and off in a frenzied way. Still, there are isolated flashes of clarity. A limping woebegone dog moves slowly down a dirt-choked street. A big-eyed, big-bellied Negroid child stands naked in a dust-swept ravine, gnawing her thumb and crying. A sag-shouldered old woman, carrying carefully wrapped bundles through the cobbled plaza of some mellow European city, gasps and clutches at her chest, letting her packages tumble as she falls. A parched Oriental-faced man with wispy white beard and tiny green skullcap emerges from a shop, coughs, and spits blood. A crowd—Mexicans? Japanese?— gathers around two boys dueling with carving knives; their arms and chests are bright with red cuts. Three children huddle on the roof of a torn-away house rushing swiftly downstream on the white-flecked gray breast of a flooding river. A hawk-faced beggar stretches forth an accusing clawlike hand. A young dark-haired woman kneels at a curb, bowed double in pain, head touching the pavement, while two small boys look on. A speeding automobile veers crazily from a highway and vanishes in a bushy gulley. Surveillance Vector One is like some vast tapestry of hundreds of compartments, each with a story to tell, a fragmentary story, tantalizing, defying comprehension. Out there in the world, out in the great big Trauma Ward that is the world, the two billion subjects of Genghis II Mao IV Khan are dying hour by hour, despite the best efforts of the Permanent Revolutionary Committee. Nothing new about that—everyone who has ever lived has died hour by hour all through his life—but the modes of death are different in these years following the Virus War; death seems ever so much more immediate when so many people are so conspicuously rotting within all at once; and the general decay out there is that much more poignant because there are these innumerable eyes to see it in its totality. The scanners of the Khan capture everything, making no comment, offering no judgment, merely filling these walls with a staggering, baffling portrait of the revised postwar early-twenty-first-century version of the human condition.

The room is a touchstone of character, drawing revealing responses from every viewer. To Mordecai the whirling stream of scenes is fascinating and repelling, a crazy mosaic of decomposition and defeat, courage and endurance; he loves and pities the sufferers who flash so quickly across the screens, and if he could he would embrace them all—lift that old woman to her feet, put coins in the beggar's gnarled hand, stroke that child's distended belly. But Mordecai is, by inclination and profession a healer. To others the brutal theater that is Surveillance Vector One serves only as a reminder of their own good fortune: how wise of them it was to attain high governmental rank and steady supplies of the Roncevic Antidote, to enjoy the favor of Chairman Genghis Mao and live free of pain and hunger and organ-rot, insulated from the nightmare of real life! To others the screens are unbearable, arousing not a sense of smug superiority but rather a feeling of intolerable guilt that they should be here, safe, while *they* are out there. And to others the screens are merely boring: they show dramas without plot, transactions without discernible purpose, tragedies without moral significance, mere stray snatches of life's scratchy fabric. What Genghis

Mao's own reactions to Surveillance Vector One may be is impossible to determine, for the Khan is, in this as in so many other things, wholly inscrutable as he manipulates the controls. But he does spend hours in there. Somehow the room feeds him.

Shadrach Mordecai takes his time this morning, giving the huge room five minutes, eight, ten. Genghis Mao still sleeps, after all. The implanted monitors tell Mordecai that. In this world no one escapes surveillance; while the many eyes of Genghis Mao scan the globe, the slumbering Khan is himself scanned by his physician. Mordecai, standing quite motionless beside the Chairman's upholstered throne, receives a flood of data within and without, Genghis Mao's metabolic output twanging and tweaking the doctor's implants, the flowing shimmer of the screens assailing his eyes. He starts to leave, but just then a screen high up and to his left shows him a glimpse of what is certainly Philadelphia, unmistakably Philadelphia, and he halts, riveted. His native city: he was a Bicentennial baby, entering the world in Ben Franklin's own town, coming forth in Hahnemann Hospital when the United States of America was four months short of its two hundredth birthday. And there is Philadelphia now, turning in the gyre of some ineffably keen satellite-mounted eye: the familiar childhood totems, City Hall, Independence Hall, Penn Center, Christ Church. It is years since he last was there. For a decade now, Shadrach Mordecai has lived in Mongolia. Once it was hard for him to believe that there really was such a place as Mongolia, fabled land of Prester John and Genghis Khan, but by this time it is Philadelphia that has started to seem a place of fable to him. And the United States of America? Do those syllables still have meaning? Who could imagine that the Constitution of Jefferson and Madison would be forgotten, and America pledge allegiance to a Mongol overlord? But that overstates the case: America, Mordecai knows, is governed like all other nations by a local wing of the Permanent Revolutionary Committee, that alliance of radical and reactionary groups functioning through a series of vestigial quasi-democratic institutions; and the aged recluse Genghis Mao is merely the Chairman of the Committee, a remote and semimythical figure who governs indirectly and has no immediate consequence in the daily lives of Dr. Mordecai's former countrymen. Probably no one in America pauses to consider Genghis Mao the embodiment of the authority of the Permanent Revolutionary Committee, and thus the true master of the body politic, any more than one considers the chairman of the board of the local electric company to be the source and controller of the power that flows when the switch is thrown. But he is. Not that many Americans would be disturbed to learn that they owed fealty to a Mongol. The whole world has abdicated; the game of politics is ended; Genghis Mao rules by default, rules because *no one cares*, because in an exhausted, shattered world dying of organ-rot there is general relief that someone, anyone, is willing to play the role of the global dictator.

Philadelphia vanishes from the screen and is replaced by an idyllic tropical scene, pink-white half-moon beach, feathery palm fronds, flowering hibiscus in scarlet and yellow, no people in view. Mordecai shrugs and moves on.

The imperial chambers are circular in layout, occupying the entire top story of the Grand Tower of the Khan except for the five wedge-shaped apartments, such as the one where Mordecai lives, that notch into the suite equidistantly around its rim. As the doctor crosses Surveillance Vector One he comes to three massive doorways, spaced some eight meters apart along the side of the room farthest from the interface through which he entered. The left-hand doorway leads to the bedroom of Genghis Mao, but Mordecai does not take it—best to let the Chairman have all the sleep he needs, today—nor does he choose the central doorway, which goes to the Chairman's private office. Instead he approaches the right-hand doorway, the one that opens into the room known as Committee Vector One, through which he must pass to reach his own office.

He waits briefly while the door scans and approves him. All the inner rooms of the imperial suite are divided one from another by such impermeable barriers, smaller in scope than the main doors at the five interfaces but similarly suspicious: no one is allowed to range freely here from room to room. After a moment the door grants him entry to Committee Vector One. This is a large, brightly lit room, spherical like all the major rooms of Genghis Mao's suite. It occupies the physical center of the apartment, the locus around which all else turns, and in a less literal sense it is the nerve center of the planetary governing structure, the Permanent Revolutionary Committee. Here, day and night, arrive urgent communiques from Committee cadres in every city; and here, day and night, Commmittee potentates sit in front of intricate switchboards glistening with terminals, making policy and communicating it to the lesser satraps in the outer provinces. All applications for Roncevic Antidote treatments are routed through this room; all requests for organ transplants, regeneration therapy, and other vital medical services are considered in Committee Vector One; all jurisdictional disputes within the regional Committee leadership are settled here according to the principles of centripetal depolarization, Genghis Mao's chief philosophical gift to humanity. Shadrach Mordecai is not a political man and he has little concern with the events that take place in Committee Vector One, but since the floor plan of the building requires him to cross the room many times a day, he does occasionally pause to observe the bureaucrats at their labors, the way he might stop to examine the behavior of bizarre insects in a crumbling log.

Not much seems to be going on here now. At times of high crisis all twleve of the switchboard seats are occupied, and Genghis Mao himself, seated at his own elaborate desk at the very center of everything, fiercely manipulating his formidable battery of sophisticated communications devices, directs the course of strategy. But these are quiet days. The only conspicuous crisis in the world is the one in the Chairman's liver, and that will soon be remedied. For weeks now Genghis Mao has not bothered to take up his post in Committee Vector One, preferring to discharge his sovereign responsibilities from his smaller private office adjoining his bedroom. And only three of the switchboards are in use this morning, operated by weary-looking vice-chairmen, one male and two female, who yawn and slouch as they take incoming messages and formulate appropriate replies.

Mordecai is halfway across the room and walking briskly when someone calls his name. He turns and sees Mangu, the heir-apparent to Genghis Mao, heading toward him from the direction of the Chairman's private office.

"Do they operate on the Khan today?" Mangu asks worriedly.

Mordecai says, nodding, "In about three hours."

Mangu frowns. He is a sleek, handsome young Mongol, unusually tall for his kind, nearly as tall as Mordecai himself. His face is round; his features are symmetrical and pleasing; his eyes are bright and alert. At the moment he seems tense, jangled, apprehensive.

"Will it go well, Shadrach? Are there any risks?"

"Don't worry. You won't become Khan today. It's only a liver transplant, after all."

"*Only!*"

"Genghis Mao's had plenty of those."

"But how much more surgery can he stand? Genghis Mao is an old man."

"Better not let him hear you say that!"

"He's probably listening right this minute," says Mangu casually. Some of the tension goes from him. He grins. "The Khan never takes what I say seriously, anyway. I believe he sometimes thinks I'm a bit of a fool."

Mordecai smiles guardedly. He also sometimes thinks Mangu is a bit of a fool, and perhaps more than a bit. He remembers Dr. Crowfoot of Project Avatar, Nikki Crowfoot, *his* Nikki with whom he would have spent this past night but for Genghis Mao's operation, telling him months ago of the dismal fate reserved for Mangu. Mordecai knows, as Mangu almost certainly does not, that Genghis Mao plans to be his own successor, through the vehicle of Mangu's strong, healthy young body. If Project Avatar is carried to a successful conclusion, and the auguries are favorable for it, the fine sturdy figure of Mangu will indeed someday sit upon the throne of Genghis Mao, but Mangu himself will not be there to enjoy the occasion. To Mordecai, anyone who marches as blithely toward his own destruction as Mangu is doing, perceiving nothing, suspecting nothing, fearing nothing, is a fool and worse than a fool.

"Where will you be during the operation?" Mordecai asks.

Mangu gestures broadly toward the main command desk of Committee Vector One. "Over there, pretending to run the show."

"Pretending?"

"You know there are many things I still have to learn, Shadrach. I'm not going to be ready to take over for *years*. That's why I wish he wouldn't undergo all these transplants."

"He doesn't do it for the exercise," Mordecai says. "The present liver's been failing for weeks. It's got to come out. But I tell you: don't worry."

Mangu smiles and grips Mordecai's forearm for a brief, affectionate, surprisingly painful squeeze. "I won't. I have faith in you, Shadrach. In the whole medical team that keeps the Khan alive. Let me know the moment it's over, will you?"

He strides away, toward the main command post, to play at being monarch of the world.

Mordecai shakes his head. Mangu is an attractive figure, genial and charming and even charismatic. In a dark time lit only by ghastly jagged flashes of nightmare-light, Mangu is something of a popular hero. In the past ten months or so he has become the Chairman's public surrogate, appearing in Genghis Mao's place at formal functions, dam dedications, Committee congresses and the like, and the dashing, gallant prince-in-waiting, so disarming, so umpretentious, so accessible to the populace, is beloved in a

way that Genghis Mao never has been, never for an
instant. Those who have observed Mangu at close
range are aware that he is essentially a hollow man,
all image and no substance, shallow and plump-souled,
an amiable athlete living an implausible charade;
but though Mangu is trivial, he is far from contemptible, and Mordecai feels genuine compassion for him.
Poor Mangu, fretting over the possibility that he might
succeed the Khan this day, with his apprenticeship
not yet finished! Does it ever occur to Mangu that he
will *never*—not in a year, not in ten years, not in a
thousand—be a fit successor to Genghis Mao, that he
is fundamentally incapable of wielding the terrible
power which he is ostensibly being groomed to inherit?
Apparently not. Or else Mangu, knowing his own
limits, would have begun to wonder what plan Genghis Mao really had for him, why the Chairman had
picked as his successor a mere handsome boy, his
own opposite in all important respects. To train him
to be supreme sovereign? No. No. To be a puppet,
merely; to dance before the people and win their
love. And then, one day, to have his identity scooped
out and thrown away, so that his body might become
a dwelling for the wily mind and dark soul of Genghis Mao, when the Chairman's own ancient patched
hull can no longer be repaired. Poor Mangu. Mordecai
shivers.

He hurries on into his own office, closes the door,
seals it.

There is a sudden sharp twanging in his left thigh,
close to the hip, the place where he receives Genghis
Mao's cerebral output. Four rooms away, the Khan is
awakening.

2

Mordecai's office is an island of tranquility for him within the tumultuous intensity of life atop the Grand Tower of the Khan. The room, a sphere ten meters in diamter, has many entrances, but they are programmed to open only for himself or Genghis Mao. One is the door through which he has just come, out of Committee Vector One. Another goes to the Khan's private dining room, and another, on the far side, to a seldom-used heavy-insulation study known as the Khan's Retreat. The last door is Interface Five, connecting the doctor's office to the two-story-high Surgery that occupies one of the five outer wedges of the tower.

In the sanctuary of his office Shadrach Mordecai enjoys a few moments of peace before proceeding on his voyage into the turmoils of the day. Though Genghis Mao is up, there is no need to hurry. Mordecai's implants tell him—by now, he can equate every trifling inner signal with some concrete aspect of the Khan's activities—that the imperial servitors have entered Genghis Mao's bedchamber, have helped the Khan to his feet, are walking him through the series of mild arm-swinging chest-stretching exercises that the old man, at Dr. Mordecai's insistence, performs every morning. Next they will bathe him, then they will shave him, finally they will dress him and bring him forth. Though there will be no breakfast for Genghis Mao today, because of the impending operation, Shadrach Mordecai has at least an hour before he must attend the Khan.

Simply being in the office buoys him. The dark, rich paneling, the subdued lighting, the curving uncluttered desk of strange exotic woods, the splendid bookcase of crystalline rods and thin travertine slabs in which he keeps his priceless library of classic medical texts, the elegant armories that house his extensive collection of antique medical instruments—it is an ideal environment for him, a perfect enclosure for the doctor he would like to be and occasionally is able to believe he is, the master of the Hippocratic arts, the prince of healers, the preserver and prolonger of life. Not that this room is a place for the practice of medicine. The only medical tools here are ancient ones, romantic and quaint apparatus, odd beakers and scalpels and lancets, bloodletting knives and cauterizing irons, ophthalmoscopes and defibrillators, early and inaccurate anatomical models, chirurgical saws, sphygmomanometers, electrical invigorators, flasks of discredited antitoxins, trephines, microtomes, relics of more innocent times. He has acquired these things eagerly in the past five years, by way of establishing his professional kinship with the great physicians of yesterday. The books, too, rare and auspicious, landmarks of medical history, talismans of scientific progress: the *Fabrica* of Vesalius, *De Motu Cordis* of Harvey, Boerhaave's *Institutiones*, Laënnec on auscultation, Beaumont on digestion—with what joy he has collected them, with what reverence he has fondled them! Not without some guilt, too, for in this battered and deflated era it is all too easy for those few who have power and wealth to take advantage of those who have not; and Mordecai, so close to the throne, has accumulated his treasures cheaply, catching them as they slip from the grasp of older, unluckier, perhaps more worthy possessors. Still, had these things not descended to him they might have been lost altogether in the chaos that surges freely through the world beyond the Grand Tower of the Khan.

Mordecai's actual medical work is done elsewhere,

in the Surgery beyond Interface Five, which serves
not only for actual surgical operations but also for
any other medical attention Genghis Mao may need.
Mordecai's office is a place for research and reflec-
tion only. Just to the right of his desk are keyboards,
compact data terminals, giving him instant access to
entire libraries of medical knowledge; he need only
touch a finger to a key or even speak a coded word,
cite symptomata, facies, tentative diagnosis, and back
will come, in neatly codified form, extracts from the
accumulated scientific wisdom of the eons, the rele-
vant distillate of everything from the Smith Papyrus
and Hippocrates and Galen down through the latest
findings of the microbiologists and immunologists
and endocrinologists who labor in the laboratories of
the Khan. It is all here: encephalitis and endocarditis,
gastritis and gout, nephritis, nephrosis, neuroma,
nystagmus, aspergillosis and bilharzia, uremia and
xanthochromia, the thousand natural shocks that flesh
is heir to. Time was when doctors were shamans in
feathers and paint, bravely pounding drums to frighten
away frightening demons, doing solitary battle against
unfathomable causes and unaccountable effects,
gamely piercing veins and ventilating skulls, grub-
bing for roots and leaves of purely magical merit.
Alone against the dark spirits of disease, no guide but
one's stock of inherited supernatural lore and one's
intuition. And now! Here! The answer machine! A
touch of the finger and behold: etiology, pathology,
symptomatology, pharmacology, contraindications,
prophylaxis, prognosis, sequelae, the whole miraculous scroll of diagnosis and treatment and cure and
convalescence unrolling at a command! In moments
of lull Shadrach Mordecai enjoys testing his wits
against the computer, setting hypothetical problems
for himself, postulating symptoms and proposing diag-
noses; he is eleven years out of Harvard Medical
School and still a student, ever a student.

Today allows few lulls. He swings to his left and
taps out the telephone number of the Surgery.

"Warhaftig," he says crisply.

A moment, and then the screen shows the flat,

homely face of Nicholas Warhaftig, surgeon to the
Khan, veteran of a hundred critical transplant operations. The camera picks up a sweeping view of the
operating room behind him, boards glittering with
measuring dials and control panels, the laser bank,
the anesthesiologist's spidery maze of needles and
tubes and pipes, and, only partly visible, the main
surgical stage itself, dais and bed and lights and
instruments, white linens and dazzling chrome-steel
fixtures, everything awaiting the imperial patient.

"The Khan's awake," Mordecai says.

"We're on schedule, then," says Warhaftig. He is
sixty years old, silver-haired, phlegmatic. He was
already the supreme organ-transplant man when
Shadrach Mordecai was an idol-worshipping under-
graduate, and though Mordecai is technically his superior on Genghis Mao's staff now, there is no doubt
in either man's mind about which one of them actually holds the greater professional authority. This
makes their relationship an uncomfortable one for
Mordecai. Warhaftig says, "Will you get him to me
by 0900 sharp?"

"I'll try."

"Try hard," Warhaftig replies dryly, mouth quirking.
"We begin perfusion at 0915. The liver's still on ice,
but coordinating defrost is always tricky. How's he
feeling?"

"As usual. The strength of ten men."

"Can you give me quick readings on blood glucose
and fibrinogen production?"

"A moment," Mordecai says. Those are not factors
on which he receives direct telemetering from Genghis Mao's body; but he has become skillful in deduc-
ing hundreds of the Chairman's lesser body functions
from clues given by the main metabolic responses.
He says shortly, "Glucose doing fine, within the expected reduced levels caused by the general hepatic
necrosis. It's harder to get the fibrinogen reading,
but my feeling is that all the plasma proteins are on
the low side. Probably the fibrinogen not as bad as
the heparin."

"And bile?"

"Off sharply since Friday. Down some more this morning. No critical breakdowns of any function yet."

"All right," Warhaftig says. He gestures brusquely to someone beyond camera range. The surgeon's hands are formidable, long and muscular, fingers like elongated pliable wands, incredible octave-devouring fingers of extraordinary power and delicacy. Shadrach Mordecai, although he is no surgeon, has strong and graceful hands himself, but the sight of Warhaftig's always makes him think of his own as coarse and stumpy, butcher-fingered hands. "We're moving well here. I'll expect you at 0900. Anything else?"

"I just wanted you to know the Khan was awake," Mordecai answers, a little sharply, and breaks the contact.

Next he phones the Chairman's bedchamber and talks briefly with one of the Khan's valets. Yes, Genghis Mao is awake, he has bathed, he is readying himself for the operation. He will begin his morning meditation in a moment. Does the doctor wish to speak with the Khan before that? The doctor does. The screen goes blank, and there is a lengthy pause during which Mordecai feels his adrenalin levels beginning to rise: not yet, not even after all this time, has the fear and awe that Genghis Mao inspires in him begun to ebb. He forces himself into calmness with a quick centering exercise, and none too soon, for abruptly the head and shoulders of Genghis II Mao IV Khan appear on the telephone screen.

The Chairman is a lean, leathery-looking man with a narrow triangular skull, powerful cheekbones, heavy brows, fierce eyes, thin harsh lips. His skin is more brown than yellow in tone; his hair is thick black, combed back straight from his forehead and descending almost to his shoulders. His face is one that readily and obviously evokes dread, but also, oddly, trust; he seems omniperceptive and omnicompetent, a man to whom all the burdens of the world can be given and who will uncomplainingly and effectually assume them. The recent deterioration of his current liver has had visible effect on him—a bronzing of his skin beyond its normal deep hue, some blotches of pigment on his cheeks, an uncharacteristic feverish brightness of the eyes—but still he seems a man of regal bearing and inexhaustible strength, a man designed by nature to endure and to rule.

"Shadrach," he says. His voice is deep, grating, with a narrow dynamic range, not really a good demagogue's voice. "How am I this morning?"

It is an old joke between them. The Khan laughs; Mordecai manages a bilious smile.

The doctor replies, "Strong, well rested, a little low in blood sugar, but everything generally as expected. Warhaftig is waiting for you. He'd like you in the Surgery by 0900 hours. Mangu's at the Committee Vector One desk. It's a quiet day so far."

"This will be my fourth liver."

"Your third, sir," Mordecai says gently. "I've been over the records. First transplant in 2005, the second in 2010, and now—"

"I was born with one also, Shadrach. We should count that. I'm human, eh, Shadrach? We mustn't forget the set of organs I was born with." Genghis Mao's inescapable eyes pierce the uneasy Mordecai. Human, yes, one must always try to keep that in mind; the Chairman is human, though his pancreas is a tiny plastic disk and his heart is constantly spurred by electric jolts delivered through fine silver needles and his kidneys were grown in bodies other than his own and his spleen his lungs and his corneas his colon his esophagus his pharynx his thymus his pulmonary artery his stomach his yes oh yes human he is human but sometimes it is hard to remember that— and sometimes, looking into those irresistible terrifying glacial eyes, one sees not the godlike flash of supreme authority, but something else, an opaque look of fatigue or perhaps terror, a look that seems at once to reveal an overwhelming fear of death and to offer warm welcome to it. Genghis Mao is death-haunted, certainly, a man whose grasp on life is so ferocious after nine decades that he will submit to any bodily torment in order to buy another month, another year; he lives in morbid dread of death and his eyes proclaim it; but he is death-loving, too, ob-

sessed with the termination that he constantly post-
pones, as much so as a man who is obsessed with
the orgasm he strives so fiercely to delay. Mordecai
has heard Genghis Mao speak of *the purity of not-
being*. Not for him the coming of *süsser Tod*, no,
never, and yet how he savors the tempting sweetness
of it even as he averts his lips from it. Mordecai
suspects that only such a man, death-haunted, death-
obsessed, would want to make himself master of the
sort of place this world has become. But how can
Genghis Mao, brooding dreamily on the delicate beauties of death, nevertheless also yearn to live forever?

"Come for me at 0900," the Chairman tells him.
Mordecai nods to a dead screen.

3

In the time remaining before he must go to fetch the
Khan, Shadrach Mordecai discharges one of his regu-
lar bureaucratic responsibilities: receiving the daily
progress reports from the directors of the three great
research schemes in which Genghis Mao has much of
the resources of the government mobilized, Project
Talos, Project Phoenix, and Project Avatar. As Genghis Mao's physician, Shadrach is ex-officio head of
all three projects, and he confers each morning with
the project leaders whose laboratories are located in
the lower levels of the Grand Tower of the Khan.

Katya Lindman of Project Talos comes on screen
first. "We coded the eyelids yesterday," she tells him
at once. "It's one of the biggest steps so far in our
analogue-to-digital conversation program. As of now

we have seven of Genghis Mao's three hundred basic kinesic traits fully graphed and equivalented." She is a short, wide-shouldered woman, a Swede, formidably intelligent, dark-haired and easily angered, a woman of considerable beauty despite or perhaps because of her thin-lipped, sharp-toothed, oddly feral and menacing mouth. Her project is the most far-fetched of the three, an attempt to develop a mechanical Genghis Mao, an analogue-entity through which he can continue to rule after bodily death—a puppet, a simulacrum, but one with a sustaining Genghis Mao-like life of its own. The technology for building such an automaton already exists, of course; the problem is to create something that transcends the Walt Disney robots that Mordecai remembers from his youth, the cunning Abe Lincoln and Thomas Edison and Christopher Columbus machines, so lifelike in their skin tones and movements and manner of speaking. Disney machines are not sufficient to the present need. A Disneyed Abe Lincoln can deliver the Gettysburg Address flawlessly, eight times an hour, but it would never be able to deal with a delegation of angry Reconstructionist congressmen; and a Genghis Mao of metal and plastic might spout the tenets of centripetal depolarization with hypnotic eloquence, but what value would that be in meeting the crises of a constantly changing, challenging society? No, they must capture the essence of the living Genghis Mao, code it, make from it a program that will continue to grow and react. Shadrach Mordecai is skeptical of success. He asks Katya Lindman, as he does every few weeks, how her department is coming on the task of digitalizing Genghis Mao's mental processes, which is rather more difficult than working out digital programs for his facial expressions and habits of posture. The question is threatening to her, and her eyes briefly flash with familiar fire; but all she says is, "We continue to attack the problem. Our best people are constantly at work on it."

"Thank you," Shadrach says, and switches to Irayne Sarafrazi's channel. The head of Project Phoenix is a young Persian gerontologist, a slight, almost fragile-

looking person, with huge dark eyes, full solemn lips,
black hair pulled back starkly from her forehead. Her
group seeks a body-renewal technique that will allow
rejuvenation of the living cellular matter of Genghis
Mao, so that he may be reborn in his own skin when
he no longer has the strength and resilience to accept
further organ transplants. The prime obstacle here is
the unwillingness of the brain to regenerate the cells
it daily sloughs off; reversing the decline of the
other organs and making them young again is a relatively simple matter of nucleic-acid reprogramming,
but no one has found a way to halt, let alone to
recoup, the constant death of the brain. Already in
Genghis Mao's long life the estimated weight of his
brain has declined by ten percent, with a correspond-
ing loss in mnemonic function and neural response
time; nevertheless he is far from senile, but what
hideous decline into idiocy might not overtake him if
he were given a further century or two of residence in
his present cerebro-cerebellar equipment? Hundreds
of hapless primates have surrendered their cranial
contents to Irayne Sarafrazi's research, and their brains
live in bell jars on her laboratory benches, alive and
responsive while she seeks ways of tickling their neu-
rons into new growth, but no progress has been made.
This morning she seems discouraged. Her glittering
Achaemenid eyes look dull and strained. The disembodied brain of Pan, a chimpanzee, has suddenly
undergone a fatal deterioration, just when it appeared
that some actual cellular growth was beginning.
"We're about to begin the autopsy," Irayne Sarafrazi
says dismally, "but we think Pan's death may mean
our whole cerebral stimulation program is a mistake.
I'm thinking of switching our emphasis away from
actual brain regeneration and toward redundancy
activation. What do you think, Shadrach?" Mordecai
shrugs. Of course he knows that the human brain has
vast redundant areas, billions of cells whose only
apparent function is to be an emergency reserve; he
knows, too, what has been accomplished by way of
rehabilitating the victims of strokes and other cerebral damage through redirecting the neural channels

into the redundant areas. But more efficient utilization of existing brain tissue only delays, does not remove, the threat of senile degeneracy. So long as cells daily die, Genghis Mao will tumble eventually into senility in his rejuvenated body, fifty or seventy or ninety years from now, a drooling Struldbrug of the mind trapped in a sturdy requickened frame. "Redundancy is a short-term measure," Shadrach tells her. "Without brain regeneration, the risks are too high. An old brain in a young body won't work. Let me see the autopsy report on the chimp tomorrow and maybe I'll have some ideas." Unable to bear the sight of her stricken face, he tunes Sarafrazi out and gets Nikki Crowfoot of Project Avatar on his screen.

She smiles tenderly. "Did you sleep well, Shadrach?"

Her strength, and the strength of her concern for him, radiates glowingly from the screen. She is a stalwart woman, an athlete, a huntress, tawny-skinned, big-breasted, nearly 190 centimeters tall, with a strong heavy-boned face, wide-set eyes, wide-lipped mouth, assertive high-bridged nose. Her parents on both sides were Amerindians, Navajo mother, detribalized Assiniboin father. She and Shadrach Mordecai have been lovers for months, friends for more than a year. Mordecai hopes Genghis Mao knows nothing of their affair, but he suspects it is a naive hope.

He says, "I slept well for a while, anyway."

"Worrying about the Chairman's operation?"

"I suppose. Or maybe just worrying in general."

"I could have helped you relax," she says with a sly grin.

"Probably you could. But I've always abstained the night before the chairman undergoes surgery. Like a prizefighter, like an opera singer. To keep the concentration absolutely clear, the mind unblurred. I know it's silly, Nikki, but it's something I do."

"All right. All right. I was only teasing. Anyway, we can make up for it tonight."

"Tonight, yes. Or this afternoon. We'll have him off the table by 0230 hours. How would you like to take the tunnel to Karakorum with me?"

Nikki Crowfoot sighs. "Can't. Don't tempt me. Critical tests this afternoon. Do you want to hear my report?"

Dr. Crowfoot's work overlaps, in some respects, both of the other projects, for Project Avatar's goal is to develop a personality-transfer technique that will permit Genghis Mao—his soul, his spirit, his persona, his anima, but no actual physical part of him—to move to another, younger body. Like Project Talos, Avatar strives to reduce the patterns of Genghis Mao's mental responses to digital—therefore programmable, therefore reproducible—codings; like Project Phoenix, Avatar intends to give the Chairman a new and healthy body in which to dwell. But where Talos would house the digital-coded analogue of Genghis Mao in a mechanical construct, Avatar would place him in one formerly inhabited by someone else, specifically Mangu. On the one hand Crowfoot's project would avoid the inhumanity of creating a robot Khan, on the other it would sidestep the problem of brain-cell deterioration by instilling the intangible and abstract essence of Genghis Mao in a young and vigorous brain. Despire the areas of overlap, the three projects conduct their research altogether independently of one another, and no attempts are made at exchanges of ideas. Redundancy, after all, is our main avenue of survival.

Shadrach Mordecai, because he is privy to the work of all three, is perhaps the only one who really knows where they stand in relation to one another. He knows that Katya Lindman's team is attempting something that is probably hopeless—instilling the soul of a man into a machine will not produce a convincing and politically viable duplicate of the original, machines ordinarily being incapable of transcending their machinehood—and that Irayne Sarafrazi's group, though it is pursuing the most plausible route toward giving Genghis Mao the eternal life he hungers for, is destined to be blocked by the apparently insoluble brain-decay difficulty. He knows, too, that Nikki Crowfoot's approach to personality coding has been more fruitful than Lindman's, and that in a matter of

months it may be possible for the scientists of Project
Avatar to infuse the essence of Genghis Mao like a
pervasive coating of paint over the mind of a donor
body whose previous occupant has been obliterated
by electroencephalographic mindpick techniques. Poor
Mangu. Poor hopeful tragic princeling, destined to be
nothing better than a *tabula rasa* for the Khan.

Mangu's fate will not be long delayed. Mordecai
listens in chilly fascination to Nikki's recitation of
the latest wonders. They have reached the stage where
they can code the souls of animals, abstracting from
them the unique electrical patterns of their minds,
transforming those waveforms into numbers, using
the numbers to replicate the electrical patterns within
the brains of donor beasts. They have coded a rooster
and pumped its soul into a mindpicked hawk; hawk
no longer flies, but runs cockadoodling around the
chickencoop, clumsily fluttering its magnificent wings
and crazily mounting the terrified hens. They have
coded a gibbon and housed its mind in a gorilla's
body; gorilla has turned berserkly arboreal, brachiat-
ing in wild desperation through the treetops, while
its evicted gorilla-essence now resides within a former gibbon that struts ponderously at ground level,
leaning on its flexed knuckles and pausing occasionally to pound its scrawny chest. And so on, and so on;
they are getting ready to attempt the first human
transfers, within a matter of weeks. Mordecai does
not ask Crowfoot where she intends to obtain her
experimental subjects. There are confusing problems
of ethics as it is in this whole business of serving
Genghis Mao; he would rather not load his conscience
with his beloved's deeds.

"Call me when the operation's over," Nikki Crowfoot tells him.

"Won't that interrupt your critical tests?"

"Not critically. Call me. I'll see you tonight."

"Tonight, yes," Shadrach says faintly. The time is
0855 hours. He must convey Genghis Mao now to the
Surgery.

4

The liver, the body's largest gland, is a useful and complex organ weighing a kilogram and a half—about two percent of the total body weight—that performs hundreds of significant biochemical functions. The liver produces bile, a green liquid essential to digestion. Through the liver passes exhausted venous blood en route to the heart, blood which the liver filters to remove bacteria, poisons, drugs, and other noxious impurities. To the blood the liver adds the plasma proteins it manufactures, among them the clotting agent fibrinogen and the anticoagulant heparin. From the blood the liver takes sugar, which it converts to glycogen and stores until the body's energy needs require it. The liver is responsible also for the conversion of fats and proteins into carbohydrates, the storage of fat-soluble vitamins, the manufacture of antibodies, the destruction of outworn red blood cells, and much else.

So many metabolic purposes does the liver serve that no vertebrate can survive more than a few hours without one. So central is it to life that it has extraordinary regenerative powers: if three quarters of the liver is removed, the remaining cells will multiply so rapidly that the gland will regain its original dimensions within two months. Even if ninety percent of the liver is destroyed, it continues to produce bile at the normal rate. Redundancy is our main avenue of survival. Nevertheless the liver is subject to many dysfunctions—the various jaundices, the various

necroses, septicemia, dysenteric abscesses, cancer of
the bile passages, and so forth. The liver's totipotence
enables it to withstand such dysfunctions for prolonged
periods, but its powers of recuperation diminish, like
most other things, with age.

Genghis Mao suffers from chronic liver trouble. To
sustain his life and the life of the assorted artificial
and transplanted organs within him, the Chairman
must pour oceans of medication through his system
each day, and even the most durable of livers would
be hard pressed to handle the constant assault of
high-powered chemicals it is asked to filter from Genghis Mao's bloodstream. Then, too, the presence of so
many alien organs sets up biochemical interaction
phenomena within the body that the liver must
counteract, and the strain is telling. The Chairman's
beleaguered liver is in a perpetually morbid state,
aggravated by his great age and the unnatural intri-
cacy of his composite internal structure, and periodi-
cally it must be replaced. That time has again come.

Two burly aides lift Genghis Mao's short, slight
figure onto a gurney and the familiar trip from the
imperial bedchamber to the operating table commences. The Khan is cheerful, feverish and frail and beady-
eyed though he looks; he nods and winks to the aides
as they position him, telling them that he is comfortable; he chuckles, he even essays a quip or two.
Mordecai is astounded, as always, by the Khan's incredible calmness at such a moment, as evidenced by
the telemetered data reaching his implanted sensors.
Surely Genghis Mao knows that there is a significant
chance of his dying during the operation, but his
somatic output registers no apparent awareness of
that—as though the Chairman's spirit is so neatly
balanced between love of life and hunger for death
that it floats in perfect metabolic equilibrium. At any
rate Shadrach is much less relaxed than his employer,
perhaps because he regards the risks of a liver transplant operation as distinctly nontrivial and is far
from ready to confront the personal uncertainties of
a post-Genghis Mao world.

On silent pneumatic treads the gurney bearing the

Chairman glides from the imperial bedchamber to the imperial office, thence via the private dining room into Shadrach Mordecai's office, and—after an eternity of suspicious scanning—through Interface Five into the Surgery. This is a magnificent tetrahedral enclosure extending through the uppermost two stories of the Grand Tower of the Khan and subtending some thirty degrees of arc along the skin of the elongated conical building. A cruciform cluster of chromed fixtures at the room's summit floods it with brilliant but not glaring light. A platform midway between floor and ceiling juts from the wall opposite the interface, dividing the great room almost in half on its far side, and atop this platform rests the dazzling aseptic transparent bubble within which the actual surgery is performed; beneath the platform that supports the bubble is the surgical stage's environment-support apparatus: a huge sinister hooded cube of dull green metal, housing what Mordecai imagines to be pumps, filters, heating ducts, reservoirs of sterilizing chemicals, humidifiers, and other equipment. On the other side of the room is a ziggurat of supplementary machinery rising step by step on smooth blue-green benches for some thirty meters—a squat brick-colored power unit at the bottom, an array of metering devices, an autoclave, a laser bank, the anesthesia console, a camera boom and associated playback screens to enable consulting doctors to follow the events inside the bubble, and much other materiel, some of it wholly baffling to Mordecai.

He does not need to understand what functions all this equipment serves. He will perform no actual surgery. His role in the operation is as part of the auxiliary equipment—for, with his capability to monitor, evaluate, and report on the moment-by-moment physiological changes within Genghis Mao's body, he is a kind of supercomputer, far more supple and perceptive than any medical machine could be. The Chairman's condition will, of course, be monitored by the usual machinery as well (redundancy is our main avenue . . .) but Shadrach, standing at Warhaftig's elbow and receiving direct bulletins from

the Khan's interior, will be able to interpret and
recommend with an intuitive and deductive wisdom
that no machine could attempt. He is neither flat-
tered nor insulted by his function as a supercomputer:
it is merely what he is here to do.

The gurney waddles onto the operating stage and
positions itself next to the table. The table's own
octopuslike, power-driven, glittering steel arms, extending telescopically, embrace Genghis Mao, lift him,
and make the transfer; the gurney marches away.
Mordecai, Warhaftig, and Warhaftig's two assistants,
all properly scrubbed and gowned, enter the aseptic
bubble; it is sealed behind them and will not open
again until the operation is over. Now a soft hissing.
the atmosphere of the bubble is being withdrawn
and replaced by a surgically clean environment.

Genghis Mao, supine but still conscious and in
high spirits, darts bright, keen glances everywhere,
alertly observing each phase of the preparations. The
assistants lay bare the Chairman's small hard torso—
Genghis Mao is light-framed but muscular, with little subcutaneous fat and sparse body hair; the fine
scars of innumerable operations crisscross his yellow-
bronze skin—and begin the laborious process of connecting the terminals of the monitoring devices.
Warhaftig thoughtfully palpates the Khan's abdomen
and adjusts the cutting angle of the surgical laser.
The anesthesiologist, whose post is outside the bubble,
runs off preliminary acupuncture combinations on
his keyboard. "Hook up the perfusion," Warhaftig
mutters absently to Shadrach Mordecai, who is
pleased to have something to do.

Since Genghis Mao will be liverless for four to six
hours, an artificial liver must be used to sustain him
during the operation. But no wholly artificial liver
has ever been perfected, not even now, after more
than fifty years of organ-transplant technology. The
squat cubical device Warhaftig employs is a mechano-
organic composite: pipes, tubes, pumps, and electro-
dialytic filters keep the patient's blood properly pure,
but the basic biochemical functions of the liver, having thus far proven impossible to duplicate mechani-

cally, are performed by the naked liver of a dog, resting in a bath of warm fluid at the core of the apparatus. Mordecai deftly slides two needles into Genghis Mao's upper arm, one tapping a vein, the other entering an artery. The arterial line seems to encounter some resistance and Shadrach hesitates. The Chairman winks. This is old stuff to him. "Go ahead," he murmurs. "I'm all right." Mordecai completes the hookup and nods to an assistant. Shortly the Chairman's blood is traveling toward the dialyzing coils, perfusing thereafter through the moist red lobes of the canine liver, and returning to the Chairman's body. Shadrach keeps careful check on Genghis Mao's telemeter reports: fine, fine, everything fine.

"Immunosuppressives," Warhaftig orders.

For several weeks, in anticipation of the operation, Mordecai has been dosing the Khan with antimetabolitic drugs, gradually raising the level in order to damp out Genghis Mao's normal graft-rejecting immune response. By now the Khan's antigenic structure has been so weakened that the chance of a graft rejection is slight, but no risks will be run: Genghis Mao receives a last jolt of antimetabolites now, as well as a dose of corticosteroids, and an aide outside the bubble activates a node that will irradiate the blood passing through the liver-surrogate, thus destroying the rejection-inducing lymphocyte corpuscles. Redundancy, redundancy, ever redundancy! The Khan's heart beats strongly. Everything is at normal throb, Mordecai perceives: blood pressure, pulse, body temperature, peristaltic rhythm, muscle tonus, pupil dilation, muscular reflexes.

"Anesthesia," Warhaftig says.

The anesthesiologist, perched high on the far wall at the keyboard of an instrument more complicated than a concert synthesizer, begins his virtuoso performance. A touch of his sensitive fingertips and the shining retractable claws of the operating table unfold and hover over the Chairman's body. The anesthesiologist seeks the acupuncture points, maneuvering the claws into place by remote control, probing with little sonic blurts until he finds the precise conduits of neural energy; when he has arranged his metal fingers to his satisfaction, he activates the ultrasonic generators and beams of sonic force rush from the hovering fingers into the Khan's relaxed, motionless body. No acupuncture needles penetrate Genghis Mao, merely a laminar flow of high-frequency sound entering the acupuncture meridians. Warhaftig, using epidermal electrodes, tests the Khan's reactions, confers with the anesthesiologist, tests again, asks Mordecai for a reading, runs a deeper test, gets no wince of pain from Genghis Mao. The steel digits of the sonipuncture equipment sparkle in the bright light of the operating chamber; they surround Genghis Mao like the bristly organs of insects, palps or stings or ovipositors. Genghis Mao never permits a general anesthetic to be administered to him—loss of consciousness is too much like death—and Warhaftig dislikes all chemical anesthetics, general or local, so sonipuncture is the method of choice both for doctor and for patient. Fully conscious still, terrifyingly alert, Genghis Mao offers reports on his deepening loss of sensation. At last Warhaftig and the anesthesiologist deem the process complete.

"We begin now," the surgeon declares.

There is a momentary dip in the illumination as all surgical devices and support systems are activated at once. Mordecai imagines a throb passing through the entire building under the sudden power demand. To the left of the operating table is the perfusion machine, quietly pumping blood from Genghis Mao and forcing it through the dialysis coils. To the right waits the new liver, which has been stored in an iced saline solution since its removal from the donor and now is being bathed by warm fluids bringing it to body temperature. Warhaftig checks his laser bank one last time and, with a quick jab of a long bony finger against the control stud, causes a flash of dazzling purple light to leap forth and cut a thin red incision in Genghis Mao's abdomen. The Khan remains entirely motionless. The surgeon glances at Shadrach, who says, "All systems placid. Keep going."

Deftly Warhaftig slices deeper. As he makes each cut, scanners record the epidermal stratifications down to the cellular level, so that all joins will be perfect when the abdominal cavity is resealed. Bright steel retractors move automatically into place to hold the widening incision. The Khan watches the early phases with deep fascination, but, as his internal organs are laid bare, he turns his head away and stares toward the domed ceiling. Perhaps he finds the sight of his viscera frightening or repellent, Mordecai thinks, but more likely the Chairman is merely bored with them, having been cut open so many times.

Now the dark diseased liver is visible, heavy, spongy, sullen in color. Warhaftig, fingers moving like unerring spindles, clamps the arteries and veins connected to it. With quick daredevil flicks of his laser scalpel he severs the portal vein, the hepatic artery, the inferior vena cava, the ligamentum teres, and the bile duct. "Done," he murmurs, and Genghis Mao's third liver is lifted from his abdomen. Away for biopsy; the fourth waits close by, large and plump and healthy, resting within a crystalline jewel-case.

The surgeon and his team commence the most taxing part of the operation. Any pigsticker can make an incision, but only an artist can execute perfect sutures. Warhaftig seals flesh to flesh with a different laser, one that welds rather than cuts. Slowly, showing no sign of fatigue, he connects the closed-off arteries, veins, and bile duct to the new liver. Genghis Mao is limp, almost comatose now, eyes glazed, lips slack: Shadrach Mordecai has seen this response before and understands it well. It is a sign neither of exhaustion nor shock. It is no more than a kind of yogic exercise by which the Chairman disassociates himself from the boredom of his long ordeal. His vital signs are still high, with a preponderance of alpha rhythms in the cerebral output. Warhaftig toils on. The liver has been installed. The Khan's pulse rate rises and corrective measures must be taken, but this is to be expected; no cause for alarm. Meticulously Warhaftig rejoins peritoneum and muscular layers and dermis and epidermis, collaborating in this process with the com-

puter that feeds him the stratification data. Every
join is flawless. Scar formation will be minimal. Now
the abdominal wall is closed. Warhaftig steps back,
cool, self-satisfied, and lesser beings take over. The
transplant has been accomplished in exactly five hours.
Mordecai leans forward to study Genghis Mao's face.
The Chairman sleeps, so it would seem, facial muscles relaxed, eyes quiescent, chest rising and falling
evenly; but no, but no, the mere shadow of Shadrach
seems to register on the Khan's consciousness, for
his thin lips pull back in a frosty smile; his left eye
opens and performs an unmistakable wink.

"Well, that's another one over with," Genghis Mao
says, his voice firm and clear.

5

And so, in early evening, the day's work done and
his Hippocratic responsibilities well discharged, it
is off to Karakorum, the playground of this weary
world's ruling class, for Shadrach Mordecai, with
Nikki Crowfoot as his playmate.

He picks her up three hours after the operation in
the Project Avatar laboratory on the seventh level of
the Grand Tower of the Khan. A great green-walled
barn of a place it is, experimental animals caged
everywhere, crazy animals, cockadoodling hawks and
tree-climbing gorillas, and colossal banks of testing
equipment wherever there are no cages. There is a
laboratory stink to the air down here, a stink Mordecai
remembers well from his Harvard Med days, a mix
of Lysol and formaldehyde and ethyl alcohol and

mouse shit and Bunsen-burner fumes and burned insulation and what-all else. Most of the Avatar staff has left for the day, but Crowfoot, in gray lab smock and battered sandals, is busy at a five-meter-high agglomeration of computers and playback heads and television screens when he comes in. She stands with her back to the door, watching pyrotechnic bursts of green, blue, and red erupt and wiggle wildly across the face of a gigantic oscilloscope. Shadrach slips up behind her and, sliding his hands under her arms, cups her breasts through the smock. Her back goes rigid at the first touch of his fingers, but then she relaxes immediately, and does not turn around.

"Idiot," she says, but there is only affection in her voice. "Don't distract me. I'm running a triple simulation. That's a real Genghis Mao tape down there, the green, and the blue above it is our April seven persona-construct, and—"

"Forget it. Genghis Mao died on the table when we pulled his liver out. The revolution started an hour ago. The city—"

She squirms in his embrace, pulling around, staring wide-eyed at him, aghast.

"—is in flames, and if you listen you can hear the explosions where they're blowing up the statues—"

She sees his expression and begins to laugh. "Idiot! *Idiot!*"

"Actually, he's doing fine, even though Warhaftig put the new liver in upside down."

"Stop it, Shadrach."

"All right. He really is in good shape. He took ten minutes off to recuperate and now he's leading Mongol-style square-dancing in Committee Vector One."

"Shadrach—"

"I can't help it. I'm in my postoperative manic phase."

"Well, I'm not. It's been a garbage day here." Indeed her depression is obvious, once he slows down long enough to perceive it: her eyes are strained, her face is tense, her shoulders are uncharacteristically slumped.

"Your tests come out bad?"

"We blew them altogether. Hit a feedback loop and wiped three key tapes before we knew what was happening. I'm trying to salvage what's left. We've been set back a month, a month and a half."

"Poor Nikki. Is there any way I can help?"

"Just get me out of here," she says. "Amuse me. Distract me. Make funny faces. How *did* the operation go?"

"Flawless. Warhaftig's a wizard. He could do a nuclear implant on an amoeba with his thumbs and bring it off."

"The great man rests well?"

"Beautifully," Mordecai says. "It's almost obscene, the way an eighty-seven-year-old man bounces back from major surgery like this every five or six weeks."

"Is that what he is, eighty-seven?"

Shadrach shrugs. "That's what the official figure is. There are stories that he's older, perhaps a lot older, ninety, ninety-five, even past a hundred, they say. Rumors that he served in World War II. What we're talking about, of course, is the brain, the epidermal integument, and the skeletal structure. The rest of him's been cobbled together relatively recently out of fresh parts. A lung here, a kidney there, dacron arteries, ceramic hip joints, a plastic esophagus, a molybdenum-chromium shoulder, a new liver every few years—how it all hangs together I don't know. But he just gets younger and younger, stronger and stronger, wilier and wilier. You ought to hear his vital signs ticking away in here."

Grinning, Nikki Crowfoot puts her hands to Shadrach's thighs as though to feel the sensor implants. "Ye-es. He's doing marvelously well for his age. At the moment he's fornicating a nurse. Wait. Wait. I think he's coming! No, it's a sneeze. And now I pick up audio input. Gezundheit, she just said. How is Genghis Mao's sex life, anyway?"

"I try not to ask."

"Doesn't your inner machinery tell you?"

"Honi soit qui mal y pense," Mordecai says. "Doubt-

less he's got a splendid sex life. Probably more active than mine."

"You didn't *have* to sleep alone last night."

"My vocation demanded it of me." He gestures toward the door. "Karakorum?"

"Karakorum, yes. But first I need to wash and change."

They go to her apartment, forty stories higher in the building. All important members of Genghis Mao's staff have lodgings in the tower; but a research-group director has far less prestige than the Chairman's personal physician, and Crowfoot's suite is not nearly as opulent as Shadrach Mordecai's, just three rooms, plain furnishings, floors of common wood, no balcony, a sliver of a view. Shadrach settles into a webfoam lounger while Nikki strips and heads for the shower. Her bare body is strikingly beautiful, and desire stirs in him at the sight of her heavy dark-tipped breasts, her powerful thighs, her flat hard belly. She is long and lean, with strong shoulders, a narrow waist, sudden flaring hips, sleek muscular buttocks; a dense flood of thick black hair descends to the middle of her back. Unclothed she sheds the laboratory aura, the tense and fatigued look of the dissatisfied scientist, and becomes something primitive, barbaric, primordial—Pocahontas, Sacajawea, moon-begotten Nokomis. Once when he made such feverish comparisons when they were in bed together she became embarrassed and self-conscious, and mockingly, defensively, called him Othello and Ras Tafari and Chaka Zulu; never again has he overtly romanticized her savage ancestry, for he does not like to be twitted about his own, but the feeling persists, whenever she bares herself to him, that she is a princess of a fallen nation, high priestess of the great plains, red Amazon of the pagan night.

She emerges and dons a floor-length robe of openwork golden mesh, blatantly provocative, the antithesis of her epicene lab smock. Chocolate nipples show through, hints of the blue-black wire-stiff pubic triangle, flashes of haunch and thigh. He would gladly bed her this moment, but he knows she is tired and hungry, still preoccupied with the failures of the day, not yet at all in the mood for making love, and in any case she usually dislikes afternoon couplings, preferring to let erotic tensions build through the evening. So he contents himself with a light playful kiss and an appreciative smile, and out they go, down to the depths of the tower, to the loading ramp of the Karakorum tube-train.

Karakorum lies four hundred kilometers west of Ulan Bator. Five years ago a nuclear-powered subterrene drilled a wide tunnel connecting the two cities beneath the Central Gobi, its invincible thermal-stress penetrator slicing serenely through the resistant deep-lying Paleozoic granites and schists. Now high-speed trains on silent inertialess tracks sweep between the ancient capital and the modern one, making the journey in less than an hour. Shadrach Mordecai and Nikki Crowfoot join the pleasure-bound throngs on the platform; the next train is due to depart in just a few minutes. Several people greet them but no one comes close. There is something formidable and intimidating about a truly impressive-looking couple, something that seals them within a zone of chilly unapproachability, and Shadrach knows he and Nikki are impressive, tall slender black man and tall sturdy copper-skinned woman, handsome of form and face, elegantly dressed, Othello and Pocahontas out for a night on the town. But there is another isolating factor at work—Dr. Mordecai's professional proximity to the Khan: these people are aware that he has face-to-face access to Genghis Mao, one of the very few, and some of the Chairman's aura has been transferred to him, a contagion of awesomeness, making Mordecai one not to be approached casually. He dislikes this but there is little he can do about it.

The tube-train pulls in. Off now to Karakorum go Shadrach and Nikki.

Karakorum. Founded eight hundred years ago by Genghis Khan. Transformed into a majestic capital by Genghis's son Ogodai. Abandoned a generation later by Genghis's grandson Kublai, who preferred to rule from Cambaluc in China. Destroyed by Kublai

Khan when his rebellious younger brother attempted
to make it the seat of his revolt. Rebuilt eventually,
abandoned again, allowed to fall into decay, forgotten entirely. Its site rediscovered in the middle of the
twentieth century by archaeologists of the Mongolian
People's Republic and the Soviet Union. And now
much restored by decree of Genghis II Mao IV Khan,
self-anointed successor to one ancient empire and
one modern one, who wishes to remind the world of
the greatness of Genghis I and to make it forget the
centuries of Mongol slumber that followed the decline of the Khans.

Karakorum by night glitters with an unearthly
brightness, a stunning lunar glow. Mordecai and
Crowfoot, leaving the tube-train station, behold the
excavated ruins of old Karakorum to their left—a
solitary stone tortoise in a field of yellowed grass, the
outlines of some brick walls, a shattered pillar.
Nearby are gray stone stupas, monuments to holy
lamas, erected in the sixteenth century; in the distance,
against the parched hills, are the white stucco buildings of Karakorum State Farm, a grandiose project
of the defunct Mongolian People's Republic, a vast
agricultural enterprise occupying half a million hec-
tares of grassland. Between the farm buildings and
the stupas lies the Karakorum of Genghis Mao, a
flamboyant reconstruction of the original city, the
great many-columned walled palace of Ogodai Khan
imagined anew, the splendid observatory with its
heaven-stabbing turrets, the mosques and churches,
the gaudy silken tents of the nobility, the somber
brick houses of the foreign merchants, all testifying
to the might and magnificence of the latter-day Prince
of Princes, Genghis Mao, who, according to a half-
suppressed legend, had once had a humbler Mongol
name, Choijamtse or Ochirbal or Gombojab—the tales
vary according to the teller—and had been a mi-
nor functionary, a very insignificant *apparatchik*, in
the bureaucracy of the old People's Republic in the
vanished Marxist-Leninist days, before the world fell
apart and a new Mongol empire was constructed on
its relict.

The resurrected Karakorum is not merely a sterile monument to antiquity, though: by Genghis Mao's decree it is an amusement park, a place of revelry and pleasures, a twenty-first-century Xanadu blazing with frantic energy. In these black and yellow and scarlet tents one may dine, drink, gamble; the latest hallucinations are for sale here; here one may find willing sexual partners of all kinds; those who indulge in the popular cults of the moment—dream-death, transtemporalism, and carpentry are the fashionable ones just now—have facilities for their rituals in Karakorum. Shadrach is a carpentry-cultist himself; Nikki Crowfoot goes in for transtemporalism, and he has dabbled in that too, though not lately. Once he came to Karakorum with Katya Lindman, and that fierce, intense woman urged him to try dream-death with her, but he refused, and she scorned him for his timidity for days afterward. Not with words. Little castrating scowls; sudden harsh flickers of her furious eyes. Mocking quiverings of her elegant nostrils.

As they pass the dream-death pavilion now, neither of them giving it more than a casual glance, Mordecai forcing the image of Katya Lindman's bare blazing body out of his mind, Crowfoot says, "Isn't it risky, your going this far from Ulan Bator only a few hours after he's had major surgery?"

"Not especially. In fact, I always go out the evening after a transplant. A little bonus I give myself after a hard day's work. If anything, it's a better time for a Karakorum trip than most."

"Why so?"

"He's in an intensive-care support system tonight. If any complications set in, alarms will go off all over the place and one of the low-echelon medics will respond instantly. You know, my job doesn't require me to hold the boss's hand twenty-five hours a day. It isn't needed and he doesn't want it."

Fireworks abruptly explode overhead. Wheels of gold and crimson, spears coursing across the night. Shadrach imagines he sees the face of Genghis Mao filling the sky, but no, but no, just self-deception, the pattern is plainly abstract. Plainly.

"If an emergency comes up, they'll summon you, won't they?" Nikki asks.

"They won't need to," Mordecai tells her. Out of the dream-death pavilion comes a weird discordant music, bagpipes gone awry. He thinks of Katya Lindman crooning in Swedish an hour before the dawn one snowy night, and shivers. He pats his thigh where the implants are and says, "I'm getting the full broadcast, remember?"

"Even out here?"

He nods. "The telemetering range is about a thousand kilometers. I'm picking him up clearly right this minute. He's resting very comfortably, dozing, I'd say, temperature about a degree above normal, pulse very slightly high, new liver integrating itself nicely and already making positive changes in his general metabolic state. If anything starts deteriorating, I'll know about it immediately, and if necessary I can always get back to him in ninety minutes or so. Meanwhile I'm covered and I'm free to amuse myself."

"Always aware of the state of his health."

"Yes. Always. Even while I sleep, the information ticks into me."

"Your implants fascinate me philosophically," she says. They pause at a sweets-vendor's booth to buy some refreshments. The vendor, a squat thick-nosed Mongol, offers them airag, the ancient Mongol beverage of fermented mare's milk, and, shrugging, Mordecai takes a flask for her and one for himself. She makes a face, but drinks, and says, "What I mean is, looking at you and the Chairman in strict cybernetic terms, it's hard to see where the boundaries of your individuality end and his begin. You and he amount to a single self-corrective information-processing unit, practically a single life system."

"That's not exactly how I see it," Mordecai tells her. "There may be a constant flow of metabolic information from his body to mine, and the information I receive from him has some impact on the course of my actions and I suppose ultimately on his, but he remains an autonomous being, the Chairman of the PRC, no less, with all the tremendous power that that entails, and I am only—"

"No. Look at it with a total-systems approach," Crowfoot urges impatiently. "Let's say you're Michelangelo, trying to turn a huge block of marble into the *David*. The figure is within the marble: you must liberate it with your mallet and chisel, right? You strike the block; a chip of marble is knocked off. You strike it again. Another chip. A few more chips and perhaps the outline of an arm begins to emerge. The angle of the chisel is slightly different for each stroke, isn't it? And maybe the intensity of the force you use to hit the chisel with a mallet is different, too. You constantly modify and correct your strokes according to the information you're receiving from the cut face of the marble block—the emerging shape, the right cleavage planes, and so on. Do you see the total system? The process of creating Michelangelo's *David* isn't one in which you, Michelangelo, simply act on a passive lump of stone. The marble's an active force too, part of the circuit, in a sense part of the mind system that is Michelangelo-as-sculptor. Because—"

"I don't—"

"Let me finish. Let me trace the whole circuit for you. A change in the outline of the marble is perceived by your eye and is evaluated by your brain, which transmits instructions to the muscles of your arm having to do with the force and angle of the next blow, and this causes a change in your neuromuscular response as you strike the next blow, producing further change in the marble that causes further perception of change in the eye and a further alteration of program within the brain, leading to another correction of neuromuscular response for the next stroke, and so on, on and on around the loop until the statue is done. The process of carving the statue is a process of perceiving and responding to change, to stroke-by-stroke difference; and the block of marble is an essential part of the total system."

"It didn't ask to be," Shadrach says mildly. "It doesn't *know* it's part of a system."

"Irrelevant. View the system as a closed universe. The marble is changing and its changes produce changes within Michelangelo that lead to further changes in the marble. Within the closed universe of sculptor-and-tools-and-marble, it's incorrect to view Michelangelo as the 'self,' the actor, and the marble as a 'thing,' the acted-upon. Sculptor and tools and marble together make up a single network of causal pathways, a single thinking-and-acting-and-changing entity, a single *person*, if you will. Now, you and Genghis Mao—"

"Are different persons," Mordecai insists. "The feedback's not the same. If his kidney conks out, I react to the extent that I perceive the malfunction and treat it and arrange for a kidney replacement, but I won't get sick myself. And if something goes wrong with *my* kidneys, it won't affect him in any way."

Crowfoot shrugs. "True but trivial. Don't you see that the causal interlock between the two of you is much more intimate? Your whole daily routine is controlled by the transmissions you get from Genghis Mao: you sleep alone or sleep with me, depending on his health, you go to Karakorum or stay by his bedside, you experience somatic anxieties if the signal from him starts going critical, you have a whole constellation of life-choices and life-responses that are governed almost entirely by his metabolism. You're an extension of Genghis Mao. And what about him? He lives or dies at your option. He may be Chairman of the PRC, but he would be just another dead man next week if you fail to pick up some key symptom or fail to take the proper corrective action. You're essential to his survival, and he controls many of your movements and actions. One system, Shadrach, one constantly resonating circuit, you and Genghis Mao, Genghis Mao and you!"

Still Shadrach Mordecai shakes his head. "The analogy's close, but not close enough to convince me. Not quite close enough. I'm equipped with some extraordinary diagnostic devices, sure, but they're not all that special; my implants help me respond faster to emergencies than an ordinary doctor might respond to an ordinary patient, but that's all. It's only a quantitative difference. You can define any doctor-patient unit as a single self-corrective information-processing system, of sorts, but I don't think the hookup between Genghis Mao and myself creates any kind of significant difference in that type of system. If I got sick when he got sick, the point would be valid, but—"

Nikki Crowfoot sighs. "Let it pass, Shadrach. It isn't worth all this palaver. In the Avatar lab we constantly have to deal with the principle that the popular notion of 'self' is pretty meaningless, that it's necessary to think in terms of larger information-handling systems, but maybe I'm extending the principle into areas where it doesn't need to go. Or maybe you and I simply aren't communicating very well right now." She closes her eyes for a moment and clenches her jaws as if trying to discharge some jangling current pulsing through her brain. Another barrage of fireworks lights up the sky with garish purple and green streaks. Savage thorny music, all snarls and shrieks, pierces the air. After a moment Crowfoot relaxes, grins, points to the shimmering tent of the transtemporalists a few meters in front of them. "Enough talk," she says. "Now some excitement."

6

"I shall explain the method of our rite, if you wish," says the transtemporalist. Deep slurred Mongol voice, monolithic face, all nose and no cheekbones, the eyes hidden in shadows.

"Not necessary," Mordecai tells him. "I've been here before."

"Ah. Of course." An obsequious little bow. "I was not sure of that, Dr. Mordecai."

Shadrach is accustomed to being recognized. Mongolia is full of foreigners but very few of them are black. The sound of his own name, therefore, gives him only the most fleeting jab of surprise. Still, he would have welcomed more anonymity here. The transtemporalist kneels and beckons to him to do the same. They are in a private little cubicle, formed by thick carpets draped over ropes, within the vast dim tent. A thick yellow candle set in a pewter cup on the earthen floor flickers between them, sending a heavy spiral of dark sour smoke toward the tent's sloping top. In Mordecai's nostrils are all sorts of primeval Mongol odors, the reek of shaggy goatskin walls, the stench of what might well be a cow-dung fire somewhere nearby. The floor is densely strewn with soft wood shavings, a luxury in this land of few trees. The transtemporalist is busy at the chemistry of his vocation, mixing fluids in a tall pewter beaker, an oily blue one and a thin scarlet one, stirring them around with an ivory swizzle-stick that makes lively swirl patterns, adding now a sprinkle of a green powder

50

and a yellow one. Hocus-pocus, all of it: Mordecai suspects that only one of these substances is the true drug, the others being mere decoration. But rites demand mystery and color, and these dour priests, claiming all of time and space for their province, must heighten their effects as best they can. Shadrach wonders how far from him Nikki is now. They were parted at the entrance to the transtemporalists' maze of a tent, each led separately into the shadows by silent acolytes. The time voyage is a journey that one must take alone.

The Mongol concludes his pharmaceutics and, holding the cup tenderly in both hands, passes it above the candle's sputtering flame to Shadrach Mordecai.

"Drink," he says, and, feeling a bit like Tristan, Shadrach drinks. Surrenders the cup. Sits back on his haunches, waiting.

"Give me your hands," the transtemporalist murmurs.

Shadrach extends them, palms upward. The Mongol covers them with his own short-fingered wide-spanned hands and intones some gibberish prayer, unintelligible except for scattered Mongol words that have no contextual coherence. A faint dizziness is beginning in Shadrach Mordecai now. This will be his third transtemporal experience, the first in nearly a year. Once he visited the court of King Baldwin of Jerusalem in the guise of a black prince of Ethiopia, a Christian Moor at the swaggering feasts of the Crusaders; and once he found himself atop a stone pyramid in Mexico, robed all in white, slashing with an obsidian dagger at the breast of a writhing Spaniard spreadeagled on the sacrificial altar of Huitzilopochtli. And now? He will have no choice in his destination. The transtemporalist will choose it for him according to some unfathomable whim, aiming him with a word or two, a skillful suggestion as he is cut loose from his moorings by the drug and sent adrift into a living past. His own imagination and historical knowledge, coupled with, perhaps—who knows?— whispered cues from the transtemporalist as his drugged body lies on the floor of the tent—will do the rest. Mordecai sways now. Everything whirls. The transtemporalist leans close and speaks, and it is a struggle to comprehend the words, but Shadrach must comprehend, he needs to hear—

"It is the night of Cotopaxi," the Mongol whispers. "Red sun, yellow sky."

The tent disappears and Shadrach is alone.

Where is he? A city. Not Karakorum. This place is unfamiliar, subtropical, narrow streets, steep hills, iron-grilled doorways, twining red-flowered vines, cool clear air, grand fountains in spacious plazas, white-fronted houses with wrought-iron balconies. A Latin city, intense, hectic, busy.

—*¡Barato aquí! ¡Barato!*

—*Yo tengo un hambre canina.*

Honking horns, barking dogs, the shouts of children, the cries of vendors. Women roasting bits of meat over charcoal braziers in the cobbled streets. A thousand strident people-sounds. Where is there a city with such vigorous life? Why does no one show signs of the organ-rot? They are all so healthy here, even the beggars, even the paupers. There are no such cities. No more, no more. Ah. Naturally. He is dreaming a city that no longer exists. This is a city of yesterday.

—*Le telefonearé un día de estos.*

—*Hasta la semana que viene.*

He has never spoken Spanish. And yet he recognizes the words, and yet he understands them.

—*¿Donde está el teléfono?*

—*¡Vaya de prisa! ¡Tenga cuidado!*

—*¡Maricón!*

—*No es verdad.*

Standing in the middle of a busy street at the top of a broad hill, he is stunned by the view. Mountains! They rim the city, great snowcapped cones, gleaming in the midday sun. He has lived too long on the Mongolian plateau; mountains such as these have become unfamiliar and alien to him. Shadrach stares in awe at the immense glaciered peaks, so huge they seem topheavy, they seem about to tumble from the sky to crush the bustling city. And is that a plume of smoke rising from the crest of that most enormous one? He is not sure. At such a distance—at least fifty kilometers—is it possible to see smoke? Yes. Yes. Beyond any doubt, smoke. He remembers the last words he heard before the dizziness took him: "It is the night of Cotopaxi. Red sun, yellow sky." The great volcano—is that it? A flawless cone, swathed in snow and pumice, its base hidden in clouds, its summit outlined in numbing majesty against the darkening sky. He has never seen such a mountain.

He halts a boy who darts past him.

—*Por favor.*

The boy is wide-eyed, terrified, but yet he stops, looks up.

—*¿Sí, Señor?*

—*¿Como se llama esta montaña?*

Shadrach points toward the colossal snowcapped volcano.

The boy smiles and relaxes. His fear is gone; obviously he is pleased by the notion of knowing something that this tall darkskinned stranger does not. He says:

—*Cotopaxi.*

Cotopaxi. Of course. The transtemporalist has given him a front row ticket to the great catastrophe. This is the city of Quito, then, in Ecuador, and that, trailing smoke to the southeast, is Cotopaxi, the world's loftiest active volcano, and this day must be the nineteenth of August, 1991, a day that everyone remembers, and Shadrach Mordecai knows that before the sun touches the Pacific tonight the world will be shaken as it rarely has been shaken in all the time of mankind, and an era will end and a reign of fire will be loosed upon civilization. And he is the only person on earth who knows this, and here he stands below great Cotopaxi and he can do nothing. Nothing. Nothing but watch, and tremble, and perhaps perish with the half million who will perish here tonight. Can one die, he wonders, while one is traveling this way? Is it not only a dream, a dream, a dream, and can dreams kill? Even if he dreams an eruption, even if he dreams tons of lava and brimstone descending on his broken body?

The boy is still standing there, staring at him.

—*Gracias, amigo.*

—*De nada, Señor.*

The boy waits, perhaps for a coin, but Shadrach has none to give him, and after a moment he runs off, pausing after ten paces to look back and stick out his tongue, then running again, sprinting into an alleyway, disappearing.

And a moment later there is a terrible noise from Cotopaxi and a white column at least a hundred meters thick rises straight up like a scepter from a secondary cone on the volcano's sloping flank.

Immediately all movement halts in the city. Everyone freezes; every head turns toward Cotopaxi. The white column, pouring from the vent with incredible velocity, rising already to a height of at least a thousand meters above Cotopaxi's summit, is spreading now, filling the sky like a broad plume of feathers, a cloak of live steam. Mordecai perceives a low droning rumbling sound, as of a train passing through the city, but a train for giants, a titanic train that makes lanterns sway and potted plants topple from balconies. The cloud of steam has turned gray on top, with tinges of red and yellow toward its outer edges.

—*¡Aie! ¡El fin del mundo!*

—*¡Madre de dios! ¡La montaña!*

—*¡Ayuda! ¡Ayuda! ¡Ayuda!*

And the flight from Quito begins. Nothing has happened yet, nothing but a roar and a hiss and a column of steam rushing skyward, but nevertheless the people of the city abandon their houses, carrying little or nothing, grasping perhaps a crucifix or a child or a cat or a handful of clothes, crowding into the streets, shuffling somberly downhill, northward, long lines of people moving with hunched shoulders, no one looking back, everyone heading out of the city, heading away from Cotopaxi, from the frightening crimson cloud that now looms over the mountain, from the death that soon will come to Quito. These are people wise in the way of volcanoes, and they do not care to stay for the show. Shadrach Mordecai is swept along in the human tide. He towers over these folk as the volcano does over the city, and they glance strangely at him, and some tug at his arms in a kind of appeal, as if they think he is a black deity come to lead them to safety. But he is leading no one. He is following, he is fleeing helplessly with all the rest. Unlike them he does look over his shoulder every few minutes. Whenever he can, whenever the press of refugees is not too powerful, he pauses and turns to see what is happening. The volcano now is spurting little bursts of pumice and light ash, wind-borne powdery stuff that changes the color of the air, staining it yellow, deepening the sun's hues to an orange-red. The earth seems to be groaning. The whole city shakes. Automobiles laden with well-dressed citizens move slowly through the streets, unable to make headway in the throngs of shuffling pedestrians; there are collisions, shouts, quarrels. Soon the cars have halted altogether and their passengers, quirky-lipped and disdainful, shoulder their way into the lines of humbler folk. Shadrach has been marching for an hour or two now, perhaps three, mechanically pushing himself along; the air has grown thin and chilly, with an acrid reek of brimstone in it, and though it is only the middle of the afternoon the falling ash has so obscured the light that the streetlamps have come on—the ash is accumulating like fine snow in the streets, already ankle-deep—and still Cotopaxi roars and hisses, and still the people straggle northward. Mordecai knows what will happen soon. With the eerie double-edged vision of the time traveler, he looks forward as well as back, remembering the future. Before long there will be the explosion that will be heard thousands of miles away, the earthquake, the clouds of poisonous gas, the lunatic outpouring of tons of volcanic ash that will blot out the sun all over the world, and on this night of Cotopaxi the ancient gods will be let loose on earth and empires will crumble. He has lived through this night once already, but not with the knowledge he now has. Somewhere far away at this moment is fifteen-year-old Shadrach,

all arms and legs and huge eyes, doing his lessons
and dreaming of medical school, and he will hear the
explosion too, dull and muffled though it will sound
after spanning the planet from Quito to Philadelphia,
and he will think it is a terrorist's bomb, perhaps,
going off downtown, but in the morning he will see
the sky tinted yellow and the swollen sun gone all
red, and then the fine dust will fall for days, bringing
early twilights on these summer evenings, and news
will trickle out of South America of the terrible
eruption, the loss of hundreds of thousands of lives.
What that young Shadrach does not know, what no
one knows except the stranger striding through the
northern outskirts of Quito under a dirty crimson
cloud, is that the eruption of Cotopaxi is more than a
natural event: it signals a political apocalypse, the
fall of the nations about to begin, the time of Genghis
Mao about to arrive.
    —*¡El fin del mundo!*
Yes. Yes. The end of the world.
And now the explosion comes.
    It happens in stages, first five quick sharp reports
like cannonfire; then a long moment of total silence
when even the persistent rumble that has gone on for
hours abruptly halts; then a violent shaking of the
earth and a single monstrous booming sound, the
loudest sound Mordecai has ever heard, a sound that
breaks windows and splits walls; then silence again;
then the rumbling once more; then more cannonfire,
bang bang bang, quick hard pops; then a second
great boom, five times as powerful as the first, that
drops people to their knees, clutching at their ears;
then silence, an ominous, sinister, nerve-tightening
silence; and then the sound of sounds, the sound of a
planet splitting apart at its core, an unending grotesque avalanche of sound that makes the neck snap
and the arms jerk wildly and the eyes jiggle in their
sockets, a sound that rolls over Quito like the tram-
pling foot of an angry god. And the sky turns black
and a torrent of red fire spills out of Cotopaxi and
burns with a hideous glare on the horizon. The mountain appears to be ripping open. Shadrach can see

huge chunks of its crest, slabs of rock that must be the size of great buildings, flying loose and soaring slowly and grandly toward Quito. The perfect cone, once as graceful as Mount Fuji's, is a ruin now, a shattered wreck, dimly visible through the dense clouds of ash and the flying balls of pumice; it is only a stump, irregular and ghastly. The air itself is burning. People still struggle onward, moving ever more slowly, dragging themselves along on leaden legs toward a salvation that is not to be reached, but they vomit, they clutch at their throats, they gasp, they choke, they fall.

—*Ayuda. Ayuda.*

But there is no help to be had. They are dying here in the early afternoon of this sparkling day, sparkling no longer.

Shadrach, trying to breathe an atmosphere that is half ash and half carbon monoxide, falls himself, gets up, falls again, forces himself to rise. He remembers that he is a doctor and kneels beside a fallen woman, a girl, really, whose face is distorted and nearly as black as his own from asphyxiation.

—*Yo soy un médico.*

—*Gracias, señor. Gracias.*

Her eyes flutter. She looks to him for aid, medicine, a drink of water, anything. How can he help her? He is a doctor, yes, but can he teach the dying to breathe poisoned air? She gags, shivers, and then—strangely—yawns. She is falling asleep in his arms. But it is a deadly drowsiness, and she will not wake. He releases her. He moves onward, handkerchief over his mouth and nose. Useless. Useless. He falls again and does not rise, he lies in a heap of weeping murmuring victims, a victim himself.

So this is how it was on the night of Cotopaxi. Night and ash, flight and death. That saucy boy, those women roasting bits of meat, the shopkeepers and the bankers, the cab drivers and the policemen, that tall black-skinned stranger, all dying together now, the hours of frenzied flight a waste, and Cotopaxi's ashy ejecta filling the heavens, giving all the world a blood-red twilight. *El fin del mundo*, yes. Shadrach claws at the ashes filling his mouth. There is another explosion, a lesser one now—for what could equal that last unimaginable apocalyptic blast?—and another, another, and he knows that the booms will continue in diminishing intensity for many hours, even for days. No one will sleep tonight in Ecuador, in Colombia, Venezuela, in all of Central America, even in Mexico; the dread thunder of Cotopaxi will resound in Canada, in Patagonia, it will reach far across both oceans, and by dawn, the dust-choked dawn, the black dawn through which no light can penetrate, the first revolution will be under way, the *putsch* in Brazil, the insurrectionists taking advantage of the strange darkness and the universal terror to launch their long-awaited coup; and then the chain reaction, the uprisings triggered by the Brazilian one in Argentina, Nicaragua, Algeria, Indonesia, one bloodbath providing the cue for the next, and all spurred by Cotopaxi, by the great symbol-freighted upheaval of the volcano; the economic crises of the 1970s and the repressions and shortages of the impoverished 1980s leading inexorably to the worldwide chaos of 1991, the global revolution, the long *Walpurgisnacht* touched off in some incalculable way by the eruption.

So this is how it was on the night of Cotopaxi. The angry gods shaking the world and bringing the nations into destruction. Shadrach bows his head, closes his eyes, surrenders to the soft warm fragrant ash that drifts peacefully upon him. This is the night of Cotopaxi, yes, *el fin del mundo*, the sounding of the last trump, the opening of the seventh seal, and he has been part of it, he has tasted the pumice of the volcano. And now he sleeps.

7

He stands in the gravel-strewn walk outside the tent of the transtemporalists, dazed, the sulphurous taste of Cotopaxi somehow still in his mouth. Nikki has not yet emerged. Other people he knows wander by, members of Genghis Mao's staff, flowing past him down the midway toward the garish cluster of gaming pavilions at the western end of the pleasure complex: there goes Frank Ficifolia, the jowly little communications man who designed Surveillance Vector One, and after him a Mongol military aide-de-camp, Gonchigdorge, all ribbons and medals in his comic-book uniform, and then two of the Committee vice-chairmen, a pallid Turk named Eyuboglu and a burly Greek named Ionigylakis. Each, as he passes, greets Shadrach in characterstic style, Ficifolia warm and effusive, Gonchigdorge offhanded and remote. Eyuboglu wary, Ionigylakis boisterous. Shadrach Mordecai manages a nod and a glassy smile in return, no more. *Yo soy un médico.* He still feels the earth rumbling. He wishes everyone would let him alone. In Karakorum one deserves a little privacy. Especially right now. The significant sectors of his consciousness are still in the suburbs of Quito, sinking under tons of fine hot ash. Coming out of transtemporalism is always something of a shock, but this is too much, it is as bad as eviction from the womb; he is vulnerable and fuddled, unable to cope with the social rituals. Those rough globules of airy pumice, that scent of brimstone, that inescapable sleepiness; above all, that crushing sense of transition, that feeling of one world falling apart and a new, strange one being formed—

Out of the transtemporalists' tent now comes a short pigeon-breasted man with crooked teeth and astonishing bushy red eyebrows. He is Roger Buckmaster, British, a microengineering expert, competent and usually sullen, a man whom few people seem to know well. He plants himself near the exit of the tent, a few meters from Shadrach Mordecai, and digs both feet firmly, flatfootedly, into the gravel as though he is uncertain about his balance. He has the stunned look of a man who has just been thrown out of a pub after five beers too many.

Mordecai, though he has only a distant acquaintance with Buckmaster and just now has especially little interest in a conversation with him, knows all too well how confusing the first moments outside the tent can be, and is sympathetic. He feels impelled to meet Buckmaster's wobbly gaze with some sort of polite gesture; he smiles and says hello, thinking that he will now retreat into his own confusion and fatigued meditations.

Buckmaster, though, blinks and glares aggressively. "It's the black bahstard!" he says. His voice is thick, phlegmy, high-pitched, not at all friendly. "The black bahstard himself!"

"Black bahstard?" Mordecai repeats wonderingly, mimicking the accent. "Black bahstard? Man, did you call me—"

"Bahstard. Black."

"That's what I thought you said."

"Black bahstard. Evil as the ace of spades."

This is ludicrous. "Roger, are you all right?"

"Evil. Black and evil."

"I heard you, yes," Shadrach says. A miserable throbbing begins along the left side of his skull. He regrets having acknowledged Buckmaster's presence; he wishes Buckmaster would disappear. The racial slur itself is more grotesque than insulting to him, for he has never had any reason to feel defensive about his color, but he is puzzled by the gratuitousness of the attack and he remains too deeply under the spell of his own powerful transtemporal experience to want any sort of interaction with a truculent clown like Buckmaster, not now, above all not now. Perhaps the thing to do is ignore him. Shadrach folds his arms and steps back against a light-pillar.

But Buckmaster says into Shadrach's silence, "You don't feel covered with shame, Mordecai?"

"Look, Roger—"

"Drenched with guilt for every filthy act of your treacherous life?"

"Come *on*. What have you been drinking in there, man?"

"The same as everyone else. Just the drug, the drug, the time-drug, whatever they give you. D'ye think they fed me hashish? D'ye think I'm high on whiskey? Oh, no, just the time-drink, and it opened my eyes, let me tell you, it opened them wide!" Buckmaster advances until he stands no more than thirty centimeters from Shadrach Mordecai, glaring up at him, shouting. The pain in Shadrach's skull is that of a spike being hammered deep. "I've seen Judas sell Him out!" Buckmaster roars. "I was there, in Jerusalem, at the Supper, watching them eat. Thirteen at the table, eh? I poured the wine with my own hands, you black devil, I watched Judas smirking, saw him whispering in His ear, even, and then out into the garden, y'know. Gethsemane, there in the darkness—"

"Would you like a trank, Roger?"

"Keep off me with your filthy pills!"

"You're getting overwrought. You ought to try to calm yourself."

"Listen to him doctoring me. *Me*. No, you won't dope me, and you'll pay heed while I tell you—"

"Some other time," Shadrach says. He is pinned between Buckmaster and the light-pillar, but he slips aside and makes broad swimming gestures in the air between them, as though Buckmaster is a noxious vapor he'd like to blow away. "I'm tired now. I've had a heavy trip in there myself. I can't handle any of this at the moment, Buckmaster, if you don't mind. All right?"

"You bloody well will handle it. I want to tell you. I've got you here and I'll tell you. I saw it, everything, Judas coming up to Him and kissing Him in the garden, and saying, Master, master, just as it is in the Book, and then the Roman soldiers closing in and arresting him—oh, the bloody betraying bahstard. I saw it, I was there, I understand now what guilt means. Do you? You don't. And you're as guilty as he was, in a different way but the same kind, Mordecai."

"I'm a Judas?" Shadrach shakes his head wearily. Drunks irritate him, even if they are drunk only on the transtemporalists' drug. "I don't understand any of this. Who is it I'm supposed to have betrayed?"

"Everyone. All of mankind."

"And you say you aren't drunk."

"Never been more sober. Oh, my eyes are open now! Who is it who keeps him alive, answer me that? Who's there by his side, giving him injections, medicines, pills, yelling for the bloody surgeon every time he needs a new kidney or a new heart, eh? Eh?"

"You want the Chairman to die?"

"Damn right I do!"

Shadrach gasps. Buckmaster has obviously been driven insane by his transtemporal experience; Shadrach can no longer be annoyed with him. The angry little man must be protected against himself. "You'll be arrested if you go on this way," Shadrach says. "He might be listening to us right now."

"He's flat on his back, half dead from the operation," Buckmaster retorts. "Don't you think I know that? You put a new liver into him today."

"Even so, there are spy-eyes everywhere, recording instruments—you designed some of them yourself, Buckmaster."

"I don't care. *Let* him hear me."

"So now you're a revolutionary?"

"My eyes are open. I've had a revelation in that tent. Guilt, responsibility, evil—"

"You think the world would be better off with Genghis Mao dead?"

Fiercely Buckmaster cries, "Yes! Yes! He's draining us all so he can live forever. He's turned the world into a madhouse, into a bloody zoo! Look, Mordecai, we could be rebuilding, we could be passing around the Antidote and healing the whole world, not just the favored few, we could go back to what we had before the War, but no, no, we're ruled by a bloody Mongol Khan, can you imagine that? A hundred-year-old Mongol Khan who wants to live forever! And he'd have been dead five years ago but for you."

Shadrach sees where Buckmaster is heading, and he presses his hands to his temples in dismay. He wants more desperately than ever to escape from this conversation. Buckmaster is a fool, and his onslaught is cheap and obvious. Shadrach has thought all this through, long ago, considered the moral problems, and dismissed them. Of *course* serving an evil dictator is wrong. No job for a nice sincere dedicated black boy from Philadelphia who wants to do good. But is Genghis Mao evil? Are there any alternatives to his rule, other than chaos? If Genghis Mao is inevitable like some natural force, like the rising of the sun or the falling of the rain, then no guilt attaches to serving him: one does what seems appropriate, one lives one's life, one accepts one's karma, and if one is a doctor then one heals, without considering the ramifications of one's patient's identity. To Shadrach this is no glib rationalization, but rather a statement of acceptance of destiny. He refuses to assume burdens of guilt that have no meaning to him, and he will not let Buckmaster, of all people, flagellate him over absurdities nor accuse him of misplacing his loyalties.

He notices that Nikki Crowfoot has come out of the transtemporalists' tent and is standing to one side, hands on her hips, waiting for him, and he says to Buckmaster, "Excuse me. I have to go now."

Nikki seems transfigured. Her eyes are aglow, her face glistens with ecstatic sweat, her whole body seems to gleam. As Shadrach strides toward her, she acknowledges him with a mere tilt of her head, but she is far away, still lost in her hallucination.

"Let's go," he says. "Buckmaster's a little crazy tonight and he's making a nuisance of himself."

He reaches for her hand.

"Wait!" Buckmaster yells, running toward them. "I'm not through with you. I've got more to tell you, you black bahstard!"

Mordecai shrugs and says, "All right. You can have one more minute. What do you want me to do, exactly?"

"Leave off tending him."

"I'm a doctor, Buckmaster. He's my patient."

"Precisely. And that's why I call you a guilty bahstard. Billions of people to care for in the world, and *he's* the one you choose to look after. Dooming us all to decades more of Genghis Mao."

"Someone else would serve him if I didn't," Shadrach says gently.

"But you do. *You.* And I must hold you responsible."

Astonished, baffled by the force and persistence of Buckmaster's attack, Shadrach says, "Responsible for what?"

"For the way the world is. The whole bleeding mess. The continued threat of universal organ-rot twenty years after the Virus War. The hunger, the poverty. Oh, don't you have any shame, Mordecai? You with your legs full of machinery that tell you every twitch of his blood pressure so you can run to him even faster?"

Shadrach glances at Nikki, appealing to her to do something to rescue him. But she still has that far-off look; she does not appear to be aware of Buckmaster at all.

Angrily Mordecai says, "Who designed that machinery, Roger?"

Buckmaster recoils. He has been hit where it hurts. His cheeks blaze; his eyes glisten with furious tears. "I! I did! You bahstard, I admit it, I built your dirty implants. Don't you think I know I share the guilt? Don't you think I understand that now? But I'm getting out. I won't bear the responsibility any longer."

"This is suicidal, the way you're carrying on." Shadrach Mordecai points to shadowy figures on the periphery of the path, high staffers who hover in the darkness, unwilling to come within range of possible spy-eyes while they enjoy Buckmaster's juicy lunatic outburst. "There'll be a report of all this on the Chairman's desk tomorrow, Roger, more likely than not. You're destroying yourself."

"I'll destroy *him*. The bloodsucker. He holds us all for ransom, our bodies, our souls, he'll let us rot if we don't serve him, he—"

"Don't be melodramatic. We serve Genghis Mao because we have skills and this is the proper place to employ them," Mordecai says crisply. "It's no fault of ours that the world is as it is. If you'd rather have been out in Liverpool or Manchester living in some stinking cellar with your intestines full of holes, you could have been."

"Don't goad me, Mordecai."

"But it's true. We're lucky to be here. We're doing the only sane thing possible in a crazy world. Guilt is a luxury we can't afford. You want to walk out now, go ahead, go, Roger. But you won't want to leave the Khan when you calm down in the morning."

"I refuse to have you patronize me."

"I'm trying to protect you. I'm trying to get you to shut up and stop shouting dangerous nonsense."

"And I'm trying to get you to pull the plug and free us from Genghis Khan Mao," Buckmaster wails, flushed and wild-eyed.

"So you think we'd be better off without him?" Shadrach asks. "What are your alternatives, Buckmaster? What kind of government would you suggest? Come on. I'm serious. You've been calling me a lot of unpleasant names, now let's have some rational discussion. You've become a revolutionary, right? Okay. What's your program? What do you want?"

Buckmaster is beyond the moment for philosophical discourse, however. He glowers at Mordecai in barely controlled loathing, framing words that will not leave his throat except as incoherent guttural growls; he clenches and unclenches his fists, he sways alarmingly, his reddened cheeks turn scarlet. Shadrach, all sympathy long gone, turns from him and reaches toward Nikki Crowfoot again. As they begin to walk away together Buckmaster rushes forward in a clumsy flailing lunge, clamping his hands on Shadrach's shoulders and trying to pull him down. Shadrach pivots gracefully, bends slightly to slip free of Buckmaster's grasp, and, when Buckmaster hurls himself at him, seizes him about the ribs, spins him around, and holds him immobile. Buckmaster squirms, kicks, spits, sputters, but Shadrach is much too strong for him. "Easy," Shadrach murmurs. "Easy. Relax. Let go of it, Roger. Let go of everything." He holds Buckmaster as one might hold a hysterical child, until at length he feels Buckmaster go slack, all the frenzy leaving him. Mordecai releases him and steps back, hands poised at chest level, ready for a new lunge, but Buckmaster is spent. He backs away from Mordecai in the slinking heavy-shouldered walk of a beaten man, pausing after a few paces to scowl and mutter, "All right, Mordecai. Bahstard. *Stay* with Genghis Mao. Wipe his decrepit arse for him. See what happens to you! You'll finish in the furnace, Shadrach, in the furnace, in the bloody furnace!"

Shadrach laughs. The tension is broken. "The furnace. I like that. Very literary, Buckmaster."

"The furnace for you, Shadrach!"

Mordecai, smiling, takes Crowfoot's arm. She still looks radiant, ecstatic, lost in transcendental raptures. "Let's go," he says. "I can't take any more of this."

Softly, in a dream-furry voice, she says, "What did he mean by that, Shadrach? About the furnace?"

"Biblical reference. Shadrach, Meshach, Abednego."

"Who?"

"You don't know it?"

"No. Shadrach, it's such a lovely night. Let's go somewhere and make love."

"Shadrach, Meshach, Abednego. In the Book of Daniel. Three Hebrews who refused to worship Nebuchadnezzar's golden idol, and the king cast them into a burning fiery furnace, and God sent an angel to walk with them in there, and they were unharmed. Strange you don't know the story."

"What happened to them?"

"I told you, love. They were unharmed, not a hair of their heads singed, and Nebuchadnezzar called them forth, and told them that their God was a mighty god, and promoted them to high office in Babylon. Poor Buckmaster. He ought to realize that a Shadrach wouldn't be afraid of furnaces. Did you have a good trip, love?"

"Oh, yes, yes, Shadrach!"

"Where did they send you?"

"Joan of Arc's execution. I watched her burning, and it was beautiful, the way she smiled, the way she looked toward heaven." Nikki presses close against him as they walk. Her voice still comes to him out of some realm of dream; that bonfire has left her stoned. "The most inspiring trip I ever had. The most deeply spiritual. Where can we go now, Shadrach? Where can we be alone?"

8

He is weary of Karakorum after his encounter with Buckmaster, and he sees now how this whole long day has drained his vigor and glazed his soul; if he could he would stagger to the tube-train and let himself be whisked off to Ulan Bator and his hammock and a night of—at last—deep, satisfying sleep. But Crowfoot, eerily exultant, glows now with insistent lusts, and he does not feel strong enough to confront her disappointment if he denies her now. Arm in arm, therefore, they go to the lovers' hospice at the north end of the pleasure grounds, a bright-skinned orange-and-green geodesic dome, and with a touch of his thumb against the credit plate he rents a three-hour room.

Not much of a room. Bed, washstand, clothes rack, within a little slope-ceilinged segment of the vast dome, annoying bluish-purple granular-finish walls, but the place suffices. It suffices. Nikki whips off the golden-mesh robe that is her only garment and from her nude body, four meters away across the room, comes such a rush of seductive energy, such a flow of force oscillating cracklingly up and down the whole electroerotic spectrum, that Shadrach's fatigue is swept away, Cotopaxi and Buckmaster recede into ancient history, and he swoops joyously toward her. Mouth seeking mouth, hands rising to breasts. She embraces him, then darts away, prudently offering her left hip to the contraceptron next to the washstand: presses the switch, receives the benevolent bath of sterilizing soft radiation, and returns to him. The tattooed no-preg symbol on her tawny flank, a nine-pointed star, glows in brilliant chartreuse, telling them that the irradiation has done its job. She strips him and claps hands in glee at the sight of his rigid maleness. This is not Joan of Arc he is bedding, oh, no; a warrior perhaps but a maiden no.

They tumble to the bed. With hands nearly as skilled as those of Warhaftig the surgeon he diligently commences the customary foreplay, but she lets him know by a quick wordless flip of her shoulders that he can skip it and get down to the main event; and he enters the taut hidden harbor between her thighs with a sudden unsparing thrust that brings grunts of pleasure from them both. Some things never change. There is a man only four hundred kilometers to the east who has had four livers and seven kidneys thus far, and in a tent just a few hundred meters from his bed they sell a drug that lets one be an eyewitness to the betrayal of the Savior, and there is a machine in Ulan Bator that flashes instantaneous pictures of virtually everything that is happening anywhere in the world, and all of these things would have been deemed miracles only two generations ago, but nevertheless in this miracle-infested world of 2012 there have been no significant technological improvements on the act of love. Oh, there are cunning drugs that are said to enhance the sensations, and there are clever devices that suppress fertility, and there are some other little biomechanical gimmicks that the sophisticated sometimes employ, but all of these are simply updated versions of peripheral equipment that has been in use since medieval days. The basic operation has not yet been digitalized or miniaturized or randomized or otherwise futurized, but remains what it was in the days of the australopithecines and the pithecanthropoids; that is, something that mere naked people do, pressing their humble natural-born bodies one against the other.

The bodies press, copper clasping ebony, acting out the ancient rite, Shadrach surprising himself with the intensity of his passions. He is not sure whether this energy comes from Nikki, via some mysterious telepathic transfer, or from some unexpected reservoir within himself, but he is grateful for it whatever the source, and rides it to an agreeable conclusion. Afterward he slips easily into a sound sleep, awakening only when the mellow but inescapable beeper tone signals the approaching end of their three-hour rental period. He finds himself cozily pillowed against Nikki's breasts. She is awake and evidently has been for some time, but her smile is beatific and no doubt she would have cradled him like that all night, an appealing idea. The night is well-nigh gone, in any case. They allow themselves a brief cuddle, rise, wash, dress, go forth with hands lightly touching into the chilly moon-dappled darkness. Like children unwilling to leave the playground, they drift into a gaming parlor, a wine house, a light studio, all three packed with raucous debauched-looking fun-seekers, but they stay no more than a few minutes in each place, drifting out as aimlessly as they went in, and finally they admit to each other that they have had enough for one night. To the tube-train station, then. Dawn will be here soon. From the ceiling above the station platform dangles a huge glowing green globe, a public telescreen showing a late-night news program,

and blearily Shadrach peers at it: the face of Mangu
looks back at him, sincere and earnest and deplor-
ably youthful. Mangu is making a speech, so it seems.
Gradually, for he is very tired, Shadrach perceives
that it is the classic Roncevic Antidote speech, the
one which Genghis Mao traditionally makes every
five or six months and which now apparently has
been delegated to the heir-apparent. ". . . major laboratory breakthroughs," Mangu is saying. ". . . encouraging progress . . . fundamental qualitative transformations of the manufacturing technology . . . the
unceasing efforts of the Permanent Revolutionary Committee . . . the diligent and persevering leadership of
our beloved Chairman Genghis Mao . . . there can be
no doubt any longer . . . large-scale distribution of
the drug throughout the world . . . the scourge of
organ-rot driven from our midst . . . stockpiles increasing daily . . . a time is approaching when . . . a
happy, healthy humanity . . ."

A florid, goggle-eyed man standing a few meters
farther down the platform says in a loud harsh whisper to the woman who accompanies him, "Certainly.
In only ninety to one hundred years."

"Quiet, Béla!" his companion cries, sounding genuinely alarmed.

"But it is the truth. He lies when he says the stockpiles are increasing daily. I have seen the figures. I tell
you, I have seen *reliable* figures."

Mordecai finds this interesting. The florid man is
Béla Horthy, a dour but volatile Hungarian physicist,
creator of the great fusion plant at Bayan Hongor
that supplies power for most of northeastern Asia. He
also happens to be minister of technology for the
Permanent Revolutionary Committee, and it is a little odd to hear so formidably well-connected a government leader uttering such scandalous subversion
in public. Of course, this is Karakorum, and Horthy,
looking boneless and out of focus just now, is obviously adrift on some potent hallucinogen, but still,
but still—

"The Antidote stockpiles are stable at best, or even
decreasing slightly," Horthy continues, framing his

words with the exaggerated precision of the extremely
intoxicated. "What Mangu tells us is a lie intended to
pacify the populace. He thinks that telling them such
things will make them happy and induce them to
love him. Pfaugh!" The woman tries desperately to
quiet him. She is short and compact, efficiently constructed with her center of gravity close to the ground;
her face is partly obscured by an ornate, flamboyant
green domino, but Shadrach, after a moment, recognizes her as Donna Labile, no less a mogul than
Horthy himself, in fact minister of demography for
the Committee, whose responsibility it is to maintain
a reasonable balance between births and deaths.
Masked or not, it is she, no mistaking that ferocious
jaw, and Shadrach observes that Horthy too has a
mask, dangling from his left hand. Perhaps he thinks
he still wears it. She struggles with him, taking the
mask from his limp hand and attempting to fasten it
in place, but he brushes her aside, and, lurching
toward Shadrach Mordecai, greets the doctor with so
grandiose a bow that he nearly pitches himself from
the platform. Donna Labile, flapping his discarded
mask about, flutters around him like an angry insect.
"Ah, Dr. Mordecai!" Horthy bellows. "Our leader's
devoted Aesculapius! I greet you!"

"... the climax of our unending struggle against
..." Mangu says from the glowing globular screen.

Horthy jerks a thumb at the image of the heir-
apparent. "Do you believe that trash, Mordecai?"

Shadrach has his own suspicions about the sincerity
of the Khan's oft-expressed plan for universal distribution of the Roncevic Antidote, but they are suspicions rather less than half formed, and in any case
this is no place to voice them. Softly he says, "I'm
not a member of the Committee, Dr. Horthy. The only
inside information I have concerns such things as the
endocrine balance of Genghis Mao."

"But you have an opinion, haven't you?"

"My opinion's an uninformed one, and therefore
worthless."

"Such a diplomat you are!" Horthy says in contempt.

"Pay no attention," Donna Labile begs. "He's had

too much tonight. Eating kot and yipka like so much
candy, drugging himself crazy, now risking his whole
career—"

"It seems to be the night for it," Shadrach remarks.

"A filthy hoax," Horthy says heavily, shaking his
fist at the screen. He is trembling, ashen-faced beneath his florid glow, sweating profusely. "Cruel,
sinister, bestial—" and he lapses into a series of unintelligible sibilant expletives, presumably Magyar, toward the end of which he begins to sob. Donna Labile,
meanwhile, has disappeared. After a moment she returns leading two tall men who wear the gray-and-
blue uniform of the Citizens' Peace Brigade. It is odd
to find a couple of Citpols here, for Shadrach thinks
of Karakorum as an open city, naturally monitored
by secret spy-eyes and the usual audio bugs but otherwise unpoliced; and these two are more than ordinarily repellent even for Citpols, for they look like
identical ugly twins, gray-faced and gray-eyed, with
flat heads and stiff close-cropped hair and strange
malproportioned bodies, all legs and no middle. They
walk in a weird clucking stride, like a couple of
poorly programmed robots, but they appear to be
human, more or less: perhaps the Committee, finding
volunteers scarce, is raising a clone of monsters to
serve as policemen. They surround Horthy and speak
to him in low, urgent tones. One of them takes the
domino from Donna Labile and with curiously fussy,
almost mincing, gestures, affixes it over the bridge
of Horthy's nose. Then, slipping their arms gently
under those of the minister of technology, they lead
him, lifting him a bit so that his feet are dragging,
toward a gray enameled door at the far end of the
platform. Shadrach Mordecai is uncertain whether
they are arresting him at Donna Labile's instigation
or—more likely—are hauling him up to some behind-
the-scenes sobering-up facility before he can compro-
mise himself further.

"... a glorious epoch in the splendid history of the
human race ..." Mangu booms.

The tube-train arrives. The survivors of the night's
revelries at Karakorum move slowly, sleepily aboard.

9

Before he heads for his hammock, Shadrach Mordecai visits the Khan. Though the implants tell him all is well, he feels obligated after his outing to make a personal call on his patient. It is early morning, and Genghis Mao lies in blissful sleep: through the electroencephalographic node in Mordecai's haunch travel the slow rhythmic quivers of the Chairman's peaceful delta waves. All the telemetered data reaching Shadrach is encouraging: blood pressure good, lungs clear of fluid, temperature back to normal, cardiac activity fine, bile production excellent. The newly installed liver has obviously established itself already and has begun to undo the deteriorations of the recent weeks. Shadrach passes through the interface and enters the bedroom where the Chairman rests within the intricate cocoon of the intensive-care support system. The biometer readings on the support system's instrument panel instantly confirm Shadrach's long-distance diagnosis: the Chairman is doing amazingly well. None of the emergency equipment has been needed, neither the oxygen tent nor the electrodialysis machine nor the heart-lung respirator nor the twelve or fourteen other instruments. There he lies, relaxed, a faint smile on his thin lips, this man of ninety years or so, only sixteen hours out of major surgery and already nearly strong enough to resume the stress of normal life. But of course there is nothing normal about Genghis Mao's body, reconstructed so many times out of so many healthy borrowed parts: like the cannibal chieftain, he has feasted on the flesh of heroes, and their strength has become his strength. And, Shadrach suspects, there is some quality of the mind within that tapering triangular skull that will not admit bodily weakness, that banishes it altogether from his metabolic cycle. The doctor stands for a few moments by the bedside, admiring Genghis Mao's toughness of constitution, half expecting Genghis Mao to wink at him, but the Khan's sleep holds him utterly.

Off to his own, then. With Genghis Mao in such fine shape, Shadrach feels free to sleep until sleep is done with him, even if that is midafternoon. Crowfoot already lies curled and dozing in his hammock; he strips, snuggles in beside her, delicately coils his belly and thighs against her back and buttocks, and lets consciousness go from him.

He is awakened some hours later by an internal jolt that nearly throws him from the hammock. A geyser of adrenalin floods his bloodstream; his heart begins to pound, his limbs tremble, all systems switching on in violent alarm reaction. Automatically he begins a process of self-diagnosis, considering and rejecting within the first fraction of a second such possibilities as a coronary thrombosis, a cerebral hemorrhage, pulmonary edema; a moment later, as the thunderous tachycardia begins to subside and his breathing starts to return to normal, he realizes that it is nothing more serious than an episode of shock leading into a classic fight-or-flight syndrome; and an instant after that he becomes aware that it is all purely vicarious, that there is nothing wrong with him at all but that he is getting an intense overload via the telemetering system that links him to Genghis Mao.

He leaps from the hammock, sending it swinging wildly. "Shadrach?" Nikki asks, her voice groggy and dim. "Shadrach, what's happening?"

Catching the hammock for a moment to stabilize it, he mutters an apology. "Trouble with the Khan," he says, groping along the floor for his casually discarded clothing. He is fully awake now, but his body is so saturated with the hormonal outpourings engendered by surprise and alarm that his hands shake and his jangled mind refuses to focus on the simple tasks of dressing. Has the Chairman's life-support system malfunctioned? Have assassins broken into Genghis Mao's bedroom? The Chairman still lives—the telemetering leaves no doubt of that—and whatever it was that gave Genghis Mao so severe a shock seems already to be over, for his biophysical output is settling back toward normal, though there are ample indications of continuing neurasthenic hyperesthesia and associated cardiovascular and vasomotor distress.

Wearing only his trousers and still feeling wobbly—never before, in all the time he has worn the implants, have the signals from Genghis Mao had such an impact on him—he approaches the interface. "Shadrach Mordecai to serve the Khan," he says, and waits, and nothing happens for nearly a minute. Dr. Mordecai repeats the password, more urgently. Still the door remains shut. "Come on!" he snaps. "The Khan might be dying in there, and I have to get to him, you idiot machine!" Lights flash, scanners scan, but nothing else occurs. Shadrach realizes that the interface system must have gone into emergency mode, under which the flow of personnel to and from the inner chambers is even more strictly controlled than usual. This supports the hypothesis of an assassination attempt. Shadrach shouts, gesticulates, pounds the interface with his fists, even makes faces at it; but the security system is obviously concerned with other matters, and it will not let him in. By the time the door finally does open, he estimates, four or five minutes have elapsed. The data coming from Genghis Mao holds firm, at least: the Khan's signals indicate that he is still disturbed and overexcited but that he is slowly recovering from his moment of alarm.

Maddeningly, Shadrach is kept another minute or so in the inner holding chamber; at last it yields, and he lopes swiftly through Surveillance Vector One, which is deserted, to Genghis Mao's bedroom. Here the secondary door scanner delays him no more than the usual microsecond, and he bursts in to find Genghis Mao alive and awake, sitting up in bed, surrounded by five or six servants and a dozen or more members of the Committee, all milling about in a frenzied excitement very much contraindicated at this phase of the Chairman's recuperation. Mordecai sees General Gonchigdorge, Vice-Chairman Ionigylakis, Security Chief Avogadro, even Béla Horthy, looking horribly liverish and hung over after his excessive night in Karakorum. And more people are constantly arriving. Shadrach is appalled. He can hear the voice of Genghis Mao, clear but weak, cutting through the overall hubbub, but there is such a mob around the bed that Mordecai is unable to reach the Khan's side.

"Terrible, terrible," Ionigylakis says, shaking his head from side to side like a wounded bear.

Shadrach turns to him. "What's going on?"

"Mangu," Ionigylakis blurts. "Assassinated!"

"What? How?"

"Out the window. Off the balcony." Ponderously the big Greek pantomimes the action with great sweeps of his arm—the open window, the draperies fluttering in the breeze, the curve of the body as it executes its swooping seventy-five-story descent, the abrupt ghastly termination of the graceful dive, the hideous impact at plaza level, the tiny final rebounding motion of the crumpled body.

Shadrach shudders. "When was this?"

"Ten, fifteen minutes ago. Horthy was just arriving at the tower. He saw the whole thing."

"Who notified the Khan? Horthy?"

Ionigylakis shrugs. "How would I know?"

"They should have waited. The shock of news like that—"

"First I heard of it, I was at my desk in Committee Vector One and the lights flash emergency mode. Then people running around everywhere, crazy. Then everyone running in here."

"Which is even crazier," Shadrach says, scowling. "Making a lot of noise, upsetting the Khan's nervous system, filling the room with potentially infectious bacteria—doesn't anyone have any sense? We're jeopardizing his life in this chaos. Help me clear the room."

"But the Khan has sent for these people!"

"Doesn't matter. He doesn't need them all. I'm responsible for his health, and I want everybody out of here except, oh, Avogadro and Gonchigdorge and maybe Eyuboglu."

"But—"

"No buts. The rest of you ought to return to Committee Vector One so you can handle more trouble if more trouble comes. What if this is the start of a worldwide revolutionary uprising? Who's going to face the crisis if you're all in here? Go. Go. I want to clear the room. Get everybody out, will you? That's an order."

Ionigylakis still looks doubtful, but after a moment's hesitation he nods and begins pushing people enthusiastically toward the door, bellowing at them that they must leave, while Shadrach, catching the attention of the security chief, tells him to post his men in the hall to keep visitors out.

Shadrach approaches the bed. Genghis Mao looks drawn and tense, his forehead moist, shiny, his skin tone pallid and grayish. He is breathing shallowly and his eyes, always restless, move now with manic intensity. The life-support system has activated itself and is feeding the Khan a steady flow of glucose, sodium chloride, and blood plasma; Shadrach, glancing quickly at the readings on the instrument panel and integrating them with his own telemetered inputs, assesses Genghis Mao's level of blood potassium and plasma magnesium, his capillary permeability, his arteriolar vasoconstriction, and his venous pressure, and makes manual adjustments in the rate of medication. "Try to relax," he tells Genghis Mao. "Sit back. Let your limbs go limp."

"They killed him," the Khan says hoarsely. "Have you heard? They threw him from his window."

"Yes, I know. Lie back, please, sir."

"The killers must still be somewhere inside this

building. I'll supervise the investigation myself. Wheel me into Surveillance Vector One, Shadrach."

"That won't be possible. You'll have to remain here, sir."

"Don't talk that way to me. Avogadro! Avogadro! Help me into the wheelchair!"

"I'm sorry, sir," Shadrach murmurs, signaling frantically behind his back to Avogadro to ignore the command of Genghis Mao. At the same time Shadrach nudges a pedal that sends a flow of tranquilizing 9-pordenone into the Chairman's body. "It could be fatal for you to leave the bed now, sir. Do you understand me? It could kill you."

Genghis Mao understands that. He sinks back against the pillow, looking almost relieved at being overruled, and as the drug takes effect his face relaxes, his demeanor becomes far less intense. Genghis Mao is much weaker, Shadrach realizes, than the instruments indicate. "They killed him," the Khan says again, ruminatingly, absent-voicedly. "Only a boy and they killed him. He had no enemies." And to Shadrach's amazement the old man's lips begin to quiver and his eyes fill with tears. Eh? What's this? A show of some genuine emotion by Genghis Mao? A kind of quasi-paternal grief seizing the old man? But how can that be, considering the bleak fate Genghis Mao had himself intended for Mangu? Either yesterday's surgery has so enfeebled the Khan that he has grown uncharacteristically sentimental, suddenly entering an inconceivable dotage, or else Mordecai is misreading the signs: not grief but fear, cognizance of personal peril, awareness that if assassins could reach Mangu they might well find a way to the sanctum of Genghis Mao. That must be it. The Khan is angry and afraid, but because he is so diminished physically by his operation, his anger and fear momentarily take the form of sorrow. And indeed, after a few moments more Genghis Mao grows calm again, and says, in a low, controlled, newly resonant voice, "This is the first successful attack against our rule that we have experienced. It is unprecedented and must be met with force to demonstrate that we have lost none of our vigor and that our authority will not be undermined." He beckons Avogadro to his bedside and begins to dictate plans for mass arrests, wholesale interrogation of suspected subversives, tightened security measures both within the Grand Tower and in Ulan Bator in general. He sounds now less like a bereaved elder than a threatened despot. The loss of Mangu, it quickly becomes clear, means little or nothing to him personally, Mangu having been such a cipher, but it is a frightening omen of a breach in the power of his regime, and will require a reign of terror.

In the midst of these grim plans Genghis Mao suddenly looks up at Shadrach as if noticing him for the first time that morning, and says amiably, "You have nothing on but your trousers, Doctor. Why is that?"

"I came here in a hurry. I got a tremendous jolt from the implants, strong enough to wake me up, and I knew there must be trouble."

"Yes. When Horthy brought me news of the assassination I became quite agitated."

"Your damned doors kept me waiting for five minutes, though. We ought to do something about that. Someday it'll be a critical matter for me to get to you in time, and Interface Three will give me the business again and it'll be too late."

"Mmm. We'll talk about that." The Khan eyes Shadrach's bare torso with some amusement and, it would seem, admiration, surveying the pronounced ridges of muscle down his belly, the long lean arms, the wide powerful shoulders. It is a pleasing body, Shadrach knows, trim and shapely and covered all over with smooth lovely chocolate skin, an athletic and graceful body, not much changed from the days nearly twenty years ago when he was a respectable college sprinter and passable basketball player, but nevertheless there is something weird and unnerving about this close inspection. After a moment the Khan says, sounding almost jolly, "You look very healthy, Shadrach."

"I try to keep in shape, sir."

"A wise doctor you are. So many of your profession

worry about everyone's health except their own. But why were you still in bed at this hour of the morning?"

"I was in Karakorum late last night," Shadrach confesses.

Genghis Mao laughs explosively. "Dissipation! Debauchery! So that's how you keep in shape, is it?"

"Well—"

"At ease. I'm not serious." The Chairman's mood has changed astonishingly in these few minutes. This badgering banter, this light teasing—it is hard to believe that he was weeping for dead Mangu just a moment ago. "You can go and get your shirt, if you like. I think I can spare you for a few minutes, Shadrach."

"I'd prefer to stay a while longer, sir. It's not chilly this way."

"As you wish." Genghis Mao seems to lose interest in him. He turns back to Avogadro, still waiting by the bedside, and rattles off half a dozen more repressive measures to be put into effect at once. Then, dismissing the security chief, the Chairman summons Vice-Chairman Eyuboglu and outlines, seemingly impromptu, an elaborate program for the virtual canonization of Mangu: a colossal state funeral, a prolonged period of global mourning, the renaming of highways and cities, the erection of costly and imposing memorial monuments in every major capital. All this for such a trifling boy? Why? Shadrach wonders. This is an outpouring of mortuary energy worthy of a demigod, an Augustus Caesar, a Siegfried, even an Osiris. Why? Why, if not that Mangu was a symbolic extension of Genghis Mao himself, his link to tomorrow, his hope of bodily reincarnation? Yes, Shadrach decides. In ordering this bizarrely inappropriate posthumous inflation of the murdered man, Genghis Mao must be mourning not Mangu but himself.

10

Was Mangu really murdered, though? Avogadro, waiting for Mordecai in the hallway when the doctor finally leaves Genghis Mao, is not so sure of that. The security chief, a big-boned, thick-bodied, quick-witted man with cool eyes and a wide, quizzical mouth, draws Shadrach aside near the entrance to Surveillance Vector One and says softly, "Is he on any medication that might be making him mentally unstable?"

"Not particularly. Why?"

"I've never seen him as upset as this before."

"He's never had his viceroy assassinated before, either."

"What leads you to think there's been an assassination?"

"Because I—because Ionigylakis said—because—" Shadrach pauses, confused. "Wasn't there one?"

"Who knows? Horthy says he saw Mangu fall out the window. Period. He didn't see anyone pushing him. We've already run playback checks on all personnel scanners and there's no record of any unauthorized individual entering or leaving the entire building this morning, let alone having reached the seventy-fifth floor."

"Perhaps somebody was hiding up here overnight," Shadrach suggests.

Avogadro sighs. He looks faintly amused. "Spare me the amateur detective work, Doctor. Naturally, we've looked through yesterday's records too."

"I'm sorry if I—"

"I didn't mean to be sarcastic. My point is simply that we've considered most of the obvious possibilities. It's not easy for an assassin to get inside this building, and I don't seriously believe that any assassins did. Naturally, that doesn't rule out the chance that Mangu was pushed by someone whose presence within the building would not seem unusual, as for example General Gonchigdorge, or you, or me—"

"Or Genghis Mao," Shadrach offers. "Tiptoeing from his bed and tossing Mangu through the window."

"You get the idea. What I'm saying is that anyone up here might have killed Mangu. Except that there's no evidence that anyone did. You know, whenever someone passes through a door up here, it's recorded. No one entered Mangu's bedroom this morning, either on the interface side or the elevator side. The tracking cores are absolutely blank. The last one to go in was Mangu himself, about midnight. Preliminary inspection indicates no traces of intruders in the room, no strange fingerprints, no flecks of someone else's dandruff, no stray hairs, no bits of lint. And no sign of a struggle. Mangu was a strong man, you know. He wouldn't have been easy to overpower."

"You're suggesting it was probably suicide?" Shadrach asks.

"I am. Obviously. No one on my staff takes any other theory at all seriously at this point. But the Chairman is certain it was an assassination, and you should have seen him before you got here. Almost hysterical, wild-eyed, raving. You know, it doesn't look good for me and my men if he believes there's been an assassination. We're supposed to make assassinations impossible up here. But it goes beyond whether I lose my job, Doctor. There's this whole fantastic purge that he's instituting, the arrests, the interrogations, restrictive measures, a tremendously messy and unpleasant and expensive enterprise, all of it, so far as I can see, absolutely useless. What I want to know," Avogadro says, "is whether you think there's some chance the Chairman will be willing to take a more rational attitude toward Mangu's death when he's further along in his recovery."

"I don't know. But I don't think so. I've never seen him change his mind about anything."

"But the operation—"

"Has weakened him, sure. Physically *and* psychologically. But it hasn't greatly affected his reason in any way that I can perceive. He's always had this thing about assassins, of course, and obviously he's assuming Mangu was murdered because it fulfills some kind of inner need for him, some fantasy projection, something very dark and intricate. I think he'd have made the same assumption even if he'd been in perfect health when Mangu went out the window. So his recovery *per se* isn't going to be a factor in getting him to reevaluate Mangu's death. All I can suggest is that you wait three or four days until he's strong enough to be getting back on the job and go in there with the findings of your completed investigation, show him conclusively that there's no evidence whatsoever of murder, and count on his basic sanity to bring him to an acceptance of the fact that Mangu killed himself."

"Suppose I bring him the report this afternoon?"

"He's not really ready for all this stress. Besides, is such a speedy investigation going to be plausible to him? No, I'd recommend waiting at least three days, preferably four or five."

"And meanwhile," Avogadro says, "suspects will be rounded up, minds will be pried into, the innocent will suffer, my staff will be wasting its energies on a foolish pursuit of a nonexistent assassin—"

"Can't you delay the purge a few days, then?"

"He ordered us to start at once, Doctor."

"Yes, I know, but—"

"He ordered us to start at once. We've done so."

"Already?"

"Already. I understand the meaning of an order from the Chairman. Within the past ten minutes the first arrests have taken place. I can try to stretch out the process of interrogation so that as little harm as possible will come to the prisoners before I can bring my findings on Mangu's death to the Chairman, but I have no authority to sidetrack his instructions altogether." Quietly Avogadro adds, "I wouldn't want to risk it, either."

"Then there'll be a purge," Shadrach says, shrugging. "I regret that as much as you do, I suppose. But there's no way to stop it now, eh? And no real hope that you'll persuade Genghis Mao to swallow the suicide theory, not this afternoon or tomorrow or next week, not if he wants to think Mangu was murdered. I'm sorry."

"I am also," Avogadro says. "Well. Thanks for your time, Doctor." He begins to move away; then, pausing, he gives Shadrach a deep, uncomfortably appraising look, and says, "Oh, one more thing, Doctor. Is there any reason you might know of for Mangu to have wanted to kill himself?"

Shadrach frowns. He considers things.

"No," he answers after a moment. "No. Not that I'm aware of."

He goes on into Surveillance Vector One. The big room is crowded with high staff personnel. He begins to feel a little odd, wandering around headquarters without a shirt. General Gonchigdorge sits at Genghis Mao's ornate throne, jabbing with stubby fingers at the enormous keyboard that controls the whole vast spy-eye apparatus. As the general pounds the buttons, images of life out there in the Trauma Ward swing jerkily in and out of focus, zooming into view and vanishing rapidly. The scene on the screens looks just as dizzyingly random as when the machine is left to its own whims; not surprising, for Gonchigdorge really does seem to be tapping the keys without system, without purpose, in a kind of sullen petulance, as though he hopes to uncover a revolutionary cadre out there by some stochastic process of nondirected scoops—dipping down into the world here and there until he comes upon a band of desperados waving a banner, WE ARE CONSPIRATORS. But the screens reveal only the usual human story, people working, walking, suffering, quarreling, dying.

Horthy, appearing silently at Mordecai's left elbow, says, with a certain glee, "The arrests have already begun."

"I know. Avogadro told me."

"Did he tell you that they have a prime suspect?"

"Who?"

Horthy delicately prods his thumbs into the corners of his bulging, bloodshot eyes. A psychedelic effluvium still hovers about him. "Roger Buckmaster," he says. "The microengineering man, you know."

"Yes. I know. I've worked with him."

"Buckmaster was heard making wild statements at Karakorum last night," Horthy says. "Calling for the overthrow of Genghis Mao, yelling subversion at the top of his lungs. The Citpols picked him up, finally, but they decided he was just drunk and let him go."

In a low voice Shadrach says, "Is that what happened to you?"

"Me? To me? I don't understand what you mean."

"At the tube-train station. I saw you there, remember? While they were running that tape of Mangu's speech. You made some remarks about the Antidote distribution program, and then the Citpols—"

"No," Horthy says. "You must be mistaken." His eyes fix on Shadrach's and lock there. They are intimidating eyes, cold and hostile, despite all their dissipated bleariness. With great precision Horthy says, "It was someone else you saw at Karakorum, Dr. Mordecai."

"You weren't there last night?"

"It was someone else."

Shadrach chooses to take the crude hint, and decides not to press the issue. "My apologies. Tell me about Buckmaster. Why do they think he's the one?"

"His eccentric behavior last night was suspicious."

"Is that all?"

"You'll have to ask the security people for the rest."

"Was he found near Mangu's apartment at the time of the murder?"

"I couldn't say, Dr. Mordecai."

"All right." On the surveillance screens, in repellent close-up, the image of a girl vomiting. It is the crimson puke of organ-rot, in glistening lifelike color. Horthy seems almost to smile at the sight, as though nothing horrid is alien to him. Shadrach says, "One more thing. You saw Mangu fall, didn't you?"

"Yes."

"And then you notified Genghis Mao?"

"I notified the guards in the lobby first."

"Of course."

"And then I went to the seventy-fifth floor. The security people had already sealed it, but I was able to enter."

"Going straight to the Chairman's bedroom?"

Horthy nods. "Which was under triple guard. I obtained admittance only by insisting on my ministerial privileges."

"Was Genghis Mao awake?"

"Yes. Reading PRC reports."

"What would you say was his general state of health?"

"Quite good. He looked pale and weak, but not unusually so, considering that he had just had a major operation. He greeted me and saw from my expression that something was wrong, and asked me, and I told him what had happened."

"Which was?"

"What else?" Horthy says snappishly. "That Mangu had fallen from his window, naturally."

"Is that how you put it? 'Mangu has fallen from his window'?"

"Something like that."

"Did you talk about his being pushed, maybe?"

"Why are you interrogating me, Dr. Mordecai?"

"Please. This is important. I need to know whether the Khan arrived at the idea that Mangu was assassinated by himself, or if you inadvertently put the suggestion in his mind."

Horthy stares balefully up at Shadrach Mordecai. "I told him exactly what I saw: Mangu falling from the window. I drew no conclusions about how it had happened. Even if someone had thrown him, how much could I have seen, four hundred meters below? At that distance Mangu himself was no bigger than a speck against the sky, a doll. I didn't recognize him until he had nearly reached the ground." A disconcerting gleam appears in Horthy's eyes. He leans close to Shadrach and says, almost crooning, "He looked so serene, Dr. Mordecai! Floating there above me—his eyes wide open, his hair straight out behind him, his lips drawn back—he was smiling, I think. Smiling! And then he hit."

Ionigylakis, who has evidently been eavesdropping, interjects abruptly, "That's strange. If someone had just flung him from the window, would he have looked so cheerful?"

Shadrach shakes his head. "I doubt that Mangu was conscious at all by the time Horthy could see his face. That serene expression was probably just acceleration stupor."

"Perhaps," Horthy says crisply.

"Go on," Shadrach tells him. "You informed the Khan that Mangu had fallen. Then what happened?"

"He sat up so sharply that I thought he would break the medical machinery all around him. He turned red in the face and began to perspire. His breath came in gasps. Oh, it was very bad, Dr. Mordecai. I thought he would die from overexcitement. He started to wave his arms, to shout about assassins— suddenly he sank back against the pillow, he put his hands to his chest—"

"You thought he would die from overexcitement," Shadrach says. "But it never occurred to you beforehand that it might be unwise to trouble him with news like that, in his state of health."

"One doesn't think clearly at a time like that."

"One ought to, if one is in a position of high responsibility."

"One's judgment is not always perfect," Horthy retorts. "Especially when one has nearly been killed oneself a few minutes before by a body plummeting from the sky. And when one realizes that the dead man is such an important figure in the government, in fact the viceroy. And when one suspects that his death may be murder, assassination, the beginning of revolution. And when—"

"All right," Shadrach says. "All right. He managed to survive the unnecessary shock. But what you did was very risky, Horthy. Worse: it was dumb. Extremely dumb." He frowns. "You think there's some conspiracy, eh?"

"I have no idea. Clearly it's a possibility."

"So is suicide, though."

Ionigylakis says, "You think so, Shadrach?"

"Avogadro certainly does."

"But Avogadro's men have arrested Buckmaster."

"I've heard. The poor crazy devil. I pity him." Gonchigdorge is still jabbing buttons. The screens are full of weirdly distorted faces, as though the spyeye lenses are getting much too close to their targets. Donna Labile, from the far side of the room, calls to Horthy, who gives Shadrach a frosty incomprehensible look and stalks away. Shadrach is altogether unable to make sense out of Horthy, but suddenly it does not matter. Nothing matters. This room is a madhouse, through which he wanders, bare-chested and feeling a bit of a chill, baffled by all the frantic activity around him. He feels too sane, too mundane, for this environment. The screens of Surveillance Vector One suddenly go blank, and then grow bright with wild jagged streaks of blue and green and red. General Gonchigdorge, in his heavy-handed pursuit of conspirators, has broken something. "Ficifolia!" the general yells. "Get Frank Ficifolia up here! The machine has to be repaired!"

Ficifolia is already present, though. Cursing softly, he shoulders through the crowd toward the enthroned general. As he passes Shadrach he pauses to murmur, "Your friend Buckmaster's in the quiz room right now. I suppose you won't weep over that."

"On the contrary. Buckmaster wasn't in his right mind when he was hassling me last night. And now he'll pay for it."

"Avogadro himself is interrogating, I hear."

"Avogadro thinks it was suicide."

"So do I," Ficifolia says, and keeps going.

Shadrach has had enough. He heads for the interface. As he reaches it, he looks back at the turmoil, the blaring jags of color on the screens, Gonchigdorge shouting like an angry child, Horthy and Labile deep in some mysterious intense discussion punctuated by fierce Italo-Magyar gesticulations, Ionigylakis looming above everyone and announcing his confusions in booming tones, Frank Ficifolia squatting by an open panel to insert a long slender wrench into a turbulent spaghetti of bubble-circuits. While somewhere in the depths of this huge building Avogadro, who does not believe a murder was committed, is nevertheless preparing to administer torture to Roger Buckmaster, suspected of having committed that murder, even though Buckmaster almost certainly could not have been capable of murdering anyone this morning. And in the great bedchamber of the Khan that old, old man, his near-fatal episode of shock all but over according to the tickety-tock pulsations and quivers running through Shadrach Mordecai's body, lies in bed scheming with calm crazy dedication how best to make sacred the memory of the departed viceroy and how to destroy his supposed slayers. Enough, enough. More than enough: too much. Shadrach requests exit from the interface, which opens with blessed promptness and admits him to the holding chamber, and then, quickly, to his own apartment on the far side.

How peaceful it is here! Crowfoot is awake and out of the hammock; she has just taken a shower, and stands, bare, beautiful, in the middle of the room, drying herself, droplets of moisture still glittering on her smooth sleek skin, nipples puckered and taut in the coolness of the air. "I'm going to be awfully late getting to the lab today," she says casually. "What's been happening?"

"Everything. Mangu's dead, the Khan nearly had apoplexy when he found out, they've arrested Buckmaster, a general purge of subversives has been ordered. Horthy is—"

"Wait," she cries, blinking. "Dead? Mangu? How?"

"Fell out the window. Pushed or jumped."

"Oh." A little sucking intake of breath. "Oh, God. When was this?"

"Half an hour ago, more or less."

She crumples her towel into a ball, hurls it into a

corner, and begins to pace the room, striding like a splendid perplexed tigress. Whirling on him, she demands, "Which window?"

"His own," he tells her, mystified by the drift of her questions.

"Fell from the top of the building? His body must have been smashed to a ruin."

"I imagine so. But what—"

"Oh, Shadrach! My project!"

"What about it?"

"This sounds terribly inhuman, doesn't it? But what will happen to my project now? Without Mangu—"

"Oh," he says dully. "I hadn't considered that."

"He was intended for—"

"Yes. Don't say it."

"It's awful of me to have that reaction."

"Was the entire project built about Mangu as the specific particular one—the recipient?"

"Not necessarily. But—oh, to hell with the project!" She crouches near the floor, folding her arms across her breasts. She is shivering. "I don't understand. Who would kill Mangu, anyway? What's going on? Is there going to be a revolution, Shadrach?"

"Mangu may have killed Mangu," he tells her. "No one knows yet. Avogadro's men didn't detect any sign of forced entry to his apartment."

"Yet they've arrested Buckmaster?"

"Because of the nonsense he was spouting last night in Karakorum, I suppose. But they haven't arrested Horthy, who was being just as subversive. Horthy's right next door in Surveillance Vector One. He was the one who brought the news about Mangu to Genghis Mao. Damn near killed him with the shock of it."

Nikki, looking up somberly, says, "Perhaps that's what he wanted to do."

11

Things grow calmer. The messages from the interior of Genghis Mao indicate that the medical crisis is past. The Khan is healing, the morning's upheavals will have no serious impact. Here at noon, Shadrach Mordecai at last dresses for the day, neutral gray doctor's clothes. He feels rootless, disoriented: too much sleep, after all these months of insomnia, the nap in Nikki's arms in Karakorum and then the long, emergency-interrupted spell in the hammock, and now his mind is foggy. But he'll fake it through the day, somehow.

Heading for his office, he passes as usual through Surveillance Vector One, much quieter now than it was fifteen or twenty minutes before. The high panjandrums are gone, Gonchigdorge and Horthy and Labile and that crowd, and no one remains except three underlings, a Citpol man and a couple of Avogadro's lieutenants, who stare moodily at the jumpy mosaic flitting across the hundreds of screens. Their eyes are glazed. Informational overkill, it is. They see so much that they know not what they see.

Bypassing Committee Vector One—Shadrach has no yearning to intrude on the politicos this tense morning—he takes the long route to his office, via Genghis Mao's own vacant office and the Khan's majestic dining room. It is, as always, comforting to be among his familiar talismans, his books, his collection of medical instruments. He wanders from case to case, getting himself together. Picks up his devaricator, sinister splay-elbowed forceps used to pry open wounds. Thinks of Mangu, splattered against the terrazzo pavement; banishes the thought. Examines the hacksaw with which some eighteenth-century surgeon accomplished amputations. Thinks of Genghis Mao, livid, beady-eyed, ordering mass arrests. *Off with their heads!* That may be next; why not? Fondles a fifteenth-century anatomical doll from Bologna, elegant ivory homunculus, female—what is the feminine of homunculus, he wonders? Homuncula? Feminacula?—the belly and breasts of which lift away at the push of a fingertip, revealing heart, lungs, abdominal organs, even a fetus crouching in the uterus like a kangaroo in the pouch. And the books, oh, yes, the precious musty books, formerly owned by great doctors of Vienna, Montreal, Savannah, New Orleans. Valesco de Taranta's *Philonium Pharmaceuticum et Cheirurgicum*, 1599! Martin Schurig's *Gynaecologia Historico-Medica*, 1730, rich with details of defloration, debauchery, penis captivus, and other wonders! Here is old Rudolf Virchow's *Die Cellularpathologie*, 1852, proclaiming that every living organism is "a cell state in which every state is a citizen," that a disease is "a conflict of citizens in this state, brought about by the action of external forces." *Aux armes, citoyens!* What would Virchow have said of transplanted livers, borrowed lungs? He'd call them hired mercenaries, no doubt: the Hessians of medical metaphor. At least they fight fair in the cellular wars, no sneaky defenestrations, no snipers on the overpass. And this huge book: Grootdoorn, *Iconographia Medicalis*, luscious old engravings—see, here, Saints Cosmas and Damian in this sixteenth-century portrait, shown grafting the dead Moor's leg to the cancer victim's stump. Prophetic. Transplant surgery circa 500 A.D., performed posthumously, no less, by the saintly surgeons. If I ever find the original of that print, Shadrach thinks, I'll give it to Warhaftig for Hanukkah.

He spends half an hour updating Genghis Mao's medical file, dictating a report on the liver operation, adding a postscript about this morning's brief alarm. Someday the printout of the Genghis Mao dossier is going to be a medical classic, ranking with the Smith Papyrus and the *Fabrica*, and he toils conscientiously over it, preparing his place in the history of his art. Just as he finishes the account of the current episode, Katya Lindman phones him.

"Can you come down to the Talos lab?" she asks. "I'd like to show you our latest mock-up."

"I suppose so. You've heard about Mangu?"

"Of course."

"You don't sound very concerned."

"What was Mangu? Mangu was an absence. Now the absence is absent. His death was more of an event than his whole existence."

"I doubt that he saw things that way himself."

"You are so compassionate, Shadrach," she says in the flat voice that he knows she reserves for mockery. "I wish I shared your love of mankind."

"I'll see you in fifteen minutes, Katya."

Her laboratory is on the ninth floor of the Grand Tower, a cluttered place festooned with cables, connectors, buses, coaxials, crates of bubble-chips, enough electronic gear to throttle a brontosaur. Out of this chaotic maze of materiel Lindman materializes, coming toward him in her customary slashing headlong stride. She is all business, very much the bustling woman of science. She wears a white blouse, a lavender lab jacket open at the throat, a short brown tweed skirt. The effect is severe, stark, and harsh, mitigated neither by the bare thighs nor the tightness of the skirt nor the exposed cleft of her breasts. Lindman is not a woman who works at projecting sexuality. Nor does she need to, with Shadrach; she holds a malign physical authority over him, the source of which he does not comprehend. He feels always when he is with her that he must be on guard—against what, he is not sure.

"Look," she says triumphantly, with a broad sweeping gesture.

He follows her pointing arm halfway across the laboratory to the one uncluttered place, a kind of dais, on which, under a dazzling spotlight, the current working model of the Genghis Mao automaton sits enthroned. A single thick yellow-and-red cable runs to it from a power unit. The automaton is half again as large as life, a massive imitation of the Chairman, plastic skin over metal armature; the face is an altogether convincing replica, the shoulders and chest look plausibly human, but below the diaphragm the robot Genghis Mao is an incomplete thing of struts and wires and bare circuitry, skinless and lacking even the internal mechanical musculature that fills its upper half. As Shadrach watches, the ersatz Chairman extends its right arm toward him and, with an altogether human impatient little flip of its hand, beckons him forward.

"Go ahead," Katya Lindman says.

He advances. When he is three or four meters away he halts and waits. The robot's head slowly turns to face him. The lips pull back in a cruel grimace—no, a grin, unmistakably a grin, the bleak and terrible grin of Genghis Mao, that self-congratulatory smirk, slowly forming at the corners of the leathery cheeks, a regal grin, a monstrous overbearing grin. Imperceptibly the features rearrange themselves, without apparent transition; the robot now is scowling, and the wrath of Genghis Mao darkens the room. *Off with their heads*, yes, indeed. And then a smile. A cold one, for there is no other sort from Genghis Mao, but yet it is a smile that puts one at one's ease, Arctic though it is; and the smile of the robot is an uncanny replica of the smile of Genghis Mao. And, lastly, the wink, the famous wink of the Khan, that sly, disarming dip of the eyelid that cancels all the seeming ferocity, that communicates a redeeming sense of perspective, of self-appraisal: *Don't take me so seriously, friend, I may not be the megalomaniac you think I am.* And then, just as the wink has achieved its effect and the terror that Genghis Mao can generate with a glance has subsided, the face returns to its original expression, icy, remote, alien.

"Well?" Lindman asks, after some while.

"Doesn't he speak?"

"Not yet. The audio is trivial to accomplish. We aren't bothering with it just now."

"That's the whole show, then?"

"That's it. You sound disappointed."

"Somehow I expected more. I've seen him do the grin already."

"But not the wink. The wink is new."

"Even so, Katya—you add a feather here and there, but you still don't have an eagle."

"What did you think I'd show you? A walking, talking Genghis Mao? The complete simulacrum overnight?" His disappointment has angered her, obviously: her mouth works tensely, the lips drawing back from the gums again and again, baring those pointed carnivorous incisors. "We still are in preliminary stages, here. But I thought you would like the wink. I like the wink. I rather do like the wink, Shadrach." Her voice grows lighter, her features soften; he can almost hear the gears shifting within her. "I'm sorry I wasted your time. I was pleased with the wink. I wanted to share it with you."

"It's a fantastic wink, Katya."

"And, you know, Project Talos will become much more important with Mangu gone. Everything that Dr. Crowfoot has been doing was aimed toward integrating the Chairman's personality with the neural responses of Mangu's living mind and body, and that's over with, now, that whole approach must be discarded."

Shadrach knows enough about Nikki's work to know that this is not literally so; apparently Mangu was indeed the template against which the Avatar personality-coding program was being plotted, but there was nothing inexorable about the use of Mangu; with the appropriate adjustments the project can readily be reshaped around some other body donor. But there is no need to tell Lindman that, if she wants to feel that her project, peripheral so far, has suddenly become Genghis Mao's prime hope of postmortem survival. She has made an obvious effort in the past minute or two to be less intimidating, less abrasive, and he prefers her that way; he will do nothing that might spur new tension and defensiveness in her.

In fact her mood has eased so much that she seems

almost coquettish. Chattering in a shrill, girlish, wholly unKatyaesque way, she leads him on a hectic and gratuitous tour of the laboratory, displaying circuit diagrams, boxes of memory chips, prototypes for the pelvis and spine of the next model of Genghis Mao, and other bits of Project Talos that are of no conceivable significance just now; and he realizes, after a time, that her only pretext for doing all this is to detain him, to have a few minutes more of his company. It puzzles him. Lindman's usual manner is aggressive and peremptory, but now she is coy, flirtatious, sidling up unsubtly to him, plenty of heavy breathing and forthright eye contact, actually grazing his elbow with her breasts as they stand close together rummaging through a table full of schematics. Does she think that such stuff will make him snort, sweat, paw the ground with his hooves, fling himself upon her throbbing body? He has no idea what she thinks. He rarely does. Nor is he going to find out now, for whatever she is organizing here is truncated abruptly by a squeaky summons from his pocket beeper, tracking him through the building. He activates his portable telephone. Avogadro is calling.

"Can you come to Security Vector One, Doctor?"

"Now?"

"If you would."

"What's happening?" Shadrach asks.

"We've been interrogating Buckmaster. Your name has arisen."

"Oh. *Oh.* Am I a suspect too, now?"

"Hardly. A witness, perhaps. Can we expect you in five minutes?"

Shadrach looks at Katya, who is flushed, excited. "I have to go," he says. "Avogadro. Something about the Mangu inquiry. It sounds urgent."

Her face darkens. Her lips compress. But she says only that she hopes to see him again soon, and, hiding her disappointment behind a mask of detachment, she releases him. As he leaves the laboratory he feels his entire body expand, as though it had been held under great pressure while he was with her.

Security Vector One is on the sixty-fourth floor.

Mordecai has never had occasion to go there, and he has little idea what to expect, other than standard police paraphernalia—magnifying glasses and finger-print pads all over the place, no doubt, photos of known subversives mounted on tacky boards, sheafs of dossiers and transcripts, rows of tap-terminals and fiber-eyes, whatever things detectives would be likely to use in protecting the physical persons of Genghis Mao and the PRC. Perhaps such things are there, but Shadrach gets no glimpse of them. A feline, soft-voiced young man, Oriental but too sinuous to be a Mongol, probably Chinese, greets him at the reception desk and guides him through a labyrinth of blank-walled hallways, past a nest of tiny offices where weary-looking bureaucrats sit at desks heaped with paper. The place could be the headquarters of an insurance company, a bank, a brokerage house. Only when he is ushered into the interrogation cell where Avogadro and Buckmaster are waiting for him does he feel that he is among the enforcers of the law.

The room is artfully claustrophobic, rectangular and windowless, with dirty green walls and a low, oppressive ceiling from which short-stalked spotlights dangle at the ends of jointed metal arms. The spotlights are trained on the forehead of Roger Buck-master, who sits uncomfortably slouched in a squat, hard narrow chair with broad aluminum armpieces and a high backrest. Electrodes are taped to Buck-master's wrist and temples; their leads disappear into the recesses of the backrest. Buckmaster looks unnaturally pale, sweaty, blotchy-faced; his eyes are glassy; his lips are slack. Clearly Avogadro has been working him over for some while.

Avogadro, who is standing next to Buckmaster as Shadrach enters, looks little better—grim, harried, frayed. "A madhouse," he mutters. "Fifty arrests in the first hour. We have every interrogation cell full and they're still coming in. Lunatics, beggars, thieves, all the riffraff of Ulan Bator. And the radicals, of course. I go from cell to cell, cell to cell. And for what? For what?" A rough-edged laugh. "There'll be plenty of meat for the organ farms before this is over." Slowly, moving his heavy frame as though doubled gravity drags it down, he turns to the man in the chair. "Well, Buckmaster? You have a visitor. Do you recognize him?"

Buckmaster stares at the floor. "You know bloody well I do."

"Tell me his name."

"Let me be."

"Tell me his name," Avogadro urges in a tone that is tired but menacing.

"Mordecai. Shadrach Bloody Mordecai. Em Dee."

"Thank you, Buckmaster. Now tell me when you last saw Dr. Mordecai."

"Last night," Buckmaster says, his voice a feeble fluting thing, barely audible.

"Louder?"

"Last night."

"Where?"

"You know where, Avogadro!"

"I want you to tell me yourself."

"I already have."

"Again. In front of Dr. Mordecai. Tell me."

"Why don't you just carve me up and be done with it?"

"You're making this hard for yourself, Buckmaster. You're also making it hard for me."

"Pity."

"I have no choice about this," Avogadro says.

Lifting his head, Buckmaster manages a cold, sullen, furious glare. "Do I? Do I? Oh, I know the game. You'll question me for a while, you'll find me guilty of conspiracy, you'll sentence me to death, and off I go to the organ farm, right? Right? And there I lie, a corpse that isn't dead, so that whenever Genghis Mao needs a lung, a kidney, a heart, someone can come and cut out mine, right? While I lie there, dead, warm, breathing and metabolizing, part of the stockpile."

"Buckmaster—"

Buckmaster chuckles. "Genghis Mao thinks the stocks are getting low, and he can't use the miserable organ-rotted people out there, so he turns on us, he tosses a few dozen of his own people to the farms, right? Very well, take me away! Turn me into canni- bal food! But let's end this farce fast, shall we? Stop asking me idiotic questions."

Avogadro sighs. "To continue. You saw Dr. Mordecai at—"

"Timbuktu."

Avogadro lifts his left hand. A security man sitting at a table in the farthest corner does something to a control console in front of him; Buckmaster jerks and twitches and the left side of his face goes into a brief ugly spasm.

"You saw him where?"

"Piccadilly Circus."

Again the left hand, higher. Again the touching of controls; again the facial spasm, much worse. Shadrach Mordecai shifts his weight uneasily from foot to foot. In a low voice he says, "Possibly it isn't necessary to—"

"It's necessary, yes," Avogadro tells him. "The forms must be observed." To Buckmaster he says, "I'm prepared to keep this up all day. It bores me, but it's my job, and if I have to hurt you, I'll hurt you, and if you make me cripple you, I'll cripple you, because I have no choice. Do you understand? *I have no choice.* Now, again: you met Dr. Mordecai in—"

"Karakorum."

"Where in Karakorum?"

"Outside the transtemporalists' tent."

"About what time?"

"I don't know. Late, but it was before midnight."

"Dr. Mordecai, is this correct? Your answers will be recorded."

"It's all correct so far," Shadrach says.

"Good. Go on, Buckmaster. Tell me what you told me before. You encountered Dr. Mordecai and you said what to him?"

"I spoke a lot of bloody nonsense."

"What kind of nonsense, Buckmaster?"

"Foolish talk. The transtemporalists jumbled my mind with their drugs."

"What exactly did you say to the doctor?"

Buckmaster, silent, stares at the floor.

The right hand of Avogadro rises almost to his shoulder. The controls are adjusted. Buckmaster leaps in his seat as though speared. His right arm thrashes about like an infuriated snake.

"Tell me, Buckmaster. Please."

"I accused him of doing evil."

"Go on."

"I called him a Judas."

"And a black bastard," Shadrach says.

Avogadro, with a gentle nudge, indicates to Shadrach that his prompting is unwelcome.

"Specifically, Buckmaster, what did you accuse Dr. Mordecai of doing?"

"Of doing his job."

"Meaning what?"

"His job is keeping the Chairman alive. I said he's responsible for keeping Genghis Mao from having died five years ago."

Avogadro says, "Is that correct, Dr. Mordecai?"

Shadrach hesitates. He doesn't particularly want to cooperate in sending Buckmaster to the organ farm. But it would be folly to try to protect the little man now. The truth about last night's incident in Karakorum has already been drawn forth and recorded, he knows. Buckmaster is condemned out of his own mouth. No lie can save him, but only imperil the liar.

"It is," he says.

"So. Buckmaster, do you regret that Genghis Mao didn't die five years ago?"

"Let me be, Avogadro."

"Do you? Do you truly want the Chairman to be dead? Is that your position?"

"I had the drug in my head!"

"You don't have the drug in your head now, Buckmaster. What are your feelings about Genghis Mao at this moment?"

"I don't know. I simply don't know."

"Hostile?"

"Perhaps. Look, Avogadro, don't force any more out of me. You have me, you'll give me to the cannibals tonight, isn't that enough for you?"

"We can end this as soon as you cooperate."

"Very well," Buckmaster says. He pulls himself upright, finding some remaining resource of dignity. "I don't care for the regime of Genghis Mao. I am not in general agreement with the policies of the PRC. I regret having devoted so much effort to their service. I was overwrought last night and I said a lot of foul things to Dr. Mordecai for which I feel shame today. *But.* But, Avogadro! But I have never done anything disloyal. And I don't know a thing about the death of Mangu. I swear I had no part in it."

Avogadro nods. "Dr. Mordecai, did the prisoner mention Mangu last night?"

"I don't think he did."

"Can you be more positive about that?"

Shadrach considers. "No," he says finally. "To the best of my recollection, he said nothing about Mangu."

"Did the prisoner make any threats against the life of Genghis Mao?"

"Not that I recall."

"Try to remember, Doctor."

Shadrach shakes his head. "You have to understand, I had just come out of the transtemporalists' tent myself. My mind was still elsewhere during most of Buckmaster's tirade. He did speak critically of the government, yes, quite strongly, but I don't think there were any direct threats. No."

"I should refresh your memory, then," Avogadro says, gesturing to his assistant in the corner. There is a hissing sound, and then, from an invisible speaker, the sound of a voice, strangely familiar but oddly strange. His own.

This is suicidal, the way you're carrying on. There'll be a report of all this on the Chairman's desk tomorrow, Roger, more likely than not. You're destroying yourself.

—*I'll destroy* him. *The bloodsucker. He holds us all for ransom, our bodies, our souls*—

"Again," Avogadro says. "That last bit."

—*I'll destroy* him. *The bloodsucker. He holds us all for*—

"Do you recognize those voices, Doctor?"

"Mine. Buckmaster's."

"Thank you. The identification is important. Who was it who said, 'I'll destroy *him*'?"

"Buckmaster."

"Yes. Thank you. Buckmaster, was that your voice?"

"You know it was."

"Making a threat against the life of Genghis Mao?"

"I was overwrought. I was making a rhetorical point."

"Yes," Shadrach Mordecai says. "That's how it seemed to me. I urged him not to shout nonsense. I can't see it as any kind of serious threat. You have a tape of the whole conversation?"

"The whole thing," Avogadro says. "Many conversations are taped, you know. And automatically screened for subversion. The computers brought this to our attention early this morning. The voiceprints told us it was you and Buckmaster, but of course your direct corroboration is useful—"

"As though you'll have a trial, a jury, lawyers," Buckmaster says bitterly. "As though I won't be meat by nightfall!"

"He didn't say anything about Mangu to me last night, did he?" Shadrach asks.

"No. Nothing on tape."

"As I thought. Then why hold him?"

"Why defend him, Doctor? According to the tape, he was insulting and offensive to you."

"I haven't forgotten. Nevertheless, I hold no grudges. He was a nuisance to me last night, but being a nuisance shouldn't be enough to make me want to see him sent to the organ farms."

"Tell him again!" Buckmaster cries. "Oh, God, tell him!"

"Please," Avogadro says. Buckmaster's outburst appears to give him pain. He signals to his man, and Buckmaster is unstrapped, freed of the electrodes, helped to his feet, led from the room. At the door Buckmaster pauses and looks back, face bleary, distorted with fear. His lips tremble; in a moment he will be sobbing. "I'm not the one!" he cries, and the security aides haul him away.

"He isn't," Shadrach says. "I'm sure of that. He

was out of his mind last night, ranting and screaming, but he's no assassin. A malcontent, maybe. But no assassin."

Avogadro, sinking limply into the interrogation chair, plays with the electrodes, winding the snaky leads around his fingers. "I know that," he says.

"What will happen to him?"

"The organ farm. Probably before morning."

"But why?"

"Genghis Mao's reviewed the tape. He regards Buckmaster as dangerous."

"Christ!"

"Go argue with Genghis Mao."

"You sound so calm about it," Shadrach says.

"It's out of my hands, Doctor."

"We can't just let him be murdered!"

"We can't?"

"I can't."

"If you want to try to save him, go ahead. I wish you well."

"I might try. I might just."

"The man called you a black bastard," Avogadro says. "And a Judas."

"For that I should let him be vivisected?"

"You aren't *letting* anything. It's just happening. It's Buckmaster's problem. Not mine, not yours."

"No man's an island, Avogadro."

"Haven't I heard that before somewhere?"

Shadrach stares. "Aren't you at all concerned? Don't you give a damn about justice?"

"Justice is for lawyers. Lawyers are an extinct species. I'm only a security officer."

"You don't believe that, Avogadro."

"Don't I?"

"Christ. Christ. Don't come on with that I'm-just-a-cop routine. You're too intelligent to mean it. And I'm too intelligent to take it at face value."

Avogadro sits up. He has coiled two of the leads around his throat in a bizarre clownish way, and his head is tilted to one side, like that of a hanged man. "Do you want me to play you the Buckmaster tape? There's a place on it where you tell him that it's not

our fault the world is the way it is, that we accept
our karma, that we all serve Genghis Mao because
he's the only game in town. The alternative is organ-
rot, nez-pah? Therefore we dance to the Khan's tune,
and we don't ask questions of morality, neither do
we unduly search our souls over matters of guilt and
responsibility."

"I—"

"Wait. *You* said it. It's on the tape, *Dottore*. Now I
say it to you. I've forfeited the luxury of having personal feelings about the righteousness of sending Bucky
to the organ farm. By entering the Khan's service
I've given up the privilege of having qualms."

"Have you ever seen an organ farm?"

"No," Avagadro says. "But I hear—"

"I've seen them. Long quiet room, like a hospital
ward, but *very* quiet. Except for the burble of the
life-support machinery. Double row of open tanks,
wide aisle between them. One body in each tank,
floating in warm blue-green fluid, a nutrient bath.
Intravenous tubes all over the floor, like pink spaghetti.
Dialysis machines between each pair of tanks. Before
they put a body in its tank, they kill the brain—spike
through the foramen magnum, *zap*—but the rest stays
alive, Avogadro. Vegetable in animal form. God knows
what it perceives, but it lives, it needs to be fed, it
digests and excretes, the hair grows, the fingernails,
the nurses shave and groom the bodies every few
weeks, and there they lie, arranged neatly by blood
type and tissue type, available, gradually being
stripped of limbs and organs, a kidney this week, a
lung the next, sliced down to torsos in easy stages,
the eyes, the fingers, the genitalia, eventually the
heart, the liver—"

"So? What's your point, Doctor? That organ farms
aren't pretty places? I know that. But it's an efficient
way to maintain organs awaiting transplant. Isn't it
better to recycle bodies than to waste them?"

"And turn an innocent man into a zombie? Whose
only purpose is to be a living storage depot for spare
organs?"

"Buckmaster isn't innocent."

"What's he guilty of?"

"Guilty of bad judgment. Guilty of bad luck. His number's up, Doctor." Avogadro, rising, lays his hand lightly on Shadrach's arm. "You're a man of conscience, aren't you, *Dottore?* Buckmaster thought you were a cynical fiend, a soulless servant of the Antichrist, but no, no, you're a decent sort, caught in a nasty time, doing your best. Well, Doctor, so am I. I quote your own words of last night: *Guilt is a luxury we can't afford.* Amen! Now go. Stop worrying about Buckmaster. Buckmaster's done himself in. If you hear the bell tolling, remember, it tolls for him, and it doesn't diminish you or me at all, because we've already diminished ourselves as much as possible." Avogadro's smile is warm, almost pitying. "Go, Doctor. Go and relax. I have work to do. I have a dozen more suspects to question before dinner."

"And the real murderer of Mangu—"

"Was Mangu himself, nine to one. What's that to me? I'll continue to find his killer and interrogate him and ship him to the organ farms until I'm told to stop. Go, now. Go. Go."

12

Word circulates, the next day, that thirteen conspirators have been sent to the organ farms, including Roger Buckmaster, the ringleader. Such rumors generally have a way of being accurate, but Shadrach Mordecai, still finding the idea unpalatable, goes to the extent of keying into the master personnel register to find out where Buckmaster is. He tries the engineering department code, but is told by the master computer that Buckmaster has been reassigned to Department 111. Shadrach tries that code next, though he knows what it is likely to be, and yes, Department 111 is the euphemism for the organ farms. Buckmaster has joined the human stockpile. Spike through the foramen magnum, *zap*. Poor silly red-faced fool.

Dr. Mordecai chooses not to bring up the subject of Buckmaster when he pays his morning call on the Chairman. Buckmaster's fate seems beside the point now. "The conspiracy is crushed!" Genghis Mao declares vehemently as Shadrach enters. "The guilty have been punished. The threat to our regime has been met. The principles of centripetal depolarization will not be challenged." His eyes gleam with lunatic satisfaction. His ancient patchwork body throbs with triumphant good health, reverberating in Shadrach's implants as furious freshets of resurgent energy.

Shadrach takes blood samples, administers medicines, checks reflexes; the Khan pays no more heed to him than if he were an orderly changing the bed linens. He is altogether preoccupied, it appears, with his proliferating schemes for the deification of Mangu. Already blueprints for Mangu monuments have been drawn up, and they are spread everywhere in rustling heaps across the Chairman's bed, over his bony upjutting knees and on both sides of him and tumbling to the floor. Humming tunelessly, Genghis Mao turns the documents this way and that, nodding, scribbling marginal notes, muttering private observations.

"Hah! I like this!" Genghis Mao exclaims sharply. "Patterned after the Great Pyramid of Gizeh, but twice the size, with statues of Mangu twenty meters high rising out of each of the four faces. What do you think?" He shoves the blueprint toward Mordecai. "It's Ionigylakis's idea. He's trying to improve on antiquity, like everyone else. How do you like it, Shadrach?"

"The statues, sir. They—ah—tend to break the line of the pyramid, wouldn't you say?"

"What's wrong with that?"

"Pyramids are so graceful," Shadrach says. "So compact."

"The original pyramid is an exhausted concept," the Chairman snaps. "What I like about this is the contrast in angles, the slope of the pyramid's face versus the upright statue working against it, do you see? Mangu rising upward, outward, away from the center—it's centripetal, Shadrach! Do you see?"

"Centrifugal, I'd say, sir."

Genghis Mao gapes as though his doctor has struck him. "Centrifugal? Centrifugal? Are you serious?" He breaks into frantic laughter. "A joke! My earnest Shadrach makes a joke! Tell me: do you think Mangu was in great pain?"

"He must have died instantly. I doubt that he was conscious as he fell. The acceleration—"

"Yes. Look at this one, will you? A helical spire, it says here, nine hundred meters high, a great metal coil through which a magnetic field flows, and a perpetual bolt of lightning flickering at the tip—"

"Sir, if you would, the tritetrazol injection—"

"Later, Shadrach."

"The absorption levels are already slightly above optimum. If I could have your arm—"

"—and here, yes, I like this. A giant sarcophagus of alabaster, inlaid with onyx—"

"—clench your fist, sir—"

"—build a tomb worthy of—"

"—if you'd hold your breath, count to five—"

"—a scale befitting Alexander the Great, Tut-ankh-Amen, even Genghis Khan himself. Yes, why not? Mangu—"

"—and relax now, sir—"

"—Ch'in Shih Huang Ti! There's our prototype! Do you know him, Shadrach?"

"Sir?"

"Ch'in Shih Huang Ti."

"I'm afraid I—"

"The First Emperor of China, the Unifier, the builder of the Great Wall. Do you know how they buried him?" Genghis Mao scrabbles through the documents on his bed and comes up with a sheaf of pale green printouts, which he brandishes wildly in Shadrach's face. "A great hill of sand, south of the River Wei, at the foot of Mount Li. Or was it Mount Wei, River Li? Wei. Li. In the mound a palace, and the palace contained a relief map of China modeled in bronze, depicting the rivers, mountains, valleys, plains. The Yangtze and the Huang Ho had channels four meters deep, filled with quicksilver. Models of cities and palaces along their banks, and a great dome of bright copper overhead, yes, with the moon and the constellations engraved on it. The coffin of the First Emperor, then, floated on one of the quicksilver rivers, Shadrach! An endless journey across China. Silent, slippery—oh, bathe me in quicksilver, Shadrach, let me sleep on quicksilver! Do you see the coffin? And a powerful bow at the coffin's side, ready to hurl an arrow at any intruder. Trapdoors and hidden knives waiting for the grave-robbers, too, and thunder-making machines—and hundreds of slaves and artisans buried in the mound with Ch'in Shih Huang Ti to serve him, yes. Grandeur! What do you think? Should I build this for Mangu?" The Khan blinks, frowns, moistens his lips. Shadrach Mordecai perceives changes in skin temperature and blood pressure. "On the other hand—if I build such a tomb for Mangu, what could I provide for myself? Surely I deserve something finer. But what—what—" Genghis Mao breaks into a broad grin. "There's time to plan it! Twenty, fifty years! Why should I think now of tombs for Genghis Mao? It's Mangu we bury. I'll give him the finest!" The old man pushes the blueprints into a heap. "Forty-one guilty conspirators to the organ farms so far, Shadrach."

"I had heard thirteen."

"Forty-one, and we're not finished. I've told Avogadro to bring in at least a hundred. Think of the livers going into storage! The kilometers of intestine. How beautiful the farms are, Shadrach. I hate waste of all kinds. You know that. To conserve. It's a kind of poetry. Forty-one more tanks filled. And the threat to the government is put down." Genghis Mao's voice grows dark, hollow. "But Mangu—what have they done to Mangu? My other self—my self-in-waiting—my prince, my viceroy—"

"Sir, perhaps you're becoming overexcited."

"I feel fine, Shadrach."

"But some rest—"

"Rest? I don't need to rest. I could get out of bed now and run from here to Karakorum. Rest, for what? Are you worried about me, Shadrach?" The Chairman's laughter bursts forth, booming, resonant. "I feel fine. Never better. Stop worrying. What an old woman you are, Shadrach. Are you a Christian?"

"Sir?" Shadrach says blankly.

"A Christian. A Christian. Do you accept the Only Begotten Son of God as your Savior? What? Can't you hear? The ears going bad? I'll ask Warhaftig to give you new eardrums. I asked you, Are you a Christian?"

Baffling. "Well—"

"You know. You know. *Pater noster qui* art in heaven. Ave Maria full of grace. Whoever eats my flesh and drinks my blood has life eternal, and I will raise him up on the last day, says the Lord. Yes? You know of this? Lamb of God you take away the sins of the world. *Ite missa est.* Well?"

"Well, my parents sometimes took me to church, but I can't really say that I—"

"Too bad. Not a believer?"

"In the narrow sense of the word, perhaps, but—"

"There's only one sense of the word, it seems to me."

"I don't think I'm a believer, then."

"Well, hallowed be thy name. Would you like to be Pope anyway?"

"Sir?"

"Is that all you can say? *Sir? Sir?*" Genghis Mao mimics his obsequiousness with devastating ferocity. The Khan's pulse is rising; his face is flushed. "The kingdom and the power. Oh, and the glory. You Christians, you understand. I am the way, the truth, and the life, says the Lord; no one comes to the Father, except through me." This manic volatility disturbs Dr. Mordecai, who surreptitiously boosts the

Khan's tranquilizer intake, hitting the 9-pordenone pedal while pretending to examine the base of the life-support system. Genghis Mao, sitting up, shouting now, cries, "Answer yes, answer no, but no more sirs! Pope! I asked you, would you like to be Pope? The Pope is dead in Rome, old Benedict. The cardinals will meet this summer. I am invited to offer a nominee. I'll send them the name of my doctor, my beautiful black doctor, yes? *Le Pape Noir. Il Papa Negro.* There have been black saints, why not a black Pope? Pick your own regnal name. It's one of the little dividends of the power and the glory. What do you say to Papa Legba? Eh? Eh?" Genghis Mao claps his hands. "Papa Legba! Papa Legba!"

The new liver, Shadrach thinks. Could it have been the liver of a madman?

He says mildly, "I'm not Roman Catholic, sir."

"You could become one. Is that so hard? A week of coaching and you'd know how to mumble the right words. *Kyrie eleison. Credo in unum deum. Om mani padme hum.*"

There is something ominous in all this crazy talk of poping. Genghis Mao's lightning shifts of subject, his hectic flow of fantasies, his volcanic verbal outpour, do not inspire confidence in Genghis Mao's mental stability. This is the man who rules the world, Shadrach reflects. Such that it is.

Shadrach says, "If I became Pope, who would be your doctor?"

"Why, you would, Shadrach."

"From Rome?"

"We'd move the Vatican to Ulan Bator."

"Even so, I don't think I could do justice to both jobs, sir."

"A young man like you? Of course you could. What are you, thirty-five years old, thirty-eight, something like that? You'd be a splendid Pope. I'd become Catholic myself, and you could hear my confession. Don't refuse the offer, Shadrach. I think you don't have enough to do as things are now. You need distractions. You spend too much of your time doctoring me, because your days are otherwise idle. You fill me with needless medicines. Why are you staring at me like that?"

"I'd prefer not to become Pope, sir."

"Final decision?"

"Final."

"All right. I'll name Avogadro."

"At least he's Italian."

"You think I'm insane, Shadrach?"

"Sir, I think you're overtaxing yourself. I prescribe two hours of total rest. May I give you a sleep tab?"

"You may not. You may leave and amuse yourself in Karakorum. Gonchigdorge will be Pope, yes, a Mongol, do you like that? I like that. You, up there, sainted old Father Genghis, old Temujin, do you like that? Leave me, Shadrach. You annoy me today. *I am not insane*. I am not overtaxing myself. The death of Mangu distresses me. I grieve for Mangu. I will make the world remember Mangu forever. Forty-one to the farms, and it's only morning! Will you take yourself to Karakorum?"

The metabolic levels are rising on a dozen fronts. Shadrach is alarmed. He manipulates the tranquilizer pedal once again. The old man must be awash in 9-pordenone now, but somehow Genghis Mao overrides it, remaining in the manic mode despite the drug. It is at last taking effect, though. At last, some sign of calming. The Khan subsides. Shadrach departs, troubled, but confident that the Khan's temperament will stabilize for a time. As he goes out, Genghis Mao calls after him, "Or King of England! What do you say? There'll be a vacancy in Windsor soon!"

13

He goes to Karakorum with Katya Lindman. Ordinarily he spends his free evenings with Nikki Crowfoot, but not always; they are not husband and wife, there is no monogamy between them. He loves Crowfoot, or believes he does, which amounts to the same thing for him. But he has never been able to escape Lindman for long. Now she is in the ascendant, like baleful Saturn rising into the house of Aquarius. This night will be hers. Nikki is elsewhere, anyway, he knows not where; he is free, accessible, vulnerable.

"You'll do the dreams with me tonight?"

Why not? Her harsh forceful contralto has maimed his will. He shall allow himself finally to be indoctrinated into the mysteries of dream-death. Her dark eyes sparkle with savage succubal glee as he nods his agreement.

The dream-death pavilion is a wide many-poled tent, black cloth with trim of rusty orange stripes. Over its entrance is mounted a great jutting image of a ram's head, heavy, glowering, aggressive, spearing the chilly spring air with massive superprepotent coiled horns. Shadrach knows the ram is Amon-Re, lord of fear, king of the sun, patron of dream-death; for this cult is said to be derived from Pharaonic Egypt, secret rites never lost since first they were practiced along the shores of the sluggish, sweltering Nile in the time of the Fifth Dynasty. Within the tent, surprisingly, all is light. The place is ablaze with glowing fixtures from floor to ceiling—hanging lamps, floor-poles, spots, cascading lavalieres of radiance, so that the air burns with a numbing blue-white brightness and all shadows are obliterated. Shadrach, remembering the murky atmosphere of the transtemporalists' tent, is taken aback by this intense luminosity. But in the realm of Amon-Re a solar brilliance must prevail.

A costumed figure approaches, a slender Oriental female who wears nothing but a twist of white linen around her hips and a huge gilded lioness-mask that rests ponderously on her slim shoulders. Between her dainty breasts hangs a pendant, the crux ansata, in fiery gold. She does not speak; but with expressive gestures she leads Mordecai and Lindman through the crowded tent, past scores of sleepers who lie on fluffy mattresses of white cotton surrounded by high barriers of golden rope strung through ebony stanchions, to a vacant cubicle that is to be theirs. Within the ring of rope lie two thick mattresses side by side, a neatly folded dreaming costume beside each one, and an ornate wooden trunk which, their guide indicates, is for their street clothes. Katya immediately begins to strip, and Shadrach, after a moment, does the same. The guide stands aside, showing no interest in their nakedness. Shadrach feels foolish in his costume—a single handkerchief-sized square of linen to cover his loins and thighs, a beaded belt with which to fasten it around his hips, and two narrow strips of cloth, one green, one blue, which the guide helps him fasten crosswise over his chest.

Katya smiles at him. He feels heavy lust, unleavened by love or even by joy, as she removes her clothes. That dense dark pubic thatch, broad and curling, spilling into the corners of her thighs, exerts a terrible pull: he longs with weird intensity to bury his sex in it, to plunge like a hatchet to her hot unforgiving depths and stay there, motionless. Lindman dons a one-piece loincloth similar to his and a looped-cross pendant identical to the guide's. These enhance, rather than mask, her nakedness. As always, her body disturbs him: wide-hipped, heavy-rumped, a peasant-woman's body, the center of gravity quite low, the navel deep, hidden in smooth slabs of belly fat, the breasts full and somewhat elongated. It is a strong and voluptuous body, powerful without being at all athletic, as exaggeratedly female as those primordial Venuses out of the Cro-Magnon caves. What bothers Shadrach most, he suspects, is the contrast between that robustly sexual earth-mother body and those thin, predatory lips, those sharp, threatening teeth. Katya's mouth is untrue to the archetype that the rest of her body projects, and that contradiction makes her a mystery to Shadrach. *Falsus in uno, falsus in omnibus*, perhaps.

The lioness-headed one invites them to kneel on their mattresses and hands each of them a polished metal talisman. It seems at first to be no more than a mirror, a bright blank planchet with quasi-Egyptian motifs around its rim, small engravings of the Horus-hawk, serpents, scorpions, scarabs, bees, the ibis of Thoth, interspersed with tiny portentous-looking hieroglyphs; but as he stares Shadrach begins to perceive a dizzying pattern of almost invisible dotted lines spiraling around the middle of the amulet; these lines, he realizes, may be seen only when the angle at which he holds the talisman in relation to a certain brilliant lamp over his head is just right; and, by moving the device ever so slightly, he can make the lines appear to move, to swirl in a counterclockwise eddy, to create a vortex—

—sucking him toward the center of the disk—

So they work by hypnotism here rather than by drugs, he thinks, feeling smug, scientific, Shadrach the scholar, the detached observer of all human phenomena, and then he feels an irresistible tug, he finds himself caught, drawn helplessly inward, a mere speck blown on the cosmic winds, a mote, a phantasm—

—one moment kneeling here admiring the cleverness of the mechanism and a moment later gripped, held, pulled, altogether incapable of objective considerations, *animula vagula blandula hospes comesque corporis*—

As he goes under, the priestess, for so he must

think of her, begins a rhythmic chant, fragmentary and elusive, a mingling of English words and Mongol and bits of what might well be Pharaonic Egyptian, invocations of Set, Hathor, Isis, Anubis, Bast. Figures out of myth surround him in the sudden shadows, the hawk-headed god, the great jackal, the dog-faced ape, the vast clicking scarabaeus, desiccated deities exchanging knowing comments in opaque tongues, nodding, pointing. Here is Father Amon, bright as solar fire, turbulent as the skin of the sun, beckoning to him. Here is the beast with no face, radiating streams of starflame. Here is the dwarf-god, the buffoon, the protector of the dead, capering and guffawing. Here is the goddess with a woman's body and the heads of three snakes. The gods dance, laugh, pass water, spit, weep, clap hands. Still the priestess chants. Her words, chasing one another round and round, seize and control him. He can barely comprehend anything any longer, all structures having dissolved and become formless, but yet he is remotely aware that he is being programmed, being propelled, being given by this slim naked yellow girl who speaks in impassive sing-song certain attitudes toward death and life that will shape his experience in the hours just ahead. She has him, she leads him, she guides and aims him as he tosses on the eschatological breeze.

He is being pulled apart. Something is gently and painlessly severing him from himself. He has never felt anything like this before, not in the tent of the transtemporalists, not when taking any of the traditional psychedelics, not on kot, not on yipka: this is new, this is unique, a shedding of mass, a dropping away of the flesh, a liberation into weightlessness. He knows he is—

—dying?—

Yes, dying. That's the commodity offered here, death, the actual experience of departing from life, of having life depart from oneself. He can no longer feel his body. He is beyond all exterior sensation. This is the true death, that ultimate sundering toward which his life has moved throughout all its days; no simulation, no hypnotic trick, but real and actual death, the

going-forth of Shadrach Mordecai. Of course, on a
deeper level he knows it is only a dream, a night's
amusement purchased for sport; but under that awareness lies the realization that he may be dreaming
that he is dreaming, dreaming the talisman and the
tent and the lioness-girl, that he may really have
fallen through the illusion of an illusion and really is
dying here tonight. It does not matter.

How easy dying is! There is a cool moist gray mist
about him, and everything dissolves in it, Anubis
and Thoth, Katya and the priestess, the tent, the
amulet, Shadrach himself, invaded and interpenetrated
by the grayness until he is part of it. He floats
toward the center of the void. Is this what Genghis
Mao fears so much? To be a balloon and nothing but
a balloon, so much helium surrounded by a nonexistent skin, to put aside all responsibility and, liberated wholly, to float and float? Genghis Mao is so
heavy. He carries so much weight. It may be hard to
relinquish that. Not for Shadrach. He passes through
the center and emerges on the far side, congealing
nicely out of the mist and resuming his human form.
He is altogether naked now, not even a scrap at the
waist. Katya, naked also, stands beside him. At their
feet lie their discarded bodies, relaxed, limp, seemingly asleep, even giving the appearance of slow rhythmic breathing, but not so: they are actually dead,
truly and really dead. Shadrach Mordecai beholds
his own corpse.

"How quiet it is here," Katya says.

"And clean. They've washed the world for us."

"Where shall we go?"

"Anywhere."

"The circus? The bullfight? The marketplace?
Anywhere?"

"Anywhere," Shadrach says. "Yes. Let's go anywhere."

Effortlessly they float into the world. The lioness
waves farewell. The air is mild and balmy. The trees
are in bloom, fireflowers, little cups of flame sprout-
ing at the tips of the branches; they break loose and
drift down, swirl about, approach them, touch them,

sink sweetly into their bodies. Shadrach watches the passage of a blazing red blossom through Katya's breastbone; it emerges between her shoulders, falls lightly to the ground, goes to seed, sprouts. A skinny sapling rises and burst into flaming flower. They laugh like children. Together they stride across the continent. The sands of the Gobi sparkle. The Great Wall stretches before them, a wriggling stone serpent humping its back.

"Why, it's Nigger Jim and Little Nell!" cries Ch'in Shih Huang Ti, who stands atop the Wall. He does a little dance of joy, doffing his silken black skullcap, letting his long elaborate pigtails wave about.

"Chop-chop," Shadrach says. "Kung po chi ding!"

"Which way to the egress?" Katya asks.

"There," says the First Emperor. "Past the chains, over the spikes."

They go through the gate. On the far side of the Great Wall are flooded rice paddies glittering in rosy sunlight. Women in black pajamas and broad coolie hats move slowly through ankle-deep water, stooping, planting, stooping, planting. Invisible chorus off screen. Swelling crescendo of celestial sound. Katya scoops rich yellow mud and hurls it at him. Glop! He throws mud at her. Glip! They plaster each other with it and embrace, slippery and wriggling. What sweet slime! They laugh; they romp; they tumble and topple, landing in the rice paddy with a splash, and the Chinese women dance around them. Huang! Ho! Lindman's legs grasp his hips. Thighs like clamps. She reaches for him. They couple in the mud like rutting buffalo. Gripping one another, rolling over and over. Snorting. Slapping flesh. Wallowing in the primeval ooze. Very gratifying. Nostalgia for the mud. Belly to belly. He does not perceive his rigid organ as anything that particularly belongs to him, but rather as something shared, an independent connecting rod that passes back and forth in swift reciprocations between their clasped bodies. Without reaching a climax they rise, bathe, move on to New York. A hot wind blows through this city of sky-stabbing towers. Confetti showers down upon them; it stings, it burns. Cheers of the inhabitants. Everyone has organ-rot here, but it is accepted; it causes no alarm. The bodies of the New Yorkers are transparent, and Shadrach sees the red lesions within, the zones of corruption and decay, the eruptions and erosions and suppurations of intestines, lungs, vascular tissue, peritoneum, pericardium, spleen, liver, pancreas. The disease announces itself in radiating waves of low-spectrum electromagnetic pulsations, hammering dully at his soul, red red red. These people are full of holes from fetlock to gunwale and yet they are happy, as why should they not be? Shadrach and Katya do a buck-and-wing down Fifth Avenue. Shadrach's skin is white. His lips are thin. His hair is straight and long; it blows across his face, momentarily blinding him, and when he clears it he sees that Katya now is black. Flat broad-flanged nose, splendid steatopygous ass, yards of chocolate skin. Ruby lips, sweeter than wine. "Poon!" she cries.

"Tang!" he replies.

"Hot!"

"Cha!"

They dance on swords. They dance on pineapples. He sells her into slavery and redeems her with his first-born.

"Are we dead?" he asks her. "Really and truly dead?"

"As doornails."

"Is it supposed to be this much fun?"

"Are you having fun?" she asks.

They are in Mexico. Frangipani, flamboyans. It is spring: the cacti are in bloom. Towering spiny green poles topped by crazy clusters of fragrant yellow petals. Loops and whorls of thorniness exploding in gaudy firecracker bursts of red and white. They sleep-walk through the prickly pears. They somnambulate among the pitahayas. The pace is frantic but restful. Often they make love. He could waltz all night. Crossing the Pyrenees, they meet Pancho Sanchez, squat and greasy, who offers them green wine out of a leather bota and giggles shrilly when they spill it on themselves. Pancho licks wine from Katya's breasts. She gives him a merry shove and he somersaults into

Andorra. They follow. Commemorative coins of high
denomination are struck in their honor by the ador-
ing populace. "I thought death would be more serious," Shadrach says.

"It is."

Dead, they can go anywhere, and they do. But the
journey is an empty one and the food at the feast is
mere spun air, less sweet than cotton candy. He wishes
for more substance and the servants bring him stones.
He is black again, and so is Genghis Mao, enthroned
in a seat of glistening jade ten meters overhead.
Ficifolia is black, Buckmaster, Avogadro, Nikki Crowfoot; Mangu is the blackest of all; but the black of
their skins is not Negro-black, not African-black, it is
black-black, ebony-black, the color of a dark closet,
the color of the air between the worlds. Black as the
pit. They look like beings from some other galaxy.
Shadrach goes among them, slapping palms, touching elbows. They speak nigger-Mongol to one another,
they laugh and sing, they shuffle and shake. Ficifolia
is on guitar, Buckmaster on jew's harp, Avogadro on
banjo; Shadrach plays the bongos, Katya the tam-
bourine.

> Drop your body off
> Step outside your bones.
> So—easy to die—
> Such—a groovy trip—
> Man, man, man, man.

"It isn't really this good," Shadrach tells Katya.
"We're fooling ourselves."

"It has its points."

"I can't help feeling suspicious."

"Even dead you can't really let yourself go, can
you?" She takes him by the wrist and pulls him
along with her, through a desert of sparkling sands,
through a river of leaping white water, through a
thicket of dense aromatic brambles, into the ocean,
the great salty mother, and they lie on their backs,
looking up into the sun. He is utterly becalmed.

"How long does it go on?" he asks.

120   *Robert Silverberg*

"Forever."

"When does it end?"

"It doesn't."

"Really?"

"Nature of the state. Death is nothing but a continuation of life by different means."

"I don't believe it. *Dopo la morte, nulla.*"

"Then where are we now?"

"Dreaming," he says.

"Sharing the same dream? Don't be a fool."

The snouts of sharks poke through the gentle surface of the sea. Toothy jaws gape. Shadrach practices fearlessness. These beasts can do him no harm. He is, after all, dead. He is also a doctor of medicine. He gulps ocean until the shining sandy floor is laid bare and the sharks, beached, morosely flop about, munching on crabs and starfish. Shadrach laughs. Death is real, death is earnest! Out of the north come frosty winds, roaring down the flanks of the Himalayas. Indefatigably they continue the ascent of the North Cwm, clawing up the rocky face piton by piton, staring constantly at the formidable tapering peak rising like a giant whelk at the head of the valley. They shiver in their parkas; they clutch their ice-axes with weary hands; their oxygen tanks press inexorably against their aching shoulders; and still they climb, now into that giddy realm above seven thousand meters, where only the splay-footed snowmen dare to go. The summit is in sight. Vast crevasses loom, but they have no meaning; where crampons and pitons will not serve, Shadrach and Katya simply launch themselves into great sky-spanning leaps. It is too easy. He had not thought death to be so frivolous a place. Indeed now the sky is darkening, the pace is slowing; he hears solemn music, he experiences a lessening of the frenetic urges that have driven him thus far, he settles into a glacial calm, an Egyptian timelessness. He is one with Ptah and Osiris. He is a twanging Memnon beside the mighty river, waiting out the eons. Katya winks at him and he scowls his disapproval. Death is serious business, not a holiday. Ah, yes, now he has it, the proper pace. He is wholly absorbed by the task of being dead. He does not move. Vital signs nil; intellection nil; he has reached the core of the event. *Hic jacet. Nascentes morimur, finisque ab origine pendet. Mors omnia solvit.* Let there be trombones, please. *Missa pro defunctis. Requiem aeternam dona eis, Domine.* It is very quiet here. When they speak at all, they speak in Sanskrit, Aramaic, Sumerian, or, of course, Latin. Thoth himself speaks Latin. Doubtless other tongues too, but the gods themselves have whims. How sweet it is to be immobile and to think, if at all, only in languages one no longer understands! *Nullum est jam dictum quod non dictum est prius.* What a good sound that has! If you would, a little more volume on the basset horns:

> *Dies irae, dies illa*
> *Solvet saeclum in favilla*
> *Teste David cum Sybilla.*

Gradually the voices diminish. The music becomes subdued and abstract as it fades; the sound of the instruments now is hollow, a mere outline of sound, blank within, the idea of sound rather than sound itself, and the chorus, far away, sings the terrible words of the ancient prayer in a faint, chittering, rustling, elegant tone, poignant and penetrating:

> *Quantus tremor est futurus*
> *Quando Judex est venturus*
> *Cuncta stricte discussurus!*

And then all is silent. Now he is at peace. He has reached the essence of the dream-death, an end to striving, an end to seeking. The chase is over. He could go, if he wished, to Bangkok, Addis Ababa, San Francisco, Baghdad, Jerusalem, traveling with no more effort than it takes to blink an eye, but there is no reason to go anywhere, for all places have become one, and it is better to remain here, at the still point, motionless, swaddled in the soft sweet woolly fleece of the grave. *Consummatum est.* He is in perfect equilibrium. He is finally, truly dead. He knows he will sleep forever.

Instantly he wakes. His mind is clear, tingling, painfully alert. Passion inflames his penis, passion or else the blind force that comes over men in dreams; at any rate it juts shamelessly against his loincloth, making a little pyramid out of his lap. Katya lies not far away, propped up on her elbows, watching him. Her smile is sphinxlike. He sees her broad fleshy bare back, her firm meaty buttocks, and instantly the tranquility of dream-death is gone; lust rules him. "Let's go," he says hoarsely.

"All right."

"It isn't far to the lovers' hospice."

"No. Not there." She has already begun to dress. The lioness-guide is across the aisle, greeting newcomers. The brightness of the air leaves Shadrach dazzled. Anubis and Thoth still lurk somewhere nearby, he is convinced. He struggles to regain that vanished equilibrium, to find his way back to the still point, but he knows it will take many more dream-death sessions before he can reach that calm place on his own.

"Where?" he says.

"At the tower. I hate making love in rented rooms. Didn't you know that?"

So he must stifle his longings another hour or two. Perhaps that's the lesson of dream-death: delay gratification, purify the spirit. Or perhaps not. It is a jolt, stepping from the radiant ambiance of the dream-death tent to the darkness without, and the night is cold, very cold even for the Mongolian May, just a hint of snow in the air, a few hard little flakes whipping on the breeze. Riding the tube-train back they say almost nothing to each other, but as they approach the Ulan Bator station he says, "Were you really there?"

"In your dream?"

"Yes. When we met Pancho Sanchez. And the First Emperor. And when we went to Mexico."

"That was your dream," she says. "I was having other dreams."

"Oh. Oh. I wondered. It seemed very real, talking to you, having you beside me."

"The dreams always seem that way."

"But I'm surprised at how playful it was. Frivolous, even."

"Is that how it was for you?"

"Until the end," he says. "It got solemn then. When things grew calm. But before then—"

"Frivolous?"

"Very frivolous, Katya."

"For me it was solemn all the time. A great quietness."

"Is it different for everybody?"

"Of course," she says. "What did you think?"

"Oh."

"You thought, when you met me in your dream, that I was actually there, talking with you, sharing your experiences?"

"I confess that I did."

"No. I wasn't there."

"No. I suppose not." He laughs. "All right. I wasn't thinking. For you it was somber. For me it was all games. What does that say about you, about me?"

"Nothing, Shadrach."

"Really?"

"Nothing at all."

"We don't express something about our inner selves in the dreams we choose for ourselves?"

"No," she says.

"How can you be so sure?"

"The dreams are chosen for us. By a stranger. I don't know more than that, but the woman in the mask told us what to dream. The broad outlines. The tone."

"And we have no choice about the content?"

"Some. Her instructions are filtered through our sensibilities. But still—still—"

"Is your dream always the same?"

"In content? In tone?"

"Tone."

"The dream is always different," Katya says. "And yet the flavor is the same, for death is always the same. Different things happen each time, but the dream brings you always to the same place, in the same way, at the end."

"To the still point?"

"You could call it that. Yes. Yes."

"And the meaning of what I dreamed—"

"No," she says. "Don't talk about meaning. Dream-death gives no oracular wisdom. The dream is without meaning." The tube-train has reached Ulan Bator. "Come," Katya says.

They go to her suite, two floors below Nikki Crowfoot's, a dark place, three small rooms furnished with stark, heavy hangings. Once more they are naked before one another, once more he feels the overwhelming pull of Katya's thick sturdy body; he moves stiffly toward her, embraces her, digs the tips of his fingers into the deep flesh of her shoulders and back. But he cannot bring himself to kiss that terrifying mouth. He thinks of the joyous couplings He shared with her in dream-death, the rice paddy, the fragrant Mexican nights, and he tugs her down with him to the bed; but, though he fills his hands with her breasts, though he imprisons his head between her smooth cool thighs, though he drives himself urgently against her flesh, he is altogether unmanned by her physical presence, helpless, limp. Not for the first time, either: their sporadic lovemaking has always been marked by such difficulties, which he rarely experiences with other women. Katya is not bothered by this: calmly she pushes him back against the pillow with a thump of her knuckles on his chest, and then, bending forward, she goes to work on him with her mouth, her sinister and ferocious sharp-fanged mouth, lovingly engulfing him, and he feels lips and tongue, lips and tongue, warm and wet, no hint of teeth at all, and under her cunning ministrations he relaxes, he puts aside his fear of her, he grows stiff at last. Deftly she slides upward over him—it is a maneuver she has clearly practiced often—and, with a sudden startling thrust, drives herself downward, impaling herself on him. She squats astraddle, peasant-strong, above him, knees flexed, buttocks taut, body rocking. He looks at her and sees her face distorted by the early spasms of ecstasy, nostrils flared, eyes tight shut, lips pulled back in a fierce grimace; then he closes his own eyes and gives himself up fully to their union. An awesome energy courses through her. She rides him, now squatting high so that their only contact is at their loins, now pressing herself full length against his body, but always remaining above him, always staying in command. He does not object to this. She writhes, grinds, pushes, twists, suddenly rears back and breaks into bizarre laughter; it is, he knows, her signal, and he seizes her breasts and joins her in the final climax.

Afterward he dozes, and wakes to find her quietly sobbing. How strange, how unlike her! He had never imagined Lindman to be capable of tears.

"What's wrong?"

She shakes her head.

"Katya?"

"Nothing. Please."

"What is it?"

Sullenly, face against pillow, she says, "I'm afraid for you."

"Afraid? Why? What about?"

She looks toward him and shakes her head again. She clamps her lips. Suddenly her mouth looks not at all fierce. A child's mouth. She is frightened.

"Katya?"

"Please, Shadrach."

"I don't understand."

She says nothing. She shakes her head.

14

Over a week goes by before Shadrach sees Nikki Crowfoot again. She claims she is very busy in the laboratory—problems of recalibration, necessary compensatory adjustments in the Avatar persona-transplant system now that the donor body will not be Mangu's—and therefore she is too tired in the evenings to want company. But he suspects she is avoiding him. Crowfoot has always been at her most sociable when she is most overworked; it is her escape from pressure. Shadrach does not know why she would want to avoid him. Surely the night he spent with Katya Lindman has nothing to do with it. He has been to bed with Lindman before, and with others; Crowfoot too has had other partners; such things have never mattered between them. It baffles him. When they speak by telephone Nikki is wary and aloof. Beyond doubt something has gone wrong in their relationship, but he has no theories.

A new Genghis Mao crisis distracts him briefly from these matters. For the past several days the Khan has been leaving his bed to work in his office, to visit Surveillance Vector One, to direct the Committee activities from the headquarters room. His recuperation was proceeding so smoothly that there seemed no reason to confine him. But now Dr. Mordecai's sensitive implants are picking up early warnings of trouble—epigastric pulsations, faint systolic murmur, general circulatory stress. Too much activity too soon? Shadrach goes to the Chairman's office to discuss the problem. But Genghis Mao, still busy with his Mangu monuments and his roundup of assassins, does not feel like conferring with his doctor, does not want to talk about symptoms. He brushes Shadrach's queries aside with a brusque declaration that he has rarely felt better. Then he turns back to his desk. The arrests, he tells Mordecai proudly, now total two hundred eighty-two. Of these, ninety-seven have already been found guilty and sent to the organ farms. "Soon," the Khan says, "the lungs and kidneys and the intestines of these criminals will serve to extend the lives of loyal members of the government. Is there not poetic justice in that? All things are centripetal, Shadrach. All opposites are reconciled."

"Two hundred eighty-two conspirators?" Shadrach asks. "Did it take that many to push one man out one window?"

"Who knows? The actual crime perhaps required no more than two or three perpetrators. But a great network of subordinate plotters must have been needed. Security devices had to be altered, guards distracted, cameras deflected. We believe it may have taken a dozen conspirators simply to remove the bodies of the killers from the plaza after they jumped."

"To do what?"

Genghis Mao smiles blandly. "We believe," he says, "that the assassins, after hurling Mangu from the window, deliberately jumped from the same window themselves to keep from being captured in the building. Confederates in the plaza immediately gathered up their bodies and drove off with them, while others removed all signs of their deaths from the pavement."

Shadrach stares. "Horthy saw only one man falling, sir."

"Horthy did not remain in the plaza to observe further developments."

"Even so—"

"If the killers of Mangu did *not* leap after him," the Khan says, eyes bright with the brightness of reason triumphant, "what did become of them? No suspicious persons were found in the tower after the crime."

Shadrach is unable to find an appropriate reply to

this. No comment he might make, he suspects, would
be constructive. After a pause he says, clearing his
throat, "Sir, if we could talk about your health again
for a moment—"

"I told you. I feel fine."

"The symptoms I've begun to detect are fairly
serious ones, sir."

"Symptoms of what?" Genghis Mao snaps.

Shadrach suspects that the Khan may be developing an aneurysm of the abdominal aorta—a defect in
the wall of the great vessel that conveys blood from
the heart. He asks Genghis Mao if he has felt any
unusual discomfort, and the Chairman grudgingly
admits recent sharp pains in the back and sides. Dr.
Mordecai does not point out how this contradicts
Genghis Mao's claim of being in good health; but the
admission does give Shadrach the upper hand, and
he orders the Chairman back to bed for rest.

Peering through the eye of a fiber probe extending
into Genghis Mao's catheterized aorta, Shadrach con-
firms his diagnosis. The recent liver surgery, perhaps,
has released emboli into the Chairman's bloodstream,
and one has somehow made its way against the arterial flow, lodging in the abdominal aorta and causing
infection. Or perhaps not, but at any rate a tumor is
taking form, and more surgery will be necessary. If it
were anyone else, the risks of an operation so soon after
a major organ transplant might be even greater than
the risks of letting the aneurysm expand. But Shadrach
has become amazingly casual about delivering up his
venerable patient to the knife. Genghis Mao's resil-
ient body has been opened so often that it accepts
frequent surgery as the natural state. Besides, the
aneurysm is not far from the liver, and Warhaftig
will be able to enter through the recent incision,
which is only now beginning to heal.

The news annoys Genghis Mao. "I have no time for
surgery now," he says, irritated. "We're still finding
new conspirators every day. I must give my full attention to the problem. And next week is Mangu's state
funeral, at which I intend to preside in person. I—"

"The danger is critical, sir."

"You always tell me that. I think you enjoy telling me that. You're too insecure, Shadrach. Even if you didn't manage to find some new crisis every few weeks I'd still keep you on the payroll. I *like* you, Shadrach."

"I don't invent the crises, sir."

"Even so. Can't this wait a month or two?"

"We'd have to make a fresh cut in healed tissue then."

"What of it? What's one more slice?"

"Aside from that, the risks—'"

"Yes," Genghis Mao says. "The risks. What risks do I run by letting this thing sit?"

"Do you know what an aneurysm is, sir?"

"More or less."

"It's a tumor containing blood or a blood clot, in direct contact with the wall of an artery and causing deteriorative changes in the tissues surrounding it. Think of it as a balloon, gradually being inflated. When balloons get too big, they explode."

"Ah."

"Eventually this aneurysm could rupture—into the intestines, the peritoneum, the pleura, or the retro- peritoneal tissues. Or it might cause an embolism of the superior mesenteric artery, producing intestinal infarction. The aorta itself could rupture spontane- ously. There are several other possibilities. All fatal."

"Fatal?"

"Invariably fatal. Agonizing pain, death usually within minutes."

"Ah," Genghis Mao says. "Ah. I see."

"It could come at almost any time."

"Ah."

"Without warning."

"I see."

"We'd be helpless, once the aneurysm goes. No way of saving you, sir."

"Ah. I see. Ah."

Does he see? Yes. Certainly, visions of erupting aneurysms are floating before Genghis Mao's basilisk eyes. The lean leathery cheeks contract in profound speculation; somber frowns furrow the bronze fore-

head. The Khan is troubled. He had not planned on
being confronted with potential extinction this morning. Now, obviously, he contemplates the going of
Genghis II Mao IV Khan from the world, and likes
the idea no more than ever. The Permanent Revolution that has transformed the aching world requires
a Permanent Leader; though Genghis Mao has often
said, echoing Mao I's similar words, that when one
participates in a revolution one attains revolutionary
immortality, one transcends the death of the individual by living on indefinitely within the permanent
revolutionary ferment one has helped to create, it is
plain that Genghis Mao prefers the other, less metaphorical species of immortality for himself. He
glowers. He sighs. He gives his consent to this latest
surgical interruption of his revolutionary labors.

Warhaftig is summoned. There are conferences;
schedules are rearranged; details of the surgery are
explained to the Khan. The blood vessels will be
clamped above and below the aneurysm to arrest
circulation temporarily while Warhaftig removes the
aneurysm and installs a dacron or teflon prosthesis.

"No," the Khan says. "Not a prothesis. You can
use a tissue graft, can't you? There's not much of a
rejection problem with arterial tissue. It's like stitching in a length of hose."

Warhaftig says, "But dacron and teflon have proven
perfectly—"

"No. I have enough plastic in me already. And the
organ banks are overflowing with new material. Give
me real aorta." Genghis Mao's eyes gleam. "Give me
aorta from one of the recently convicted conspirators."

Warhaftig looks at Shadrach Mordecai, who shrugs.

"As you wish," the surgeon says.

Shadrach has lunch soon afterward with Katya
Lindman. When they have eaten, they stroll in Sukhe
Bator Square. He has spent more time than usual
with Lindman since the night they went to Karakorum,
although he has not slept with her again. He finds
her more gentle, less threatening now, and is not
sure whether she has changed or simply his attitude
toward her; waking up and finding her sobbing may

have had something to do with it. Certainly she has become warm and friendly, so much so that he suspects and fears she may even be falling in love with him: yet there is something reserved at her core, some ineluctable holding back, a zone of silence within her that strikes him as the enemy of love. There never were such sealed places in Nikki Crowfoot when Shadrach's relationship with her was going well.

The midday sun is bright, the air soft, the day warm; golden flowers gleam in the terra-cotta tubs of shrubbery that decorate the plaza. Katya walks close to him, but their bodies do not touch. She has already heard of the new crisis. News of all sorts travels inordinately swiftly through the Grand Tower of the Khan, but especially news of the health of Genghis Mao. "Tell me what an aneurysm is," she says. He gives her an elaborate explanation and describes the operation that will be performed. They are standing near the place where Mangu fell. When he finishes, Shadrach looks up and tries to imagine two or three assassins plummeting in Mangu's wake, while lurking confederates spring forth to sweep up the shattered bodies and escape with them. Madness, Shadrach thinks. And this is the carefully considered theory propounded in all seriousness by the ruler of the world. Madness. Madness.

He says, "There've been almost three hundred arrests so far. Ninety-seven sent to the organ farms. Last week Roger Buckmaster was alive, healthy, his own master as much as any of us is. Tomorrow we may be using his aorta to patch Genghis Mao's. And still the arrests continue."

"So I gather. Avogadro's men bring them in, day and night. When will the Khan be satisfied?"

"When he decides that all the conspirators have been caught, I suppose."

"Conspirators!" Katya says scathingly. For a moment she has the old frightening intensity again. "What conspirators? What conspiracy? The whole thing is insane. Mangu killed himself."

"You think it was suicide too, then?"

"Think? I know it was," she says in a low voice,

turning away from the Grand Tower as though to avoid cameras that might read her lips.

"You talk as if you were there when he jumped."

"Don't be silly."

"How can you know it was suicide, then?"

"I know. I know."

"*Were* you there when he—"

"Of course not," Lindman says.

"Then why are you so sure you're right?"

"Good reasons. Sufficient reasons."

"You know something that the security people don't?"

"Yes," she says.

"Then why don't you speak up about it, before Avogadro arrests the whole world?"

She is silent a moment. "No," she says at last. "I can't. It would destroy me."

"I don't follow."

"You would if I told you the story." She studies him. "If I told you, would it stop with you?"

"If that's what you wanted."

"I feel I should tell someone. I'd like to tell you. I trust you, Shadrach. But I'm afraid."

"If you'd rather not—"

"No. No. I'll tell you. Walk with me across the plaza. Keep your back to the tower."

"There are cameras everywhere. It doesn't matter which way we face. But they can't pick up everything, I guess."

They start across the plaza. Lindman raises her arm, holding it across her face as though to scratch her nose with the back of her wrist, and says, mouth covered, voice muffled, "I saw Mangu the night before he jumped. We talked about Project Avatar. I told him he was going to be the donor."

"Oh, Jesus. You didn't!"

She nods grimly. "I couldn't keep it to myself any longer. It was a Monday night, just before Genghis Mao's liver transplant, right? Yes. Mangu had made a speech that night, something about worldwide distribution of the Antidote. Then he and I went for drinks somewhere. He was afraid Genghis Mao might die during the operation and he'd have to take charge of things—*I'm not ready*, Mangu kept saying, *I'm not ready*. And then we started talking about the three projects, and he began to speculate about Avatar. What his role would likely be in the government if they transplanted Genghis Mao's mind into some other body. Whether Genghis Mao would still want him as viceroy after the transition, things like that. It was so sad, Shadrach, so fucking sad, so filthy sad, the way he kept poking at it, trying to figure out what was in store for him, working up all sorts of hypotheses and scenarios. Finally I couldn't stand it and I told him to stop worrying about it, that he was wasting his time, that after the transition he wasn't going to be around, that Genghis Mao was going to use his body as the donor."

Shadrach is stunned by this confession. He can barely speak; his legs tremble, his skin is chilled.

He says, "How could you have done it?"

"The words just came out. I mean, here was this man, this pitiful doomed man trying to understand his future, trying to see what his role would be, and I knew that he had no future. Not if Project Avatar worked out. We all knew it, all but him. And I couldn't hold it back any longer."

"What happened then?"

"His face seemed to cave in. His eyes went dead—blank—empty. He sat for a long time and didn't say anything. Then he asked me how I knew. I said it was known to a lot of people. He asked if you knew and I said I thought so. I want to talk to Nikki Crowfoot, he said. She's at Karakorum with Shadrach, I told him. Then he asked me if I thought Avatar really would work out, and I said I didn't know, I had a lot of faith in my own project, with any luck Talos would head Avatar off. It's all a matter of time, I said. Avatar's ahead of Talos now, and if anything serious happens to Genghis Mao in the next few months they might have to activate Avatar, because the Talos automation needs at least a year of further development work and Project Phoenix isn't getting anywhere. He thought about that. He said it didn't matter to him whether he actually became the donor or not, the thing was that Genghis Mao had let him think he was the heir-apparent while secretly approving what amounted to his murder. That was what hurt, he said, not the idea of dying, not the idea of giving up his body to Genghis Mao, but being tricked, being treated like a simpleton. And then he got up, he said goodnight, he went out. Walking very slowly. After that I don't know. I suppose he spent the whole night thinking things over. Thinking about how he had been duped. The prize lamb, fattened for the slaughter. And in the morning he jumped."

"And in the morning he jumped," Shadrach says. "Yes. Yes. It sounds right. Some truths can't be faced."

"So there are no conspirators. The conspiracy exists only in Genghis Mao's paranoia. Those three hundred arrested people are innocent. How many sent to the organ farms so far? Ninety-seven? Innocent. All innocent. I've watched it happen, but there's nothing I can do. I can't speak out. They say the Khan refuses even to consider the suicide hypothesis."

"He wants there to have been a conspiracy, yes," Shadrach says. "He enjoys punishing the guilty."

"And if I told him what I've just told you, the Khan would have me killed."

"You'd be in the organ farm tomorrow. Yes. Or else maybe he'd pick you as the new Avatar donor."

"No," Katya says. "That isn't likely."

"It would suit his philosophy. It would be very centripetal, wouldn't it? Your loose tongue costs him Mangu's body, so you become Mangu's replacement. Very fitting. Very neat."

"Don't be foolish, Shadrach. It's unimaginable. He's a barbarian, isn't he? He's a Mongol. He thinks he's the reincarnation of Genghis Khan. He'd never let himself be transplanted into a woman's body."

"Why not? The old Mongol khans weren't sexists, Katya. As I recall, the Mongols let themselves be ruled by female regents now and then when the male line gave out. Of course, there are problems of adaptation he'd have, changing sexes, all the bodily reflexes,

all the million little masculine things that he'd have
to unlearn—"

"Stop it, Shadrach. It isn't a serious possibility,
the Khan's taking my body."

"But it's amusing to consider—"

"It doesn't amuse me." She halts and swings around
to face him. She is pale, drawn, tense. "What can we
do? How can we stop these hideous arrests?"

"There's no way. The thing has to run its course."

"Suppose an anonymous tip is sent to the Khan,
telling him merely that Mangu had learned what was
in store for him, that some unnamed person had
revealed to him that he would be used for—"

"No. Either Genghis Mao will ignore it, or else
he'll begin a vast and bloody interrogation of everybody who might have had knowledge of the Avatar
plan."

"What if the arrests don't stop, though?"

Shadrach says, "Avogadro's running out of suspects.
It's almost over."

"And the prisoners awaiting sentence?"

Shadrach Mordecai sighs. "We can't help them.
They're lost. Nothing can be done, Katya. One way
or another, we're all awaiting sentence."

He is haunted all afternoon by the vision of Mangu,
pitiful deluded Mangu, stripped of all delusions, confronted at last by frosty reality. Why had Lindman
tipped him to his true fate? Out of compassion? Did
she really think she was helping him, for God's sake?
Had she thought that receiving such knowledge could
do Mangu any good? Could she have failed to see
how cruel, how merciless, she was being? No. She
must have known that a man like Mangu, genial,
shallow, unquestioning, a man who was living an
impossible fantasy of eventual succession to the
world's most powerful office, believing he enjoyed
the esteem, even the love, of Genghis Mao, would
collapse totally if that structure of fantasy was ripped
away.

She must have known.

Of course. An hour after lunching with Katya
Lindman, Shadrach finally grasps the pattern. Lind-

man, good chess player that she is, had forseen all
the consequences of her move. Tell Mangu the truth,
pretending compassion and claiming a compulsion
to frankness. Mangu—out of humiliation, chagrin,
fear, even vengefulness, whatever—reacts by putting
his body beyond Genghis Mao's reach. No Mangu,
and Project Avatar is dealt a mighty blow. Nikki,
Lindman's rival, is discomfited; Avatar, set back by
many months, loses its primacy to Lindman's Project
Talos; Shadrach, already mysteriously estranged from
Nikki, is drawn inevitably closer to Katya as her star
rises. Of course. Of course. And all the rest, Katya's
pretense of concern for the hapless victims of the
mass arrests, Katya's show of grief for poor pathetic
Mangu—all part of the game. Shadrach shivers. Even
in the harsh and perverse climate of the Grand Tower
of the Khan, this seems monstrous, and Lindman a
baleful and alien figure, malevolent enough to make
a suitable consort for Genghis Mao himself. Or, if not
a mate, then a fitting housing for the old ogre's devi-
ous and sinister mind. Yes! For a moment Shadrach
does seriously consider urging the Khan to take
Lindman's body in place of Mangu's: *An appropriate
choice, sir, very centripetal, very apt.* Though he is
puzzled by one still-obscure motive: why has Lindman
revealed all this to him? If she is so calculating a
monster, would she not have calculated the likelihood
that he would sooner or later come to see her for
what she is? Can that have been her ultimate aim?
Why? He is dizzied by the multiplicity of speculations.

He wants to turn to Nikki, but Nikki has continued
to hold herself aloof, and he has not even spoken to
her by telephone for two or three days. He phones
her now, on the pretext that he needs an update on
Project Avatar progress, but one of her assistants
appears on the screen, a Dr. Eis from Frankfurt. Eis,
classically Teutonic, pale blue eyes and soft golden
hair, does an odd little take of—surprise? dismay?
distaste?—at the sight of Shadrach, forehead furrowing and corner of mouth pulling in, but he recovers
quickly and gives him a cool, formal greeting.

Shadrach says, "May I speak with Dr. Crowfoot, please?"

"I'm sorry. Dr. Crowfoot is not here. Perhaps I can be of assis—"

"Will she be back this afternoon?"

"Dr. Crowfoot has left for the day, Dr. Mordecai."

"I need to reach her."

"She is in her apartment, Doctor. An illness. She has asked that she not be disturbed."

"Sick? What's the matter?"

"A mild upset. A fever, headaches. She has asked me to tell you, if you called the laboratory, that we are still studying the recalibration problem, but that at present there is nothing to report, no—"

"*Danke*, Dr. Eis."

"*Bitte*, Dr. Mordecai," Eis replies crisply, as Shadrach blanks the screen.

He starts to phone Nikki's apartment. No. He's had enough of evasions, excuses, procrastinations, deflections. It's too easy for her to run numbers like that when he calls. He'll simply go down there and ring the doorbell, uninvited.

She lets him stand in the hallway a long time before she responds, though she must know, from her doorscreen, who's there. Then she says, "What do you want, Shadrach?"

"Eis told me you were ill."

"It's nothing serious. Just a bad case of the lousies."

"May I come in?"

"I'm trying to take a nap, Shadrach."

"I won't stay long."

"But I feel so awful. I'd rather not have visitors."

He starts to turn away from the door, but, although he knows his maniac persistence can do him no good, he finds it too painful to leave without seeing her. Helplessly he hears himself saying, "At least let me see if I can prescribe something for you, Nikki. I *am* a doctor, after all."

Long silence. Desperately he prays that no one he knows will come upon him here, out in the hall like a lovesick Romeo pleading to be let in.

The door opens, at last.

She is in bed, and she really does look sick, face flushed and feverish, eyes bloodshot. The air in the bedroom has that stale sickroom quality, stuffy and congested. He goes at once to open the window; Crowfoot shivers and asks him not to, but he ignores her. He sees when she sits up that she is naked under her blanket. "I'll find your pajamas for you if you're cold," he says.

"No. I hate wearing pajamas. I don't know if I'm cold or hot."

"May I examine you?"

"I'm not all that sick, Shadrach."

"Even so, I'd like to make certain."

"You think I'm coming down with organ-rot?"

"There's no harm in checking things out, Nikki. It'll take only a moment."

"Pity you can't diagnose me the way you do Genghis Mao, just by reading your own internal gadgets. Without having to bother me at all."

"No, I can't," he says. "But this'll be quick."

"All right," she tells him. She has not once met his eyes during this interchange, and that bothers him. "Go ahead. Play doctor with me, if you have to."

He uncovers her, and finds himself curiously reticent about exposing her body this way, as though their recent estrangement has somehow deprived him of a doctor's traditional privileges. But of course he has had only one patient in his career, having gone straight from medical school to the service of Genghis Mao, having done nothing but gerontological research until being elevated to serve as the Khan's personal physician, and he has never developed the practicing doctor's traditional indifference to flesh: this is no anonymous patient, this is Nikki Crowfoot whom he loves, and her naked body is more than an object to him. After a moment he attains some impersonality, though, transforms her breasts into mere globes of meat, her thighs into sexless columns of flesh and muscle, and checks her over without further unsettling himself, reading her pulse, tapping her chest, palpating her abdomen, all the routine things. Her self-diagnosis turns out to have been accurate: no incipient organ-rot, just a trifling upset, some fever, nothing remarkable. Plenty of fluids, rest, a couple of pills, and she'll be back to normal in a day or so.

"Satisfied?" she asks mockingly.

"Is it so hard for you to accept the fact that I worry about you, Nikki?"

"I told you I didn't have anything serious."

"I still worried."

"So examining me was really therapy for you?"

"I suppose," he admits.

"And if you hadn't rushed over to give me the benefit of your high-powered medical skills, I might be asleep now."

"I'm sorry."

"All right, Shadrach."

She turns away from him, curling up sullenly under the bedclothes. He stands by the bed, silent, wanting to ask a thousand unaskable questions, wanting to know what shadow has fallen between them, why she has become so mysteriously remote, so cool, why she will not even look straight at him when she speaks to him. After a moment he says, instead, "How's the project going?"

"Didn't Eis speak to you? We're recalibrating. It'll take us a while to gear up for a new donor. The whole thing's a colossal pain in the ass."

"How much of a setback is it, actually?"

She shrugs. "A month, if we're lucky. Or three. Or six. It all depends."

"On what?"

"On—on—oh, Christ! Look, Shadrach, I don't really want to talk shop right now. I feel sick. Do you know what being sick means? My head hurts. My belly hurts. My skin tingles. I want to get some rest. I don't want to discuss my current research problems."

"I'm sorry," he says again.

"Will you go now?"

"Yes. Yes. I'll phone you in the morning to see how you're coming along, okay?"

She mutters something into her pillow.

He starts to leave. But he makes one last attempt

to reach her before he goes. At the door he says lamely, "Oh—have you heard the newest rumor making the rounds? About Mangu's death?"

She groans stoically. "I haven't heard anything. But go on. Go on. What is it?"

He frames his words, carefully, so that he will not feel he is breaching Katya Lindman's confidence: "The story that's going around is that Mangu committed suicide because somebody connected with Project Talos tipped him that he was to be the Avatar donor."

Nikki sits upright, eyes wide, face animated, cheeks blazing in excitement.

"What? What? I hadn't heard that!"

"It's just a story."

"Who's the one who's supposed to have tipped him?"

"They don't say."

"Lindman herself, was it?" Nikki demands.

"It's only a rumor, Nikki. Nobody specific has been named. Anyway, Katya wouldn't do anything so unprofessional."

"Oh no?"

"I don't think so. If it happened at all, it was probably some ambitious underling, some third-echelon programmer. If it happened at all. There may not be a shred of truth to it."

"But it *sounds* right," she says. Her breasts are heaving, her skin is glossy with new sweat. "What better way could Lindman find to sabotage my work? Oh, why didn't I think of it! How could I not have seen—"

"Stay calm, Nikki. You aren't well."

"When I get hold of her—"

"Please," Shadrach says, "Lie down. I wish I hadn't said a word. You know what sort of wild rumors go floating around this building. I absolutely don't believe that Katya would—"

"We'll see," she says ominously. She grows more calm. "You may be right. Even so. Even so. We should have had much tighter security. However many people knew that Mangu was the donor, five, six, ten people, that was too many. Much too many. For the next donor—" Crowfoot coughs. She turns away again, huddling into her pillow. "Oh, Shadrach, I feel lousy! Go away! Please go away! Now you've got me all stirred up over something altogether new, and I—oh, Shadrach—"

"I'm sorry," he says once more. "I didn't mean—"

"Goodbye, Shadrach."

"Goodbye, Nikki."

He bolts from the apartment. He plunges through the hall, fetching up finally against a stanchion near the stairs. He grasps it, steadies himself. The visit to Nikki has hardly improved his state of mind. Her attitude toward him, he realizes, ranged from indifferent to irritated; never once did she express any pleasure that he had come to see her. He was tolerated at best.

And now, he knows, he must hurry back to Katya.

She seems surprised to see him again so soon. She greets him warmly, unsubtly, as though automatically assuming he has come here to make love. His mood is far from sexual, though. He disengages himself from her embrace as soon as is politic, and gently but firmly establishes a psychic distance between them. In quick earnest blurts he reports the essence of his conversation with Nikki, stressing that the "rumor" he had invented did not in any way incriminate Katya herself in the tipping off of Mangu.

"But of course Crowfoot immediately guessed I was the one, right?"

"I'm afraid so. I argued that it was inconceivable you'd do any such thing, but she—"

"Now she knows I did, and will hold the grudge against me forever, and will do whatever she can to pay me back. Thanks a lot."

Quietly Shadrach says, "If she's angry, you can't entirely blame her. You have to admit there was an aspect of sabotaging Avatar in your passing the word to Mangu."

"I passed the word to Mangu out of pity for him," Lindman says flintily.

"Pity and nothing but pity? You didn't consider at

all that he might react in a way that would upset the
Avatar program, and that that would create problems for Nikki Crowfoot?"

Katya is silent for some while.

At length she says, in a more yielding voice, "I suppose that that crossed my mind too. But it was very
secondary. Very very secondary. Mainly I couldn't
bear to face Mangu any more, listening to him talking about his future and knowing what I knew. I had
to warn him or I'd saddle myself with full responsibility for what was going to happen to him. Can
you believe that, Shadrach? How evil do you think
I am? Do you think my life begins and ends with
these insane projects of Genghis Mao's? Do you
think that the only motivations that operate in
me are Talos motivations, how I can push my own
career, how I can wreck Nikki Crowfoot's? Do you?"

"I don't know. I suppose not."

"You suppose?"

"I don't think you're like that, no."

"Fine. Splendid. Thank you. And what happens
now? Will she denounce me to Genghis Mao?"

"There's no proof you ever said anything to Mangu,"
Shadrach Mordecai replies. "She knows that. She
knows also that whatever accusations she makes
against you will be discounted as professional jeal-
ousy. I don't think she'll take any action at all,
actually. Except that she did say she'd maintain
tighter security on the identity of the *next* Avatar
donor, so that there'd be no chance the same thing
would—"

"It's too late," Lindman says.

"The next donor's already been picked?"

"Yes."

"And you know his name?"

"Yes."

"I don't suppose you'd care to tell me," Shadrach
says.

"I don't think I should."

"Are you planning to tell *him*?"

"Would you say it was sabotage again if I did?"

"It depends on the circumstances, I guess. Who is
he?"

Katya Lindman trembles. Her lips quiver.

"You," she says.

15

It seems like a joke, and not a very good joke. He is
unable to accept it at all, despite the strident note of
conviction in Katya's voice, that shrill, almost desperate note of certainty that Shadrach had also heard
when Roger Buckmaster was trying to deny his com-
plicity in Mangu's death, that tone that says, *You
won't believe this no matter how heavy an oath I swear,
but what I'm telling you is true, is true, is true, is true!*

Yet if he *has* been selected as the new donor, it
would explain why Nikki has been avoiding him,
why she is remote and short-tempered when they
speak, why her eyes will not meet his—

"No," he says. "I don't believe you."

"So don't believe me."

"It's absurd, Katya."

"Undoubtedly it's absurd. And it'll be just as absurd the day they come for you and put the electrodes
on your head and obliterate every trace of Shadrach
Mordecai and pour the soul of Genghis Mao into your
pretty brown body."

"My pretty brown body," Shadrach says, "is full of
complicated and irreplaceable medical devices that
register every twitch of Genghis Mao's metabolism.
It took Roger Buckmaster a couple of years to design
and build that system, it took Warhaftig weeks to

implant it in me, it took me a year to learn how to use it. Using it, I can protect Genghis Mao's health in a way that was never before possible in medical history. With all the warm bodies Avatar has to choose from, do you think Genghis Mao would let them choose the one body that's indispensable to his—"

"Think, Shadrach, *think!* Avatar won't be activated unless Genghis Mao's present body is on the threshold of death. He won't *need* all your fancy implants once he moves into your body. He won't need you as his doctor; he won't really need a full-time doctor at all, not for many years. And he can find another doctor. He can find another Buckmaster to build a new set of implants when the time comes. He's probably got a replacement for you in training already, somewhere in Bulgaria or Afghanistan. Remember what he always says about redundancy, Shadrach? The avenue of survival. Genghis Mao understands survival very well. Better than you, I'm afraid."

Shadrach Mordecai's mouth opens. Says nothing. Closes.

"If Avatar is activated," Katya says, "you go. I swear it."

"When was this decided?"

"More than a week ago. I found out about it a few hours before we left for Karakorum."

Which was just about the time Nikki Crowfoot began finding excuses for not keeping company with him, Shadrach reflects. He remembers waking up in this very room, Katya's room, the night of the dream-death excursion, and discovering Katya sobbing beside him in bed, and hearing her tell him that she was afraid for him, without offering further explanation. Yes. And he remembers all that lunatic talk of Genghis Mao's about nominating him for Pope, for King of England—what was that about? Disguised and displaced intimations of the real nomination? He remembers, too, and the memory chills him, running shirtless into Genghis Mao's bedroom just after the news of Mangu's death had broken, remembers seeing the Khan eyeing his bare torso with interest, with admiration, Genghis Mao saying, *You look very healthy, Shadrach.* Yes. Shopping for a new body already, was he, minutes after learning of the loss of Mangu?

He thinks of Buckmaster screaming. *You'll finish in the furnace, Shadrach, in the furnace, in the bloody furnace!*

No. No. No.

"I can't believe this," he says.

"Start learning how."

"It makes no sense to me. I literally can't grasp the meaning of the whole thing."

"Does it frighten you, Shadrach?"

"No. Not at all." He holds out his hands, Steady. As steady as Warhaftig's. "See? I'm entirely calm. I am without affect. It doesn't register on me. It's unreal."

"But it isn't, Shadrach."

"Nikki knows?"

"Of course."

"She's not the one who picked me, is she?"

"Genghis Mao picked you."

"Yes. That figures. Yes." He laughs. "Do you notice how I begin to talk as though I believe this? As though I accept it, on some level?"

"What will you do, Shadrach?"

"Do? Do? What should I do? Should I do what Mangu did?"

"You're not Mangu."

"No," he says. "Even if I had absolute proof, even if they came to me with an engraved scroll signed by Genghis Mao, nominating me for Avatar, I wouldn't choose Mangu's way. I'm not in the least a suicidal person. Maybe it sets in later, Katya. First I have to feel something. I don't feel anything yet. I don't feel betrayed, I don't feel endangered, I don't think I even feel surprised."

"Could it be that you want to be the Avatar donor?"

"I want to be Dr. Shadrach Mordecai. I want to go on being him for a long time."

"Then keep Genghis Mao healthy. So long as his body is functioning, he won't need yours. Meanwhile, it'll be my task to make Avatar altogether superfluous by bringing Talos quickly to perfection. You know, Genghis Mao may actually prefer the Talos idea. I think it suits his particular brand of paranoia to be transferred into a machine, an imperishable, flawless machine. After all, even your beautiful body is going to decay and crumble. He knows that. He knows he might have twenty or thirty good years in you, and then it'll be the same route all over again, organ transplants, drugs, constant surgery, whereas the Talos simulacrum will spare him all that. So Avatar is just a contingency plan for him, a redundancy that he hopes not to have to use, and that's why he can pick people he values as the donors—Mangu, you—a kind of honor, in its way, the blessing of the Khan, not at all the jeopardy that it might be thought to be. I tried to tell that to Mangu, too, that Avatar wouldn't necessarily happen, but he—"

"Why did you tell me about this, Katya?"

"For the same reason I told Mangu."

"To help wreck Avatar?"

Her eyes flash the old Lindman fire. "Don't be a bastard. Do you think I want you to jump out a window too?"

"What good is it, telling me?"

"I want you to be on guard, Shadrach. I want you to know what danger you're in now. So long as there's even a slight likelihood that Avatar will have to be used, you—"

"What does it matter to you, though? A sore conscience? You don't like hanging out with men who you know are secretly earmarked for destruction?"

"That's part of it," Katya says quietly. "I hate living a lie."

"What's the rest?"

"I love you," she says.

He stares with glassy eyes. "What?"

"I'm not capable of it? I'm good only for building automatons, is that it? I have no emotions?"

"I didn't mean that. But—you seemed so cold all the time, so businesslike, so matter-of-fact. Even when—" He pauses, decides to finish. "Even when we would have sex. I never felt any emotional warmth from you; only, well, physical passion."

"You were Nikki's. Getting involved with you would only have been painful to me. You didn't want me except for the occasional fling in Karakorum, except for the occasional meaningless screw."

"And now?"

"Do you still love Nikki? She helped sell you out, you know. She went to Genghis Mao, she heard him select you for Avatar, she probably tried to get him to change his mind—we ought to give her that much credit—and she failed, and then she accepted the order. Her career comes before your life. She could have come to you and said, *This is what Genghis Mao wants to do, but I can't do it, I rebel, let's both get out of this hideous place.* She didn't, though, did she? She simply started keeping away from you. Because of the guilt she felt, right? Not out of love, but out of guilt, out of shame."

Numbly Shadrach shakes his head.

"This is unreal, Katya."

"I have told you no lies today."

"But Nikki—"

"Is afraid of Genghis Mao. As am I, as are you, as is everyone in this city, everyone in the world. That's the measure of her love for you: her fear of that crazy old man is greater. If I'd been in her position, I might have made the same choice. But it's not my project. I'm not faced with the option of betraying you versus defying the Khan. I'm free to go behind his back, to warn you, to let you make your own decisions. But it's strange, isn't it? The warm tall beautiful loving Nikki agrees to sell you out. And the bitter vengeful squat ugly Katya risks her life to warn you."

"You aren't ugly," he murmurs.

Katya laughs. "Come here," she says. She sits on the edge of the bed, tugs him down beside her, roughly presses his head against her breasts. "Rest. Think. Make plans, Shadrach. You're lost if you don't." She caresses his aching forehead.

They sit that way in silence for a long while. Then, shakily, he rises, he removes his clothes, he gestures to her, and she disrobes as well. He must operate on the Khan tomorrow, but for once he does not let that matter to him. He reaches for her. He covers her strangely submissive body with his own, locking his long lean dark-skinned arms around her wide meaty shoulders, pushing his thin bony chest into the soft cushions of her bosom, and her legs open and he plunges deep within her, and stays like that, immobile, gathering strength, pasting himself together, until at last he is ready to move.

The next day is the day of Genghis Mao's aorta transplant. Shadrach, after the usual brief fitful sleep, awakens, exercises, breakfasts, dresses, negotiates passage through Interface Three, pauses to inspect the doings in the Trauma Ward by means of Surveillance Vector One—the standard morning routine. The dancing lenses display for him the world's two billion, perhaps twenty percent of them stricken with organ-rot, the walking dead, shambling about with perforations and lesions and corruptions, and most of the others who are still whole living in the shadow of the universal disease, going through a semblance of ordinary life with sullen courage, waiting for the spitting of blood and the fire in the guts, looking toward the demigods of Ulan Bator in envy and bewilderment. While he, light-footed Shadrach Mordecai, the pretty doctor of the Khan, has nothing worse to worry about than being evicted from his own nimble body, being kicked out on his black ass so that a Mongol usurper can move into his skull. Other than that, Shadrach, everything's fine, right? Right. Yassuh, boss.

Shadrach wonders, as he goes to fetch Genghis Mao for the traditional and familiar gurney ride from the imperial bedchamber to the Surgery, how he will react when he comes face to face with the Khan. Surely his expression will betray his new knowledge; surely Genghis Mao, nearly ninety years canny, will see at once that his designated victim is in on the scheme. But Shadrach discovers that his mysterious tranquility of spirit does not desert him even when he is eye to eye with the Khan. He feels nothing, neither fear nor anger nor resentment: the Chairman is the patient, he is the doctor, the sensors are twitching away, loading him with information, and that's all, no change in their relationship. He looks at Genghis Mao and thinks, *You have secretly plotted to steal my body*, and there is no effect, none. It remains unreal to him.

"And how am I this morning, Shadrach?" Genghis Mao booms jovially.

"Splendid, sir. Never better."

"Going to cut out my heart, are you?"

"Only the aorta this time," Shadrach says. He signals to the attendants. They wheel the Chairman away.

And there they all are once more gathered in the Surgery—the Chairman, the physician, the chief surgeon, the anesthesiologist, the nurses and other miscellaneous medical spear-carriers, everyone scrubbed and gowned and masked, the bright lights gleaming, the transparent aseptic bubbles sealed, the filters and pumps pumping and filtering, the computers flashing green and red and yellow like gaudy movie props, the new aortal section—Buckmaster's?—sitting in its container, fresh and plump, ready to be installed in Genghis Mao's abdomen.

Warhaftig, confident, serene, prepares once more to open the spare, slight body of Genghis Mao.

"Blood pressure?" he asks.

"Normal," Shadrach says.

"Respiration?"

"Normal."

"Platelet count?"

"Normal. Normal. Everything normal."

Shadrach is aware that if Genghis Mao should die on the operating table, there would be no Project Avatar to menace him: none of the three projects is ready yet to be put into effect, and if the Khan does not survive the transplant, that will be the end of him, without hope of reincarnation, perhaps even the end of the Permanent Revolutionary Committee, the entire fragile society of centripetal depolarization polarizing and centrifuging into chaos the instant the legendary figure of Genghis Mao vanishes from the scene. It would not be hard to manage it. Jostle

Warhaftig's elbow, maybe, as he aims the surgical laser at the Chairman's gut; apologize profusely afterward, but the damage will be done. Or, more subtly, feed the operating team misleading information, cockeyed reports from Genghis Mao's ostensible interior: they trust Dr. Mordecai, they will follow his data without bothering to check it against the numbers on the scopes and meters, and he could probably cause irreversible injury to the Chairman, fatal oxygen shortage or the like, before Warhaftig realizes what is taking place. And then the apologies, I simply can't *understand* why my readings were off so badly. He has no need to worry about a malpractice suit: topple the Khan and the whole fabric comes apart, every man for himself in the aftermath. But he will not. No harm will come to Genghis Mao by way of Shadrach Mordecai today, not even if he knows the Khan intends to activate Project Avatar before next Tuesday. Dr. Mordecai, in a peril or not, is nevertheless a doctor, a dedicated doctor, still young and naive enough to take his Hippocratic oath seriously. He was sworn to keep pure and holy both his life and his art. He has vowed to help the sick and to abstain from all intentional wrongdoing and harm. So be it. Shadrach Mordecai, MD, Harvard '01, is no traducer of sacred trusts. Genghis Mao is his patient; Genghis Mao will not die at Shadrach Mordecai's hands this day. Perhaps this is foolishness, but there is also a certain grace in it.

The operation proceeds smoothly. Snip, and the weakened section of Genghis Mao's aorta comes out. Stitch stitch, and the replacement is grafted in. Heart-lung machines keep the circulation bubbling. The Khan watches, conscious and beady-eyed, through the whole thing, now and again nodding to himself as Warhaftig executes some particularly admirable veronicas and entrechats and passades. He seems to know what is going on; he has spent more time observing surgeons at their trade than I have, Shadrach realizes, and can probably do the job pretty well by himself by now. Warhaftig's elegant fingers elegantly close the incision. The tissues are raw and reddened, having been cut into for the liver transplant less than two weeks earlier, and this calls for some special prophylactic measures, but the surgeon brings every-thing off with his customary finesse. Genghis Mao grins approval when all is over. "Good show," he tells Warhaftig. "Two ears and the tail!"

Shadrach makes off with the Khan's discarded ab-dominal aorta. He tells Warhaftig, not that Warhaftig cares, that he intends to run some tests on it, but what tests would tell him anything about this droop-ing length of ancient tissue, this tired hose, that he doesn't already know? He covets it because it's an authentic piece of the body of the authentic Genghis II Mao IV Khan, and Shadrach has the collector's itch: this will be an ornament to his little museum of medical memorabilia. A relic of one of history's most famous patients. There is a tale Shadrach knows, probably apocryphal, of how the doctor who per-formed the autopsy on Napoleon removed the impe-rial penis and kept it as a souvenir of the late emperor, bequeathing it to a fellow physician who ultimately sold it at an immense price, and so on and on, pass-ing from one doctor's collection to another, until it disappeared altogether during the confusions of some twentieth-century war. Similar stories, he knows, have been told of odd scraps of Hitler, Stalin, George Washington, Catherine the Great. Shadrach regrets that he attained his present post too late to collect some of the really significant organs of Genghis Mao—a kidney, say, or a lung, the liver, the pancreas—but all of them were gone long before Shadrach's time, the native organs of the Khan's body removed and replaced, sometimes several times over, with trans-planted substitutes. Shadrach does not see much value in preserving Genghis Mao's fourth liver in his collection, his eighth spleen, his thirteenth kidney, though he recognizes that these temporary residents of the Khan are more intimate artifacts of Genghis Mao than, say, his bedroom slippers or his wristwatch. But he prefers the genuine somatoplasm, and a piece of authentic aorta is the best he can do just now.

There's the aneurysm, big and ripe, ready to pop.

Another few days and it might have ruptured, *poof!*
and no more Genghis Mao. The Chairman and Mangu
might have shared the same funeral, come Saturday,
if Shadrach hadn't felt odd twitterings in the circula-
tory-system sensors and correctly guessed their import.
So I have saved the Khan's life, not for the first time,
and he is once more restored to perfect health. Fine.
Fine. May he live five hundred years, and may I be
his physician always!

16

Alone in his office, ruminating over his medical
treasures, his books and old instruments and now
this bit of bottled aorta, Shadrach feels safe and
comfortably entrenched. This Avatar disturbance will
blow over. The Khan, after all, is conservative; he
will cling to his own Mongol body, the well-loved
and sturdy patchwork carcass, as long as he can,
whatever the temptations may be for him to jump
into Shadrach's strong, young, and vital frame. So
there will be no precipitous exit for Shadrach, and in
the months or perhaps years ahead he can try to shift
the Khan's fantasies entirely away from Project Avatar and toward Project Talos. Which will mean abort-
ing the researches of Nikki Crowfoot, but Shadrach
can't feel too guilty about that, all things considered.
   He gives the aorta pride of place on his shelves.
Centuries from now it may be sacred, enshrined in a
reliquary of ivory and platinum, and the groveling
faithful will chant thanks to the sainted Shadrach
Mordecai for having saved for posterity this shred of

divine meat. Who knows? There is an apocryphal story that many of Genghis Mao's original organs are preserved in some labyrinthine secret tunnel, kept in cold storage or perhaps maintained in vivo, for eventual use in cloning the Khan. Shadrach doubts this. If Genghis Mao had any serious interest in being cloned, huge budgetary appropriations would be going to support tissue-culture research, and, so far as Shadrach knows, not much is going on in that area. Or, more likely, there would already be a battalion of genetically perfect duplicates of Genghis Mao lying in suspension tanks on five or six continents, waiting to be summoned into life.

Mordecai has often thought of writing a scientific monograph on his patient, a medical biography of Genghis Mao, a full record of the myriad transplants and implants, the infinity of surgical jugglements, that are responsible for the Khan's longevity and perhaps for his terrifying vitality. There would be nothing in the literature to compare with it, not even Beaumont on Alexis St. Martin's digestive tract, not even Lord Moran on Churchill: had ever there been so single-minded and long-sustained a medical effort, spanning so many decades, to keep one human being alive and well? Already the achievement verges on the miraculous, but the real miracles still lie ahead, as Genghis Mao, ageless and eternally renewed, lives on to be a hundred, a hundred ten, a hundred twenty—

There is another, greater temptation—to write not merely a medical study but a full-scale account of Genghis Mao's life. No biography of the Chairman exists, other than vague, sanitized publicity pamphlets, mere recitals of his political accomplishments and other exterior events, avoiding all details of his private life. It is as though the Khan has a superstitious fear of having his soul captured on paper. And so Shadrach's impulsive fantasy: to nail the Khan in words, to pin him down with literary juju. It is one means of gaining control over the world's most powerful man, at least in a metaphorical way.

The trouble is, no source material is available. The computer banks of Ulan Bator are gorged with inti-

mate data about every human being alive—except
Genghis Mao. Press the right button and platoons of
facts march forth—but none about Genghis Mao. The
facts of his life are unknown and maybe unknowable,
beyond the most elementary public milestones, his
promulgation of the philosophy of centripetal depolarization, his founding of the PRC, his election to the
Chairmanship. All the rest has been suppressed, even
obliterated. When was he born? In what obscure
village? What was his childhood like, what were his
boyhood ambitions? What was his original name, in
the old People's Republic days before he proclaimed
himself to be Genghis Mao? What was the early course
of his career? What sort of education did he have?
Did he ever travel abroad? Was he ever married? A
father? Yes, that's a good question—are there, somewhere in Mongolia, middle-aged men and women
who are in fact the blood children of Genghis Mao,
and, if so, do they know who their father is? No one
can answer these questions. No one can answer any
questions about Genghis Mao except with hearsay,
apocrypha, and myth. He has very carefully covered
his traces, so carefully that the utter success of the
attempt at total concealment argues a kind of madness.

But is anyone, even Genghis Mao, really willing to
expunge from the world all traces of his private self?
Criminals are said to return compulsively to the scene
of the crime; possibly those who seek to shroud themselves in mystery tend also to undo their own mystifi-
cations by burying, for history's sake, a full account
of all they have tried to hide. Is there no place where
Genghis Mao has secreted a concealed record of everything he has kept from the knowledge of his
subjects? Say, a diary, an intimate and revealing
diary, a repository for the essence of Genghis Mao's
masked soul. Shadrach imagines himself stumbling
across such a document among the Khan's effects—a
single billion-bit bubble-chip, smaller than a fingertip,
on which is implanted the raw red stuff of Genghis
Mao's life, his confessions, his unvarnished memoirs,
out of which the faithful doctor Shadrach Mordecai
will construct the first and only true account of the

strange and sinister man who came to dominate the dying civilization of the early twenty-first century.

Of course there is no such diary. Ordinary thieves and felons may compulsively jeopardize their own safety, but Shadrach knows Genghis Mao well enough to realize that if he wants to live in secrecy, he will leave no hidden memoirs around for others to find. The private Genghis Mao is just as secretive as the public one: open one empty box and another, even more empty, lies within. No matter. In his fantasy role as the biographer of Genghis Mao, Shadrach will fantasize the Khan's memoirs as well, inventing the source material that Genghis Mao has neglected to provide. He closes his eyes. He lets his imagination slip free of the leash. He creates the diary of the Khan within the crucible of his own throbbing brain.

November 11, 2010
My birthday. Genghis Mao is eighty-five today. No. No. Genghis Mao is—what—twenty years old? About that. It's Dashiyin Choijamste who is eighty-five today. Dashiyin Choijamste, whom I carry about within me like an internal twin. Who remembers him, that fat little babe in his proud father's arms? So long ago, in the village of Dalan-Dzadagad on a snowy night in 1925. That's down in the province of Southern Gobi, Dalan-Dzadagad. I haven't been there in fifteen years. My birthplace, but who knows that? Who knows anything? I know, Dashiyin Choijamste is eighty-five today. How many others are still alive, of those born on 11 November 1925? Not many, no. And those who remain are ancient doddering wrecks. Whereas I am still in my prime, I Dashiyin Choijamste of Dalan-Dzadagad, son of Yumzhaghiyin Choijamste, director of the camel-breeding station at Bogdo-Goom. I Genghis Mao. I feel strong today, oh, yes, eighty-five and robust. Not altogether because of the transplants, either. It's heredity that does it. The good old Tatar blood. Don't forget, you were almost seventy when the Virus War broke out, and yet not at all old, tremendous vigor, all your teeth, jet-black hair, twenty-kilometer hikes every week; you hadn't had any transplants yet. You were still Dashiyin

Choijamste then. Strange syllables, awkward now on the tongue, though that was your name for more than six decades. And I lived right through the Virus War untouched by the rot. People fell apart all around me. Sickening to behold. I didn't go in for transplants until later, much later, natural ravages of time, eventually, but not until after the power had come to me. The power. I have attained the highest power. And now clever doctors aid my natural Tatar vigor. I might live another fifty years.

I might live much longer than that.

Do I remember my childhood? How much snow piles up in eighty-five years! I think I can see my father's face, lean like mine, strong eyebrows, strong cheekbones. Yumzhaghiyin Choijamste of the camel-breeding station at Bogdo-Goom, Hero of the Order of Lenin, later. Wounded at the battle of Khalkhin Gol in 1939, afterward third secretary of the Agricultural Agency—see, Father, I remember, I remember! The father of Genghis Mao killed in 1948 in a plane crash, between Moscow and Ulan Bator, coming home from a wheat conference. Those miserable Soviet jets, forever falling from the sky. Or was it a jet? So long ago: the jets were already in service then, weren't they, the Ilyushins, the Tupolevs? I could look it up. You are dead sixty-two years, Yumzhaghiyin Choijamste. Babies born the night your plane fell are old people now. And I am still here, Father. I am Genghis Mao. I remember you at the camel station. I am standing in new snow and my father tugs on a camel's halter. The camel looms above me like a mountain, long homely face, rubbery lips, sweet dull eyes with undertones of subtle contempt. The camel leans toward me and its enormous tongue slurps across my cheeks, my lips. A kiss! Its sour breath. My father's laughter. He scoops me in his arms, gives me a crushing hug. How huge he is! Bigger than the camel, to me. I am three, four years old.

And my mother? My mother? I never knew her. Trampled by yaks in a wild snowstorm when I was an infant. I have forgotten even your name, Mother. I could look it up. But where . . . where . . . ?

*   *   *

Shadrach pauses, reflects, reconsiders. Is it plausible? Does it have internal consistency? The tone is right, but what about the "facts"? He will test them. Shall he alter some significant details? Will that make any difference? Let's see—

October 17, 2012.
My birthday. Genghis Mao is ninety-two today, though officially I am said to be a mere eighty-seven. On the other hand, some of them believe I'm well over one hundred. Meaning that I was born in 1905 or so. Can they believe that? Isn't 1920 bad enough? Wilson, Clemenceau, Henry Ford, General Pershing, Lloyd George, Lenin, Trotsky, Sukhe Bator . . . men of my time. And I am still here, anno domini 2012, I, the former Namsan Gombojab, born in Sain-Shanda, youngest son of the yak-herder Khorloghiyin Gombojab, who—

No. Changing the details is trivial. Let his original name be Choijamste, Gombojab, Ochirbal, whatever; let him have been born in 1925, 1920, 1915, even 1910; let him have spent his career in the Ministry of Defense, the Agency for Agrarian Redistribution, the Commissariat of Telecommunications; slather on any kind of factual decoration you like; none of it will make any difference. The essential patterns of the soul of Genghis Mao run deep and heavy, and they, his perceptions, his world view, are your subject, Shadrach. Not the trivia of time and place.

May 14, 2012.
Just two hours ago the liver transplant was finished, and here lies Genghis Mao, old and leathery, not dead yet, no, not by much; he is alert, full of energy, wide awake. I am proud of him. The unquenchable vitality of him. The insufferable resilience of him. I hail you, Genghis Mao! Ha! I feel pain in my abdomen, but it's nothing to moan about. Pain is the signal that we live, we feel, we respond to stimuli. The heaviness that came over me when the old liver began to fail is already going. I feel my system flushing itself clean. It is as if I

*float two meters above my own bed. Hovering over all
the beautiful machinery that pumps healing fluids into
my earthly husk. How beautiful is the pain. That throb,
low and to one side ... boom, boom, boom, a bell
tolling within old Genghis Mao, urging him on to long
life. Ten thousand years to the Emperor! My clever
doctors triumph again. Warhaftig, Mordecai.*

*My doctors. Warhaftig is a mere machine. He bores
me, but he is perfect. I love to see his hands disappear
into the hole in my belly. And come forth grasping
some limp red lump full of disease, throw it aside,
stitch a new organ into its place. Warhaftig never fails.
But he is ugly, with that flat nose, those downturned
lips. Sick dead white skin. A genius, but ugly and boring,
a mere machine. Was Warhftig ever young? Crouching
behind a bush to spy on the naked women bathing in a
stream? Not him. Oh, no, not him. Laughing, tumbling
on the grass? Warhaftig? Never.*

*Shadrach is more interesting. Graceful, witty, a fine
strong body, a clear cool mind. He is pleasing to look
at. His black skin. I never saw a black until I was forty
and a delegation from Guinea visited my department.
Their shiny faces, almost purple, their dense knotty
hair, their tribal robes. Dazzling white eyes, pink palms
like gorillas, deep voices, strange, strange. They spoke
French. Shadrach is not like those Africans except that
he has the same sort of keen, serious intelligence. He is
brown, not black, very tall, very American, nothing of
the jungle about him. Sometimes he lectures me as if I
am a child, a naughty babe. Always worrying about my
health. Conscientious, he is, earnest, dedicated, boyish.
He is too sane for us here. He lacks—what? Darkness,
can I say that of him? Yes. Interior darkness is what he
lacks: there are no demons in him. Or do I underesti-
mate him? There must be demons in everyone, even the
robot Warhaftig, even the calm and good-humored
Shadrach Mordecai. He is very young. I like that. He is
at least fifty years younger than I am, and yet we are
contemporaries, we are both men of the present moment,
both of us unknown until relatively recently, though I
waited so long to become who I am and he became
himself so young. He smiles well. There is nothing*

cynical about him yet. He has lived through the Virus War and all the ugly things that followed and yet he is tranquil, he has faith in the future, he thinks only of healing people. He would heal those who enslaved his ancestors, even. Whereas I would avenge myself against the oppressors a thousand times over; but then, I am of Tatar stock, and we are fierce, we are Gobi wolves, while he is the child of placid jungle farmers. Every morning he goes into Surveillance Vector One and stares at the rotting people all over the world. Thinks I don't know. I watch him watching. His lean mobile face, his sad intelligent eyes. He feels such sorrow for the rotting ones. A man of compassion. Childlike. Not saintly, but he has the stuff of martyrs in him.

January 23, 2012.
The Committee in plenary session. Horthy, Labile, Ionigylakis, Eyuboglu, Lapostolle, Farinosa, Parlator, Blount. All the finest bureaucrats. Drone, drone, drone, and I listened, not listening, to it all. They are machines. The Committee itself is a machine which I have constructed, a delicate and useless mechanism, like a clock without hands. When I die it will fall apart, if I die when I die. I allowed Mangu to preside. Bit by bit I ease him into the pretense of responsibility, the shadow of authority. He is fascinated by that mob of dreary bureaucrats, those apparatchiks, *as a boy is fascinated by the buzzing of dung-flies, and never mind the dung. Was this what I had in mind when I seized the reins of the world, that I would father upon it a Permanent Revolutionary Committee of dung-flies? Revolutionaries! Lapostolle sleeps; Farinosa longs for Karakorum and sits twitching his long nose; Ionigylakis's belly rumbles. I should have named more Mongols to the Committee; these white foreigners have no fire. But I need my Mongols elsewhere. I should not let them turn into drones. Snore, snore, snore! It snows again today. I could slip from the Committee room, out of the building, secretly into the snow, lie in it, roll in it, throw handfuls in the air. Summon a horse and ride all night, no saddle, hooves silent on the whiteness, a man and beast crossing the steppe without a pause, crust of*

bread for me, a goatskin full of airag to gulp along the way—aye, I am still a boy, I who am so ancient, and they are old men! But of course Shadrach would forbid it. I rule the world, he rules me. What if I insisted? Must I endure these droning flies when there is fresh snow on the Gobi? You can replace a crumbled kidney, I will tell him; surely you can repair an old man's frostbit nose. Yes. Yes. I will go. I will. I must escape from this boredom.

Is this what I had in mind when I seized the reins?

What did I have in mind? Did I have anything in mind, except that everything was falling apart, and it was my task to hold it together? I think that was it. The world had descended into chaos. How I abhor disorder! Such turmoil, such confusion: the dying people, the dead nations, hordes of wild men sweeping across the land, nothing simple, all simplicity gone from the world. I love simplicity, a neatly organized structure, harmonious and satisfying, one nation, one government, one code of laws, everything one, onward to the horizon. I was seventy-three years old, and strong. The world was millions of years old, and weak. I could not bear the chaos. I think all those who have ruled the world were basically haters of chaos rather than mere lovers of power. Napoleon, Attila, Alexander, great Genghis, even poor crazy Hitler, all of them wanted things to be neat, to be simple, they had a vision of order, that is, and saw no other way to attain that order except to impose it themselves upon the world. As did I. Of course, most of them eventually spawned more chaos than they were removing, and they had to be removed themselves. Hitler, for example. I have not made that mistake. To the end, I do battle against entropy, I offer myself, Genghis II Mao IV, as the symbol of oneness, the focus of world-wide energy, the crystal of simplicity. But oh, Father Genghis, these plenary sessions, this droning, these dung-flies! Father Genghis, did you have a Horthy to harangue you? Did you sit idle, dreaming of a swift horse and an icy wind, listening to a Parlator and a Blount? Oh! Oh! Was it for this that I took upon myself the chaos of the crumbling rotting world?

*   *   *

Shadrach rises. He can sit here in reverie no longer; he has responsibilities, obligations, reports to file, projects to oversee. To begin with, he must update the Genghis Mao dossier with a concise account of today's aorta transplant, which means collating a vast sheaf of printouts and selecting from that mass of raw and fragmentary data the significant outlines of a useful medical profile. Very well. He taps keys, summoning the outtakes of this morning's operation. But as he works, he finds his mind invaded at times by the spurious voice of Genghis Mao, dictating stray shreds of imaginary memoir:

May 27, 1998.
The People's Republic is leaderless this morning and I think the government will collapse before noon. Shirendyb, the fifth prime minister in the past six weeks, succumbed to the organ-rot late last night. No one is left in the politburo; the presidium has been decimated; the streets of Ulan Bator are choked with refugees, a slow steady stream of oxcarts and dilapidated trucks heading—where? It is the same everywhere. The old society is dying. Only ten years ago I thought fundamental change was impossible; then came the volcano, the terror, the uprisings, the Virus War, the organ-rot, and three billion human beings are dead and institutions are crumbling like shoddy buildings struck by earthquakes. I will not leave Ulan Bator. I think my time is at last at hand. But the government I will proclaim will not be called a people's republic.

November 16, 2008.
To celebrate the tenth year of my reign I journeyed to Karakorum and dedicated the new pleasure complex. They invited me to experience the amusements they call "dream-death" and "transtemporalism." I chose dream-death. The irresistible fascination of the morbid. Especially the illusion of the morbid. It takes place in a tent full of pseudo-Egyptian motifs. The ugly old monster-gods, hovering like gargoyles over the place; you can practically smell the reek of Nile mud, hear the buzzing

*of the flies. Attendants with masks. Bright lights. Much
fuss made over me. Naturally I was the only one having
the experience at that time. I allowed myself to be hyp-
notized behind a phalanx of picked security guards. A
sensation as of dying, very convincing, I think. (What
does any of us know about it?) And then a dream. But
in my dream the world was exactly as it is when I am
awake. They promised me gaudy illusions and surreal
fantasies. None. Have they deceived me? Are they afraid
to let Genghis Mao taste the true experience?*

June 4, 2010.
*Today the new physician began his duties. Shadrach
Mordecai, a strange name. American, bright, earnest.
He is terrified of me but that may pass. He holds himself so stiffly when he is with me! His training is in
gerontology and he has been on the staff of Project
Phoenix for several years. I told him this morning: "We
make a deal, you and I. You keep me healthy, I keep
you healthy, all right?" He smiled but behind that he
was plainly upset. Too heavy-handed of me, I suppose.*

Somehow Shadrach finishes dictating the profile
and moves along to the next task, which is to look
over a project report from Irayne Sarafrazi. Nothing
much new there; her project continues to wrestle
with the brain-cell-deterioration problem and, as
Shadrach has foreseen, is getting nowhere. All the
same, he must read the report through and find some
encouraging comment to make. Still the insidious
voice resonates in his head, distracting him with
bursts of fantasy. Doggedly he works on, trying to
ignore the mental static.

May 15, 2012.
*The most terrible news! Assassins have murdered Mangu.
Comes now Horthy, bleating hysterically about falling
bodies. How could this have happened? Into Mangu's
bedchamber, silently, seize him, to the window, out!
Oh, my fury. Oh, my bitter grief. What will I do now?
My plans for Mangu thwarted. Shadrach tells me Proj-
ect Phoenix is stymied, probably forever, on biological*

problems. Project Talos moves slowly, and Talos I have never really liked. Which leaves Avatar, and Avatar without Mangu is—

Ah. I will use Shadrach. A fine body—I'll be happy in it. And black. A novelty. I should experience all the varieties of humanity. Perhaps when Shadrach's body is old I should move on into a white one—even a woman, perhaps—perhaps a giant someday, or a dwarf—all possibilities—

Shadrach has been a good doctor and a pleasant companion. But there are other doctors, and companionship becomes ever less important to me. Shall I feel guilty about snuffing him out? For a while, perhaps a day, two days. But I must put myself beyond such feelings.

May 16, 2012.
More thoughts on the choice of Shadrach to replace Mangu. Obviously some residual guilt lurking in me. But why? I propose not to murder him but to ennoble him by making his body the vehicle for immense power. Of course he might object that what I propose for him is, if not murder outright, then at best a form of slavery, and his kind has endured slavery enough. But no: Shadrach is not his ancestors, and all old debts have been canceled by the Virus War, which destroyed slaves and masters indiscriminately, struck down generals as well as babes, and left those who survived in the condition of pure survivors, pastless, liberated into a new dispensation in which history is born fresh and virgin each day. What do the sins of the slavemasters mean to anyone today? The society, the network of relationships, that evolved under the stimulus of slavery and its consequences, even of emancipation and its consequences, is wholly gone. And I am Genghis Mao and I require his body. I need not vex myself with the guilt of others. I am not German; I can send Jews to the oven if the need arises, without making apologies for past sins. I am not white; therefore I am free to enslave a black. The past is dead. History is blank pages now. Besides, if historical imperatives do still

exist, I am a Mongol: my forefathers enslaved half the world. Can I do less? I will have his body.

May 27, 2012.
I monitor this week's conversation tapes and find that Katya Lindman has told Shadrach the truth, that he is the next Avatar donor. Katya talks too much. It wasn't my intention to have him find that out, but let it go. I will watch him closely, now that he possesses the knowledge. The sufferings of humanity instruct me in the arts of government. Or, to put it more harshly, I enjoy watching them squirm. Is that not ugly? But I have earned the right to indulge in some ugly pastimes, I who have borne the burdens of power for fourteen years. I haven't been Hitler, have I? I haven't been Caligula. Yet power does entitle one to certain amusements. By way of compensation for the murderous burden, the awful responsibility. The odd thing is that Shadrach isn't squirming, yet. He is oddly calm. Doesn't yet believe that what Katya told him is true, I guess. Doesn't accept it in the viscera. He will. Wait. Just wait. It'll hit him, sooner or later.

Suddenly this game is not in the least amusing to Shadrach. There is no fun, any longer, in these subtle exercises in ironic parallax, these experiments in psychological perspective. The distance between himself and what he has been inventing has narrowed abruptly, and indeed it is all suddenly very painful, it cuts much too close to the nerve, it hurts, it hurts with astonishing intensity. He has managed in the last ten minutes to puncture his own affectless equanimity, and he is not merely squirming now, he is bleeding. Pain, fear, and anger assail him. He feels that everyone has conspired to sell him down the river. He—witty, urbane, handsome, humane, dedicated Shadrach Mordecai—is just another expendable nigger, it turns out. If what Katya has told him is true. If. If. Shadrach is in anguish. This, now, here is the furnace, and he is in it for sure. The heavy shadow of Genghis Mao weighs upon him. One day they will come for him, they will put the electrodes to him, they will wipe

out his unique and irreplaceable soul, and shortly
thereafter they will pump that crafty old Mongol into
his skull. Is that how it really will be? Yes, Katya
says. And can he believe that? Should he believe
that? He trembles. Terror whips through him like a
cold gale. He craves peace; he could use a jolt of
Genghis Mao's tranquilizer now, a hefty jolt of 9-
pordenone or maybe something stronger. But Shadrach dislikes drugging himself in crisis. He needs his
sharpest wits now.

What shall he do?

The first step is one he knows he should have taken
yesterday. He will go to Nikki Crowfoot again. And
ask her some questions.

17

She is pale and peaked-looking, still in the grip of
yesterday's illness, but on the mend, definitely on the
mend. She seems to know why he has come, and it
takes only half a dozen harsh words from him to get
from her the answer he did not really want to hear.
Yes, it is true. Yes. Yes. Shadrach listens for a while
to her stammering confession, full of circumlocutions
and evasions, and then he says, quietly, reproachfully,
"You could have told me before this." He is staring
straight at her, and now, finally, she returns his stare:
now that it is all out in the open between them, now
that she has admitted the monstrous truth, she is at
last able to meet his eyes again. "You could have told
me," he says. "Why didn't you tell me, Nikki?"

"I couldn't. It wasn't possible."

"Wasn't possible? Wasn't possible? Sure it was possible. All you had to do was open your mouth and let words come out. 'Shadrach, I think I ought to warn you that you—' "

"Stop," she says. "It didn't seem that easy to me."

"When was it decided?"

"The day they sent Buckmaster to the organ farm."

"Did you have any part in selecting me?"

"Do you think I could have had any part in it, Shadrach?"

He says, "One thing I learned a long time ago is that guilty people have a way of answering a trouble-some question with another question."

But she does not seem wounded by his thrust, and instantly he regrets having made it. She is a strong woman, quite calm now that she has been unmasked by him, and in an altogether steady voice she says, "Genghis Mao chose you all by himself. I wasn't consulted."

"Very well."

"You might as well believe that."

Shadrach nods. "I believe it."

"And so?"

"When you learned I was the one, did you make any attempt to change his mind?"

"Has anyone ever changed Genghis Mao's mind about anything?"

"You notice how you parry my question with a question of your own?"

This time the jab hurts. She loses some of her newly regained poise. Her eyes slip from his, and she says hollowly, "All right. All right. I didn't try to argue with him, no."

Shadrach is silent a moment. Then he says, "I thought I knew you pretty well, Nikki, but I was wrong."

"What does that mean?"

"I believed you were the sort of person who sees human beings as ends, not means. I didn't think you'd let a—ah—a close friend—be nominated for the junkheap, and not lift a finger to save him, and not even say a word to him about it, no hint of what's been decreed for him. And start to avoid him, even. As if you had written him off as an unperson the moment he was chosen. As if you were afraid that his bad luck might be contagious."

"Why are you lecturing me, Shadrach?"

"Because I hurt," he says. "Because someone I loved sold me out. Because I can't bring myself to hurt you back in any way that's real."

"What would you have wanted me to do?" Nikki asks.

"The right thing."

"Which was?"

"You could have stood up to Genghis Mao. You could have told him you wouldn't participate in your lover's slaughter. You could have let him know that there was a relationship between us, that you weren't capable of—oh, Christ, Nikki, I shouldn't have to be explaining all this to you!"

"I'm sure Genghis Mao was quite aware of the relationship between us."

"And picked me deliberately, by way of testing your loyalty? To find out how you would react if you were made to choose between your lover and your laboratory? One of his little psychological games?"

She shrugs. "That's entirely conceivable."

"Maybe you made the wrong choice, then. Maybe he was trying to measure your fundamental humanity rather than your loyalty to Genghis Mao. And now that he sees how cold-blooded, soulless, unfeeling you are, he may decide that he can't take the chance of having a person like you in charge of—"

"Stop it, Shadrach." She is giving ground under his steady assault, his quiet, measured, remorseless voice; her lips are trembling, she is visibly fighting back tears. "Please," she says. "Stop. Stop. You're getting what you want."

"You think I'm being unkind? You think I've got no call being angry with you?"

"There was nothing I could have done."

"Nothing?"

"Nothing."

"What about threatening to resign?"

"He'd have let me resign, then. I'm not indispensable. Redundancy is—"

"And your successor would have continued with the project, using me as the donor."

"I imagine so."

"Still, even if it changed nothing at all, wouldn't you have felt cleaner putting up some kind of resistance?"

"Perhaps," she says. "But it would have changed nothing at all."

"You could have warned me, at least. I might have fled from Ulan Bator. We might have fled together, if your resignation got you in trouble with Genghis Mao. Wasn't worth destroying your career over me, though, was it?"

"Flee? Where to? He'd be watching us. On Surveillance Vector One, or some other spy gadget. In a day or two he'd decide we had had a long enough holiday, and the Citpols would pick us up and bring us back."

"Maybe."

"Not maybe. And I'd end up in the organ farm. And you'd still become the Avatar donor."

Shadrach considers that scenario. "You're telling me that it wouldn't have mattered whether you had warned me or not?"

"Not to you," Nikki replies. "It would have mattered to me. One way I lose my job and maybe my skin. The other way I get to survive a little longer."

"I still wish you had been the one to tell me."

"Instead of Katya?"

"When did I say Katya was the one?"

Nikki smiles. "You didn't need to, love."

August 19, 2009.
A mild summer day in Ulan Bator. Across half the world it is summer now. The time of lovers. Surveillance Vector One shows me the lovers going arm in arm through the streets of Paris, London, San Francisco, Tokyo. The fond gazes, the little kisses, the nudges of hip against hip. Even the ones with organ-rot shuffling along together, slowly dying but still doing the dance of

*love. Fools! I think I remember how that dance goes,
though it's forty or fifty years behind me. Yes, yes, the
first meeting, the preliminary tensions and assessments,
the probing and parrying, the spark of contact, the
dissolving of barriers, the first embrace, the tender words,
the pledges, the sense of conspiracy, two against the
world, the assumption that all this will last forever, the
discovery that it will not, the falling apart, the falling
out, the parting, the healing, the forgetting—oh, yes, the
man who is Genghis Mao once danced that dance, long
before he was Genghis Mao, he once played that game.
Long ago. What purpose does it serve? An anesthetic for
the aching ego. A lubricant for the biological necessities.
A diversion, a distraction, a foolishness. When I saw it
for what it was I renounced it, and no regrets. Look at
them strolling together. "Eternal love." As if anything's
eternal, but love? Love? It's an unstable state, thermody-
namic nonsense, two energy sources, two suns, trying
to establish orbits around one another, each one striving to give light and heat to the other. How pretty it
sounds, how implausible. Naturally the system breaks
down under gravitational stress sooner or later, and one
pulls the other to pieces, or they spiral into collision, or
they go tumbling away from one another. A waste of
energy, a futile spilling of the life-force. Love? Abolish
it! If only I could.*

January 4, 1989
*The text of my doctrine is complete, and when the
appropriate moment comes I will reveal it to the world.
Today, as I finished the last passages, a name for it
came to me:* centripetal depolarization. *Defined as the
forging of a consensus of irreconcilables through the
illusion of the attainment of everyone's mutually exclu-
sive goals. And it will sweep the world as irresistibly as
once did the hordes of old Father Genghis.*

Shadrach takes momentary refuge in carpentry.
Until now that fashionable cult has been mere amusement for him, a source of relaxation and release rather
than the quasi-mystical focus that it is for many of
its adherents, but now, frayed and desperate, no longer

the calm and detached Shadrach of yore, he surrenders to its full intensity. The world has tightened around him. Ostensibly, all is as it has been, and is not going to change; his routines will continue, his doctoring and his calisthenics and his collecting and his trips to Karakorum; but in these past two days, aware now of the dread subtraction of self that Genghis Mao has covertly ordained for him, Shadrach finds the familiar and comfortable rhythms of life no longer enough to keep him together. Fear and pain have begun to seep into his soul, and the only antidote he knows for that is submission to some force greater than himself, greater even than Genghis Mao, some all-encompassing power. If he can, he will make carpentry the vehicle of that submission. With hammer and nails, then, with chisel and adze, with plane and saw and awl, he seeks, if not salvation, then at least temporary freedom from anguish.

Usually Shadrach attends the large and majestic carpentry chapel in Karakorum. But there is always a carnival atmosphere in Karakorum, and that tends to trivialize whatever he does there, be it carpentry or dream-death or transtemporalism or mere fornication. Now, in genuine spiritual need, he wants not the fanciest chapel but the one most readily accessible, the one that will enable him most quickly to find surcease from pain, and he goes to a place here in Ulan Bator, down by the Tuula River, in one of those streets of formidable blocky white-stucco buildings constructed in the latter days of the Mongolian People's Republic.

It is a starkly functional no-nonsense sort of chapel, lacking in any religious or pseudoreligious iconography. Big bare rooms, sputtering fluorescent lights, the smell of sawdust and lemon oil—it could be an ordinary carpenters' shop, but for the silence and the peculiar concentration with which the men and women at the benches are going about their tasks. Shadrach pays a fee at the entrance—strictly a service charge, covering the cost of tool rental, lumber, and maintenance, never a fee for worship itself—and is shown to a locker where he exchanges his street

clothes for clean coveralls. Then he selects a vacant
bench. Shining well-oiled tools have been arranged
along and around it with an eye for symmetry and
neatness that is positively Japanese: chisels of many
sizes in a precisely ordered row, an assortment of
hammers and mallets, a cluster of gauges, augers,
pincers, compasses, bevels, files, try squares, and rules.
The equipment is deliberately varied and copious, to
impress upon the worshipper the hieratic nature of
the craft, the ancient lineage of its practice, the complexity of its scope.

   No one speaks to him. No one looks at him. No one
will; those who enter here must remain alone with
their tools and their wood. A strange solemnity steals
over him as he makes ready to enter the customary
initial state of meditation. In the past, having come
to the chapel for nothing more than a relaxing couple
of hours of cutting and joining, seeing the whole
experience as an amusement on the same level as a
round of golf or a game of billiards, he has approached
this stage of the ceremony in a casual and amiable
way, accepting it as part of the tradition, something
that one does merely to get into the spirit of the
thing, the equivalent of a golfer's ritualized practice
swings or a billiards player's careful chalking of the
cue; but this time, as he presses both hands flat
against the workbench and bows his head, he feels
neither flippant nor stagily ostentatious; he is aware
of a numinous presence all about him, and he grows
somber and reflective as it enters his soul.

   In the meditation one first must consider the tools,
their form and divine essence. One must visualize
them and name them: this is a tenon saw, this a
dovetail saw, this a gimlet, this a bradawl. One then
must dwell on their purpose, which requires one to
imagine each tool in action, and this in turn calls for
contemplation of certain basic techniques of carpentry and joinery: the making of mortises and tenons,
the construction of joists and frames, the fitting of
veneers, the setting of braces and struts and wedging.
This phase of the meditation is the most prolonged
and the most intense. Shadrach has heard that some

adherents to the cult devote the entire energy of their worship to it, and never actually take tools and wood into their hands, but carry out a completely satisfying communion in their minds alone. Until today he has never really understood how this could be accomplished, but now, scribing and mitring and butting as he sits with closed eyes, mentally fitting tenon into mortise and tongue into groove, he sees that actual manual labor can be extraneous to this experience if one is able fully to enter into the meditative phase.

He perceives this, but he moves on anyway into the terminal stage of the meditation, which is the entry into the wood, the mother-stuff. This too is a highly structured exercise, which one must begin by imagining trees, not merely any trees but specific timber trees of one's own choice, ordinarily pine or spruce or fir for Shadrach, occasionally more exotic woods, according to his whim, ebony, palisander, mahogany, teak. One must *see* the tree; one must imagine it felled; one must carry it onward to be milled and seasoned; one must at last behold the finished board, and contemplate its grain, its texture, its moisture content, its vulnerability to shrinkage and warpage, all its characteristics and special beauties. And then, only then, when one can taste the wood on one's tongue, when one feels the tool hot and eager in one's hand, then does one rise and go to the bin and select one's lumber and begin at last to work.

Shadrach knows, by the time he has reached this stage, exactly what the form of his worship will be today. He will do no fancy joinery this day, but simple heavy carpentry, simple but pure, a job that strikes to the essence of form: he will construct the centering for a brick arch. It has sprung entire into his mind, the ribs, and ties, the braces and struts, the laggings, the wedges; he has calculated the curvature, the span, the height of the crown, the springing line, all in one rush of inner vision, and now he need only cut and fit and hammer, and when he is done he will disassemble everything, carry out the ceremonial burning of the sawdust, and depart, drained and eased of tension.

He works quickly. A kind of wild feverish energy has come over him. He hastens from bin to bench, from bin to bench; his mouth bristles with nails of half a dozen lengths; he does not pause for an instant. Yet there is nothing rushed about his labor. To rush would be folly; the point here is to attain calmness of spirit. The work should be accomplished swiftly but without haste. Serenely Shadrach builds. The work contains its own purpose and has none beyond the immediate spiritual fulfillment, for one never *uses* anything one constructs in the carpentry chapel, one never takes anything away that one has put together, any more than one would bring in one's own tools. This is not a substitute for the home workshop, after all. The idea here is solely to exercise skill in joining, and thus to experience the fundamental connectivity of the universe; what one actually makes is incidental, a means to a higher end, and must not be allowed to become a goal in itself. Shadrach has never fully understood that part of it before today, either. He has enjoyed the physicality of the work, the hammering and the sweat, and he has enjoyed the aesthetic reward, the pleasure of watching something sturdy and attractive take shape under his hands, and he has always felt mildly distressed at the necessary disassembling that follows; because he has never seen the carpentry cult as anything more profound than tennis or golf or bicycle riding, he has never attained those farther reaches of the spirit which he has heard are available to the communicants here. Now he does attain those reaches, at least their nearer fringes, and, penetrating unexpected realms, he finds that his fears and resentments fall away, and he is purified. So it must have been for the Creator, shaping worlds on quiet afternoons, experiencing a total sense of identification with the task, a sense of utter selflessness, of being no more than a conduit for the great shaping force that flows through the universe. No doubt one can just as readily attain the same tranquil place through tennis or golf or bicycle riding, Shadrach realizes. The means is unimportant; only the state of consciousness toward which one journeys matters.

He sees his arch acquiring form; it is not *his* arch but *the* arch, the prototype of all arches, the ideal arch, the arch on which the vault of the heavens rests, and he and the arch have become one, and he, Shadrach Mordecai of Ulan Bator, bears all the weight of the cosmos and feels no burden. Does an arch complain of the load? The arch, if the arch is a proper arch, merely transmits the weight to the earth, and the earth does not complain either, but imparts the thrust of its burden to the stars, which accept it unprotestingly, for there is no burden, there is no weight, there is simply the ebb and flow of substance between the joined members of the one great entity that is the matrix of everything; and when one has perceived that, can it be such a serious matter that one's body, which at the moment houses a pattern of responses that calls itself "Shadrach Mordecai," may soon house instead something calling itself "Genghis Mao"? Such transformations are meaningless. Change does not occur; there are only transfers, not transformations; the only reality is the reality of eternal flux. He is purged of all discord and all dismay.

The arch is done. Shadrach briefly admires its perfection of form; then, calmly, he knocks it apart and carries the pieces to the salvage bin.

Does the arch no longer exist, simply because its components have been dismembered? No. The arch exists, shining as brightly in his mind as when he first conceived it. The arch will always exist. The arch is indestructible. Shadrach restores his tools to their original immaculate order, and gathers his sawdust, and makes the ceremonial pyre of it in the urn in the aisle. When his bench is as clean as he first found it, he kneels, bows his head, and remains that way a minute or two, altogether untroubled, mind blank, a *tabula rasa*, healed and made whole. Then he goes out.

Images of Mangu are everywhere in the streets, the handsome Mongol face looking down from the facade of every building and staring out from great banners strung from lampposts high above the roadways. At the intersection of three grand boulevards workmen

are diligently erecting the armature for what is undoubtedly going to be a vast statue of the dead viceroy.
The process of canonization is well advanced; day by
day, departed Mangu is thrust more visibly into the
consciousness of the citizens of the world capital,
and doubtless everywhere else as well. Mangu dead
has taken on a power and a presence never possessed
by Mangu alive: he has indeed become a fallen
demigod, he is Baldur, Adonis, Osiris, the slaughtered
promise of spring, and he is due to rise again.

Shadrach, cool and bouncy, wanders toward the
river, whistling some lush romantic melody—a tune
out of Rachmaninoff, he suspects. He is being followed,
he realizes, by a man who emerged from the carpentry chapel a moment after he did. This does not
worry him. For the moment, nothing worries him.
He is charmed by everything, the steppe, the hills,
the faintly chilly spring air, the idea of being followed.
He is charmed even by the silly ubiquity of Mangu,
whose bland symmetrical features have been plas-
tered to everything, and sprout from mailboxes, from
trashbins, from the low smooth white wall of the
promenade that runs along the river; there are Mangu
pennants and streamers hanging all around, and everything is done to a background of the Mongol mourning color, which is yellow and lends an oddly bright
and festive tone to the display, as though there is
shortly to be a parade in Mangu's honor, followed by
the viceroy's glorious second coming. Shadrach smiles.
He leans his long body over the promenade wall to
admire the lovely turbulent flow of the river, quick-
ened by its spring freshets and humming along with
rare energy, swirling and dancing. He imagines fila-
ments and tendrils of tributary streams spreading
outward from the channel below him, lacing this
arid land together, carrying water joyously from the
mountains, sweeping it to the river and thence to the
sea, a vast arterial system serving the living, throbbing entity that is the earth, and the image pleases
the doctor in him. If he listens carefully, he tells himself,
he can hear the breathing of the planet, and even the
rhythms of its heart, *lub*-dub, *lub*-dub, *lub*-dub.

The man who has been following him appears now on the promenade and takes up a position just to Shadrach's left. Side by side they watch the river in silence. After a moment Shadrach risks a furtive glance and discovers that the man is Frank Ficifolia, the communications expert, the designer of Surveillance Vector One. Ficifolia is a short, rotund, capable man, perhaps fifty years old, good-natured and talkative, and his uncharacteristic silence now is significant. Upon entering the carpentry chapel Shadrach had had a glimpse of someone he thought might be Ficifolia, but the etiquette of the cult had kept him from taking a second look; his guess is now confirmed. But a different etiquette controls Shadrach here. In the bugged and spy-eyed world of Genghis Mao, one is frequently approached by people who wish to talk without outwardly seeming to be holding a conversation. Many times Shadrach has carried on long interchanges with someone who is staring in another direction, even with someone whose back is to him. He continues, therefore, to study the rushing flow of the river, offering Ficifolia no greeting, and waiting.

Eventually Ficifolia says, apropos of nothing and without looking at Shadrach, "I don't understand why you're still hanging around here."

"Pardon me?"

"In Ulan Bator. Waiting for the ax to fall. If I were you I'd go into hiding, Shadrach."

"So you know about—"

"I know, yes. Several people know. What are you going to do?"

"I'm not sure. Stay put for a while, I guess, and think things over. There's a lot I have to evaluate."

"Evaluate? *Evaluate?* Of course you'd say something like that!" Ficifolia, though plainly trying to be unobtrusive, cannot control his emotions; he raises his voice; he gesticulates passionately. "You know, man, you never belonged in this town. You aren't crazy enough to qualify. You're so calm, so reasonable, you always want to think things out, you want to stop and evaluate when they've got the knife to your throat—how did you ever land here, anyway? This is a place for madmen. I mean that seriously, Shadrach. The lunatics are running the asylum, and the head lunatic is the craziest one of all, and you just don't fit in. Can you think of anything crazier than a world full of rotting people governed by a few thousand Antidote-filled bureaucrats and ruled by a ninety-year-old Mongol warlord who's planning to live forever? This is sanity? This is the logical outcome of five hundred years of Western imperialism? And the spy-eyes everywhere? The surveillance vectors taping my very words right now and feeding them to God knows what kind of machine where they may not be digested and acted upon for three thousand years? The robot policemen? The organ farms? Anyone who begins to take this world at face value has to be a madman, and that's what we are, all of us, top to bottom, Avogadro, Horthy, Lindman, Labile, me, the whole crew. Except you. So solemn, so contained, so accepting. Doing your job, doing your job, you and Warhaftig, stitching the new liver into the Khan, never cracking a smile, never saying to each other, This is a crazy way of making a living, never even perceiving the craziness because you're so fundamentally sane—not Warhaftig, he's either a robot or a lunatic, but you, Shadrach, deadpan, full of weird microelectronic gear and even that doesn't upset you. Don't you ever want to scream and rant? Do you have to accept everything? Do you even accept the idea that Genghis Mao is going to evict you from your own fucking *head*? Do you—" Abruptly Ficifolia checks himself, reining himself in with a little shudder and a quick series of jerking tics of the facial muscles. More calmly, in an entirely different voice, he says, "Really, Shadrach, you're in big trouble. You ought to disappear while you still can."

Shadrach shakes his head. "Hiding's not my style."

"Is dying?"

"Not particularly. But I won't hide. That's not like me. My people are done with hiding. The old Underground Railway days are gone forever."

" '*My people are done with hiding*,' " Ficifolia says, doing his mimicry in a harsh, high-pitched tone.

"Jesus. Je*sus!* Maybe I underestimated you. Maybe you're as crazy as the rest of us here. Genghis Mao has fingered you for doom, has put the old black spot right on you, and you put racial pride ahead of survival. Bravo, Shadrach! Very noble. Very dumb."

"Where could I go? The Khan's spy gadgets will find me anywhere. Gadgets that you helped invent for him."

"There are ways."

"Disguise myself? Paint my skin white? Wear a blond wig?"

"You could disappear the way Buckmaster did."

Shadrach coughs. "I don't need sick jokes just now, Frank."

"I'm not talking about organ farms. I mean *disappearing*. We disappeared Buckmaster. We could do the same for you."

"Buckmaster isn't dead?"

"Alive and well. We altered the master personnel register the day he was sentenced. Transposed half a dozen binary digits and the records show that Roger Buckmaster went to the organ farms on such-and-such day and was duly carved up. Once it's in the record, it's realer than real. Machine reality is a higher order of reality than reality reality. If Buckmaster shows up on any of the Khan's scanners now, the computer will reject the data as nonsense, because Buckmaster is known to be dead, and dead men by definition aren't found walking around."

"Where is he?"

"That's not important now. What's important is that we saved him, and we can save you."

"*We?* Who's 'we'?"

"That's not important either."

"Should I believe any of this, Frank?"

"No. Of course not. It's all lies. Actually, I'm spying for the Khan, trying to trap you. Jesus, Shadrach, use your head! Do you think I'm trying to get you into trouble? You *are* in trouble. I'm risking my ass to—"

"All right. Let me think, Frank."

"So think, already."

"You do your hocus-pocus and I disappear. Now

I'm without an identity and without a profession. Can I practice medicine if I'm hiding out in some cellar? I was meant to be a doctor. Maybe not Genghis Mao's doctor, but somebody's doctor, Frank. If I'm not working at that, I'm nobody, I'm a waste of skills and talent. In my own eyes I'll be nothing. Is there any point in disappearing into that kind of life? And how long would I have to stay underground? If I'm going to spend the rest of my life locked up in a cellar, I wouldn't be a whole lot worse off letting Genghis Mao use me for Avatar. Better off, maybe."

"You might have to stay out of sight until Genghis Mao dies. But afterward—"

"Afterward? What afterward? Genghis Mao might live another hundred years. I won't."

"He won't either," Ficifolia says, strange undertones of menace in his voice.

Shadrach stares in wonder. He is not sure he believes a syllable of this. Buckmaster alive? Ficifolia a subversive? Conspiratorial plans afoot to do away with the Khan? Questions bubble in him, and he hungers for a thousand answers; but from the corner of his eye he perceives men in gray and blue, two Citpols on patrol. So there will be no answers now. Ficifolia sees them too and nods ever so slightly and says, "Think about it. Do your evaluating, let me know what you want to do."

"All right."

"Have you ever seen the river as high as this?"

"It was an unusually snowy winter," Shadrach says, as the Citpols saunter past.

18

Troublesome dreams last night. Mouth full of cobwebs, fingers growing roots. Premonitions of death. Is the end of Genghis Mao drawing nigh? Morbid, morbid, morbid. To wake and not to be there. The great crash of silence. It pains me. To wake and not to be there. To have gone somewhere else. Or to have gone nowhere at all, the big black hole. The longer one lives, the tighter one grasps life: living becomes a habit that's hard to break. How empty the world would be if I were to leave it. Poof, no more Genghis Mao. Such a vacuum! The winds rushing in from the four corners to fill my place. Tornado. Hurricane.

    Oh I love to dwell on death.

    Dying can be so instructive. Dying can tell you so very much about your true self. Dying can even be pleasurable, I imagine. Dying as a healing experience, yes, the battered old body gladly giving up the ghost! For some people, I imagine, it is the sharpest ecstasy they have ever known.

    Oh I dread it.

    How shall I die, what will the manner of my going be? I think I fear assassins most of all. To leave the world is one thing, natural and inevitable; to be sent from it is altogether other, an affront to the self, an insult to the ego. I will not be able to bear that awareness of dismissal. Or the sense of transition, the moments just before the going, the confrontation with the killer, the contemplation of loss as he moves toward me with his knife or his gun or whatever. Let it be a bomb, if it comes. Let it be instant poison in my soup. But there will be no assassins. I am guarded too well. The mistake was in not protecting Mangu the same way. Still, Mangu wasn't Genghis Mao: his loss was not to him what my loss will be to me. The idea of dying is alien to me. I am too large of spirit, I occupy too great a place in the consciousness of mankind; the subtraction of me from the world is more than the world can accept. Certainly more than I can accept.

But why all this morbidity? Strange, considering how healthy I feel. Tremendous surge of vitality since the aortal transplant. I thrive on surgery. I should get some sort of organ work done every week. Change kidneys the first of every month, new spleen on the fifteenth. Yes. Meanwhile, healthy though I am, death plays games with my soul as I sleep. I think that it is an amusement, a delicious sport, to toy with fantasies of death. We require some tension in our lives to relieve that unbearable onwardness of existence. That flow of event, day following day, sunrise, noon, sunset, dark, it can be crushing, it can stultify. And so. The delight of dwelling on the end of all perception, that is, the end of all things. There is joy in thinking about the dismal. Especially though not exclusively as it applies to others. There is a German term, schadenfreude, the joy of gloom, the pleasure to be had from the contemplation of the misfortunes of others. This sorry century has been the golden age of schadenfreude. We have known the ecstasy of living at the end of an era, we have shared many blessed moments of decline and collapse. The shelling of the cathedrals in 1914, the English troops dying in the mud, the Soviet massacres, the first great economic disaster, the war that followed it, Auschwitz, Hiroshima, the time of the assassinations, the toppling of the governments, the Virus War, the organ-rot, so much to weep about, though of course always it was others who suffered more than one's self, which makes the weeping sweeter; nine dark decades and I have tasted them all, and why not now achieve a bit of interior distance and turn the principle inward, why not weep for the death of Genghis Mao? There is

*more pleasure in mourning than in dying. Let me in
fantasy savor my own lamentable passing. How much
I regret my going! I am my own most griefstricken
mourner. I love these fantasies; I feel so exquisitely
sorry for myself. But am I in fact dying? I summon
Shadrach. He tells me my morning readings. Everything normal, everything healthy. I am a phenomenon.
I will not go from the world today. Long life to the
Khan! Ten thousand years to the Khan!*

Béla Horthy seeks him out in a corridor on one of
the lower floors of the Grand Tower of the Khan and
says, pretending not to be looking at him, "Frank
tells me that you intend to stay here."

"For the time being," Shadrach says. "I need to
think."

"Thinking is useful, yes. But why do your thinking
in Ulan Bator?"

"It's where I live."

"For the time being," says Horthy. He swings around
and looks straight at Shadrach—boldly, daringly. His
wild hyperthyroid eyes are veiled with concern. He
must be one of the conspirators too, Shadrach realizes,
and that doesn't seem terribly surprising at all. Horthy
says softly, "Run, Shadrach."

"What's the use? They'll catch me."

"Are you sure? They haven't caught Buckmaster
yet."

"Aren't you afraid to say things like that? When
there might be—"

"Scanners in the walls?"

"Yes."

"Everything gets scanned. Everything gets taped.
So what? Who can run through all the tapes? The
Citpols are drowning in data. Every spy-channel is
choked with rivers of conspiracy, most of it insane
and imaginary. There's no filtering system to elimi-
nate the useless noise." Horthy winks. "Go. As Buckmaster went."

"Useless."

"I don't think so. I advise running. I *strongly* advise

running. You know, some people think better when they're on the run."

Horthy smiles. He takes Shadrach's hand for a moment.

As Horthy walks away, Shadrach calls after him, "Hey, are you part of it too?"

"Part of what?" Horthy asks, and laughs.

May 28, 2012.
More dark dreams. I went down to Sukhe Bator Square and found they had erected a statue of me in the center of the plaza, a colossus, at least a hundred meters high, made of bronze that was already developing a green patina. My arms outspread in benediction. My face looked awful: wrinkled, cavernous, hideous, the face of a man five hundred years old. And the statue had no legs. It ended at mid-thigh, Genghis Mao on stumps, but the statue floated in mid-air, as though the legs had once been there but had been chopped away and the statue had remained at its original height. There was an old workman, sweeping up faded flowers, and I said to him, "Is Genghis Mao dead?" and he said, "Dead and gone, they sent the pieces back to Dalan-Dzadagad, and good riddance." The pieces. They sent the pieces back. I don't like this. There is too much death in my head these days. The game has lost its savor. I must take steps.

After breakfast I decided to make an inspection of the project laboratories. When preoccupied with death, drop in on those who would help you live forever.

Wise idea. Immediately felt better. First personal visit in months. Should go more often.

Called on Phoenix first, the dainty Sarafrazi woman in charge, marvelous eyes, beautiful face. Terrified of me. Showed me her monkeys, her bubbling vats of chemicals, her pickled brains in bell jars. Optimistic forecasts from her, delivered in tense throaty voice. She'll make me young again, so she claims. Am not so sure of that but told her to keep at it. Paralyzed with awe, she was. I thought she was almost going to kneel as I left.

Went from there to Talos. Came in unannounced, but the Lindman woman cool as ice anyway. The report is

*that she's Shadrach's new lover. Can't understand what
he sees in her. Something about her mouth I don't like,
spoils her face. Looks like the mouth of some ferocious
gnawing creature. She's got a plastic Genghis Mao in
her lab, very large, nothing finished below the waist,
just framework there, no legs. No legs. The Genghis
Mao Memorial Statue. "Finish the legs," I told her. She
gave me a peculiar look. Told me the legs were the final
job, more important now to get the internal engineering
done. Knows her own mind, won't take nonsense from
me. Even if I am Chairman of the Permanent Revolutionary Committee. I Genghis II Mao IV Khan do
command—no. Her robot can wink, smile, wave its
arms. Gonchigdorge was with me and said, "It's just
like you, sir, a remarkable likeness," but I can't agree.
Ingenious but mechanical. I wouldn't want it to succeed me. I will not terminate Project Talos, not yet at
any rate, but I don't think it's going to be able to
produce what I need.*

*Went on to Nikki Crowfoot's lab, Avatar. Ah! Yes!
Beautiful woman, though tense, depressed, withdrawn,
these days. Guilty about Shadrach, I imagine. She ought
to be. But she remains a loyal servant of the Khan. Is
this a good thing? "When will you be ready to make the
transfer?" I asked her. She said, "It's just a matter of
months." I felt such a surge of excitement at that that
Shadrach phoned from upstairs to find out if I was all
right. Told him to mind his own business. But I am his
own business. Anyway, Avatar gives me hope. Soon I
will put on new healthy flesh. Before the first snows
come I will speak to the world with Shadrach's lips, I
will breathe the air with Shadrach's lungs.*

Entering the Project Avatar laboratory unannounced
in midafternoon, Shadrach is confronted immediately
by Manfred Eis, Nikki Crowfoot's chief assistant, who
emerges out of a maze of equipment and strides pur-
posefully toward him like Thor on the warpath, halt-
ing with a crispness just short of a heel-click.

"We are very busy just now," Eis announces, making a challenge out of it.

"I'm glad to hear it."

"You have come because—?"

"A routine inspection visit," Shadrach answers mildly. "To check on progress. I haven't been here for a while."

In fact it is several weeks since he was last in the Avatar lab, not since just before Mangu's death, and the rhythm of his schedule has usually brought him to each project at least once a month. But Eis hardly makes him feel welcome now. He is a cold-mannered, humorless man at best, a cliché-Teuton, stiff and square-jawed and square-shouldered and very Nordic, with frosty blue eyes, pearly teeth, long yellow hair, everything but the dueling scar. Shadrach is accustomed to Dr. Eis's Aryan brusqueness, but today there is something new in his manner, something gratuitously hostile, almost patronizing, vaguely contemptuous, that Shadrach finds disturbing because he suspects it has to do with his own suddenly significant personal involvement in the destinies of Project Avatar.

Eis is *pleased* that Shadrach has been chosen. Eis is *gratified*. Eis thinks it altogether *proper* that Shadrach should be the one. That's it. Perhaps it was Eis who actually sold Genghis Mao on the idea of selecting Shadrach. No, no, an underling like Eis would never have had access to the Chairman; but still, Eis must have rejoiced, seems still to be rejoicing right now. Shadrach does not like being gloated over. He wonders if it is possible to find some appropriate experimental use for Eis's fine Nordic body.

Nevertheless, Shadrach is nominally in charge here, and Eis must give ground. Busy though the lab is, he will have to let Shadrach make his inspection. The place really is busy, too, frantic, all sorts of experiments with all sorts of animals under way, while electronic gear is hauled from room to room by sweating cursing technicians, and men and women in lab smocks run around wild-eyed, brandishing sheafs of printouts—a real circus, altogether manic and comic, mad scientists at work, desperately striving to square the circle before the onrushing deadline arrives.

It makes Shadrach queasy to realize that *he* is the circle they must square. He is the patsy, the sucker, the victim, whose life is eventually going to be swallowed by all this equipment, and the manic tone of the current Avatar operations is entirely the result of the need to convert everything, fast, from Mangu-parameters to Shadrach-parameters. Probably a dozen people here know as much about his body, his brain-wave patterns and his neural circuitry and his serotonin levels, as he does himself. Quite likely he has been under covert scrutiny for days. (Do they steal nail parings? Hair clippings?) Shadrach wonders how many of these technicians know of the host substitution. He imagines that they all do, that they are eyeing him with secret fascination even as they rush to and fro—that they are sizing him up, comparing the authentic actual Shadrach Mordecai to the clusters of abstract and synthetic Shadrach-simulation pulsations that they have been working with. But maybe not. Apparently only a few of the Avatar people knew that Mangu was going to be the body donor in the first place, and most likely even fewer have been allowed to learn the identity of Mangu's replacement.

Nikki, at any rate, is not caught up in the general manic mood. Summoned by Eis, she greets Shadrach quite calmly. The project, she tells him, is making steady progress. Her gaze is steady, her voice is centered and composed. "Progress," in this laboratory, can only mean the daily process of bringing Shadrach closer to destruction, and certainly she is aware that he will put that interpretation on it; but it seems that she has decided not to feel guilty or act evasive any longer. They have already had their showdown; she has admitted that she was willing to betray her lover for the sake of Genghis Mao; now life continues—for however long—and she has her job to do. All this passes between them within the space of ninety seconds, and none of it is communicated in words, only in tone of voice and expression of eyes. Shadrach is relieved. He does not enjoy making people feel guilty; it makes him feel obscurely guilty himself.

"I should look at the equipment," Shadrach says.

"Come."

She takes him on a guided tour. She demonstrates for him the zoo of metempsychosized animals, the latest triumphs of electronic transmigration: here is a dog with the soul of a raccoon, diligently dipping its dinner in a pan of water, and here is an eagle with a coded peacock-construct in its skull to make it strut and preen and spread its wings, and here they have slipped the essential sheepness of a sheep into a young lioness, who sits placidly munching fodder, to the probable detriment of her digestive system. All these reborn beasts have a trapped, bewildered look, as though they are being gnawed from within by some insatiable parasite, and Shadrach asks Nikki if this is going to be a characteristic of human avatars as well, if the expunged soul of the body donor will not linger as a miasma to complicate the life of his supplanter.

"We don't think so," Nikki says. "Remember, all the animals I've shown you have undergone implant codings across species lines, in fact across generic lines. A peacock is *never* going to be comfortable in an eagle's body, or a sheep in a lion's. Eventually the animal gets the hang of operating its new body, but it'll always tend to keep reverting to the old reflex patterns."

"Then why bother with transgeneric switches? What's the point, other than showing off how clever you are?"

"The point is that the disparities between the implanted entity and the host are so gross that we can instantly confirm the success of the implant. If we put a spaniel's mind into another spaniel's body, if we put a chimp into a chimp, a goat into a goat, how do we know if we've accomplished anything? The goat can't tell us. The spaniel can't tell us."

Shadrach frowns. "Surely the electrical pattern of one spaniel's brain is different from another's, and that can readily be detected. If brain-wave patterns aren't unique to the individual, what's your whole project all about?"

"Of course the patterns are unique," Crowfoot says. "But we need confirmation on gross behavioral level.

We *have* done intraspecies coding and implants, plenty of them, but the behavioral differences after the implant are too subtle to prove very much when we put one chimp into another, say, and the brain-wave changes that we can detect are, for all we know, just artifacts of our own meddling. Whereas if we code a sheep and feed her into a lioness, and the lioness is thereupon transformed into a grazing animal, we have very dramatic confirmation that we've achieved something. Yes?"

"But it would be very much more dramatic, naturally, if the minds you were switching around were human ones. And much easier to confirm that a switch has actually been induced."

"Naturally."

"Only you haven't done any of that."

"Not yet," Nikki says. "Next week, I think, we'll tackle our first human implant."

Shadrach feels a faint chill. He has managed an admirable impersonality thus far on this tour, he has carried on this conversation exactly as though his interest in Project Avatar is a purely professional one; but it is not that easy to escape an awareness of the ultimate consequences of all this painstaking research, now that he and Crowfoot have begun talking of moving human minds from one body to another. He is unable to ignore the final goal of Avatar, the transmigration of tiger into gazelle: Genghis Mao is the tiger, and he himself the hapless gazelle. What becomes of the gazelle when the tiger invades? Shadrach examines, briefly, one avenue of escape that he had not previously considered: if they can move sheep-mind to lioness-body and Genghis Mao-mind to Shadrach-body, they can just as easily move Shadrach-mind to some other body, and leave him to proceed from there. But the fantasy fades in the instant of its birth. He does not want to move to another body. He wants to keep his own. How like a dream this is, he thinks. Except that there is no awakening from it.

"How long will you do experiments in human

implants," Shadrach asks, "before you'll be ready
to—to—"

"To transplant the Chairman?"

"Yes."

Shrugging, Nikki says, "That's hard to answer. It
depends on the problems we encounter in the early
human transplants. If there are unexpectedly difficult problems of psychological adaptation, if transplant leads to psychotic freak-outs or cerebral breakdown or identity bleed-throughs or anything like that,
it might be months or even years before we dare shift
Genghis Mao to a new body. Our animal experiments
haven't indicated that such things are going to happen,
but human minds are more complex than spaniel
minds, and we have to allow for the possibility that
complex minds will react in complicated ways to
something as traumatic as a shift of bodies. So we'll
proceed cautiously. Unless, of course, the imminent
bodily death of Genghis Mao makes an emergency
mind-transplant necessary, in which case, I suppose,
we'll just plunge ahead and see what happens.
We're not eager to do that, of course."

"Of course," Shadrach echoes dryly.

"We'd much rather be orderly about it. A period
of experimentation with human subjects, and then, if
all goes smoothly there, we'd like to do two or three
preliminary Genghis Mao transplants before we—"

"*What?*"

"Yes. Insert the Genghis Mao-construct into several temporary host bodies, simply to find out how
the Chairman reacts when transplanted, what adap-
tations may be required in order to—"

"And what will you do with all these extra Genghis
Maos?" Shadrach asks. "It's beautiful redundancy, I
know, to keep a stockpile of them around. But if they
all start giving orders at once we might—"

"Oh, no," Crowfoot says. "We don't intend to let
the Genghis Mao material remain in any of the experimental subjects. That sort of redundancy is absolutely not wanted here. We'd expunge each subject
once we were done testing him. We'd do a complete
mindpick after we've run our tests."

"Ah. Yes. Assuming the subject will let you."

"What do you mean?"

"Remember, you won't be dealing with a helpless flunky, once you've done your transplant. You'll be dealing with Genghis Mao wearing a new body. You'll be up against the dominant spirit of the age. You might have problems."

"I doubt it," Nikki says breezily. "We'll take precautions. Come this way, will you?"

She leads him forward, to a vast computer bank, a wall of gray-green metal studded with incomprehensible apparatus. In here, she tells him, the coded essence of Genghis Mao is stored, everything that has been recorded so far, a nearly complete digital persona-construct that is capable of responding to a stimuli precisely as the living Genghis Mao would, to a probability of seven or eight decimal places. Nikki offers to demonstrate the construct's Genghis Mao-ness with a few quick simulation runs, but Shadrach, suddenly disheartened, shows little interest; she marches him on to some of the other Avatar wonders to which he reacts with no greater enthusiasm, and, as though at last noticing that Shadrach has ceased to pretend to be delighted by her technological miracles, she ushers him into her private office and locks the door.

They stand facing each other, less than a meter apart, and he feels sudden surprising excitement, physical, intense. The intensity astounds him. He had thought all desire for her had gone from him forever, once he discovered how she had betrayed him. But no. Still there, strong as ever. The lure of her sleek tawny body, the memory of her fragrance, the glitter of her huge piercing dark eyes. His Indian princess, Pocahontas, Sacajawea. Even now he is drawn to her, even now. He ceases to see the ingenious woman of science whose ingenuity has altogether undone him; he sees only the woman, beautiful, passionate, irresistible. He feels the pull of her body and he is sure she feels the pull of his.

It ought not to be such a surprise. Here they are, man and woman; they have been lovers for many months; they are alone, the door is locked. Why should desire not come over them, despite everything? But still, this sudden shifting of gears into the erotic mode amazes him. Somehow sex, unexpectedly obtruding itself against this background of betrayal, depression, impending doom, seems irrelevant and inappropriate, bizarre and unwelcome.

He pretends he feels nothing. He makes no move.

"How are you managing, Shadrach?" she asks tenderly, after a moment. "Is it very bad?"

"I'm holding on."

"Are you frightened?"

"A little. More angry than frightened, I guess."

"Do you hate me?"

"I don't hate anyone. I'm not a hater."

"I still love you, you know."

"Quit it, Nikki."

"I do. That's what's been ripping me apart for weeks."

The force of Crowfoot's concern for him is like a tangible presence in the small office.

"I don't want to hear about it," he says.

"You do hate me."

"No. I'm just not interested in your remorse."

"Or my love?"

"Such that it is."

"Such that it is."

"I don't know," he says. "I don't want my head messed up any more than it already has been."

"What will you do, Shadrach?"

"What do you mean, what will I do?"

"You aren't going to stay in Ulan Bator."

"Everybody's been telling me to run."

"Yes."

"It wouldn't do any good."

"You could save yourself," Crowfoot tells him.

He shakes his head. "I wouldn't get away. The whole planet's bugged, Nikki. Watch Surveillance Vector One for fifteen minutes and you'll realize that. You know that already. You've told me yourself that escape's impossible. There's a tracer on everyone.

Anyway, it would spoil your project again if I disappeared."

"Oh, Shadrach!"

"I mean, I'm the key man, right?"

"Don't be an idiot."

"You'd have to find another host for Genghis Mao. Then you'd have to recalibrate all over again. You—"

"Stop it. Please."

"All right," he says. "At any rate, it's futile to try to escape from the Khan."

"You won't even try?"

"I won't even try."

Crowfoot regards him levelly for a long silent moment. Then she says, "I should feel relieved about that, I suppose."

"Why?"

"If you won't take responsibility for saving yourself, then I don't have to take responsibility for—for—"

"For what's going to happen to me if I stay here?"

"Yes."

"That's right. You don't need to feel any guilt at all. I've had fair warning, and nevertheless I freely choose to stay and face the music. You're absolved, Nikki. Your hands are washed of my blood."

"Are you being sarcastic, Shadrach?"

"Not particularly."

"I can never tell when you're being sarcastic."

"Not this time," he says.

They stare at each other strangely again. He still feels that mysterious sexual tension, that grotesque and inappropriate lust. He suspects that if he reached for her and dragged her down on the carpeted floor, down between the desk and the filing cabinets, he could have her right here, right now, in her own office, one last crazy and frantic screw. Then he thinks of Eis and his colleagues running around on the other side of the locked office door, busy with their computers and their chimps, doing simulated transfers of the persona of Genghis Mao into the bodily hull of Shadrach Mordecai, and his ardor cools a little. But only a little.

Nikki laughs.

"What's funny?" he asks.

"Do you remember," she says, "that time we spoke about the concept of you and Genghis Mao being one life system, one self-corrective information-processing unit? That was before any of this happened. Mangu was still alive, I think. I talked about how the chisel and the mallet and the stone are aspects of the sculptor, or, more precisely, that the sculptor and his tools and materials together make up a single thinking-and-acting entity, a single *person*, and how you and Genghis Mao—"

"Yes. I remember."

"It's going to be even truer now, won't it? In the most literal sense. That seems awfully ironic to me. Your nervous system and his, entwined, interlocked, indistinguishable. When we spoke then, you said no, it wasn't a true analogy, that Genghis Mao can send data to you but you can't send it to him, so that there's a limitation on the information flow, a discrete boundary. That'll change, now. It'll be impossible to tell where one of you leaves off and the other begins. But even then, I wanted to tell you that you weren't really grasping the idea—that the marble can't design a sculpture but is nevertheless part of the total sculpture-making system, and that you can't feed metabolic data into Genghis Mao but are nevertheless part of the total Genghis Mao system; there *is* an interaction, there *is* a feedback relationship that links you to him and he to you, there is—" She has been talking very rapidly, a torrential flow of words. Now she halts and in an altogether different voice says, "Oh, Shadrach, why don't you want to hide yourself?"

"I told you. It's useless. I keep telling people that, but they don't seem to want to believe me."

He thinks about himself as part of the total Genghis Mao system. He considers the analogies. No doubt of it, his sensors and implants link him to the Khan in a very special way. But he is no more—and no less—important to the total Genghis Mao system than Michelangelo's lump of marble was to the total statue-making system. Michelangelo, if he felt that a given lump of marble was no longer necessary to the needs

of the total system, would casually discard it and
introduce another into the system.

Nikki is trembling.

"If you won't try to save yourself," she says, "then
nobody else can do anything for you."

After he and Genghis Mao come to share one body,
they will truly be an integrated information-processing
unit. Of course, such a unit needs only one bio-
computer, one brain, one mind, one self. And that
self will not be the self of Shadrach Mordecai.

He says, "I know that. We've already discussed
that. I take full responsibility."

"Don't you *care?*"

"Maybe not. Not any longer. I don't know."

"Shadrach—"

She starts to reach toward him, a tentative gesture,
perhaps sexual, perhaps merely some sort of reflex-
ive grab at a sinking man. He pulls back. There is a
wall between them, an impermeable barrier of words
and fears and doubts and hesitations and guilts. He
does not mind that. He takes refuge behind that wall.
But still there is that sexual pull between them, that
taut hot line of erotic tension, spanning the barrier,
drilling through it, eroding it, breaching it. And then
the barrier is gone. He loves her, he hates her, he
wants her, he loathes her. He makes a tentative gesture toward her and halts. They are like two adoles-
cents, absurdly unsure of themselves, feinting foolishly,
making silly false starts and finicky nervous with-
drawals. He smiles tensely. So does she. She is obviously as conscious as he is of the minute shifts of
balance that are rapidly occurring within them and
between them. It is as though they are voyagers aboard
an ocean liner that is struggling through turbulent,
stormy waters, and they are trapped together in a
tiny cabin with a massive metal safe that slides wildly
about, careening across the floor with every convul-
sion of the waves, crashing into the walls as they
jump about, threatening to crush them if they do not
succeed in scampering out of its way as it bears
down on them. There is something undeniably comic
about their predicament, but the peril is real, too,

and not at all funny. How much longer can they hold out? The safe is so heavy, the sea so rough, the cabin so small, and they are getting weary—

And suddenly they come together, embracing, grappling, mouth seeking mouth, fingers digging furiously into flesh. He is terrified by the power of the blind, irrational force that has been unleashed in him, that he has unleashed in himself. "No," he mutters, even as he claws at her clothes, even as he pushes himself against her, even as he finds the fullness of her breasts beneath the sexless lab smock. "No," she whimpers, seemingly equally appalled. But neither of them resist. They stumble about ridiculously, sway, topple to the floor. On the carpet, between the desk and the filing cabinet.

Neither of them undresses. Down with zipper, up with skirt; this is no tender act of love, this is not even a display of sexual athleticism, this is mere savage coupling, a desperate and unsophisticated cleaving-together of flesh. His hands slide along the smooth firm columns of her thighs and his fingers find and probe the secret slit between them, already hot and moist, and she gasps and thrusts her pelvis at him and, quickly, blindly, he drives himself into her. There is barely room for their bodies to move on the floor; she tilts herself upward, feet pointed at the ceiling, and he reaches below to grasp her buttocks, supporting her, and rams himself against her with lunatic vigor. Almost at once, so it seems to him, she comes with unfamiliar little shivers and giggles, and moments later so does he, in wild galvanic spasms that wrench a hoarse strained cry from him. Inelegantly Shadrach slumps down on her chest, exhausted, and she holds him tightly, with loving rocklike patience, as if she would be willing to hold him this way for hours or weeks, but after two or three minutes he pulls free, stunned, dazed, hardly believing what has just passed between them.

They look at each other. He blinks; so does she. There are thin faint smiles of embarrassment.

Shakily he rises. Nikki lies there, her legs lowered now but still spread wide, her rumpled skirt pushed up around her hips, her face shiny with sweat, her eyes bloodshot, unfocused. Shadrach averts his glance from her body in peculiar fastidiousness: he is not exactly repelled by the sight of her exposed loins, but somehow he does not want to look. Perhaps he is frightened by the power that that dark hairy humid cavern has over him, the primordial female chasm, irresistible, all-engulfing. At any rate he adjusts his clothes, coughs self-consciously, stoops to offer Nikki a helping hand. She shakes him off gently and gets to her feet unaided, and they stand facing each other. He has nothing to say. It is a sticky moment, but she rescues them from it by taking his hand, by giving him a warm loving smile, by pulling him toward her for a quick chaste kiss, lips lightly brushing lips, a kiss that simultaneously acknowledges the intensity of what has just taken place and brings down a curtain on it. It is time for him to go.

"Save yourself," she whispers. "No one can do it for you."

"I need to think about things some more."

"Go, then. Do your thinking. I love you, Shadrach."

He knows what he is supposed to reply to that, but the words are impossible. He squeezes her fingers instead. And swiftly leaves.

19

He has been saying for days that he will not run away. He has said it to Ficifolia, to Horthy, to Nikki, to Katya, to all of the well-meaning friends who want him to try to save himself. But then he decides to get out of Ulan Bator after all.

It is not exactly an escape attempt, for Shadrach still believes there is no way ultimately of avoiding the spy-eyes of Genghis Mao. He will not try to be secretive about it: he intends even to notify the Chairman himself that he is going. No, it is more like a holiday trip, a vacation. Shadrach is going to go because of that remark of Horthy's—*some people think better when they're on the run*—and because Nikki, once again bringing up her notion that he and Genghis Mao constitute a single system, has given him some ideas. He is not sure how useful the ideas may be, and he needs to consider them at length. Perhaps he really will think better on the run. He will go, at any rate. He looks forward to the trip. It will be a diverting entertainment, and possibly instructive as well. He feels buoyant and cheerful. Shadrach the Glorious, striding splendidly from continent to continent in what may very well be the last great adventure of his life.

In the evening he visits Genghis Mao. The Khan is making his usual magnificent recovery from his latest surgery. He looks a little feverish, a trifle flushed, his keen narrow eyes unnaturally glossy, but generally he appears hale, vigorous, alert. He has spent much of the day going over the plans for the spectacular state funeral of Mangu, postponed on account of the aortal transplant and now scheduled for ten days hence. As Shadrach runs through his brisk diagnostic routines, the palpation and the auscultation and all the rest, Genghis Mao, shuffling documents and paying no attention to his physician's earnest probings, speaks with bubbling boyish enthusiasm of the great occasion. "Fifty thousand troops massed in the plaza, Shadrach! Rockets going back and forth overhead, flights of military planes, a thousand flags, six separate marching bands. Lights, color, excitement. The whole Committee on the dais under a tremendous purple-and-gold spotlight. The catafalque drawn by thirteen wild Mongol mares. Platoons of archers, a canopy of fiery arrows. An immense pyre on the very spot where Mangu fell. Teams of gymnasts who—" The Khan pauses. "You aren't going to find something new to slice out of me, are you? I don't want any more surgery just now. The funeral mustn't be postponed a second time."

"I see no reason why it should be, sir."

"Good. Good. It's going to be an event to be remembered for centuries. Whenever a great man dies, they'll talk about giving him a funeral 'as great as the funeral of Mangu.' You'll sit beside me on the dais, Shadrach. At my right hand. A special mark of my favor, and everyone will know it."

Shadrach takes a deep breath. This may be difficult.

"With your permission, sir, I intend not to be in Ulan Bator when the funeral takes place."

The imperial eyebrows lift in surprise, but only for a moment.

"Oh?" says Genghis Mao, finally.

"I want to get away for a while," Shadrach tells him. "I've been under a lot of stress lately."

"You do look pale," the Khan says dryly.

"Very tense. Very tired."

"Yes. Poor Shadrach. How devoted you are."

"You've grown much stronger since the liver transplant, sir. You won't be needing me on a day-by-day basis in the weeks just ahead. And of course I could get back to Ulan Bator in a hurry if there's any emergency."

The beady eyes study him calmly. The Khan is oddly undisturbed by Shadrach's announcement, it would seem. There is something mildly disquieting about that. Shadrach does not want to be indispensable, with all the burdens that indispensability entails, but on the other hand he wishes the Khan would *think* of him as indispensable. His only salvation now lies in indispensability.

"Where will you go?" Genghis Mao asks.

"I haven't decided that yet."

"Not even tentatively?"

"Not even tentatively. Away from here, that's all I know."

"I see. And for how long?"

"A few weeks. A month, at most."

"It will be strange, not having you at my side."

"Then I have your permission to go, sir?"

"You have my permission. Of course." The Khan smiles serenely, as if very satisifed with his own graciousness. And then a sudden mercurial shift, a darkening of the face, furrowing of the forehead, a tense fretful gleam coming into the eyes. Second thoughts? Yes. "But what if I do fall ill? Suppose I have a stroke. Suppose my heart. My stomach."

"Sir, I can return at once if—"

"It worries me, Shadrach. Not having you close by." The Khan's voice is hoarse, ragged, almost panicky now. "If organ rejection starts. If there's some intestinal obstruction. If my kidneys begin to fail. You know of trouble so soon, you react so swiftly. If—" The Khan laughs. His mood seems to be shifting again; the fears of a moment ago vanish abruptly, and a strange blank smile plays across his face. In a new, sweet voice he says, almost crooning, "Sometimes I hear voices, Shadrach, did you know that? Like the saints, like the prophets. Invisible advisers come to me. Whispering. Whispering. They always have, in time of need. To warn me, to guide me."

"Voices, sir?"

Genghis Mao blinks. "Did you say something?"

"*Voices*, I said. You were telling me that you sometimes hear voices."

"I said that? I said nothing about voices. What voices? What are you talking about, Shadrach?" Genghis Mao laughs again, a low, harsh, baffling laugh. "Voices! What madness! Well, let's not trouble ourselves with such foolishness." He cranes his neck and peers straight up at Shadrach. "So you'll be having a vacation from the old man and his complaints soon, will you?"

Shadrach is sweating. Shadrach is terrified. Is this some kind of psychotic break, or merely one of Genghis Mao's games?

"A short vacation, yes, sir," he says uncertainly.

The Chairman looks momentarily wistful. "Yes. But to miss the funeral, though—such a pity—"

"I regret that," Shadrach says. "But I do need to get away."

"Yes. Yes. By all means. Take your trip, Shadrach. If you do need to get away. If you do. Need to get away."

There. Done. Shadrach sighs. An uneasy moment or two, but he has his permission to depart.

Strange. That wasn't really so difficult at all.

May 29, 2012

Such a long face on Shadrach when he came out with the business about his vacation. Terrified of me. Afraid I'd refuse, I guess. What would he have done if I'd said no? Go anyway? He might. He seems desperate. Had that look in his eye, trapped man fighting in a corner. One must always be wary of those. Control your opponent, yes, but don't trap him in corners. Give him plenty of space. That way you give yourself plenty of space, too.

I wonder why he's going.

Tired, he said. Tense. Well, maybe so. But there's more to it than that. It has to have something to do with Avatar. Is he thinking of disappearing? He's too bright for that. Must know he can't disappear. What then? Rebelliousness? Wants to see what happens if he walks in and tells the old man he's taking off for a month to points unknown? Naturally I wouldn't refuse. Much more interesting to let him go and see what he does.

First flicker of independence poor Shadrach's ever shown. About time, too.

What if I get seriously ill while he's gone?

Heart. Liver. Lungs. Kidneys. Cerebral Hemorrhage. Pleurisy. Acute pericarditis. Toxic uremia. So fragile, so flimsy, so vulnerable this body, just chunks of meat strung together. Capable of falling apart overnight.

Mustn't worry about that. I feel fine. I feel fine. I feel fine. I am in extraordinarily good health.

I am not dependent on Shadrach Mordecai.

I am not dependent on Shadrach Mordecai.

And what if he knows some way of actually disappearing? I suppose there's at least a slight chance of that. What becomes of Avatar then? Find another donor? But I want him. Whenever I see him, I think of how

*fine his body is, how agile, how elegant. I mean to wear
that body someday, oh, yes!*

Should I therefore let him get out of my sight?

No one can get out of my sight. Right.

*Anyway, I know Shadrach. It doesn't worry me, this
trip of his. He'll go, he'll have his fling, and then he'll
come back to me. Of his own free will. He'll come back,
all right. Yes. Of his own free will.*

It is time to think of the choosing of destinations.
Shadrach can go anywhere in the world, and no
concern for the cost; he is a member of the ruling
elite, is he not, Antidote-blessed, an aristocrat in a
world of rotting plebes. But where shall he go?

He heads for Surveillance Vector One to consider
his options.

Though he has often paused before the screens of
Surveillance Vector One for a random dip into the
activities of the outer world that he calls the Trauma
Ward, this is the first time that Shadrach has actually seated himself in the imperial throne from which
the great spy-eye apparatus is controlled. Scores, perhaps hundreds, of colored buttons confront him: a
bank of red ones, a wedge of green ones, yellow, blue,
violet, orange. His hands hover above them like those
of a novice organist approaching a full keyboard for
the first time. Nothing is labeled. Is there a system?
All about the room, images whirl and flit on the
myriad screens, zipping by at unfathomable variable
rates. Shadrach pokes a green button. Has anything
been accomplished? The screens still seem random.
He covers dozens of green buttons with both palms
outstretched. Ah. Now there seems to be a detectable
pattern of response. One slice of screens high up and
to his right is showing unmistakably European cities—
Paris, London, maybe Prague, Vienna, Stockholm.
The color-coding, then, may be keyed to continents.

Leaving the green keys depressed, Shadrach punches
a bunch of orange ones. A systematic search through
the whirling madness of the blinking screens shows
him, eventually, a bloc of North American scenery

far to his left—glimpses of Los Angeles, surely, and New York, and Chicago, Boston, Pittsburgh. So. Yes.

Half an hour of patient, absorbing work and he has mastered the system: he is a quick study. Violet is Africa, yellow is Asia, red is Latin America, and so on. He discovers, also, that there are certain master buttons—the red of red, so to speak, the blue of blues— which, when punched, wipe from the screens all data on continents other than the one covered by keys of that color, so that one need not contend with the crazy oversufficiency of information that the whole of Surveillance Vector One is capable of supplying. He learns, also, how to summon images of particular cities: the keys within each color group are arranged in a geographical analogue of their actual positions, and by activating a screen at his left elbow he can call for maps, divided into grids that show him which buttons to push. And then he systematically examines the Trauma Ward to see where he wants to go.

The famous cities of the world, yes. The ancient capitals. Rome? Of course. He punches for it. The Colosseum flashes by, the Forum, the Spanish Steps. Yes. And Jerusalem, yes, one glimpse is enough. He considers Egypt and punches for Cairo, but rejects it when he sees the beggars shambling about the base of the Great Pyramid, their blind eyes crusted with swarming flies. He has heard rumors about Egypt, and they seem to be true: organ-rot does not frighten him, but he has no antidotes for that ghastly trachoma, for the endemic bilharziasis, for the thousand other Cairene plagues that the screens show him. The healer in him might be willing enough to go to Eygpt for a laying on of hands, a spraying on of medicines, but this is meant to be a holiday, he is going abroad not as a doctor but as an anti-doctor, and he shies from that challenge. No Egypt. But he chooses Istanbul after a view of the plump mosques rising from the hills; he picks London; bypasses his native Philadelphia and, with a shudder, New York; elects San Francisco; and finally Peking. The grand tour. The great adventure.

He sleeps alone that night, and for a change he

sleeps well, as if the prospect of world-girdling travel has perversely calmed his restless spirit. Before dawn he awakens, does some perfunctory calisthenics, packs quickly, taking little with him. The green face of the data screen tells him it is

FRIDAY
1 June
2012

He does not bother with farewells. Just as the sun breaks the horizon he summons a car and is taken to the airport.

June 1, 2012
I did tell him about the voices after all. Despite earlier resolves. Should I have told him? But he didn't take me seriously. Do I take me seriously? Do I take them seriously? Perhaps they are symptoms of some grave mental disorder. But were the saints mad too, then? The voices whisper to me. They have always come to me in times of crisis. During the Virus War I heard them most clearly. One voice said, I am Temujin Genghis Khan, and you are my son, and you shall be Genghis II. A voice of thunder, though he only whispered. And I am Mao, another voice said, smooth as silk. You are my son, Mao said, and you shall be Mao II. But we had already had a Mao II, nasty little coward, completely destroyed his country with his idiocies, and there was even a Mao III, briefly, during the days just before the outbreak of the Virus War, so I answered Mao, I told him he was behind the times, it was too late for me to be Mao II, I must become Mao IV. He understood. So they blessed me and anointed me. Genghis II Mao IV, I became. So my voices dubbed and ordained and anointed me. And they have guided me. Is it a sign of schizoid disturbance to hear disembodied voices? It could be. Am I schizoid, then? Very well, I am schizoid. But I am also Genghis II Mao IV, and I rule the world.

20

No flights are due to depart that morning, Shadrach learns, for Jerusalem, Istanbul, Rome, or any plausible connecting points to those destinations. There is a flight to Peking soon, but Peking is too close to Ulan Bator and Chinese look too much like Mongols; just now he needs a total change of scene. There is a flight a little later on to San Francisco, but San Francisco is awkwardly placed in respect to the rest of his itinerary. And there is a flight leaving almost immediately for Nairobi. Somehow Shadrach had not considered going to Nairobi at all, nor any other black African city, despite the vaguely felt ancestral ties. But spontaneity, he tells himself, is good for the soul. Right at this moment the idea of going to Nairobi seems oddly appealing. Impulsively, unhesitatingly, he boards the plane.

He has not left Mongolia for two and a half years, not since the time Genghis Mao unexpectedly decided to preside in person over a vast and meaningless Committee congress being held at the dilapidated old United Nations headquarters in New York. Shadrach was not yet the Khan's personal physician then—a shrewd, diplomatic Portuguese internist named Tcixeira had that job—but Teixeira was placidly dying of leukemia and Shadrach was being phased in slowly as his replacement. Ostensibly Shadrach went to New York as a mere junior medic, a spear carrier in the Khan's huge retinue, but when Genghis Mao came down with a hypertensive attack after delivering a six-hour harangue from the podium of the former General Assembly chamber, it was Shadrach who coped with the problem while Teixeira lay doped and useless in his suite. Genghis Mao, having subsequently invented Mangu to handle such ceremonial chores as Committee congresses, had stayed close to Ulan Bator ever since. So has Shadrach. But now he finds himself watching through the porthole of a supersonic transport plane as the bleak Mongol steppe rapidly retreats far below. In just a few hours he will be in Africa.

Africa! Already the telemetered signals from Genghis Mao blur and fade as Shadrach approaches the thousand-kilometer boundary. He still picks up data, feeble clicks and bleats and pops out of the implant system, but as the plane streaks southwestward it becomes harder and harder for Shadrach to translate them into comprehensible analogues of the Chairman's bodily processes: Genghis Mao, his kidneys and liver and pancreas, his heart and lungs, his arteries, his intestines, have become remote, are becoming unreal. And soon the signals are gone altogether, dropping below the threshold and leaving Shadrach suddenly, amazingly, alone in his own body. That crash of silence! That absence of subliminal input! He had forgotten what it was like, not to have those steady burbling pulses of information flowing through his consciousness, and in the first moments after leaving telemeter range he feels almost bereft, as if he has lost one of his major senses. Then the inner silence begins to seem normal and he relaxes.

The plane is comfortable—a wide rump-gripping cushion of a seat, plenty of leg room. Probably it is about twenty years old; certainly it is pre-Virus War. Many industries have disappeared since the War, and the aircraft industry is one of them. The greatly reduced postwar population can easily make do, given a proper maintenance program, with the planes it inherited from the crowded, hectic world of the 1980s, when the old industrial economy was going through its last great period of convulsive expansion amid, paradoxically, dreadful shortages and dislocations. Not that the War and the organ-rot have brought an end to technological progress: in Shadrach's time fusion power has rescued the world from its energy crisis, subterrene borers have created an entirely new mass-transit-tunnel system for most urban areas, communications systems have become immensely sophisticated, the computerization of civilization has been well-nigh completed, and so on. Progress continues. Things are different but not utterly different. Even corporations and stock exchanges have survived. There has not been a total break with the old days, merely because two thirds of the former population has perished and a wholly new quasi-dictatorial political structure has been imposed upon the remnant. But this is a contracting society, daily diminished by the inroads of organ-rot and oppressed by a certain sense of stagnation and futility that the regime of Genghis Mao does not appear to know how to dispel, and such a society does not need new jet transports while the old ones still can fly.

June 1, continued
If the ruler of the world is schizoid, doesn't this have serious consequences for his subjects? I think not. I've studied history closely. Throughout all of history people have gotten the rulers they deserved, the appropriate rulers. A sovereign mirrors the spirit of his times and expresses the deepest traits of his people. Hitler, Napoleon, Attila, Augustus, Ch'in Shih Huang Ti, Genghis Khan, Robespierre: none of them accidents or anomalies, all of them organic outgrowths of the needs of the time. Even when a ruler imposes his will by conquest, as I have not, the historical imperative is at work: those people wanted to be conquered, needed to be conquered, or they would not have fallen to him. So too now. Schizoid times demand schizoid government. The people of the world are dying lingering deaths of organ-rot; an antidote exists but we do not put it into widespread distribution; the people of the world accept this situation. I define that as madness. A mad government, then, for a mad citizenry, a government that offers promises of antidotes but never delivers. Of course there isn't enough of the Antidote to go around. But there's some to spare.

We do not give priority to expanding the supply. We offer hope but no injections, and this somehow sustains our subjects. Madness. A world that destroys itself with cloud-borne antigens is mad; one that gives itself over to an oligarchy of strangers is mad; fitting then that the oligarchs themselves are mad.

But are we? Am I? I have done more research into the symptoms of schizophrenia this morning, consulting Shadrach's medical library in Shadrach's absence. Here I have a text that says that two of the most common symptoms are delusions and hallucinations. "A delusion," I am told, "is a persistently held belief, contrary to reality as it is perceived by most people, that is not dispelled by logical arguments. Delusions in schizophrenia often have a grandiose or a persecutory theme: the individual may express a belief that he is Jesus Christ or that he is the object of a worldwide search by a supersecret organization." I have never expressed the belief that I am Jesus Christ. I do frequently believe with great conviction that I am Genghis II Mao IV Khan. Is this belief delusive? I believe that this belief is congruent with reality as it is perceived by most people. I believe that my belief in this belief is founded in reality. I believe I genuinely am Genghis II Mao IV Khan, or that at least I have genuinely become Genghis II Mao IV Khan, and that therefore this belief is not schizophrenic, not delusive. On the other hand, I also believe I am in imminent danger of assassination, that there is a worldwide conspiracy against my life. Classic schizoid delusion? But Mangu is really dead. They pushed Mangu from a window seventy-five stories above the ground. Do I imagine Mangu's death? Mangu is really dead. Do I misconstrue it? I know there are those who believe he committed suicide. This is delusive. Mangu was murdered. They might come for me at any time. Despite all my precautions. Am I deluded? Then I accept my delusions. As appropriate to my position in history. And if the danger is real, how wise of me to have barricaded myself behind the interfaces!

Let us go on. Hallucinations. "A hallucination is a perception of sight, sound, smell, or touch that is not 'real.' In schizophrenia, hallucinations most frequently

take the form of voices." Aha! *"A patient may be tor-
mented by voices ordering him to jump out of a window or accusing him of heinous crimes."* What's this
about windows? Could Mangu have been schizoid too?
No. No. It doesn't apply. Mangu wasn't intelligent enough
to be schizoid. I'm the one who hears voices, and my
voices don't advise lunacy. *"Sometimes the hallucination consists only of noises or isolated words, or the
patient may seem to 'hear his thoughts.' Other hallucinations include frightening visions, strange smells, and
odd bodily sensations."*

I think this applies. If so, I accept it freely. But
there's more. *"Delusions and hallucinations are not
limited to schizophrenia,"* it says. *"They may occur in
a wide range of organic conditions (e.g., infections of
the brain substance or a decreased flow of blood to the
brain caused by arteriosclerosis)."* Is that the explanation? When Father Genghis whispers to me, it's nothing but a bug in my cerebellum? When Mao whispers in
my ears, it's merely a clotted artery? I should speak to
Shadrach about this when he returns. He worries about
my arteries. He might want to do another transplant.
After all, I still have some of my own original blood
vessels, and they're getting old. I'm what, eighty-seven
years old? Eighty-nine, ninety-three? Yes, perhaps ninety-
three. So hard to keep the numbers straight. But old,
very old.

Great Father Genghis, am I old!

In Nairobi the air is clear, dry, cool, not at all
tropical although the city is only a degree or so from
the equator, just about the same latitude, indeed, as
fiery Cotopaxi and ravaged Quito. Quito, high in
mountainous country, was cool also, but that was
only a dream, a transtemporal illusion. Whereas
Shadrach actually is, so far as anything is actual, in
Nairobi. "We are much above sea level," explains the
taxi driver. "It is never too hot here." The taxi man is
hearty, outgoing, talkative: a Kikuyu, he says, this
being his tribe. He wears huge dark sunglasses and a
blue uniform that looks fifty years old. He seems
healthy, although Shadrach had been half expecting

to find everyone outside Ulan Bator afflicted with organ-rot. "I speak six languages," the driver announces. "Kikuyu, Masai, Swahili, German, French, English. You are British from England?"

"American," Shadrach says, though the label sounds odd in his ears. What else is he to answer, though? Mongol?

"American? Ah! New York? Los Angeles? Once we had plenty Americans here. Before the big death, you know? That plane they come in, it was big, too big, it was always full, all those Americans! They come to see the animals, you know? Out in the bush. With cameras. Not any more. Long time, no Americans here. No anybody here." He laughs. "Different times, now. Too bad, these times. Except for the animals. Good times for the animals. You see, there, by the road? Hyena. Right by the road!"

Yes, Shadrach sees: a lumpy, sinister beast, like a small ungainly bear, squatting at the edge of the highway. The driver tells him that there are wild animals everywhere now, ostriches strutting down Nairobi's main streets, lions and cheetahs preying on the suburban farmers, gazelles moving in huge fluttery herds across the university campus. "Because there are not enough people now," he says. "And most of them too sick. Not much hunting now. Last week, big elephant, ripped up thorn tree in front of New Stanley Hotel. Very old thorn tree, very famous. Very big elephant." Of course. With the world's population cut back now to early nineteenth-century levels, the animals would be starting to reclaim their domain. The Virus War had left them unscathed, even the primates closest to man: only the unlucky human chromosomes could harbor the rot.

On the way to the city he sees more animals, two stunning zebras, some wart-hogs, and a group of heavy-humped spindle-shanked antelopes; these are wildebeests, the driver informs him. It pleases Shadrach to observe this resurgence of nature, but the pleasure is tainted by sadness, for if wildebeests graze on the margins of great highways and grass grows in

city streets, it is because the time of man is coming
to its end, and Shadrach is not ready for that.

Actually not much grass is growing in the streets of
Nairobi, at least not on the broad, elegant boulevard
on which the taxi enters town. Flowering shrubs erupt
in beauty on all sides. After monochromatic Ulan
Bator, Nairobi is a visual delight. Bougainvillea, red
and purple and orange, cascades over every wall;
some creeping succulent with densely packed lavender blossoms carpets the islands in the roadway;
thick, many-tentacled aloe trees stand like sentinels
at streetcorners; he recognizes hibiscus and jacaranda,
but most of the bushes and trees that fill the streets
with such gaudy masses of color are unknown to
him. The effect is gay and sparkling and unexpectedly moving: who could feel despair, he wonders, in
a world that offers such intensity of beauty? But in
that moment of transcendent joy that the glowing
flowers of neatly manicured Nairobi create comes its
own instant negation, for Shadrach asks himself also
how, having been turned loose in this beautiful world,
we could have contrived to make such a woeful mess
out of so much of it. Nevertheless this serendipitous
city inspires more pleasure than gloom in him.

Through flowery sun-loved Nairobi rides Shadrach
Mordecai in an old rump-sprung taxi to his hotel, the
Hilton, an aging cavernous place where he may well
be the only guest. The hotel staff treats him with
extraordinary deference, as though he is some visit-
ing prince. In a way he is, to these people. They know
he lives at the capital and travels on a PRC passport;
probably they conclude from that that he must sit at
the right hand of Genghis Mao, which in truth he
does, though he is not a part of the government at
all. Yet even those who have not seen his passport
regard him with awe, here. They pause at their work
in corridors, and turn and look. They whisper among
themselves. They nod, they point. Shadrach is re-
minded again of what he tends often to forget: that
he is a man of great presence and dignity, capable
and self-assured and of striking physical appearance,
who radiates an aura that leads others to defer to

him. It is hard, living in the shadow of Genghis Mao, to remember that one is a person oneself, even a considerable person, and not merely an extension of the Chairman. In Nairobi he learns it anew.

Strolling about the city half an hour after checking in, he makes another discovery of the obvious: everyone here is black. Almost everyone, at any rate. He notices a few Chinese shopkeepers, a couple of Indians, a few elderly whites, but they are exceptions, and they stand out as clearly as he does in Ulan Bator. Why should the negritude here surprise him? This is Africa; this is where people are black. And it was the same, really, when he was a boy in Philadelphia— whites rarely ventured into his neighborhood, and at least in early childhood it was easy for him to assume that the ghetto was the world, that black was the norm, that those occasional creatures with pink faces and blue eyes and loose, lank hair were freakish rarities, like the giraffes in his picture book. But this is no ghetto. It is a nation, a universe, where the policemen and the schoolteachers and the Committee delegates and the firemen are black, the engineers at the fusion plant are black, the brain surgeons and the optometrists are black, black through and through. Brothers and sisters everywhere, and yet he is apart from them, he feels not kinship but surprise at the universality of the blackness. Possibly he has lived in Mongolia too long. Living in that polyglot multiracial amalgam that surrounds Genghis Mao, he has lost some degree of his own racial identity; and, living amid millions of Mongols, he has developed some heightened sense of himself as outsider, as freak, that leaves him alienated even among his own kind. If these people, speakers of Swahili, intimates of ostrich and cheetah, bloodlines undiluted by slavemaster genes, can be said to be his own kind.

He discovers yet another obviousness: that Nairobi is not just beautiful boulevards and clear vibrant air, not just bowers of bougainvillea and hibiscus. This place is, however lovely it may be, still very much a part of the Trauma Ward, and he does not need to walk far from the precincts of his hotel to find the sufferers. They straggle through the streets, scores of them, in all phases of the disease, some merely pallid and sluggish, showing the first bafflement at the on-rushing crumbling of their bodies, and some bowed and shrunken and dazed, some already hemorrhaging, dizzy with pain and flecked with the shiny sweat of imminent death. Those in the late stages travel in solitary orbits, each shambling alone through the streets, God knows why, struggling with incomprehensible determination to reach some unattainable destination before the final breakdown overtakes them. Often the organ-rot victims pause and stare at Shadrach, as if they know he is immune and want from him some gift of strength, some charismatic infusion that will clothe them in the same immunity, that will heal their lesions and make their bodies whole. But there is nothing particularly reproachful or envious in their gaze: it is the calm, steady, equable look that one sometimes gets from grazing cattle, unreadable but not threatening, with no hint in it that they hold you guilty of the slaughterhouse.

At first Shadrach cannot meet that level stare. He was taught, long ago, that a doctor must be able to look at a patient without feeling apologetic for his own good health, but this is a different case. They are not his patients, and he is healthy only because his political connections give him access to protection they cannot have. He is curious about organ-rot—it is the great medical phenomenon of the age, the latter-day Black Death, the most terrible plague in history, and he studies its effects wherever he encounters them—but neither his curiosity nor his medical detachment is enough to let him look straight at these people. He gives them only darting sidewise glances until he realizes that his feelings of guilt are irrelevant. These lurching wrecks don't care if he looks at them. They are beyond caring about anything. They are dying, right out here in public; their bellies are ablaze, their minds are fogged; what does it matter to them if some stranger stares? They look at him; he looks at them. Invisible barriers screen him from them.

Then the barriers are breached. Shadrach turns away momentarily from the procession of the damned to investigate the window of a curio shop—grotesque wood carvings, zebra-skin drums, elephant's-foot ashtrays, Masai spears and shields, all manner of native artifacts mass-produced for the tourists who no longer come—and someone gives his elbow a sharp stinging blow. He whirls, instantly on guard. The only person at all near him is a small withered old man, chalky-skinned, rag-clad, white-haired, fleshless, who is moving back and forth in front of him in an erratic semicircle, making little harsh clicking noises deep in his throat.

A terminal case. Eyes blotched and dim, belly distended. The disease eats slowly through epithelial tissue, indiscriminately ulcerating any flesh in its path; the lucky ones are those whose vital organs are pierced quickly, but only a few are lucky. Eighteen years have passed since the Virus War launched the organ-rot upon mankind; Shadrach has read that many who were infected in the first onslaught are still waiting for the end to come. This man looks like one of those eighteen-year cases, but he can't have long to wait now. Every interior mechanism must be seared and corroded; he must be nothing but a mass of holes held together by frail ropes of living fabric, and the next erosion, wherever it strikes, will surely be fatal.

He seems to want Shadrach's attention, but he is unable to come to a halt in the proper place. Like a robot with rusty contacts he keeps overshooting, going by Shadrach in jerky convulsive motions, stopping, clashing internal gears, pivoting with a wild flapping of slack dangling arms, coming back for another try. At last on one desperate pass he succeeds in clapping his hand around Shadrach's forearm and anchors himself that way, standing close by him, leaning on him, rocking gently in place.

Shadrach does not pull away. If he can do no more for this maimed creature than give him support, he will at least do that.

In a terrible apocalyptic caw of a voice, a sort of

whispered shriek, the old man says something to him
that appears to be of high importance.

"I'm sorry," Shadrach murmurs. "I can't understand you."

The old man leans closer, straining to reach his
face up to Shadrach's, and repeats his words with
even greater urgency.

"But I don't speak Swahili," Shadrach says sadly.
"Is that Swahili? I don't understand."

The old man searches for a word, wrinkled lips
moving, throat bobbing, face taut with concentration.
There is a sweet, dry odor about him, the odor of
faded lilies. A lesion in one cheek seems nearly to go
completely through the flesh from inside to out; probably he could thrust the tip of his tongue through it.

"Dead," the old man says finally, in English, delivering the word like a monstrous weight that he drops
at Shadrach's feet.

"Dead?"

"Dead. You—make—me—dead—"

The words fall one after another from the ravaged
throat without expression, without inflection, without emphasis. *You. Make. Me. Dead.* Is he accusing
me of having given him the disease, Shadrach wonders, or is he asking for euthanasia?

"Dead! You! Make! Me! Dead!" Then more Swahili.
Then some strained rheumy coughs. Then tears, amazingly copious, flooding in deep channels down the
dusty cheeks. The hand that grips Shadrach's forearm tightens with sudden incredible strength, crushing bone against bone and wringing a sharp yelp of
pain from him. Then the unexpected pressure is
withdrawn; the old man stands free for a moment,
tottering; from him comes a hoarse clucking noise,
an unmistakable death rattle, and life leaves him so
instantly and completely that Shadrach has a quasi-
hallucinatory vision of a skull and bones within the
old man's tattered clothes. As the body falls Shadrach
catches it and eases it to the pavement. It weighs no
more than forty kilos, he guesses.

What now? Notify the authorities? Which authorities? Shadrach looks about for a Citpol, but the street,

busy a few minutes ago, is mysteriously empty. He
feels responsible for the body. He can't simply abandon it where it dropped. He enters the curio shop to
find a telephone.

The proprietor is a sleek, plump Indian, sixty years
old or so, with large liquid eyes and thick dark silver-
flecked hair. He wears an old-fashioned business suit
and looks dapper and prosperous. Evidently he has
witnessed the little curbside drama, for he bustles
forward now, palms pressed together, lips clamped in
a fussy oh-dear expression.

"How regrettable!" he declares. "That you should
be troubled in this way! They have no decency, they
have no sense of—"

"It was no trouble," Shadrach says quietly. "The
man was dying. He didn't have time to think about
decency."

"Even so. To importune a stranger, a visitor to
our—"

Shadrach shakes his head. "It's all right. Whatever
he wanted from me, I couldn't provide it, and now
he's dead. I wish I could have helped. I'm a doctor,"
he confides, hoping the disclosure will have the right
effect.

It does. "Ah!" the shopkeeper cries. "Then you understand these things." The sensibilities of doctors
are not like those of ordinary beings. It no longer
embarrasses the proprietor that one of his shabby
countrymen has had the poor taste to inflict his death
on a tourist.

"What shall we do about the body?" Shadrach
asks.

"The Citpols will come. Word gets around."

"I thought we might telephone someone."

A shrug. "The Citpols will come. There is no
importance. The disease is not contagious, I understand. That is, we are all infected from the days of
the War, but we have nothing to fear from those who
display actual symptoms. Or from their bodies. Is
this not true?"

"It's true, yes," Shadrach says. He glances uncomfortably at the small sprawled corpse, lying like a

discarded blanket on the sidewalk outside the store. "Perhaps we ought to phone anyway, though."

"The Citpols will come shortly," the shopkeeper says again, as if dismissing the subject. "Will you have tea with me? I rarely have the opportunity to entertain a visitor. I am Bhishma Das. You are American?"

"I was born there, yes. I live abroad now."

"Ah."

Das busies himself behind the counter, where he has a hotplate and some packets of tea. His indifference to the body on the street continues to distress Shadrach; but Das does not seem to be an unintelligent or insensitive man. Perhaps it is the custom, out here in the Trauma Ward, to pay as little attention as possible to these reminders of the universal mortality.

In any event Das is right: the Citpols do indeed arrive swiftly, three black-skinned men in the standard uniforms, riding in a long somber hearselike vehicle. Two of them load the body into the car; the third peers through the shop window, staring long and intently at Shadrach and nodding to himself in an unfathomable, oddly disturbing way. The Citpols finally drive away.

Das says, "We will all die of the organ-rot sooner or later, is this not true? We and our children as well? We are all infected, they say. Is this not true?"

"True, yes," Shadrach replies. Even he carries the killer DNA enmeshed in his genes. Even Genghis Mao. "Of course, there's the Antidote—"

"The antidote. Ah. Do you believe there is indeed an antidote?"

Shadrach blinks. "You doubt it?"

"I have no certain knowledge of these things. The Chairman says there is an antidote, and that it will soon be given to the people. But the people continue to die. Ah, the tea is ready! Is there, then, an antidote? I have no idea. I am not sure what to believe."

"There is an antidote," says Shadrach, accepting a delicate porcelain cup from the merchant. "Yes, truly there is. And one day it will be given to all the people."

"You know this to be fact?"

"I know it, yes."

"You are a doctor. You would know."

"Yes."

"Ah," Bhishma Das says, and sips his tea. After a long pause he says, "Of course, many of us will die of the rot before the antidote is given. Not only those who lived in the days of the War, but even our children. How can this be? I have never understood this. My health is excellent, my sons are strong—and yet we carry the plague within us too? It sleeps within us, waiting its moment? It sleeps within everyone?"

"Everyone," Shadrach says. How can he explain? If he talks of the structural similarities between the organ-rot virus and the normal human genetic material, if he describes how the virus liberated during the long-ago war was capable of integrating itself into the nucleic acid, into the germ plasm itself, becoming so intimately entwined with the human genetic machinery that it is passed from generation to generation with normal cellular genes, a deadly packet of DNA that can turn lethal at any time, how much of this will Bhishma Das comprehend? Can Shadrach speak of the inextricability of the lethal genetic material, the inexorable way in which it must be incorporated into the genetic endowment of any child conceived since the Virus War, and get the meaning across? The intrusive organ-rot gene has become as intimate a part of the human heritage as the gene that puts hair on the scalp or the one that puts calcium in the bones: our tissues now are automatically programmed at birth to deteriorate and slough off when some unknown inner signal is given. But to Bhishma Das this may be as baffling as the dreams of Brahma. Shadrach says at last, after a moment's pause, "Everyone who was alive when they turned the virus loose absorbed it into his body, into the part of his body that determines what he transmits to his children. It can't be eradicated once it enters that part. And so we pass the virus along to our sons and daughters the way we do the color of our skins, the color of our eyes, the texture of our hair—"

"A dreadful legacy. How sad. And the antidote, Doctor? Would the antidote free us from this legacy?"

"The antidote they have now," Shadrach says, "keeps the virus from having a harmful effect on the body. It neutralizes it, stabilizes it, holds it in a state of latency. You follow me?"

"Yes, yes, I understand. In the deep freeze!"

"So to speak. Those who receive the antidote have to take a new dose every six months, at present. To hold the virus in check, to keep the organ-rot from breaking out in them."

"More tea, Doctor?"

"Please."

"You have received this antidote yourself?"

Shadrach replies uneasily, after a moment's consideration, "Yes. I have."

"Ah. Because you are a doctor. Because we must keep the healers alive. I understand. It seemed to me you must have the antidote. There is something about you; you are like a man apart from us. You do not wake up every day wondering if this is the day when the rot will start in you. Ah. And someday we will have the antidote too."

"Yes. Someday. The government is working on increasing the supply." The lie sours his mouth. "I wish you could have your first injection today."

"It is not important for me," Das says calmly. "I am old and I have enjoyed good health, and my life has been a happy one even in the most troubled times. If the rot begins in me tomorrow, I will be ready for it. But my sons, and the sons of my sons, I would spare them. What do old wars mean to them? Why should they die horrible deaths for the sake of nations that were forgotten before they were born? I want them to live. My family has been in Kenya for a hundred fifty years, since we first came from Bombay, and we have been happy here, and why should we perish now? Sad, Doctor, sad. This curse on mankind. Will we ever cleanse ourselves of what we have done to ourselves?"

Shadrach shrugs. There is no way to comb the murderous new gene out of the genetic package; but in theory a permanent antidote is possible, a hybrid DNA that can be integrated into the contaminated genes to absorb or detoxify the lethal genetic material. Somewhere in the PRC organization they are at work on such an antidote, Shadrach has been told. Of course, the rumor may be false. The research group may be only a myth. The permanent antidote itself may be only a myth.

He says, "I think these last twenty years have been a purge that mankind necessarily had to undergo. A punishment for accumulated idiocies and foolishness, perhaps. The whole history of the twentieth century is like an arrow pointing straight to the Virus War and its aftermath. But I believe we'll survive the ordeal."

"And things will be again as they once were?"

Shadrach smiles. "I hope not. If we go back to where we were, we'll only arrive again eventually at the same place we've reached now. And we may not survive the next version of the Virus War. No, I think we'll build a better world out of the ruins, a quieter, less greedy world. It'll take time. I'm not sure how we're going to accomplish it. Many bad things will happen first. Millions will die needless, horrible deaths. But eventually—eventually—the suffering will be over, the dying will be done, and those who remain will live in happiness again."

"How refreshing to hear such optimism."

"Am I an optimist? I've never thought of myself that way. A realist, maybe. But not an optimist. How strange suddenly to find myself an apostle of faith and good cheer!"

"Your eyes were glowing when you said what you said. You were already living in that better world as you spoke. Do you want to withdraw your prophecy? Please, no. You believe that that happier world will come."

"I hope it'll come," Shadrach says soberly.

"You know it will."

"I'm not sure. Perhaps I sounded sure a moment

ago, but—" He shakes his head. He makes a determined effort to recapture that unexpected strain of positive thinking that had come so surprisingly from him a moment ago. "Yes," he says. "Things *will* get better." Already there is something forced about it, but he goes on. "No trend continues downward forever. The organ-rot can be defeated. The smaller population that exists now will be able to live comfortably in a world that couldn't support the numbers of people who lived before the War. Yes. A purge, an ordeal by fire, a necessary corrective to old abuses, leading to better things. Dawn after the long darkness."

"Ah. You *are* an optimist!"

"Perhaps I am. Sometimes."

"I would like to see a man like you as the leader of that new world," Bhishma Das exclaims rapturously.

Shadrach recoils. "No, not me. Let me live in that world, yes. But don't ask me to govern it."

"You will change your mind when the moment comes. They will offer you the government, Doctor, because you are wise and good, and you will accept. Because you are wise and good." Das pours more tea. His naive faith is touching. Shadrach takes a sip; then he has a sudden morbid vision of Bhishma Das, a year or two from now, crying out in surprise and delight as the new Chairman of the Permanent Revolutionary Committee appears for the first time on his television screen, and the face of the new Chairman is the finely wrought brown-skinned face of that wise and good American doctor who once visited his store. Shadrach coughs and sputters and nearly spills his cup. The face will be the face of Dr. Mordecai, yes, but the mind behind the warm searching eyes will be the cold dark mind of Genghis Mao. Shadrach has almost managed to forget Project Avatar, this day in Nairobi. Almost.

"I should be going," Shadrach says. "It's late in the day. You'll want to close the shop."

"Stay awhile. There is no hurry." Then: "I invite you to my home for dinner this evening."

"I'm afraid I can't—"

"Another engagement? Oh, how regrettable. We

would provide a fine curry in your honor. We would open a fine wine. Some close friends—the most stimulating members of the Hindu community, professional people, teachers, philosophers—intelligent conversation—ah, yes, yes, a delightful evening, if you would grace our home!"

A temptation. Shadrach will dine alone, otherwise, at his hotel, a stranger in this strange city, lonely and in peril. But no: impossible. One of those stimulating Hindu professional persons will surely ask him where he lives, what kind of doctoring he does, and either he must lie, which is repugnant to him, or he must let it all spill out—member of privileged dictatorial elite, physician to the terrifying Genghis Mao, etc., etc., and so much for his new reputation as a humanitarian benefactor: the truth about him will sicken the friends of Bhishma Das and humiliate poor Das himself. Shadrach mumbles sincere-sounding excuses and regrets. As he edges to the door, Das follows him, saying, "At least accept a gift from me, a remembrance of this charming hour." The merchant glances hastily about his shelves, searching among the spears, the beaded necklaces, the wooden statuettes, everything apparently too crude, too flimsy, too inexpensive, or too awkwardly large to make a fitting offering for such a distinguished guest, and it seems for an instant that Shadrach will get out of the place ungifted; but at the last moment Das snatches up a small antelope horn in which a hole has been drilled at the pointed end and plugged with wax. A cupping horn, Das explains, used by a tribe near the southern border to draw pain and evil spirits from the bodies of the sick: one applies the cup to the skin, sucks, creates a vacuum, seals it with the wax plug. He urges it on Shadrach, saying it is an appropriate gift for a healer, and Shadrach, after a conventional show of reluctance, accepts gladly. He has no East African medical devices in his collection. "They still use these," Das informs him. "They use them very much just now, to draw forth the organ-rot spirit." He bows Shadrach from the store, telling him again and again

what an honor his visit has been, what pleasure has
come from hearing the doctor's words of hope.

On the seven-block journey back to the hotel
Shadrach counts four dead bodies in the streets, and
one that is not quite dead, but will be soon.

21

In the morning he flies onward, toward Jerusalem.
He is aware of the curve of the planet below him, the
enormous belly of the world, and he is amazed anew
by its complexity, its richness, this globe that holds
Athens and Samarkand, Lhasa and Rangoon, Timbuktu, Benares, Chartres, Ghent, all the fascinating
works of vanishing mankind, and all the natural
wonders, the Grand Canyon, the Amazon, the Himalayas, the Sahara—so much, so much, for one small
cosmic lump, such variety, such magnificent multi-
tudinousness. And it is all his, for whatever time
remains before Genghis Mao calls upon him to yield
up the world and go.

He is not, like Bhishma Das, ready to go whenever
his marching orders arrive. The world, now that he is
again out in the midst of it, seems very beautiful, and
he has seen so little of it. There are mountains to
climb, rivers to cross, wines to taste. He who has been
spared from organ-rot does not want to succumb to
another man's lust for immortality. Shadrach's pas-
sivity has fallen from him: he does not accept the
fate in store for him. Bhishma Das called him an
optimist, a wise and good man whose face glows
when he speaks of the better days that are coming,

and though that was not how Shadrach had ever
seen himself, he is pleased that Das saw him that
way, pleased that those unexpectedly hopeful words
tumbled from his lips. It is agreeable to be thought
of as a man of sunny spirit, to be a source of hope
and faith. He tries the image on and likes the fit. It is
a little like smiling when one is not in a smiling
mood, and feeling the smile work its way inward
from the facial muscles to the soul: why *not* smile,
why *not* live in the hope of a glorious resurrection? It
costs nothing. It makes others happier. If one is proven
wrong, as no doubt one will be, one has at least had
the reward of having dwelled for a time in a warm
little sphere of inner light rather than in dank dark
despair.

But it is hard to put much conviction into one's
optimism when the threat of immediate doom hangs
over one. I must deal somehow with the problem of
Project Avatar, Shadrach resolves.

December 8, 2001
*So I am not to suffer the organ-rot after all. Today I
had my first dose of Roncevic's drug. They say that if
your smears have shown no trace of the virus in its
active state before your first injection, you are safe, but
the antidote can do nothing for you if the thing has
already entered into the lethal phase. My smears were
clean: I am safe. I never doubted that I would be
spared. I was not meant to perish in the Virus War, but
rather to endure, to survive the general holocaust and
enter into my own true time. Which now has come.
"You will live a hundred years," Roncevic said to me
this morning. Does he mean a hundred more years? Or
a hundred all told? In which case I have only about
twenty-five years left. Not enough, not enough.*

*No matter what, I'll outlive poor Roncevic. He has
the rot already. It glistens and glazes in his belly. How
hard he worked to develop his drug, how eager he was
to save himself! But not in time. The disease went
active in him too soon, and he will go. He goes, I stay:
he plays his appointed role in the drama and leaves the
stage. While I live on, perhaps another hundred years.*

My physical vitality has always been extraordinary. No doubt my bodily energies are of a superior order, for here I am, past seventy, with the vigor of a young man. Resisting disease, deflecting fatigue. They say that Chairman Mao, when he was past seventy, swam eight miles in the Yangtze in an hour and five minutes. Swimming is of no interest to me; yet I know that if there were need, I could swim ten miles in those sixty-five minutes. I could swim twenty.

Jerusalem is colder than Shadrach expects—almost as chilly as Ulan Bator on this late spring morning—and smaller, too, amazingly compact for a place where so much history has been made. He settles in at the International, a sprawling old mid-twentieth-century hotel stunningly located high on the Mount of Olives. From his balcony he has a superb view of the old walled city. Awe and excitement rise in him as he looks out upon it. Those two great glittering domes down there—his map tells him the huge gold one is the Dome of the Rock, on the site of Solomon's Temple, and the silver one is the Aqsa Mosque—and that formidable battlemented wall, and the ancient stone towers, and the tangle of winding streets, all speak to him of human endurance, of the slow steady tides of history, the arrivals and departures of monarchs and empires. The city of Abraham and Isaac, of David and Solomon, the city Nebuchadnezzar destroyed and Nehemiah rebuilt, the city of the Maccabees, of Herod, the city where Jesus suffered and died and rose from the dead, the city where Mohammed, in a vision, ascended into heaven, the city of the Crusaders, the city of legend, of fantasy, of pilgrimages, of conquests, of layer upon layer of event, layers deeper and more intricate than those of Troy—that little city of low buildings of tawny stone just across the swooping valley from him counsels him that apocalyptic hours are followed by rebirth and reconstruction, that no disaster is eternal. The mood that came upon him when he was with Bhishma Das has survived the journey out of Africa. Jerusalem is truly a city of light, a city of joy. He remembers his hymn-singing great-aunts Ellie and Hattie clapping their hands and chanting—

> Jerusalem, my happy home
> When shall I come to thee?
> When shall my sorrows have an end?
> Thy joys when shall I see?

—and suddenly he is again a boy of six or seven, wearing tight blue trousers and a starched white shirt, standing between those two colossal black women in their Sunday finery, singing with them, clapping his hands, humming or making up words where he does not know the right ones, oh, yes, Jerusalem, Jerusalem, lead me unto Jerusalem, Lord! That promised land, long ago, far away, that city of prophets and kings, Jerusalem the golden, with milk and honey blest, and here he is at its gates, trembling with anticipation. He calls for a cab.

But when he actually enters the city, passing through St. Stephen's Gate and stepping forth onto the Via Dolorosa, that romance and fantasy begins unexpectedly to evaporate, and he wonders how he could have babbled so blithely to Das of the good times a-coming. Jerusalem is undeniably picturesque, yes—but to call a place picturesque is to damn it—with its narrow steep streets and sturdy age-old masonry, its crowded stalls piled high with pots and pans, fish and apples, pastries and flayed lambs, its scents of strange spices, its hawk-faced old men in Bedouin regalia, but a cold wind whistles through the filthy alleyways and everyone he sees, children and beggars and merchants and shoppers and porters and workmen alike, has that same look of dull despair, that same hollow-eyed broken-souled expression that is the mark not of endurance but of anticipated defeat and surrender: *The Assyrians are coming, the Romans are coming, the Persians are coming, the Saracens are coming, the Turks are coming, the organ-rot is coming, and we will be crushed, we will be everlastingly annihilated.*

It is impossible to escape the twenty-first century

even within these medieval walls. Climbing toward
Golgotha, Shadrach sees the standard mourning poster
of Mangu pasted up all over, the bland young face
against the brilliant yellow background. Mangu's presence was not absent from Nairobi, naturally, but in
that spacious and airy city the posters were less
oppressive, easily obscured by the dazzle of the bou-
gainvilleas and the jacarandas. Here the heavy stone
walls sweat garish images of Mangu over passageways barely wide enough for three to go abreast,
yellow blotches impossible to escape, and, seeing them,
one feels the malign hand of Genghis Mao passing
over the city, imposing on it an unfelt grief for the
dead viceroy. Genghis Mao is more immediately
present, too, the familiar sinister leathery features
glowering from breeze-bellied banners at every major
intersection. The natives take these alien images as
casually as, no doubt, they once took the posters and
banners of Nebuchadnezzar, Ptolemy, Titus, Chosroes,
Saladin, Suleiman the Magnificent, and all the other
transient intruders, but to Shadrach these reduplicated
Mongol faces toll against his consciousness like so
many leaden bells counting out his dwindling hours.
   Then too the organ-rot is here. Not as conspicuously as in Nairobi, perhaps, for on the broad avenues of that city the terminal cases walked alone,
stumbling and lurching through private zones of vacant space. Old Jerusalem is too congested for that.
But there is no scarcity of victims, shivering and
sweating and groping along the Via Dolorosa. Occasionally one halts, sags against a wall, digs his fingers between the stones for support. The Stations of
the Cross are indicated by marble plaques set into
walls: here Jesus received the cross, here He fell the
first time, here He encountered His Mother, and so
on. And here, up the Via Dolorosa, go the dying, lost
in their own crucifixions. As in Nairobi, they stare
without seeming to see. But a few stretch their hands
toward him as if imploring his blessing. This is a
town where miracles have not been uncommon, and
the black stranger is a man of dignity and stature:
who knows, perhaps a new Savior walks these streets?

But Shadrach has no miracles to offer, none. He is helpless. He is as much a dead man as they are, though he still walks about. As they do.

He feels much too conspicuous, too tall, too black, too alien, too healthy. Beggars, mostly children, cluster about him like flies. "*Dol-lar*," they implore. "*Dol-lar, dol-lar, dol-lar!*" He carries no coins—he uses a government credit planchet to cover all expenses—and so there is no way he can get rid of them. He scoops one five-year-old into the air, hoping to make a piggyback ride serve in lieu of baksheesh, but the expression of terror in the child's huge eyes is so pitiful that Shadrach quickly puts him down, and kneels, trying to give comfort. The child's fright passes at once: "*Dol-lar*," he demands. Shadrach shrugs and the child spits at him and runs. There are too many children here, too many everywhere, unattended, running in packs through the cities of the world. They are orphans, running wild, a feral generation. Shadrach has seen Donna Labile's demographic surveys: the worst impact of the organ-rot has fallen upon those who would now be between the ages of twenty-five and forty, Shadrach's own contemporaries, those who were children during the Virus War. Slower to succumb than their parents were, they survived into adulthood—just long enough, most of them, to marry and bring forth young; then they died, having seeded the world with little savages. The PRC has begun to establish camps for these abandoned children, but they are not much more attractive than prisons, and the system is not working well.

It is too much for Shadrach—the fierce children, the woeful staggerers, the dirt, the unfamiliar density of the populace that throngs this tiny walled city. There is no way to escape the overwhelming sadness of the place. He should never have entered it; it would have been better by far to look out from his hotel balcony and think romantic thoughts of Solomon and Saladin. He is pushed, prodded, pawed, and elbowed; harsh-sounding things are said to him in languages he does not understand; he is beleaguered by offers to buy his clothing, to sell him jewelry,

to take him on tours of the great religious sites.
Without the help of guides he makes his way to the
Church of the Holy Sepulchre, a grimy and graceless
building, but he does not go in, for some kind of
pitched battle seems to be under way at its main
entrance between priests of different sects, who shout
and shake fists and tug one another's beards and
shred one another's cassocks. Turning aside, he finds,
just back of the church, a busy bazaar—more accurately a flea market—where shreds and tatters of the
former era are for sale: broken radios, antique television tubes, outboard engines, a miscellany of gears
and wheels and cameras and electric shavers and
telephones and pumps and gyroscopes and vacuum
cleaners and batteries and lasers and gauges and
tape recorders and calculators and microscopes and
phonographs and washing machines and prisms and
amplifiers, all the debris of the affluent twentieth
century washed up on this strange shore. Everything
is seemingly broken or defective, but the traders are
doing a brisk business anyway. Shadrach is unable
even to guess what uses these remnants and fragments may now be finding in the Palestinian hinter-
lands. He actually spies something he wants for his
own medical collection, a gleaming little ultramicro-
tome once used to prepare tissue sections for the
electron microscope, but when he produces his credit
planchet rather than haggle, the trader merely gives
him a blank, sullen stare. The PRC has decreed that
government planchets must be accepted as legal tender everywhere, but the old Arab, after examining
the glossy strip of plastic without much interest, hands
it silently back to Shadrach and turns away. There is
a Citpol at the edge of the marketplace who appears
to be watching the aborted transaction. Shadrach
could call the policeman over and get him to make
the trader honor the planchet, but he decides against
it; perhaps there will be unforeseeable complications,
even dangers, and he does not want to attract attention in this place. He abandons the microtome and
walks off to the south, through quieter streets, a
residential district.

In a few minutes he comes to steps that lead downward to a great opened space, a cobblestoned plaza, at the far end of which stands an immense wall made of titanic blocks of roughhewn stone. Shadrach ambles across the plaza, heading toward the wall as he studies his map and tries to get his bearings. He remembers turning left, then left again at the Street of the Chain—perhaps he is in the old Jewish Quarter, heading back toward the Dome of the Rock and the Aqsa, in which case—

"You should cover your head in this place," says a quiet voice at his right elbow. "You stand on holy ground."

A small compact man, seventy years old or more, tanned and vigorous-looking, has approached him. He wears a round black skullcap, and, with a courteous but insistent gesture, has produced another from his pocket which he extends toward Shadrach.

"Isn't this whole city holy ground?" Shadrach asks, taking the skullcap.

"Every inch is holy to someone, yes. The Arabs have their places, the Copts, the Greek Orthodox, the Armenians, the Syrian Christians, everyone. But this is ours. Don't you know the Wall?" There is no mistaking the capital letter in his voice.

"The Wall," Shadrach says, embarrassed, staring at the great stone blocks, then at his map. "Oh. Of course. You mean this is the Wailing Wall? I didn't realize—"

"The Western Wall, we called it, after the reconquest in 1967, when the wailing stopped for a time. Now it is the Wailing Wall again. Though I myself do not believe much in wailing, even in times such as these." The little man smiles. "Under whatever name, it is for us Jews a holy of holies. The last remnant of the Temple." Again the capital letter.

"Solomon's Temple?"

"No, not that one. The Babylonians destroyed the First Temple, twenty-seven hundred years ago. This is the wall of the Second Temple, Herod's Temple, leveled by the Romans under Titus. The Wall is all that the Romans left standing. We revere it because it is for us a symbol not only of persecution but of endurance, of survival. This is your first time in Jerusalem?"

"Yes."

"American?"

"Yes," Shadrach says.

"I am also. So to speak. My father brought me here when I was seven. To a kibbutz in the Galilee. Just after the proclamation of the State of Israel, you know?—in 1948. I fought in the Sinai in '67, the Six Day War, and I was here to pray at the Wall in the first days after the victory, and I have lived in Jerusalem ever since. And the Wall to me is still the center of the world. I come here every day. Even though there is no longer really a State of Israel. Even though there are no longer any states at all, any dreams, any—" He pauses. "Forgive me. I talk too much. Would you like to pray at the Wall?"

"But I'm not Jewish," Shadrach says.

"What does that matter? Come with me. You are a Christian?"

"Not particularly."

"No religion at all?"

"No official religion. But I would like to go to the Wall."

"Come, then." They stride across the plaza, the short old man and the tall young one. Shadrach's companion says suddenly, "I am Meshach Yakov."

"*Meshach?*"

"Yes. It is a name from the Bible, the Book of Daniel. He was one of the three Jews who defied Nebuchadnezzar when the king ordered them to—"

"I know," Shadrach cries. "I know!" He is laughing. Delight bubbles in him. It is a delicious moment. "You don't have to tell me the story. I'm Shadrach!"

"Pardon me?"

"Shadrach. Shadrach Mordecai. It's my name."

"Your name," says Meshach Yakov. He laughs too. "Shadrach. Shadrach Mordecai. It is a beautiful name. It could be a fine Israeli name. With a name like that you aren't Jewish?"

"The wrong genes, I think. But I suppose that if I

converted I wouldn't need to bother changing my name."

"No. No. A beautiful Jewish name. *Shalom*, Shadrach!"

"*Shalom*, Meshach!"

They laugh together. It is almost a vaudeville routine, Shadrach thinks. That Citpol lurking over there—is he Abednego? They are right by the Wall, now, and the laughter goes from them. The enormous weatherbeaten blocks seem incredibly ancient, as old as the Pyramids, as old as the Ark. Meshach Yakov closes his eyes, leans forward, touches his forehead to the Wall as though greeting it. Then he looks at Shadrach. "How shall I pray?" Shadrach asks.

"How? How? Pray any way you want to pray! Speak with the Lord! Tell Him things. Ask Him things. Do I need to tell a grown man how to pray? What can I tell you? Only this: it is better to give thanks than to ask favors. If you can. If you can."

Shadrach nods. He turns toward the Wall. His mind is empty. His soul is empty. He glances at Meshach Yakov. The Israeli, eyes closed, is rocking gently back and forth, murmuring to himself in what Shadrach assumes is Hebrew. No prayers come to Shadrach's lips. He can think only of the wild children, the organ-rot, the blank despondent faces along the Via Dolorosa, the posters of Mangu and Genghis Mao. This journey of his has been a failure. He has learned nothing, he has achieved nothing. He might as well get himself back to Ulan Bator tomorrow and face what must be faced. But the moment he articulates those thoughts, he rejects them. What of that sudden upwelling of optimism as he sipped tea with Bhishma Das? What of the moment of delight, of warm fellow-feeling, that he experienced on first hearing Meshach Yakov's name? These two old men, the Hindu, the Jew, both so sturdy of soul, so patient and steady under the weight of the world catastrophe—has nothing of their strength rubbed off on him?

He stands a long while, listening to the silence within his body that is the absence of Genghis Mao's outputs, and decides that it is not yet time to return to Ulan Bator. He will go onward. He will complete his tour.

He says, under his breath, too self-conscious to let Meshach Yakov hear it, "Thank you, Lord, for having made this world and for having let me live in it as long as I have." *Better to give thanks than to ask favors*. Even so, asking favors is not forbidden. To himself Shadrach adds, "And let me stay in it a while longer, Lord. And show me how I can help make it more like the place you meant it to be." The prayer sounds foolish to him, mawkish, ingenuous. And yet not contemptible. And yet not contemptible. If it were given to him to live this one moment over, he would not revise that prayer, although he would not like to admit to anyone, either, that he had uttered it.

When they are done at the Wall, Meshach Yakov invites Shadrach to dinner; and Shadrach, who has come to regret having refused Bhishma Das's invitation, accepts. Yakov lives in the modern sector of Jerusalem, far to the west of the old city, out beyond the parliament buildings and the university campus, in a high-rise atop a bare lofty hill. The apartment house, one of a complex of twenty or so, has the glossy, glassy look favored in the late twentieth century, but the marks of decay are all over it. Windows are dusty, even broken, doors are out of true, the balconies are splotched with rust, the elevator creaks and groans. The place is more than half empty, Yakov tells him. As the population dwindles and services deteriorate, people have deserted these once-choice suburbs to live closer to the center of town. But he has been here forty years, he says proudly, and he intends to stay another forty, at the very least.

Yakov's apartment itself is small, well kept, furnished sparsely in a tasteful, old-fashioned way. "My sister Rebekah," he says. "My grandchildren, Joseph, Leah." He tells them Shadrach's name, and they all have a hearty laugh over the coincidence, the close biblical association. The sister is in her seventies, Joseph about eighteen, Leah twelve or thirteen. There are black-framed photographs on the wall—Yakov's wife, Shadrach assumes, and three grown children, probably all victims of the organ-rot. Yakov does not say, Shadrach does not ask.

"Are you Jewish?" Leah demands.

Shadrach smiles, shakes his head.

"There *are* black Jews," she says. "I know. There are even Chinese Jews."

"Genghis Mao is a Jew," Joseph says, and bursts into wild laughter. But he laughs alone. Meshach Yakov glares at him; Yakov's sister looks shocked, Leah embarrassed. Shadrach finds himself shaken by the sudden intrusion of that alien name into this serene self-contained household.

Stiffly Yakov says to the boy, "Don't talk nonsense."

"I didn't mean anything," Joseph protests.

"Then save your breath," Yakov snaps. To Shadrach he says, "We are not great admirers of the Chairman here. But I would not like to discuss such things. I apologize for the boy's silliness."

"It's all right," Shadrach says.

Leah says, "Why do you have a Jewish name?"

"My people often took first names from the Bible," Shadrach tells her. "My father's father was a minister, a religious scholar. He suggested it. I have an uncle named Absalom. Had. And cousins named Solomon and Saul."

"But the last name," the girl persists. "That's what I mean. It's Jewish too. There once was a great rabbi named Mordecai, in Germany, long ago. We heard about him in school. Do black people pick their own last names too?"

"They were given to us, by our owners. My family must once have been owned by someone named Mordecai."

"*Owned?*"

"When they were slaves," Joseph whispers harshly.

"You were slaves too?" the girl says. "I didn't know. We were slaves in Egypt, you know. Thousands of years ago."

Shadrach smiles. "We were slaves in America. More recently."

"And your owner was a Jew? I don't believe a Jew would own slaves, not ever!"

Shadrach wants to explain that the slavemaster Mordecai, if ever he existed and gave his name to his blacks, was not necessarily Jewish, but might have been, for even Jews were not beyond owning slaves in the days of the plantation; but the discussion is making Meshach Yakov uncomfortable, apparently, and with such abruptness that the children are left gaping he changes the subject, asking his sister whether dinner will be ready soon.

"Fifteen minutes," she says, heading for the kitchen. As though heeding an unspoken warning to leave the guest in peace, Joseph and Leah withdraw to a couch and begin a stilted, awkward conversation about events in school—a worldwide holiday has been proclaimed, it seems, for the day of Mangu's funeral, and Joseph, who is at the university, will be deprived of a field trip to the Dead Sea, which annoys him. Leah cites some remark made by Jerusalem's PRC chief about the importance of paying respect to the fallen viceroy, bringing a derisive hoot from Rebekah in the kitchen and a brusque comment about the official's intelligence and sanity, and soon things degenerate into a noisy, incomprehensible discussion of local political matters, involving all four Yakovs in a fierce bilingual shouting match. Meshach, at the outset, attempts to explain to Shadrach something about the cast of characters and the background, but as the dispute goes along he becomes too embroiled in it to keep up his running commentary. Shadrach, baffled but amused, watches these articulate and spirited people wrangle until the arrival of dinner brings a sudden halt to the debate. He has no idea what the battle was about—it has to do with the replacement of a Christian Arab by a Moslem on the city council, he thinks—but it cheers him to see such a display of energy and commitment. In Ulan Bator, bugged and spy-eyed to an ultimate degree, he has never witnessed such furious clashes of opinion; but perhaps the spy-eyes have nothing to do with it, perhaps it is only because he has lived outside the framework of the nuclear family for so long that he has forgotten what real conversation is like.

The advent of dinner is worrisome—should he don the skullcap? What other customs are there that he does not know?—but no problems arise. Neither Meshach nor his grandson wears a skullcap; there is no prayer before eating, only a moment of silent grace observed by the two old people; the food is rich and plentiful, and Shadrach does not notice any special dietary customs in force at the Yakov table. Afterward Joseph and Leah retire to their rooms to study, and Shadrach, warmed by red Israeli wine and strong Israeli brandy, settles down with old Yakov to study maps of the vicinity, for they have agreed at dinner to go on a sightseeing tour in the morning. The old city, certainly, its towers and churches and marketplaces, and the supposed tomb of Absalom in the Kidron Valley nearby, and the tomb of King David on Mount Zion, and the archaeological museum, and the national museum where the Dead Sea scrolls are kept, and—

"Wait," Shadrach says. "All this in one day?"

"We'll take two, then," Meshach says.

"Even so. Can we really cover so much ground so fast?"

"Why not? You look healthy enough. I think you can keep up with me." And the old man laughs.

22

In Istanbul a few days later he has no guide, and he wanders that intricate city of many levels alone, confused, defeated by the complexities of getting from one place to another, wishing that some Meshach Yakov would discover him here, some Bhishma Das. But none does. The map he gets at his hotel is useless, for there are few street signs, and whenever he veers off a main boulevard he immediately gets lost in a maze of anonymous alleyways. There are taxis, but the drivers seem to speak only Turkish, tourism having perished during the Virus War; they can follow self-evident instructions—"Haghia Sophia"—"Topkapi" —but when he wants to go to the ancient Byzantine rampart on the outskirts of the city he is unable to make any driver understand, and in the end he has to resort to asking to be taken to the Kariya Mosque on the city's outskirts, and getting from there to the nearby wall on foot, by guesswork.

Istanbul is gritty, grimy, archaic, alien, and irritating. Shadrach is fascinated by its architectural mix, the opulent Ottoman palaces and the glorious many-minareted mosques and the eighteenth-century wooden houses and the sweeping twentieth-century avenues and the battered fragments of the old Constantinople that jut like broken teeth from the earth, bits of aqueducts and cisterns and basilicas and stadiums. But the city is too chaotic for him. It depresses and repels him despite the powerful appeal of its rich-textured history. Even now more than a million people live here, and Shadrach finds it hard to cope with such a density of humanity. There are the usual dismaying organ-rot tragedies on display in the streets, and an extraordinary number of feral children, some only three or four years old, trooping like desperate scavengers everywhere. And there are Citpols moving in wary pairs wherever he turns. Watching him, he is convinced. Is it just paranoia? He doesn't think so. He thinks that Genghis Mao, unhappy over having given his physician leave to roam the world, is keeping him under surveillance so that he can be brought back to Ulan Bator at the Khan's whim. Shadrach had not expected to be able to vanish totally—indeed, returning to Ulan Bator is definitely central to his emerging plan of action, though he still does not know when the right moment to go back will arrive— but he does not like the idea of being spied upon. After two days in Istanbul, a perfunctory tour of the standard sights, he flies abruptly to Rome.

He spends a week there, making his headquarters in an ancient hotel, mellow and luxurious, a few blocks from the Baths of Diocletian. Rome too is densely populated, and its urban pace is frenetic, but for some reason there are fewer scars of the Virus War and its nightmare aftermath here, and Shadrach begins to relax, to ease himself into a comfortable Mediterranean rhythm of life: he strolls the splendid streets, he sips aperitifs at sidewalk cafes, he gorges himself on pasta and young white wine at obscure trattorias, and all the traumas of the Trauma Ward become insignificant. Truly this is the Eternal City, capable of absorbing all of time's heaviest blows and never losing its resilience. He sees, of course, the imperial monuments, the Arch of Titus that commemorates the Roman sacking of Jerusalem, the temples and palaces of the Capitoline and Palatine, the magnificent jumble that is the Forum, the haunted wreck of the Colosseum. He visits St. Peter's, and, looking up toward the Vatican, muses on Genghis Mao's mocking, corrosive offer to make him Pope. He does the Sistine Chapel, the Etruscan collection in the Villa Giulia, the Borghese gallery, and a dozen of

the best baroque churches. His energies seem to grow
rather than flag as he pursues the infinite antiquities
of Rome. Oddly, he finds himself responding most
intensely not to the celebrated classic monuments
but to the ancient gray tenements, steep and gaunt,
in Trastevere and the Jewish quarter. Are these the
very tenements of Caesar's time, mansions once, slums
now? Is it possible that they are still inhabited after
two thousand years? Why not? The old Romans knew
how to build six stories high, and even higher, and
built of durable stone. And it would not have been
hard, despite the sackings and the fires and the
revolutions, to keep those buildings intact, to rebuild,
replaster, patch the old and make it new, constantly
to refurbish and restore. So these gray towers may
once have housed the subjects of Tiberius and Caligula,
and Shadrach gets a pleasant little shiver from the
thought that they have been continuously occupied
across the ages. On second thought, it probably is not
so; nothing, he decides, endures that long in daily
use. These are more likely twelfth-century buildings,
fourteenth-, even seventeenth-. Old enough but not
truly ancient. Except in the sense that anything that
antedates the rise of Genghis Mao, that has survived
out of that former world, that prediluvian epoch, is
ancient.

He wishes he could stay in Rome forever. A pity, he
thinks, that Genghis Mao wasn't serious about the
papacy. But after a week Shadrach resolves to go
onward. It is too pleasant here, too comfortable;
besides, as he downs a Strega at his favorite cafe one
warm humid evening, he notices two Citpols at a
table at a cafe on the opposite corner, not drinking,
not talking, merely watching him. Are they closing
in, tightening their net? Will they pick him up tomorrow or the day after and tell him he must return to
his master in Ulan Bator? He buys a ticket to London,
cancels it at the last moment, and boards a plane
that is about to leap over the pole to California.

And suddenly he is in San Francisco. A toy city,
white and precious, rising on formidable hills and
girdled by a sparkling bay. He has never been here

before. Odd how he expects famous cities to be gigantic: this one, like Jerusalem, is surprisingly small. Drop it down in Rome, in Nairobi, in crazy sprawling Istanbul, and it would vanish altogether. Surprisingly cold, too. California to him has always been a place of swimming pools and palm trees, of football games played in bright warm sunshine on wondrous January afternoons, but that California of the mind must be somewhere else, probably down by Los Angeles; San Francisco in June has a sullen late-winter feel, with sharp insistent winds and gray, clinging fogs. Even when the fog burns away in the afternoon and the city glitters in brilliant light under an intense cloudless sky, the air still carries the chill of the ocean breezes, and Shadrach huddles into his inadequate summer jacket.

There are no ancient palaces to see here, no gazelles and ostriches running wild, no medieval ramparts or baroque churches. But there are elegant streets of Victorian houses, from grand mansions down to wooden bungalows, all of them delicately ornamented with scrollwork and cornices and friezes and gables and spires and even some stained-glass windows, most of the buildings in fine preservation, survivors of fire, earthquake, insurrection, biochemical warfare, and the collapse of the United States of America itself. There are trees and shrubs everywhere, many in bloom; this city, chilly or not, is nearly as flowery as Nairobi, and he looks with delight on trees that are great blazing masses of red blossoms, on giant tree ferns and contorted wind-sculptured cypresses, on hillsides dark with fragrant groves of eucalyptus. One long day he walks clear across the city from the bay to the ocean, emerging out of a lush dreamlike park to stand at the edge of the Pacific, staring toward Mongolia. Somewhere thousands of kilometers to the northwest Genghis Mao is awakening and beginning his morning exercises. Shadrach wonders about the current kidney functions of Genghis Mao, his pulse rate, his calcium-phosphate levels, his endocrine balances, all the myriad twitching bits of information he was so accustomed to receiving. He

realizes that he has begun to miss the broadcasts
from Genghis Mao's body. He misses the daily challenge of sustaining the Chairman's indomitable but
increasingly vulnerable inner mechanisms. He may
even miss Genghis Mao himself. Ah, strange, dark,
mysterious! Ah, the Hippocratic compulsions!

How goes it with the Khan? The Khan still lives
and thrives, judging by the newspaper Shadrach
buys— the first he has bothered to look at in all the
weeks of his journey—which is strewn with photographs of Mangu's funeral, held last week with Pharaonic pomp and majesty. There is Genghis Mao himself,
in full mourning regalia, riding in the vast procession.
There he is again, benevolently blessing the millions
crammed into Sukha Bator Square. (*Millions?* Well,
so it says. Thousands, more likely.) And again, and
again, the Khan doing this, the Khan doing that, the
Khan orchestrating all the remaining energies of this
bedraggled planet in a global outpouring of grief.
Ulan Bator, Shadrach discovers, is to be renamed
Altan Mangu, "Golden Mangu." This seems comi-
cally excessive to Shadrach, but he supposes he will
get used to the new name in time; the old one, which
means "Red Hero," has been obsolete anyway since
the fall of the People's Republic in 1995, and Genghis
Mao has been thinking for years of changing it to
something more appropriate. Well, Altan Mangu will
do well enough, Shadrach decides. A noise in place of
a noise.

Pages and pages of coverage of the funeral rites!
Not even a President of the United States would have
received such a spread. And the funeral was *last* week;
have they been running batches of photos like this
every day since then? Probably. Probably. The funeral is the big story of the month, bigger even than
the news of Mangu's death, which happened too
quickly, which lacked the linear extension in time
that makes for really big news. What other news is
there, anyway? That people are dying of organ-rot?
That the Committee is nobly endeavoring to insure a
major increase in the supplies of the Antidote, real
soon now? That the Chairman's personal physician is

loose on an aimless jaunt around the world while, in some corner of his woolly skull, he plots ways to thwart the Chairman's scheme to take possession of his body? Funeral pictures are much more interesting than any of that.

So much fuss, in an American newspaper, about a funeral in Mongolia. Shadrach finds himself thinking about the final president of the United States—someone named Williams, he thinks, or maybe Richards, at any rate a first name turned into a last name—and what sort of funeral *he* had. Seven mourners and a muddy grave on a rainy day, most likely. (Roberts? Edwards? The name has slipped through his memory, beyond recapture.) There still were presidents of the United States when Shadrach was a boy, even a living ex-president or two. He tries to remember who the president was when he was born. A man named Ford, wasn't it? Yes, Ford. Most people liked Ford, Shadrach remembers. Before him there was one named Nixon, whom people did not like, and one named Kennedy, who was shot, and Truman, Eisenhower, Johnson, Roosevelt—resonant names, sturdy American-sounding names. Our leaders, our great men. What is the name of our leader now? Genghis II Mao IV Khan. Who would believe that, in the old United States before the Virus War? Would George Washington have believed it? Would Lincoln? The final year before the PRC took over there were seven presidents, some of them simultaneously. It used to be that the country needed thirty or forty years to run through seven presidents, but there were seven all in one year, in 1995. There used to be emperors in Rome, too, and Augustus or Hadrian would probably have been surprised at the quality and racial origin of some of them toward the end of the imperial era, the ones who were Goths and the ones who were boys and the ones who were madmen and the ones who ruled six days before their own palace guards strangled them in disgust. Well, Lincoln would have been surprised to find Americans accepting someone named Genghis II Mao IV Khan as their leader. Or maybe not. Lincoln might have believed that people got the

governments they deserve, and that we must have
deserved Genghis Mao. Lincoln might even have liked
the gaudy old monster.

San Francisco is a fine city for walking. The scale
of the place is modest and human, so that one can
move from one neighborhood to another, from the
mansions of Pacific Heights to the sunny fantasy-
Mediterranean of the Marina, from Russian Hill to
the Wharf, from the Mission to the Haight, in a single
short brisk jaunt, with a constantly changing and
always agreeable urban texture all the way. Neither
wind nor fog nor steepness of hill is a serious handi-
cap in such an amiable environment. And the city is
alive. There are shops, restaurants, coffeehouses; the
waterfront districts offer half a dozen big carpentry
chapels of competing sects, a dream-death house, a
den of transtemporalists; the people in the streets
give the illusion of good health and high spirits, and
though Shadrach knows it must be only an illusion,
it is a persuasive one. The only thing wrong with San
Francisco is the profusion of Citpols.

There are more policemen here than he has ever
seen in any one place, more even than in Ulan Bator
itself. It is as though every ninth San Franciscan has
enrolled in the Citizens' Peace Brigade. Maybe it is
only a delusion of his troubled mind, or maybe the
unusual vitality of this city requires a correspond-
ingly unusual quota of policing: at any rate, there are
gray-and-blue uniforms everywhere, *everywhere*, usually in pairs but not infrequently in clumps of three,
four, five. Most of them have that mechanical insectoid
look that seems to be characteristic of their kind,
that makes Shadrach suspect that Citpols are not
born and trained but rather are stamped out in some
ghastly factory deep in the Caucasus. And they all
are watching him. Watching, watching, watching—it
can't be mere paranoia. Can it? Those dull gray watch-
ful eyes, hard, stupid, purposeful, studying him from
all angles as he strides through the city? Why are
they looking at him so intently? What do they want
to know?

They are going to arrest me soon, Shadrach tells himself.

He is certain that he has been under surveillance since his departure. He is positive that Avogadro is receiving information on his movements and is filing daily reports with Genghis Mao; and—is it his own growing tension that makes it seem that way, or is the tension in Genghis Mao?—the intensity of the surveillance appears to have been increasing, from Nairobi to Jerusalem, from Jerusalem to Istanbul, from Istanbul to Rome, first a casual Citpol or two glancing offhandedly at him, then more overt scrutiny, then teams of them following him about, hovering, staring, conferring, charting his movements, until, perhaps in San Francisco, perhaps not until he reaches Peking, they get the orders from the capital and make their move, dozens of them on the housetops, in doorways, on street-corners: *All right, Mordecai, come quietly and you won't get hurt—*

And then, when he is at Broadway and Grant, about to turn downhill into teeming Chinatown and speculating darkly about the three Citpols clustered outside an Oriental grocery store across the street, someone shouts at him from the far side of Broadway, "Mordecai? Hey, Shadrach Mordecai!"

At the sound of his name Shadrach freezes, impaled in mid-fantasy, knowing that the game is up, that the moment he has feared is at hand.

But the man approaching him, moving in awkward dragging lurches through the traffic, is no Citpol. He is a burly, balding man with a seamed weary face and a thick unkempt gray-streaked beard, who is clad in threadbare green overalls, a heavy plaid shirt, a faded red cloak. When he reaches Shadrach's side he puts his hand on Shadrach's forearm in a way that seems to be asking for support as much as for attention, and thrusts his face close to Shadrach's, assuming intimacy so brazenly that Shadrach does not resist the encroachment. The man's eyes are watery and swollen: one of the organ-rot symptomata. But he is still capable of smiling. "Doctor," he says.

His voice is warm, furry, insinuating. "Hey, Doctor, how's it going?"

A drunk. Probably not dangerous, though there is a vague sense of menace about him.

"I didn't know I was such a celebrity here."

"Celebrity. Celebrity. Yeah, you're fucking famous. At least to me you are. I spotted you from all the way across Broadway. Not that you've changed so much." The man is definitely drunk. He has that heavy, overly ingratiating warmth; he is practically hanging from Shadrach's arm. "You don't recognize me, do you?"

"Should I?"

"Depends. You knew me pretty well once."

Shadrach searches the jowly, ravaged face. Distantly familiar, but no name comes to mind. "Harvard," he guesses. "It must have been Harvard. Right?"

"Two points. Keep going."

"Medical school?"

"Try the college."

"That's harder. That goes back better then fifteen years."

"Take fifteen years off me. And about twenty kilos. And the beard. Shit, you haven't changed at all. Of course you live an easy life. I know what you've been doing." The man shuffles his feet and, without relinquishing his grip on Shadrach's arm, twists away, coughs, hawks, spits. Bloody sputum. He grins. "Piece of my gut there, eh? Lose a little more every day. You really don't recognize me. What the hell, all us white boys look alike."

"Want to give me more hints?"

"Big one. We were on the track team together."

"Shotput," Shadrach says instantly, feeling the datum rise out of God knows what recess of his memory banks and certain that it is correct.

"Two points. Now the name."

"Not yet. I'm groping for it." He transforms this ruin into a young man, beardless, brawn where he has fat today, in T-shirt and shorts, hefting the gleaming metal globe, going into the bizarre little wind-up dance of the shotputter, making his heave—

"The NCAA meet, Boston, '95. Our sophomore year.

You won the sixty-meter sprint in six seconds even. Very nice. And I took the shotput at twenty-one meters. Our pictures in all the newspapers. Remember? The first big track event after the Virus War, a sign that things were getting back to normal. Hah. Normal. You were one hell of a runner, Shadrach. I bet you still are. Shit, I couldn't even *lift* the shot now. What's my name?"

"Ehrenreich," Shadrach says immediately. "Jim Ehrenreich."

"Six points! And you're the big man's doctor now. You said you'd be of some use to humanity, you weren't going into medicine just to make a buck, eh? And you were right on. Serving humanity, keeping our glorious leader alive. Why do you look so surprised? You think nobody knows the name of the Chairman's doctor?"

"I don't try to get much publicity," Shadrach says.

"True. But we know a little about what goes on in Ulan Bator. I was Committee, you know. Until last year. Where are you heading? Chinatown? Let's walk together. Standing still like this, it's bad for my legs, the varicose veins. I was Committee, third from the top in Northern California, even had a vector-access rating. Of course they dropped me. But don't worry: you won't get into trouble talking to me. Even with those Citpols standing over there watching. I'm not a fucking pariah, you know. I'm just ex-Committee. I'm allowed to talk to people."

"What happened?"

"I was dumb. I had this friend, she was Committee too, very low echelon, and her brother caught the rot. She said to me, Can you jigger the computer, get a bigger requisition of the Antidote, save my brother? Sure, I said, I would, I'll do it, only for you, kid. I knew this computer man. He could jigger the numbers. So I asked him, and he did it, at least I thought he was doing it, but it was only a trap, a sucker deal, pure entrapment—the Citpols stepped in, asked me to account for the extra Antidote allotment I had requested—" Ehrenreich blinks cheerfully. "They sent her to the organ farm. Her brother died. Me they simply dropped, no further punishment. Very fucking lucky. On account of my years of devoted service to the Permanent Revolution. I even get a little allowance, enough to keep me in vodka. But it was a waste, Shadrach, a stupid waste. They should have sent me to the organ farm too, while I was still whole. Because now I'm dying. You know that, don't you?"

"Yes."

"They say that if you've been on the Antidote, and you go off it, you generally get the rot right away. It's like the pent-up force of the disease busts loose and conquers you."

"I've heard that, yes," Shadrach says.

"How long do I have? You can tell that, can't you?"

"Not without examining you. Maybe not even then. I'm not exactly an expert on the rot."

"No. No, you wouldn't be. Not in Ulan Bator. You don't get enough exposure there. I've had it six months. My beard was black when I got it. I had all my hair then. I'm going to die, Shadrach."

"We're all going to die. Except maybe for Genghis Mao."

"You know what I mean. I'm not even thirty-seven years old and I'm going to *die*. I'm going to rot and die. Because I was dumb, because I wanted to help the brother of a friend. I had it made, I was home safe, the Antidote in my arm every six months—"

"You really were dumb," Shadrach tells him. "Because nothing you could have done would have helped your friend's brother."

"Eh?"

"The Antidote doesn't cure. It immunizes. Once the lethal stage sets in, that's it. The disease can't be reversed. Didn't you know that? I thought everybody knew that."

"No. No."

"You smashed your career for nothing. Threw away your life for nothing."

"No," Ehrenreich says. He looks stunned. "It can't be true. I don't believe it."

"Look it up."

"No," he says. "I want you to save me, Shadrach. I want you to prescribe the Antidote for me."

"I just told you—"

"You knew what I was going to ask. You were trying to head me off."

"Please, Jim—"

"But you could get the stuff. You're probably traveling with a hundred ampoules in your little black bag. Shit, man, you're Genghis Mao's own doctor! You can do *anything*. It's not like being third from the top in a regional office. Look, we were on the same team, we won trophies together, we had our pictures in the paper—"

"It wouldn't work, Jim."

"You're afraid to help me."

"I ought to be, after what you just told me. You got dropped for illegal diversion of the Antidote, you say, and then you turn around and ask me to do the same thing."

"It's different. You're the doctor of—"

"Even so. There's no point in giving you the Antidote, for reasons that I've just explained. But even if there were, I couldn't get any for you. I'd never get away with it."

"You don't want to risk your ass. Even for an old friend."

"No, I don't. And I don't want to be made to feel guilty for refusing to do something that doesn't make any sense." There is nothing gentle in Shadrach's voice. "The Antidote is useless to you now. Absolutely entirely useless. Get that straight and keep it straight."

"You wouldn't even try some on me? Just for an experiment?"

"It's useless. Useless."

After a long pause Ehrenreich says, "You know what I wish, old buddy? That you find yourself in bad trouble someday, that you find yourself right on the edge of the cliff and you're hanging on by your fingernails. And some old buddy of yours comes along, and you yell out to him, Save me, save me, the shits are killing me! And he tromps on your hand and keeps on walking. That's what I wish. So you'd find out what it's like. That's what I wish."

Shadrach shrugs. He can feel no anger toward a dying man. Nor does he choose to talk about his own problems. He says simply, "If I could heal you, I would. But I can't."

"You won't even try."

"There's nothing I can do. Will you believe that?"

"I was sure you'd be the one. You if anybody. Didn't even remember me. Won't lift a finger."

Shadrach says, "Have you ever done any carpentry, Jim?"

"You mean, in the chapels? Never interested me."

"It might help you. It won't cure what you have, but it might make it easier for you to live with it. Carpentry shows you patterns that you can't necessarily see for yourself. It helps you sort what's real and important from what doesn't matter much."

"So you're a carpentry nut?"

"I go now and then. Whenever things cut too close. There are some chapels down by Fisherman's Wharf. I wouldn't mind going now. Suppose you come down there with me. It'll do you some good."

"There's a bar at Washington and Stockton that I go to a lot. Suppose we go there instead. Suppose you buy me some drinks on your PRC card. Do me even more good."

"Bar first, then chapel?"

"We'll see," Ehrenreich says.

The bar is dark, musty, a forlorn place. The bartender is an automatic: card in slot, thumb to identification plate, punch for drinks. They order martinis. Ehrenreich's truculence subsides after his second drink; he grows morose and maudlin, but he is less bitter now. "I'm sorry I said what I did, man," he mutters.

"Forget it."

"I really thought you'd be the one."

"I wish I could be."

"I don't wish any trouble on you."

"I'm in trouble already," Shadrach says. "Hanging

on by my fingernails." He laughs. A new round of
drinks comes from the machine. He lifts his glass.
"Never mind. Cheers, friend."

"Cheers, man."

"After this one we'll go the chapel, right?"

Ehrenreich shakes his head. "Not me. It's not for
me, you know? Not now. Not right now. You go
without me. Don't nag me about it, just go without
me."

"All right," Shadrach says.

He finishes his drink, touches Ehrenreich's arm
lightly in farewell—the man is glassy-eyed, inartic-
ulate—and finds a cab to take him down to the
Wharf. But the chapel gives Shadrach no ease today.
His fingers tremble, his eyes will not focus, he is
unable to slip into the meditative state. After half an
hour he leaves. He sees a car full of Citpols in a lot up
the block. They're still watching him. There is a
bearded man in street clothes in the car, also. Ehrenreich? Is that possible? At this distance he can't make
out faces, but the heavy shoulders look about right,
the thinning hair is familiar. Shadrach scowls. He
hails a taxi, goes back to his hotel, packs, heads for
the airport. Three hours later he is on his way to
Peking.

23

In Peking, ensconced at the Hundred Gates Hotel
in the old legation quarter adjoining the Forbidden
City district, where Kublai Khan and Ch'ien-lung
once held court, Shadrach begins once more to de-

tect emanations from Genghis Mao. He is still some twelve hundred or thirteen hundred kilometers from Ulan Bator, he calculates—beyond the optimum telemetering range, and so the incoming impulses are blurred and faint. Then, too, after these weeks of separation Shadrach is no longer as much in concord with the broadcast from Genghis Mao's body as he had been. But when he sits very still, when he tunes his attention perfectly to the task, he finds himself able to read the old warlord's biodata with gradually sharpening clarity.

The gross functions come in best, of course: heartbeat, blood pressure, respiration, body temperature. The Khan's major systems all seem to be thundering along at their usual level of irrepressible vitality. Liver and kidney action register in their normal range. Basal metabolic expenditure normal. Neuromuscular responses normal. It never ceases to amaze Shadrach how healthy, how strong, the old man is. He takes a certain vicarious pride in Genghis Mao's heroic durability and resilience.

Some unexpected puzzles begin to develop, though, as Shadrach extends his reach and starts to bring in the subtler, more refined data. These tend to contradict some of the gross indications. The muscle-firing responses do not seem quite right—phosphate breakdown appears weak, enzyme activity off. Blood viscosity is lower than normal and blood pH is nudging slightly toward the alkaline. Intestinal absorption is minutely down, cholesterol accumulation up, perspiration a trifle above normal.

None of these things is cause for real alarm in a man of the Chairman's age who has recently undergone so much radical surgery—it is hardly reasonable to expect him to be in perfect health—but the combination of factors is peculiar. Shadrach wonders how much of what he is reading is simply an artifact of distance and noise on the line: he is straining for some of these inputs, and he may not be getting them accurately. Still, the distortions, if distortions they are, are remarkably consistent. He gets the same reading whenever he returns to any sensor.

And a hypothesis is starting to take shape.

Diagnosis at more than a thousand kilometers' range is tricky. Shadrach misses his medical library and his computers. But he has an idea of what the problem may be, and he knows what data he needs to confirm his theory. What he does not know is whether Buckmaster's implant system is good enough to transmit analogues of such small-scale phenomena across so great a distance.

If blood viscosity is down and blood pH is alkaline, plasma protein levels are probably subnormal, and osmotic pressure, which draws fluids from the tissues to the capillaries, is going to be low. If the hydrostatic blood pressure is normal, as the gross-function modulator is telling him, and the osmotic blood pressure is off, Genghis Mao's tissues may be building up an accumulation of excess fluids—not serious, not dangerous, not yet, but such fluid accumulations may be leading toward the development of edemas, of watery swellings, and edemas can be symptomatic of impending failure in the kidneys, the liver, perhaps the cardiac system. Bearing down in intense concentration, Shadrach roves Genghis Mao's body in search of signs of excess fluid. The lymphatic-system checkpoints give him nothing but normal levels, though. The reports from the pericardial, pleural, and peritoneal outposts are positive. Renal and hepatic functions, as before, are fine. Nothing seems to be wrong. Shadrach begins to abandon his hypothesis. Perhaps the Khan is not in difficulties. Those few negative indications were probably just noise on the line, and therefore—

But then Shadrach notices that something is not quite right in Genghis Mao's skull. Intracranial pressure is unusually high.

The implant monitors in the Chairman's cranium are not as comprehensive as they are elsewhere. Genghis Mao has no history of stroke or other cerebrovascular events, and surgeons have never had reason to invade the imperial skull. Since most of the telemetering equipment in Genghis Mao has been installed during the course of routine corrective surgery,

Shadrach must make do with relatively skimpy coverage of the state of the Chairman's brain. But he does have a sensor that reports to him on intracranial pressure, and, as he makes his total scan of Genghis Mao's body, the rise in that pressure catches his attention. Is that where the fluid buildup is taking place?

Struggling, stretching for the data, Shadrach pulls in whatever correlative information he can grab. Osmotic pressure of the cranial capillaries? Low. Hydrostatic pressure? Normal. Meningeal distension? High. Condition of the cerebral ventricles? Congested. Something is awry, very marginally awry, in the system that drains cerebrospinal fluid from the interior of Genghis Mao's brain to the subarachnoid space, next to the skull wall, where it normally passes into the blood.

What this means, at the moment, is that Genghis Mao probably has been having bad headaches for a few days, that he will have worse ones if Shadrach Mordecai does not return to Ulan Bator at once, and that he may suffer brain damage—possibly fatal—if prompt corrective action is not taken. It means, also, that Shadrach's holiday is at its end. He will not do the sightseeing tour of Peking. Not for him the visit to the Forbidden City, the historical museum, the Ming tombs, the Great Wall, the temple of Confucius, the Working People's Palace of Culture. Those things are unimportant to him now: this is the moment for which he was waiting during his wanderings from continent to continent. The unstable system that is Genghis II Mao IV Khan has, in the absence of the devoted physician, begun to break down. Shadrach's indispensability has been made manifest. He is needed. He must go to his patient immediately. He must take the appropriate actions. He has his Hippocratic obligations to fulfill.

He has his own survival to think about, besides.

Shadrach descends to the hotel lobby to arrange for a seat aboard the next flight to Ulan Bator—there is one that evening, he learns, leaving in two and a half hours—and to check out of the room he so recently checked into. The clerk, a gaunt young Chinese who is unable to contain his fascination with the color of Shadrach's skin, staring and staring with surreptitious sideways glances, comments on the brevity of his stay in Peking.

"Change of plan," Shadrach declares resonantly. "Urgent business. Must return at once."

He glances down the length of the lobby—a dim, fragrant space, like the vestibule of some enormous Chinese restaurant, cluttered with mahogany screens and porcelain urns and huge lacquer bowls on rosewood pedestals—and sees, towering above a pair of porters, the husky, hulking figure of Avogadro. Their eyes meet and Avogadro smiles, nods his head in salute, waves a hand. He has just arrived at the hotel, it seems. Shadrach is not at all surprised to discover the security chief here. It was inevitable, he decides, that Avogadro would show up to make the arrest in person.

Neither of them remarks on the coincidence of their presence in this exotic place. Avogadro asks amiably, "How have you been enjoying your travels, Doctor?"

"I've seen a great deal of the world. Most interesting."

"That's the best word you can choose? Interesting? Not overwhelming, illuminating, transcendental?"

"Interesting," Shadrach repeats deliberately. "A very interesting trip. And how is Genghis Mao bearing up in my absence?"

"Not too badly."

"He's well looked after. He likes to think I'm indispensable, but the relief staff is quite capable of handling most of what's likely to come up."

"Probably so."

"But he's been having headaches, hasn't he?"

Avogadro looks mildly startled. "You know that, do you?"

"I'm just at the edge of the telemetering range here."

"And you can detect his *headaches?*"

"I can pick up certain causal factors," Shadrach says, "and deduce a headache from them."

"How clever that system is. You and the Khan are practically one person, wouldn't that be so? Connected the way you are. He aches and you feel it."

"Well put," Shadrach says. "Actually, Nikki was the first one to make that point to me. Genghis Mao and I are one person, yes, one united information-processing unit. Comparable to the sculptor and the marble and the chisel."

The analogy does not appear to register with Avogadro. He continues to smile the fixed, determinedly affable smile that he has been smiling since they first approached one another in the lobby.

"But not united closely enough," Shadrach goes on. "The system could be linked even more tightly. I plan to talk to the engineers about building some modifications into it, when I get back to Ulan Bator."

"Which will be when?"

"Tonight," Shadrach tells him. "I'm booked on the next flight out."

Avogadro's eyebrows rise. "You are? How convenient. Saves me the trouble of—"

"Asking me to return?"

"Yes."

"I thought you might have had something like that in mind."

"The truth is that Genghis Mao misses you. He sent me down here to talk to you."

"Of course."

"To ask you to come back."

"He sent you to ask me that. Not to *bring* me, but to *ask* me. If I would return. Of my own free will."

"To ask, yes."

Shadrach thinks of the Citpols keeping tabs on him all around the world, huddling, conferring, passing bulletins on to their colleagues in distant cities. He knows, and he is sure that Avogadro knows that he knows, that the real situation is not as casual as Avogadro would have him believe. By buying that ticket on this evening's flight, he has spared Avogadro the embarrassment of having to take him into custody and return him to Ulan Bator under duress. He hopes Avogadro is properly grateful for that.

He says, "How bad are the Khan's headaches?"

"Pretty bad, I'm told."

"You haven't seen him?"

Avogadro shakes his head. "Only on the telephone. He looked drawn. Tired."

"How long ago was this?"

"The night before last. But there's been talk in the tower all week about the Chairman's headaches."

"I see," Shadrach says, "I thought it might be like that. That's why I've decided to go back ahead of schedule." His eyes rest squarely on Avogadro's. "You understand that, don't you? That I bought my return ticket as soon as I realized the Khan was in discomfort? Because it was my responsibility to my patient. My responsibility to my patient is always the controlling factor in my actions. Always. Always. You're aware of that, aren't you?"

"Naturally," Avogadro says.

June 23, 2012

What if I had died before my work was done? Not an idle question at all. I am important to history. I am one of the great reconstituters of society. Subtract me from the scene in 1995, in 1998, even as late as 2001, and everything tumbles into chaos. I am to this society as Augustus was to the Roman world, as Ch'in Shih Huang Ti was to China. What kind of world would exist today if I had perished ten years ago? A thousand warring principalities, no doubt, each with its own pathetic army, its own legislature, currency, passports, border guards, customs levies. A host of petty aristocracies, feudal overloads, secret cabals of malcontents, constant little revolutions—chaos, chaos, chaos. New outbreaks of virus warfare, very likely. And ultimately the extinction of mankind. All this if you subtract Genghis Mao at the critical moment in history. I am the world-savior.

It sounds obscenely boastful. World-savior! Culture-hero, myth-figure, I, Krishna, I, Quetzalcoatl, I, Arthur, I, Genghis Mao. And yet it is true, truer for me than for any of them, for without me all of mankind might be dead today, and that is new in the history of the savior-myth. To end the strife, to seal away the virus, to sponsor Roncevic's work—yes, no doubt of it, this could have been a dead planet by now if I had gone into the tomb ten years ago. As history will recognize. And yet, and yet, what does it matter? I will not be forgotten when I die—I will never be forgotten—but I will die. Sooner, later, my subterfuges will exhaust themselves. Neither Talos nor Phoenix nor Avatar can sustain me indefinitely. Something will fail, or boredom will conquer me and I will terminate my own systems, and I will die, and then what will it have meant to have saved the world? What I have done is ultimately meaningless to me. The power I have attained is ultimately empty. Not immediately empty—here I sit, do I not, among splendor and comfort?—but ultimately empty. I pretend that there is meaning in empire, but there is none, no meaning anywhere. This is a philosophy common among the very young, and, I suppose, among the very old. I must pretend that power is important to me. I must pretend that the reckoning of history is the all-consoling consolation. But I am too old to care. I have forgotten why it mattered to me to do what I have done. I am playing out a foolish game, unwilling to let it reach its end, but unsure of the nature of the winning gambit. And so I go on and on and on. I, Genghis II Mao IV Khan, savior of the world, taking care to conceal from those around me the profound and paralyzing vacancy that lies beneath the subcellars of my spirit. I think I have lost the thread of my own argument. I am tired. I am bored. My head hurts.

My head hurts.

"Shadrach!" Genghis Mao roars. "This filthy headache! Fix me, Shadrach!"

The old buccaneer forces a grin. He sits propped up against triple pillows, looking weary and frayed. His jaws are set in a rigid grimace; his eyes have a harsh glare and they waver frantically as though he is struggling to keep them in focus. At this close range Shadrach can easily detect a dozen different symptoms of the pressure building up in the recesses of the Chairman's brain. Already there are many tiny signs of deterioration in Genghis Mao's cerebral functions. No doubt of the diagnosis now. No doubt of it.

"You were away too long," the Khan mutters. "Enjoying yourself? Yes. But the headache, Shadrach, the miserable hideous headache—I shouldn't have let you go. Your place is here. Beside me. Watching me. Healing me. It was like sending my right hand on a voyage around the world. You won't go away again, will you, Shadrach? And you'll fix my head? It frightens me. The throbbing. Like something trying to escape in there."

"There's no reason to worry, sir. We'll fix you soon enough."

Genghis Mao rolls his eyes in torment. "How? Chop a hole in my skull? Let the demon escape like a whiff of foul gas?"

"This isn't the Neolithic," Shadrach says. "The trephine is obsolete. We have better methods." He touches the tips of his fingers to the Khan's cheeks, probing for the sharp, upthrusting bones. "Relax, sir. Let the muscles go slack." It is late at night, and Shadrach is exhausted, having flown this day from San Francisco to Peking, from Peking to Ulan Bator, having gone at once to Genghis Mao's bedside without pausing even for fresh clothing. His mind is a muddle of time zones and he is not sure whether he is in Saturday, Sunday, or Friday. But there is a sphere of utter crystalline clarity at the core of his spirit. "Relax," he croons. "Relax. Let the tension flow out of your neck, out of your shoulders, out of your back. Easy, now, easy—"

Genghis Mao scoffs. "You aren't going to cure this with massages and soothing talk."

"But we can ease the symptoms this way. We can palliate, sir."

"And then?"

"If necessary, there are surgical remedies."

"You see? You *will* chop open my skull!"

"We'll be neat about it, I promise." Shadrach moves around behind Genghis Mao, so he will not be dis-

tracted by the need to maintain eye contact with the
fierce old man, and concentrates on diagnostic perceptions. Hydrostatic imbalance, yes; meningeal congestion, yes; some accumulation of metabolic wastes
about the brain, yes. The situation is far from critical—
action could be deferred for weeks, perhaps for many
months, without great risk—but Shadrach intends to
deal swiftly with the problem. And not only for Genghis Mao's sake.

Genghis Mao says, "It's good to have you back."

"Thank you, sir."

"You should have been here for the funeral. You
would have had a front-row seat. It was magnificent,
Shadrach. Did you watch the funeral on television?"

"Of course," Shadrach lies. "In—ah—in Jerusalem.
I think I was in Jerusalem then. Yes. Magnificent.
Yes."

"Magnificent," says Genghis Mao, dwelling lovingly
on the word. "It will never be forgotten. One of
history's great spectacles. I was proud of it. The
Assyrians couldn't have done better for old Sardana-
palus." The Khan laughs. "If one can't attend one's
own funeral, Shadrach, one can at least satisfy the
urge by staging a splendid funeral for someone else.
Eh? Eh?"

"I wish I could have been there, sir."

"But you were in Jerusalem. Or was it Istanbul?"

"Jerusalem, I think, sir." He touches Genghis Mao's
temples, pressing lightly but firmly. The Chairman
winces. When Shadrach presses the sides of Genghis
Mao's neck, just below and behind the ears, the Chairman grunts.

"Tender there," Genghis Mao says.

"Yes."

"How bad is it, really?"

"It's not good. No immediate danger, but there's
definitely a problem in there."

"Explain it to me."

Shadrach moves out where Genghis Mao can see
him. "The brain and spinal cord," he says, "float,
literally float, in a liquid we call cerebrospinal fluid,
which is manufactured in hollow chambers within

the brain known as ventricles. It protects and nourishes the brain and, when it drains into the spaces surrounding the brain, it carries off the metabolic wastes resulting from the brain's activity. Under certain circumstances the passageways from the ventricles to these meningeal spaces become blocked, and cerebrospinal fluid accumulates in the ventricles."

"Is that what's happening to my head?"

"So it seems."

"Why?"

Shrugging, Shadrach replies, "It's usually caused by infection or by a tumor at the base of the brain. Occasionally it comes on spontaneously, without observable lesion. A function of aging, maybe."

"And what are the effects?"

"In children, the skull enlarges as the ventricles swell. That's the condition known as hydrocephalus, water on the brain. The adult cranium isn't capable of expansion, of course, so the brain must bear all the pressure. Severe headaches are the first symptom, naturally. Followed by failures of physical coordination, vertigo, facial paralysis, gradual loss of eyesight, periods of coma, general impairment of cerebral functions, epileptic seizures—"

"And death?"

"Death, yes. Eventually."

"How long from first to last?"

"It depends on the degree of the blockage, the vigor of the patient, and a lot of other factors. Some people live for years with mild or incipient hydrocephalic conditions and aren't even aware of it. Even acute cases can drag on for years, with long periods of remission. On the other hand, it's possible to go from first congestion to mortality in a matter of months, and sometimes much more quickly even than that, if something like a medullary edema develops, an intracranial swelling that disrupts the autonomic systems."

These recitals of symptomatology and prognosis have always fascinated Genghis Mao, and intense interest is evident in his eyes now. But there is something else, a haunted look, a flashing look of dismay verging on terror, that Shadrach has never observed in him before.

The Chairman says, "And in my case?"

"We'll have to run a full series of tests, of course. But on the basis of what the implants are telling me, I'm inclined toward quick corrective surgery."

"I've never had brain surgery."

"I know that, sir."

"I don't like the whole idea. A kidney or a lung is trivial. I don't want Warhaftig's lasers inside my head. I don't want pieces of my mind cut away."

"There's no question of our doing that."

"What will you do, then?"

"It's strictly a decompressive therapy. We'll install valved tubes to shunt the excess fluid directly into the jugular system. The operation is relatively simple and much less risky than an organ transplant."

Genghis Mao smiles icily. "I'm accustomed to organ transplants, though. I think I *like* organ transplants. Brain surgery is something new for me."

Shadrach, as he prepares a sedative for the Chairman, says cheerfully, "Perhaps you'll come to like brain surgery as well, sir."

In the morning he seeks out Frank Ficifolia at the main communications nexus deep in the service core of the tower. "I heard you'd returned," Ficifolia says. "I heard it, but I didn't believe it. For Christ's sake, why'd you come back?"

Shadrach eyes the banks of screens and monitors warily. "Is it safe to talk here?"

"Jesus, do you think I'd bug my own office?"

"Someone might have done it without telling you about it."

"Talk," Ficifolia says. "It's safe here."

"If you say so."

"I say so. Why didn't you stay where you were?"

"The Citpols knew where I was, every minute. Avogadro himself dropped in on me in Peking."

"What did you expect? Taking commercial transport all around the world. There are ways of hiding, but—did Avogadro make you come back here, then?"

"I had already bought my ticket."

"Jesus, *why?*"

"I came back because I saw a way of saving myself."

"The way to save yourself is to go underground."

"No," Shadrach says emphatically. "The way to save myself is to return and continue to carry out my functions as the Chairman's doctor. You know that the Chairman is ill?"

"Bad headaches, they tell me."

"Dangerous headaches. We'll need to operate."

"Brain surgery?"

"That's right."

Ficifolia compresses his lips and studies Shadrach's face as though examining a map of El Dorado. "I once told you that you weren't crazy enough to survive in this city. Maybe I was wrong. Maybe you're plenty crazy. You *have* to be crazy if you think you can intentionally bungle an operation on Genghis Mao and get away with it. Don't you think Warhaftig will notice what you're doing and stop you? Or turn you in, if you actually do pull it off? What good is killing the Khan if you end up in the organ farms yourself? How—"

"Doctors don't kill their patients, Frank."

"But—"

"You're jumping to conclusions. Projecting your own fantasies, perhaps. I'm simply going to operate. And cure the Chairman's headaches. And see to it that he stays in good health." Shadrach smiles. "Don't ask questions. Just help me."

"Help you how?"

"I want you to find Buckmaster for me. There's a special piece of equipment I'll need, and he's the right man to build it. Then I'll want you to help me rig the telemetering circuits to run it."

"Buckmaster? Why Buckmaster? There are plenty of capable microengineering people right here on the staff."

"Buckmaster's the one I want for this job. He's the best in his field, and he happens to be the one who built my implant system. He's the one who ought to

build any additions to that system." Shadrach's gaze
is uncompromising. "Will you get me Buckmaster?"

Ficifolia, after a moment, blinks and brusquely nods.
"I'll take you to him," he says. "When do you want to
go?"

"Now."

"Right now? Right this literal minute?"

"Now," Shadrach says. "Is he very far from here?"

"Not really."

"Where is he?"

"Karakorum," Ficifolia replies. "We hid him among
the transtemporalists."

January 2, 2009

*I insisted, and they allowed me to sample the trans-
temporal experience. Much talk of risks, of side effects,
of my responsibilities to the commonwealth. I overruled
them. It is not often that I have to insist. It is rare that
I can speak of being allowed. But this was a struggle.
Which of course I won, but it was work. Visited
Karakorum after midnight, light snow falling. The tent
was cleared. Guards posted. Teixeira had given me a
full checkup first. Because of the drugs they use. Clean
bill of health: I can handle their most potent potions.
And so, into the tent. Dark place, foul smell. I remember
that smell from my childhood—burning cow-chips,
uncured goathides. Little slump-backed lama comes forth,
very unimpressed with me, no awe at all—why be awed
by Genghis Mao, I guess, when you can gulp a drug
and visit Caesar, the Buddha, Genghis Khan?—and
mixes his brews for me. Oils, powders. Gives me the
cup to drink. Sweet, gummy, not a good taste. Takes my
hands, whispers things to me, and I am dizzy and then
the tent becomes a cloud and is gone and I find myself
in another tent, wide and low, white flags and brocaded
hangings, and there he is before me, thick-bodied, short,
a man of middle years or more, long dark mustache,
small eyes, strong mouth, stink of sweat coming from
him as if he hasn't bathed in years, and for the first
time in my life I want to sink to my knees before
another human being, for this is surely Temujin, this is
the Great Khan, this is he, the founder, the conqueror.*

I do not kneel, except within myself. Within myself I fall at his feet. I offer him my hand. I bow my head.

"Father Genghis," I say. "Across nine hundred years I come to do you homage."

He regards me without great interest. After a moment he hands me a bowl. "Drink some airag, old man."

We share the bowl, I first, then the Great Khan. He is dressed simply, no scarlet robes, no ermine trim, no crown, just a warrior's leather costume. The top of his head is shaven and in back his hair reaches his shoulders. He could kill me with a slap of his left hand.

"What do you want?" *he asks.*

"To see you."

"You see me. What else?"

"To tell you that you will live forever."

"I will die like any man, old one."

"Your body will die, Father Genghis. Your name will live in the ages."

He considers that. "And my empire? What of that? Will my sons rule after me?"

"Your sons will rule over half the world."

"Half the world," *Genghis Khan says softly.* "Only half? Is this the truth, old man?"

"Cathay will be theirs—"

"Cathay is already mine."

"Yes, but they will have it all, down to the hot jungles. And they will rule the high mountains, and the Russian land, and Turkestan, Afghanistan, Persia, everything as far as the gates of Europe. Half the world, Father Genghis!"

The Khan of Khans grunts.

"And I tell you this, also. Nine hundred years from now a khan named Genghis will rule everything from sea to sea, from shore to shore, all souls upon this world naming him master."

"A khan of my blood?"

"A true Tatar," *I assure him.*

Genghis Khan is silent a long while. It is impossible to read his eyes. He is shorter than I would have thought, and his smell is bad, but he is a man of such strength and purpose that I am humbled, for I thought I was of his kind, and in a way I am, and yet he is more than I could ever have been. There is no calculation about him; he is altogether solid, unhesitating, a man who lives in the moment, a man who must never have paused for a second thought and whose first thought must always have been right. He is only a barbarian prince, a mere wild horseman of the Gobi, to whom every aspect of my ordinary daily life would seem the most dazzling magic: yet put him down in Ulan Bator and he would understand the workings of Surveillance Vector One in three hours. A barbarian he is, yes, but not a mere barbarian, not a mere anything, and though I am his superior in some ways, though my life and my power are beyond his comprehension, I am second to him in all the ways that matter. He awes me. As I expected him to do. And, seeing him, I come close to a willingness to yield up all my authority over men, for, next to him, I am not worthy. I am not worthy.

"Nine hundred years," he says at last, and the shadow of a smile crosses his face. "Good. Good." He claps for a servant. "More airag," he calls. We share another drink. Then he says he must depart; it is time to ride out from Karakorum to the camp of his son Chagadai, where the royal family is to hold a tourney today. He does not invite me to join him. He has no interest in me, though I come from out of the realm of distant time, though I bring him bright tales of Mongol empires to come. I am unimportant to him. I have told him all he cares to know; now I am forgotten. Only the tourney matters now. He leaps to his mare; he rides away, followed by the warriors of his court, and only the servant and I remain.

24

Two robed acolytes bring Roger Buckmaster to Shadrach out of the depths of the tent of the transtemporalists in Karakorum. Buckmaster is robed too, but not in the coarse black horsehair garb of a transtemporalist. He wears a heavy hooded cassock of thick brown wool, smoothly woven. His feet, bare, are clad in open sandals. A massive cruciform pendant dangles at his throat. He pushes back his hood to reveal a tonsured scalp.

Buckmaster has become some sort of monk.

His new asceticism of clothing is not the only change in him. Before, he had been a blurting, impatient, angry man, with some kind of sullen furious energy circulating within him that seemed dammed at every plausible point of exit. Now he is eerily calm, self-contained, a man inhabiting an unfathomable kingdom of solitude and peace. He is pale, very thin, almost spectral. He stands silently before Shadrach, fingering his beads but otherwise motionless, waiting, waiting.

Shadrach says at last, "I never expected to see you alive again."

"Life brings many surprises, Dr. Mordecai." Buckmaster's voice is different too, deeper, sepulchral, more resonant, all the sputter and frenzy burned out of it.

"Word went around that you'd been sent to the organ farm. Dissected, dismembered."

Piously Buckmaster says, "The Lord chose to spare me."

His piety is hard for Shadrach to take. "Your friends saved your skin, you mean," he retorts, instantly regretting his bluntness. Not a wise way to talk to someone whose services you need.

But Buckmaster does not seem offended.

"My friends are His agents. As are we all, Dr. Mordecai."

"Have you been here the whole time?"

"Yes. Since the day after you saw me under interrogation."

"And the Citpols haven't come sniffing around for you?"

"I am officially dead, Doctor. My body has officially been distributed to ailing members of the government: the computer will tell you so. The Citpols don't search for dead men. To them I'm no more than a set of scattered parts—a pancreas here, a liver there, a kidney, a lung. Forgotten." For a moment mischief gleams in Buckmaster's oddly solemn face. "If you told them I was here, they would deny it."

"And what have you been doing?" Shadrach asks.

"The transtemporalists regard me as a holy man. I take their cup each day. Each day I retrace the days of the life of our Lord. I have attended His Passion upon Calvary many times, Doctor. I have walked among the apostles. I have touched the hem of Mary's robe. I have beheld the miracles: Cana, Capernaum, Lazarus raised at Bethany. I have watched Him betrayed in Gethsemane. I have seen Him brought before Pilate. I have seen it all, Dr. Mordecai, everything of which the Gospels tell. It is all true. It is literally the truth. My eyes bear witness."

The unexpected intensity of conviction in Buckmaster's eyes, the unearthly sound of Buckmaster's voice, leave Shadrach speechless a moment. It is impossible not to believe that this scruffy little man has strolled through the Galilee with Jesus and Peter and James, that he has heard the sermons of John the Baptist and the lamentations of the Magdalene.

Illusion, hallucination, self-deceit, fraud: no matter. Buckmaster has been transformed. He is radiant.

With deliberate bluntness Shadrach asks, "Can you still do microengineering work?"

The irrelevance of the question catches Buckmaster off balance. He is lost in holy reveries, shrouded in mystic serenity and transcendental joy, and Shadrach's words bring a gasp of amazement from him, as though he has been jabbed in the ribs. He coughs and frowns and says, obviously baffled, "I suppose I could. It's never entered my mind."

"I have work for you now."

"Don't be preposterous, Doctor."

"I'm being altogether serious. I've come to you because there's a job that you and only you can do properly. You're the only one I'd trust to do it."

"The world has expelled me, Doctor. I have expelled the world. Here is where I dwell. The concerns of the world are no longer my concerns."

"You once were concerned about the injustices perpetrated by Genghis Mao and the PRC."

"I am beyond justice and injustice now."

"Don't say that. It sounds impressive, Roger, but it's dangerous nonsense. The sin of pride, isn't it? You were rescued by your fellow men. You owe your life to them. They took risks for you. You have obligations to them."

"I pray for them daily."

"There's something more immediately useful you can do."

"Prayer is the highest good I know," Buckmaster says. "Certainly I place it higher than microengineering. I fail to see how any microengineering job you give me can help my fellow men."

"One job can."

"I fail to see—"

"Genghis Mao is soon to undergo another operation."

"What's Genghis Mao to me? He's forgotten me. I've forgotten him."

"An operation on his brain," Shadrach continues. "Fluid now accumulates within his skull. Unless it's

drained, it could kill him. Shortly we'll install a
drainage system with a valve through which the fluid
can be removed. At the same time a new telemetering
implant will be installed in me. Which I want you to
design for me, Roger."

"What will it do?"

"Allow me to control the action of the valve,"
Shadrach says.

Two hours later Shadrach is in the great carpentry
chapel at the far end of the Karakorum pleasure
complex, surrounded by chisels and mallets and saws,
trying to enter into the initial meditative state. He is
not doing well at it. Now and then he feels just a bit
of it, the beginnings of the proper degree of concentration, but he holds it no more than an instant and
then, as he congratulates himself for having attained
the state at last, he loses it, again and again he loses
it. It is Buckmaster's fault. Buckmaster will not recede from the forefront of Shadrach's consciousness.
If Buckmaster had had his way, Shadrach would
not be among the carpenters at all now, but rather
still would be in the transtemporalists' tent, lying
drugged and limp while his soul journeyed back
through the millennia to attend the bloody rite of
Calvary. "Take the cup with me," Buckmaster had
urged. "We will visit the Passion together." But
Shadrach had declined. Some other time, he told
Buckmaster gently. Transtemporal jaunts consume
too much energy; he needs all his strength for the
difficult enterprise that lies just ahead. Buckmaster
had understood, or at least was willing to forgive
him for not caring to make the journey just then. And
Shadrach went forth from the tent, with Buckmaster's
promise that he would have the design of the new
implant ready in a day or so. And still Buckmaster
haunts him.

How astonishing it was to see Buckmaster's monk-
ishness fall away from him the moment he grasped
the implications of Shadrach's request—his breath
quickening, color coming to his cheeks, eyes bright
with the old frenzy. Asking a hundred questions, de-

manding specifications and performance thresholds, size parameters, preferred bodily placement for the device. Scribbling notes furiously. Half an hour was all it took him to work out the rough schematics. He would need computer assistance to do the final, he said, but that would be no problem: Ficifolia could hook up a telephone relay for him, keying right into Genghis Mao's own master computer. And Buckmaster laughed stridently. Abruptly his expression shifted. Serenity returned. He had put microengineering aside; suddenly he was a monk again, calm, remote, glacial, saying, "Take the cup with me. We will visit the Passion together."

Poor crazy Buckmaster.

Shadrach, struggling to regain his own serenity, picks up an awl, lays it down, picks up an auger, runs his fingers along the curved blade of a chisel, presses a bastard file against his forehead. Better. A little better. The touch of cool metal soothes him. Poor crazy Buckmaster has drained the cup by now, no doubt. And has gone off on wings of dream to see them put the crown of thorns in place, hammer in the nails, ram home the spear. Crazy? Buckmaster is a happy man. He has placed himself beyond all pain. He has outsmarted the minions of Genghis Mao. He has emerged out of his torment into holiness, and he will walk daily with the apostles and the Savior. To Buckmaster, the Palestine of Jesus is more real than the Mongolia of Genghis Mao, and who can quarrel with that? Shadrach might make the same choice, if he could. Of course, reality will eventually intrude on Buckmaster's fantasy: a time will come, and come soon, when Buckmaster's most recent Antidote treatment will cease to be effective, and he is not likely to be able to obtain a booster dose. But plainly he does not worry about that.

Thinking of Buckmaster's newfound tranquility allows Shadrach to find a glimmering of it himself. This time he sustains it, voyaging inward to that clear bright place beyond the reach of storms. Buckmaster disappears; Genghis Mao disappears; Shadrach disappears. For hours he works peacefully at his bench,

wholly at one with his tools, his lumber. When he
departs from the chapel late in the day he is in a
state near ecstasy.

He reaches Ulan Bator an hour after nightfall. As
soon as he arrives he phones Katya Lindman.

"I want to see you," he says.

"I was hoping you'd call. I knew you were back."

They meet in a recreation lounge on the fiftieth
floor, a rendezvous favored by middle-echelon staffers.
Service is discreet there. The room is a dazzling high-
vaulted oval, decorated with shining golden metallic
streamers only a few molecules thick that dangle
from the ceiling and twirl gently in the currents of
air. A giant portrait of Genghis Mao occupies the
entire east wall of the lounge, and there is one of
Mangu at the other end.

Katya is wearing what is, for Katya, an unusually
slinky costume, a clinging tight-woven wrap of some
soft rust-colored fabric, low-cut to display her strong
broad shoulders and her heavy breasts. She may even
have used perfume. Shadrach has never seen her
make the slightest concession to conventional femi-
ninity, and he is surprised and disappointed to see
her opting for such unsubtle seductiveness now. It is
not at all in character for her, and not at all necessary.
But perhaps Katya is weary of staying in character,
hard eyes, sharp teeth, cruel mouth, cool efficient
mind, brisk and capable woman of science. She has
already confessed her love for him; perhaps now she
wants to play at being the sort of woman for whom
love is a plausible event. Foolish of her, if that's her
game; he much prefers the Katya he knows. Or thinks
he knows. Love is not a costume party.

She says, "I didn't think you'd ever come back."

"I never intended not to. I wasn't trying to disappear. Only to get away for a while and think things
out."

"And did you succeed?"

"I hope so. I'll know soon enough."

"I won't ask."

"No. Don't."

She smiles. "I'm glad you're back. Except that I worry about the danger you're in."

"If I'm not worrying, why should you?"

"I don't need to answer that." Her voice is husky, almost stagy. She leans forward and says, "I missed you, Shadrach. It amazed me how much I missed you. You don't like me to say things like that, do you?"

"What gives you that idea?"

"Your face. You look so uncomfortable. You don't want to hear soft words from me. You don't think it's proper for mean, tough Dr. Lindman to talk that way."

"I'm just not used to you that way. It's a side of you that's unfamiliar to me."

"You probably don't even like the way I'm dressed tonight. But I can be the other Katya again, if you want. Wait. I'll go and change into my lab smock."

She sounds almost serious.

"Stop it," he says. He takes her hand. "You look lovely tonight."

"Thank you." Her voice is steely. She withdraws the hand.

"Well, you do. And I'm supposed to say so, and I did. That's how the game is played. Now you're supposed to say—"

"Let's not play any more games, Shadrach. Okay?"

"Okay. Did you dress like that for me or for you?"

"For both of us."

"Ah. Just for the hell of it, right? Because you just felt like coming on sexy. Right?"

"Right," she says. "Okay?"

"Okay. Okay."

"Is it okay to tell you that I missed you? Don't force me to be some kind of machine, Shadrach. Don't make me be whatever your image of me is. I'm not asking you to tell me you missed me. But give me the right to express what *I* feel. Give me the right to be silly once in a while, to be soft, to be inconsistent, if I want to be. Without worrying about which one the real Katya is. I'm always the real Katya, whoever I am at the moment. Okay?"

"Okay," he says, and takes her hand again, and she does not pull it away. After a moment he says, "What's been happening here while I was gone?"

"You know about the Khan's headaches, I assume."

"Sure. That's why I came back when I did. The moment I picked up the telemetering impulses from him, in Peking."

"Is it something serious?"

"We're going to have to operate," he says. "As soon as some special equipment I've ordered is ready."

"Is brain surgery especially risky?"

"Not as risky as you might think. But the Khan doesn't like the idea of it at all, lasers poking into his skull, et cetera, et cetera. I've never seen him look so spooked about an operation. But he'll be all right. What else has been going on here?"

"There was the funeral."

"Yes. I know. I was in Jerusalem then, or Istanbul. I saw some photographs later."

"It was monstrous," Katya tells him. "It went on for days and days. God knows how much it must have cost. Everything stopped, practically, while we had the speeches, the parades, the brass bands, the planes flying in formation, all kinds of rituals and celebrations. And Genghis Mao sitting in the middle of the plaza drinking everything in."

"What a pity I missed it."

"I'm sure you were heartbroken."

"Yes. Terribly." They laugh. He is beginning to think he rather likes the way she looks in that dress. He says, "What else? How's your project going?"

"Very well. Seventeen kinesic traits are equivalented now. We've made more progress in the past three weeks than in the previous three months."

"Good. I want to see that automaton of yours finished fast. I want your project to be the first one ready to go."

"Have you talked to Nikki since you've been back?"

"No," he says. "Not yet."

"I hear that Avatar's been moving fast too. They say that they're practically done converting from

Mangu's parameters to—to those of the new donor. Weeks ahead of schedule. It scares me, Shadrach."

"It shouldn't."

"I can't help thinking—what if—if they ever actually do—"

"They won't," he says. "It's not going to happen. I'm much too valuable to Genghis Mao as I am."

" 'Redundancy is our main avenue of survival,' remember. How many other doctors do you think he has waiting? Complete with telemeter implants and everything?"

"None."

"Can you be sure?"

"Buckmaster would know if a duplicate set of implants had ever been built. He never heard anything about that."

"Buckmaster's dead, Shadrach."

He lets the point pass. "I know that there's no duplicate Shadrach Mordecai waiting somewhere to take over when I go. I realize now how dependent Genghis Mao is on me, exclusively on me, irreplaceable me. And I have a notion I'm going to be a lot less redundable in the near future, a lot more indispensable. I'm not worrying about Avatar, Katya."

"I hope you know what you're doing."

"So do I," he says. He gestures toward the lounge exit, just below the vast blank-eyed portrait of sad silly Mangu. "Let's go upstairs," he suggests, and she smiles and nods.

Now it is the morning of the operation. Genghis Mao lies face down upon the operating table, awake, fully conscious, occasionally turning his head to stare sourly at the doctors assembled about him—Shadrach, Warhaftig, and Warhaftig's neurological consultant, an Israeli named Malin. There is no mistaking the Khan's look: he is frightened. He is trying to cover his fear with his usual swagger, but he is not succeeding. In ten minutes the surgical lasers will be drilling into his skull, and the prospect does not charm him. But for the headaches—whose effects are visible now,

as imperial grimaces and winces—none of this would
be happening.

The Chairman's head has been shaved. Without his
thick black mane he looks, strangely, much younger,
more vigorous: that sturdy knob of a skull, bare, speaks
of the immense strength of the man, the intensity of
the driving forces within him. The musculature of his
scalp is powerful and conspicuous, hills and valleys
outlined in bold relief, a rugged landscape of cords
and ridges nurtured and developed through nearly
ninety years of ferocious talking, thinking, biting,
chewing. The surgeons' angles of entry have been
marked on his skin in luminous ink.

Warhaftig is ready to make the first incision. The
strategy of the operation has evolved during three
days of conferences. They will not go near the cerebral centers. The skull is to be opened high on the
occipital curve, and the drainage device is to be inserted in the brain stem, the pons, just below the
fourth ventricle near the medulla oblongata. This,
everyone has agreed, is the optimum site for the
valve, and not incidentally will keep the lasers away
from the seat of reason—though any surgical slip
could do damage to the medulla, which controls vasomotor and cardiac functions and other vital autonomic responses. But Warhaftig is not one who slips.

The surgeon glances at Shadrach. "Is all well?"

"Fine. Go when ready."

Warhaftig lightly touches Genghis Mao's neck. The
Khan does not react, nor does a sharp pinch at the
base of his skull bring any response from him. He is
under local anesthesia, induced as customary through
sonipuncture.

"Now," Warhaftig says. "We begin."

He makes the initial cut.

Genghis Mao closes his eyes—but, Shadrach's inner monitors tell him, the Khan is still at full
awareness, tense, poised like a wary leopard on a
high branch. The skin is peeled back and clamped by
retractors. Warhaftig steps aside and allows Malin to
make the cranial incision. The neurosurgeon's touch
is not as deft as Wharhaftig's, but Malin has spent

thirty years slicing into skulls, and he knows as Warhaftig cannot possibly know just how much margin for error his cuts can have. There, now: there is a window into the Khan's head. Shadrach, peering on tiptoes, stares in awe at the very brain that conceived the theories of centripetal depolarization, that hatched the Permanent Revolutionary Committee, that carried mankind out of the chaos of the Virus War. There, there, right there, in that mysterious gray lump, it all was spawned, yes.

They are searching now for a site for the drainage valve. Warhaftig has resumed command. Instead of a laser, he uses at this point a hollow needle filled with liquid nitrogen, cryostatically cooled to a temperature of −160° C. The needle, sliding to the depths of the Khan's brain stem, freezes the brain cells on contact, and if contact is prolonged it will kill them. While Malin calls off instrument readings and Shadrach supplies telemetering data on the state of Genghis Mao's autonomic activities, Warhaftig, reassured that he is not destroying vital neural centers, opens a space for insertion of the drainage device. Everything goes smoothly. The Khan continues to breathe, to pump blood, to generate the normal array of electroencephalographic waves. There is lodged within him now a tube to shunt excess cerebrospinal fluid into his circulatory system, a valve through which the fluid can be drawn, and a telemetering implant that will relay to his physician constant reports on the functioning of that valve and the fluid levels of his cranial ventricles. Bone and skin are restored to place; the Khan, haggard and pallid but smiling now, is wheeled to the recovery station.

Warhaftig turns to Shadrach. "As long as we have everything set up, let's proceed to the next operation immediately. Yes?" He reaches for Shadrach's left hand. "You want the telemetering implant to go here, is that correct? Embedded in the thenar muscles. But not at the base of the thumb, eh? Over here, closer to the center of the palm, do I have it? All right. Let's scrub you up and get along with it, then."

*   *   *

Shadrach and Nikki, meeting for the first time since his return, are ill at ease with each other. He tries to smile, but he doubts that his face is doing a very good job of it, and her cordiality seems equally forced.

"How is the Khan?" she asks finally.

"Healing," Shadrach says. "As per usual."

She glances at his bandaged left hand. "And you?"

"A little sore. This implant was larger than the others. More complex. Another day or two and I'll be fine."

"I'm glad everything went well."

"Yes. Thank you."

They go through the ritual of forced smiles again.

"It's good to see you," he says.

"Yes. Very good to see you."

They are silent. But though the conversation has faltered, neither begins to depart. He is surprised how unmoved he is by her beauty today: she is as splendid as ever, but he feels nothing, nothing at all, only a kind of abstract admiration, as he might feel for a marble statue or a spectacular sunset. He tests it. He summons memories. The coolness of her thighs against his lips. The solidity of her breasts cupped in his hands. The little grunt as he thrusts himself into her. The fragrance of her dark torrent of hair. Nothing. The all-night conversations, when there was so much to tell each other. Nothing. Nothing. Thus does treason carbonize love. But she is still beautiful.

"Shadrach—"

He waits. She is groping for words. He suspects he knows what she wants to say: to tell him once more that she is sorry, that she had no choice, that although she betrayed him it was only out of a sense of the inevitability of what would befall. It is an endless awkward moment.

At last she says, "We're doing well on the project."

"So I've been told."

"I have to go on with it, you know. There's no other way for me. But I want you to realize that I hope it never is used. I mean, it's valuable research, it's a tremendous breakthrough, but I want it to remain just a laboratory achievement, just a—a—"

She falters.

"That's all right," he tells her, and hears an odd tenderness creeping into his voice. "Don't torment yourself about it, Nikki. Do your work, do it well. That's all you need to think about. Do your work." For an instant, only an instant, he feels a flicker of what he once felt for her. "Don't worry about me," he says gently. "I'm going to be all right."

On the third day the bandage comes off his hand. There is only a faint pink line to mark the place where the implant was inserted, a barely perceptible furrow against the darker pink of his palm. Like his master, Shadrach is a swift healer. He flexes his hand—slight muscular soreness, he notes—but is careful not to clench it into a fist. He is not yet ready to test the new device.

At the end of the week, with Genghis Mao rapidly mending, Shadrach allows himself an evening in Karakorum. He goes alone, on a mild summer night with the scent of new blossoms and the hint of rain in the air, and hires a cubicle in the dream-death pavilion, strips and dons the loincloth and the chest bands, takes the polished talisman from the lioness-headed guide, looks upon the pattern of spiraling lines, disappears into the hallucination. Once more he dies. He gives up hope and fear and striving and dismay and anxiety and need, he gives up breath and life, he dies to the world and is reborn in another place, rising above his hollow outworn husk, looking down upon it, that long brown empty form with its spidery sprawl of limbs hanging out uselessly, and floats out, out into the fragrant void, where time and space are cut loose from their moorings. Everything is accessible to him, for he is dead. He enters a city of ox carts and alleyways and low wooden buildings strung out in rambling impenetrable mazes, a place of picturesque squalor and medieval filth, and sees the lords and ladies in their green and scarlet bro-

caded robes tumbling in the unpaved streets, howling,
sobbing, trembling, sweating, crying to the Lord,
clutching at the throbbing swollen places under their
arms and between their legs. Yes, yes, the Black
Death, and Shadrach goes among them saying, I am
Shadrach the healer, come from the land of the dead
to save you, and he touches their fiery swellings and
lifts them to their feet and sends them forth into life,
and they sing hymns to his name. And he moves onto
another city, a place of bamboo and silk, of gardens
rich with chrysanthemums and junipers and small
contorted pines, and in the stillness of the day a
fireball bursts in the sky, a great mushroom cloud
bellies toward the roof of heaven, houses break into
flame, the people rush into the blazing streets, small
folk, almond-eyed, yellow-skinned, and Shadrach,
standing like an ebony tower among them, tells them
in soft tones not to be afraid, that it is only a dream
that afflicts them, that pain and even death may yet
be rejected, and he spreads forth his hands to them,
soothing them, draining the fire from them. The sky
fills with ash and soot and pumice and it is the night
of Cotopaxi once more, the volcano rumbles and hisses
and drones, the air turns to poison, and the young
black doctor kneels in the streets, breathing in the
mouths of the fallen, raising them, comforting them.
And he moves on. The howling Assyrian hordes ride
through the streets of Jerusalem, slashing without
mercy, and Shadrach patiently sews together the sun-
dered bodies of the fallen, saying, Rise, walk, I am
the Healer. The great woolly beasts flee as the glacial
snows melt beneath the suddenly colossal sun, and
the people of the caves grow thin and feeble, and
Shadrach teaches them to eat grasses and seeds, to
collect the berries of the newly sprouted thickets, to
string weirs across the streams to snare the frisky
fishes, and they worship him and paint his image on
the walls of the holy cave. He takes Jesus from the
cross when the Roman soldiers go off to the tavern,
slinging the limp body over one shoulder and hurry-
ing into a dark hut, where he wipes the blood from
the maimed hands and feet, he applies ointments

and unguents, he mixes a healing draft of herbs and juices and gives it to Him to drink, telling Him, Go. Walk. Live. Preach. He seines the fragments of Osiris from the Nile, he rejoins the severed members, he breathes life into the fallen god and summons Isis, saying, Here is Osiris. I, Shadrach, restore him to you. The sky grows green with strange cloudbursts, and the Virus War breaks above the cities of mankind, and the alien rot enters the bodies of mankind, and as the people groan and fall Shadrach raises them, saying, Fear nothing. Death is transient. Life awaits you. And in the heavens is the smiling face of Genghis Mao. Shadrach drifts across the centuries, moving freely in space and time, and gradually he becomes aware that he is no longer alone, that there is a woman beside him, plucking at his sleeve, trying to tell him something. He ignores her. He hears celestial choirs singing his name: "Shadrach! Shadrach!" And the heavenly voices cry, "O Shadrach! You are the true healer, you are the prince of princes! Shadrach who was, Genghis to be! All hail Shadrach!" And a voice like thunder cries out, "You henceforth shall be known as Genghis III Mao V Khan!"

And the woman plucks at his sleeve, and he sees that she is Katya, and he says, "What do you want?" She says, *It's too late*. He says, "The next donor's already been picked?" *Yes*. "I don't suppose you'd care to tell me his name." *I don't think I should*. "Who is he?" *You*, she says. The world erupts in flame and flood. The laughter of Genghis Mao rolls through the heavens, shattering mountains.

Shadrach awakens. He sits up.

He clenches his fist and holds it tightly clenched.

Out of Ulan Bator, four hundred kilometers to the east, comes the terrible jolt of Genghis Mao's agony, the silent scream of the sensors reporting the wave of pain that is sweeping through the Khan.

Shadrach approaches Interface Three and announces, "Shadrach Mordecai to serve the Khan."

He is scanned. He is approved. He is admitted.

It is close to midnight. Shadrach goes at once to

the Khan's bedroom, but Genghis Mao is not there.
Shadrach frowns. The Khan has been strong enough
to leave his bed for the past several days, but it is
odd that he should be wandering around this late at
night. Shadrach finds a servitor who tells him that
the Khan has spent most of the evening in the se-
cluded study known as the Khan's Retreat, on the far
side of the seventy-five-story compound, and is probably there now.

Onward, then. Into the Khan's office—he is not
there—and thence to the private imperial dining room,
empty, and then Shadrach goes into his own office,
where he pauses a moment, collecting himself amid
his familiar and beloved possessions, his sphygmomanometers and scalpels, his microtomes and trephines. Here, in a flask, is the authentic abdominal
aorta of Genghis II Mao IV Khan. Surely a treasure
of medical history, that one. And here, the newest
addition to Shadrach's museum, is a lock of Genghis
Mao's thick, rank, preternaturally dark hair, an ex-
hibit perhaps more fitting for a museum of witch-
craft and voodoo than one of medicine, but yet
appropriate, for it was removed in the course of preparations for brain surgery carried out successfully in
the celebrated patient's ninetieth (or eighty-fifth, or
ninety-fifth, or whatever) year of life. And so. Onward.
He presents himself to the door of the Khan's Retreat
and asks entry.

The door rolls back.

The Khan's Retreat is the room least used on the
floor, accessible only through Shadrach's office and
insulated against the intrusion of even the loudest
external distractions. Its ceiling is low, its lights are
dim, its furnishings are ornate and oriental, running
toward thick draperies and elaborate carpets. Genghis Mao lies on a cushioned divan along the left-
hand wall. Already his shaven scalp is covered by a
thin black stubble. The vitality of the man is irre-
presible. But he looks shaken, even dazed.

"Shadrach," he says. His voice is thick and scratchy.
"I knew you'd get here. You felt it, didn't you?

About an hour and a half ago. I thought my head was going to explode."

"I felt it, yes."

"You told me you were putting a valve in me. To drain off the fluid, you said."

"We did, sir."

"Doesn't it work right?"

"It works perfectly, sir," Shadrach says mildly.

Genghis Mao looks confused. "Then what made my head hurt so much a little while ago?"

"This did," says Shadrach. He smiles and stretches forth his left hand and clenches his fist.

For a moment nothing happens. Then Genghis Mao's eyes widen in shock and amazement. He growls and clamps his hands to his temples. He bites his lip, he bows his naked head, he drives his knuckles against his eyes, he mutters anguished guttural curses. The implanted sensors that report on the bodily functions of the Khan tell Shadrach of the intense reactions within Genghis Mao: pulse and respiration, rates climbing alarmingly, blood pressure dropping, intracranial pressure severe. Genghis Mao coils into a huddled ball, shivering, groaning. Shadrach lets his fingers relax. Gradually the pain recedes from Genghis Mao, the tense crumpled body uncoils, and Shadrach ceases to feel the broadcast of shock symptoms.

Genghis Mao looks up. He stares at Shadrach for a long moment.

"What have you done to me?" Genghis Mao asks in a harsh whisper.

"Installed a valve in your skull, sir. To drain away the dangerous accumulations of cerebrospinal fluid. However, I should tell you that the action of the valve has been designed to be reversible. Upon telemetered command it can be made to pump fluid *into* the cranial ventricles instead of draining it from them. I control the action of the valve, here, by a piezoelectric crystal implanted in my palm. A twitch of my hand and the fluid ceases to drain. A harder twitch and I can pump it upward. I can interrupt your life processes. I can cause you instant pain of the kind you have now experienced twice, and in a surprisingly short span of time I could cause your death."

Genghis Mao's facial expression is entirely opaque. He considers Shadrach's declaration in silence.

Eventually he says, "Why have you done this to me, Shadrach?"

"To protect myself, sir."

The Khan manages a glacial smile. "You thought I would use your body for Project Avatar?"

"I was certain of it, sir."

"Wrong. It wouldn't ever have happened. You're too important for me as you are, Shadrach."

"Yes, sir. Thank you, sir."

"You think I'm lying. I tell you that there was never any possibility we would have activated Project Avatar with you as the donor. Don't misunderstand me, Shadrach. I'm not pleading with you now. I'm simply telling you how things really stand."

"Yes, sir. But I know your teachings concerning redundancy, sir. I feared I was about to be made dispensable. I have made myself indispensable now, I think."

"Would you kill me?" Genghis Mao asks.

"If I felt my life was in danger, yes."

"What would Hippocrates say about that?"

"The right of self-defense is allowed even to physicians, sir."

Genghis Mao's smile grows warmer. He seems to be enjoying this discussion. There is no trace of anger on his face.

He says calmly, merely raising a speculative hypothesis, "Suppose I have you seized by stealth, immobilized before you can clench your fist, and put to death?"

Shadrach shakes his head. "The implant in my hand is keyed to the electrical output of my brain. If I die, if I'm mindpicked in any way, if there's any sort of significant interruption in my brain waves, the valve automatically begins pumping cerebrospinal fluid to your medulla. The moment of my death is the automatic prelude to your own, sir. Our fates are joined. Guard my life, sir, for your own sake."

"And if I have the valve removed from my head and replaced by one that isn't quite as—ah—versatile?"

"No, sir. There's no way you could enter surgery without my implant system notifying me of it. I'd take defensive action, naturally, at the first moment. No. We have become one entity in two bodies, sir. And we'll remain that way forever."

"Very clever. Who built this mechanical marvel for you?"

"Buckmaster did, sir."

"Buckmaster? But he's been dead since May. You couldn't have known then—"

"Buckmaster is still alive, sir," Shadrach says softly.

Genghis Mao considers that. He grows extremely thoughtful. He is silent a long while.

"Still alive. Strange."

"Yes."

"I don't understand."

Shadrach makes no reply.

After a time Genghis Mao says, "You've planted a bomb in me."

"So to speak, sir, I have."

"I have power over all of mankind. And you have power over me, Shadrach. Do you realize what that makes you? You are the true Khan now! All hail, Genghis III Mao V!" Genghis Mao laughs savagely. "Do you understand that? Do you know what you have achieved?"

"The thought has crossed my mind," Shadrach admits.

"You could force my resignation. You could compel me to name you as my successor. You could kill me and assume the Chairmanship, perfectly legitimately. You see that? Of course you see that. Is that what you mean to do?"

"No, sir. The last thing in the world I want is to be Chairman."

"Go ahead. Wiggle your hand at me, stage a coup d'etat. Take power, Shadrach. I'm old, tired, bored, crumbling. I'm willing to be overthrown. I admire your shrewdness. I'm fascinated by what you've done. No one has ever fooled me so thoroughly before, do you know that? You've accomplished what thousands of enemies have utterly failed to do. Quiet Shadrach, loyal Shadrach, dependable Shadrach—you have me beaten. You own me. I am your puppet now, do you see that? Go on. Make yourself Chairman. You've earned it, Shadrach."

"It's not what I want."

"What do you want, then?"

"To continue as your physician. To protect your health and strive to extend your life. To remain by your side and serve you according to my oath."

"That's *all?*"

"That's all. No, there's one thing more, sir."

"Let's hear it."

"I request a place on the Committee, sir."

"Ah."

"Specifically, I want authority in the sphere of public health. Government medical policy."

"Ah. Yes."

"Control over distribution of the Antidote, sir. I mean to develop a program for immediate world-wide treatment of the healthy population," Shadrach says. "And expansion of whatever programs currently exist for research into a permanent cure for the organ-rot. That is, a total reversal of what I understand is existing PRC policy."

"Ah!" Genghis Mao begins to laugh. "Now it emerges! You *do* intend to be Khan, then! I keep the Chairmanship, but you call the tunes. Is that it, Shadrach? Is that what you've engineered? Very well. You have me. I'm yours, Shadrach. You'll join the Committee at the next meeting. Draw up your policy statements and submit them." He glances somberly at Shadrach's left hand. "All hail," the Chairman cries. "Genghis III Mao V!"

When he leaves the Khan's Retreat, Shadrach's route back to his own suite takes him through his office, through Committee Vector One, and into Surveillance Vector One, where he halts awhile, as is his habit, to watch the show on the winking screens. All is quiet in the Grand Tower of the Khan. It is the depth of night; all Asia sleeps. But across the planet, out there in the Trauma Ward, life goes on, and also death. Shadrach stands before the multitude of screens, following the random flow, the suffering, the striving, the struggling, the dying. The walking dead, wandering the streets of Nairobi, Jerusalem, Istanbul, Rome, San Francisco, Peking, shambling across all the continents, the procession of the damned, the lost, the tortured, the condemned. Somewhere out there is Bhishma Das. Somewhere, Meshach Yakov. Somewhere, Jim Ehrenreich. Shadrach wishes them joy and good health for such of life as is left to them. To all, joy! To all, good health!

He thinks of the laughter of Genghis Mao. How amused the Khan seemed at his predicament! How relieved, almost, at having the ultimate authority stolen from him! But the Khan is beyond comprehension; the Khan is alien, mysterious, unfathomable, ultimately inscrutable. Shadrach does not really know what will happen now. He cannot imagine what counterploy Genghis Mao may already have conceived, what traps he is even now devising. Shadrach will walk warily and hope for the best. He has planted a bomb in Genghis Mao, yes, but he has also seized a tiger by the tail, and he must be careful lest he stumble between the metaphors and be destroyed.

He stands mesmerized before the dazzling dance of the screens of Surveillance Vector One. It is the fourth of July, 2012. Wednesday. Gentle rain is falling in Ulan Bator, which next week shall be renamed Altan Mangu in honor of the slain viceroy, who already has been forgotten by most of mankind. In this night death will travel the globe, harvesting his thousands; but in the morning, Shadrach Mordecai vows, things will begin to change. He stretches forth his left hand. He studies it as though it be a thing of precious jade, of rarest ivory. Tentatively he closes it, almost but not quite clenching his fist. He smiles. He touches the tips of his fingers to his lips and blows a kiss to all the world.